THE WALL

www.penguin.co.uk

Also by Douglas Jackson

CALIGULA
CLAUDIUS
HERO OF ROME
DEFENDER OF ROME
AVENGER OF ROME
SWORD OF ROME
ENEMY OF ROME
SCOURGE OF ROME
SAVIOUR OF ROME
GLORY OF ROME
HAMMER OF ROME

THE WALL

Douglas Jackson

BANTAM PRESS

TRANSWORLD PUBLISHERS
Penguin Random House, One Embassy Gardens,
8 Viaduct Gardens, London SW11 7BW
www.penguin.co.uk

Transworld is part of the Penguin Random House group of companies
whose addresses can be found at global.penguinrandomhouse.com

First published in Great Britain in 2022 by Bantam Press
an imprint of Transworld Publishers

A CIP catalogue record for this book
is available from the British Library.

ISBNs 9781787634848 (cased)
9781787634855 (tpb)

Typeset in 11.5/15.25pt Electra by Jouve (UK), Milton Keynes
Printed and bound in Great Britain by Clays Ltd, Elcograf S.p.A.

The authorized representative in the EEA is Penguin Random House Ireland,
Morrison Chambers, 32 Nassau Street, Dublin D02 YH68.

Penguin Random House is committed to a sustainable
future for our business, our readers and our planet. This book
is made from Forest Stewardship Council® certified paper.

This one's for Florence,
the bright new star in our universe.

Author's Note

PLACE NAMES

Author's note – The *Notitia Dignitatum* indicates that by the beginning of the fifth century when this book is set, the names of a number of forts on Hadrian's Wall had altered slightly, at least in official documents: for example, Segeduno, Cilurno, Borcovicio. In the interests of clarity and continuity I have chosen to stay with the more traditional spellings, Segedunum, Cilurnum and Borcovicium.

*indicates a major fort on Hadrian's Wall

Aesica* – Great Chesters Roman fort
Ail Dun – Selgovae fortress, Eildon Hills, Melrose (see Trimontium)
Alona – fictional township, south of Slaggyford, Cumbria
Arbeia – Roman fort and port, South Shields
Augusta Treverorum – Trier, France
Banna* – Birdoswald Roman fort
Barcum – fictional settlement on the high ground between Great Chesters and Haltwhistle
Bodotria – the Firth of Forth
Borcovicium* – Housesteads Roman fort
Braboniacum – Roman fort, Kirkby Thore, Cumbria, home to the Numerus Defensorum
Bremenium – abandoned Roman outpost fort north of the Wall on Dere Street, High Rochester, Northumberland
Brocolitia* – Carrawburgh Roman fort, also location of the Carrawburgh Mithras and Coventina's Well
Caer Eidinn – tribal capital of the northern Votadini, Edinburgh Castle rock
Camboglana* – Castlesteads Roman fort
Castra Exploratum – abandoned Roman fort, Netherby, Cumbria
Cataractonium – Roman fort, Catterick, North Yorkshire
Cilurnum* – Chesters Roman fort, home to Second Asturum cavalry wing
Condercum* – Benwell Roman fort
Constantinopolis – Istanbul, Turkey

Corstopitum – Corbridge Roman fort and township

Din Gefrin – tribal capital of the southern Votadini, Yeavering Bell, Northumberland

Eboracum – Roman York; its fortress is home to the Sixth Legion Victrix

Epiacum – Roman fort in the Pennine Hills south of the Wall, near Alston, Cumbria

Fanum – abandoned Roman outpost fort north of the Wall, Bewcastle, Cumbria

Grabant – fictional royal estate of the Brigantes, East Yorkshire

Habitancum – abandoned Roman outpost fort north of the Wall on Dere Street, Risingham, Northumberland

Hibernia – Ireland

Hunnum* – Roman fort, home of the Ala Sabiniana cavalry wing, Halton Chesters

Isurium Brigantum – Roman fort and tribal capital, Aldborough, Yorkshire

Lavatris – Roman fort, Bowes, Co. Durham

Londinium – London, capital of the Roman province of Britannia

Longovicium – Roman fort, on Dere Street, Lanchester, Co. Durham

Luguvalium* – Carlisle Roman fort

Lutetia Parisiorum – Paris, France

Mamucium – a Roman fort situated in what is now the Castlefields area of Manchester.

Mediolanum – Milan, Italy

Morbium – Roman fort on Dere Street, Piercebridge, Co. Durham

Petriana* (aka Uxelodunum) – Roman fort, Stanwix, Carlisle

Pons Aelius* – Newcastle Roman fort and first Tyne crossing point

Saxonia – land of the Saxons, now coastal north Germany

Segedunum* – Wallsend Roman fort

Tinan River – the River Tyne

Tivyet River – River Teviot

Trimontium – Roman fort (abandoned), Newstead, Melrose

Verteris – Roman fort, Church Brough, Cumbria

Vindobala* – Rudchester Roman fort

Vindolanda – Roman fort a mile south of Hadrian's Wall, near Borcovicium (Housesteads)

Vindomora – Roman fort on Dere Street, Ebchester, Co. Durham

Vinovium – Roman fort on Dere Street, north of Bishop Auckland, Co. Durham

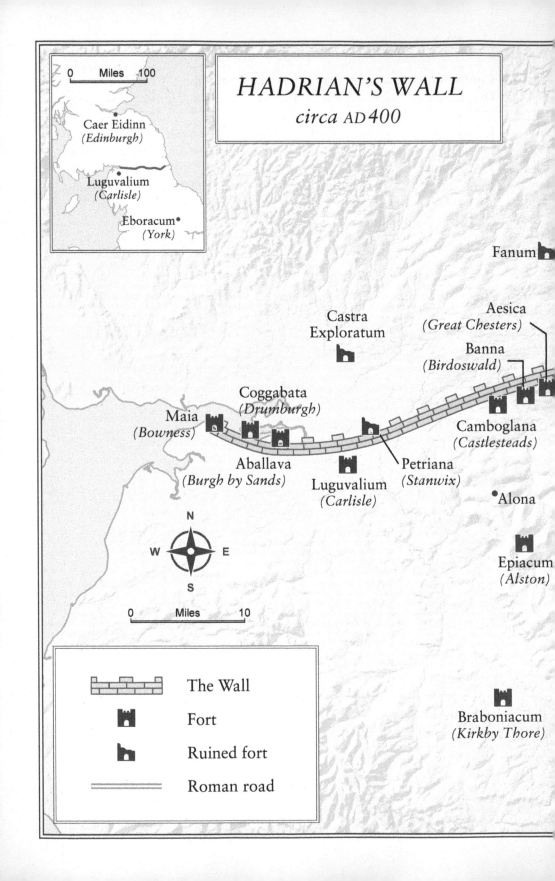

HADRIAN'S WALL
circa AD 400

0 Miles 100

Caer Eidinn
(Edinburgh)

Luguvalium
(Carlisle)

Eboracum
(York)

Fanum

Castra
Exploratum

Aesica
(Great Chesters)

Banna
(Birdoswald)

Coggabata
(Drumburgh)

Maia
(Bowness)

Camboglana
(Castlesteads)

Aballava
(Burgh by Sands)

Luguvalium
(Carlisle)

Petriana
(Stanwix)

Alona

N
W E
S

Epiacum
(Alston)

0 Miles 10

The Wall

Fort

Ruined fort

Roman road

Braboniacum
(Kirkby Thore)

To
Caer Eidinn
(Edinburgh)

MARE
GERMANICUM

Bremenium
(High Rochester)

Habitancum

Brocolitia
(Carrawburgh)

Hunnum
(Halton Chesters)

Cilurnum
(Chesters)

Vindobala
(Rudchester)

Condercum
(Benwell)

Segedunum
(Wallsend)

Vindolanda

Corstopitum
(Corbridge)

Pons Aelius
(Newcastle)

Arbeia
(South Shields)

Borcovicium
(Housesteads)

Vindomora
(Ebchester)

Longovicium
(Lanchester)

Lavatris
(Bowes)

To
Eboracum
(York)

Verteris
(Church Brough)

*Emperor Hadrian
Reigned* AD 117–138

Dramatis Personae

Marcus Flavius Victor – prefect commanding First Pannonian Wing of Sabinus, the Ala Sabiniana

Caradoc – decurion, squadron commander Ala Sabiniana

Luko – *draconarius* (bearer of the *draco* standard) Ala Sabiniana

Janus – a Pict, captured as a young boy, now serving as a trooper, Ala Sabiniana

Julius – his twin brother

Velanos – *curator* of Alona

Zeno – a Greek, former *medicus* to the Emperor of the East, now serving with the Ala Sabiniana

Melcho – a young Pictish warrior

Keother – Pictish tribal chieftain

Gofanon – the Ala Sabiniana's armourer

Demetrius – Marcus's deputy commander

Liberalis – head of Hunnum's civilian authority

Senecio – a Numidian cavalryman and expert archer

Valeria – squadron commander Ala Sabiniana and Marcus's half-sister

Brenus – Marcus's father, a prince of the Brigantes and Roman cavalry commander

Bren – Marcus's eight-year-old son, abducted and carried off into slavery by a Saxon war band

Leof – Valeria's Saxon prisoner

Rufus Arrius – commander of Vindobala Roman fort

Septimus Iuventius – commander at Condercum

Julius Postumus Dulcitius – *dux Britanniarum*, commander of all Roman military forces in the north of Britannia

Cassius – commander of the fort at Segedunum

Pompeius Canalius – commander at Cilurnum

Justus – commander at Corstopitum

Sempronius – commander of Second Asturum

Tullius Nepos – tribune, commander of First Batavians, Brocolitia

Calista – keeper of Coventina's Well

Clarian Apollo – commander at Borcovicium

Ramios – leader of German mercenaries

Claudius Dexter – commander at Aesica, First Asturians

Hostilius Geta – junior officer of the Sixth Legion Victrix

Magnus Maximus – Roman general and usurper serving in Britannia who declared himself Emperor in AD 383

Count Theodosius – saviour of Britannia during the Great Barbarian Conspiracy of AD 367, later Emperor Theodosius I

Flavius Stilicho – Rome's pre-eminent general and adviser to the young Emperor Honorius

Honorius – Emperor of the West

Arcadius – Emperor of the East

King Coel – ruler of the southern Votadini

King Luddoc – ruler of the northern Votadini

King Corvus – ruler of the Selgovae

Queen Briga – ruler of the northern Picts

Nechtan – Briga's cousin, commander

Lucti – Briga's predecessor as king of the northern Picts

Ciniath – elder of Keother's people

Drosten – Ciniath's younger son

Duna – Drosten's wife

Breth – Ciniath's elder son

Niall of the Nine Hostages – Hibernian raider and pirate whose kingdom takes in Anglesey and part of Wales

Ninian – slave and former priest, later trooper of the Ala Sabiniana

Gordianus – master builder and the young Marcus's mentor
Antonius Felix – fort commander at Vindolanda
Blaid – keeper of Queen Briga's wolves
Antonius Vitalis – tribune commanding the Roman fort at Vindomora
Terentius Cantaber – legate of the Sixth Legion Victrix
Arelius Verinus – tribune, commander at Banna, First Dacians
Julius Pastor – commander First Herculaea
Emeritus – *centurio regionarius*, Luguvalium
Rufius Clemens – commander at Verteris
Senilis – Rufius's cavalry commander
Rhuin, Alpin – Pictish scouts
Aurelius Quirinus – commander at Longovicium
Burrius – commander Numerus Defensorum
Publius – commander of Fourth Gauls squadrons with Marcus

Military units

First Pannonian Wing of Sabinus, Ala Sabiniana, cavalry wing (Hunnum)
Sixth Legion Victrix (Eboracum)
Fourth Lingonum, part-mounted cohort (Segedunum)
First Frisians, auxiliary infantry (Vindobala)
Second Asturum (Cilurnum)
First Tungrians (Borcovicium)
First Asturians (Aesica)
First Batavians (Brocolitia)
First Dacians (Banna)
Fourth Gauls, part-mounted (Vindolanda)
First Herculaea (Epiacum)
Numerus Defensorum (Braboniacum)
Numerus Exploratorum (Lavatris)
Numerus Directorum (Verteris)

There was no respite from the barbed spears flung by their naked opponents, which tore our wretched countrymen from the walls and dashed them to the ground.

Gildas the Wise, *De Excidio Britanniae*
(On the Ruin of Britain) *c.* AD 500

Prologue

The northern frontier, AD 400

The screams of the raped and the dying carried through the night like the distant cries of squabbling gulls on a windswept shore.

Somewhere close by in the trees a man cursed and the commander of the Ala Sabiniana hissed a demand for silence. He understood their frustration. The victims of the Pictish murder raid were neither nameless nor faceless. Many of the riders around him on this Saint Jude's Eve had sat in the little forum of the settlement not a fortnight past, drinking companionably with the men, teasing the children and flirting with the women; greeted as protectors.

Yet for all the ear-grating suffering of innocents it suited Marcus Flavius Victor that the people of Alona should be reminded what could happen if that protection did not exist. Velanos, the village's *curator*, had been somewhat reluctant of late to part with the supplies due the frontier garrisons as a portion of his village's tax obligations. Next time he would be less so. If he lived.

His mount tossed its head and Marcus patted the animal's neck in an automatic gesture of reassurance. Other horses sensed the animal's tension and he heard the soft jingle of horse brass as their riders gentled them. On another night that sound might have been enough to get them all killed, but they were far enough away from the village for it not to matter. Besides, the Picts and their victims were making enough noise to conceal a cavalry charge.

At least four houses were already burning, identifiable as individual glowing pyres through the trees. Now they were joined by a fifth. A spectacular eruption of flame sent a shower of sparks high into the night sky and spoke of some highly combustible substance stored for the winter. An unearthly shrieking accompanied the flames, evidence the unfortunate occupants remained trapped inside.

'Prefect?' The word emerged from between an unseen trooper's gritted teeth.

'I told you to be silent,' Marcus snarled. 'The next man to speak will have the skin off his back by sundown tomorrow. We wait until Caradoc is in position.'

Someone laughed, but he chose not to hear it. They knew Caradoc and his four squadrons had been in position these many minutes past. Alona was a settlement of two hundred souls that lay ten miles south of *linea valli* – the line of the Wall – and an hour's march from the fort at Epiacum. Marcus had tracked the Picts for two days after they'd slipped into the province through an unguarded gap between two watchtowers. The raiders were the menfolk of newly arrived settlers from the High Lands who'd set up home in a remote valley north-east of Castra Exploratum, a long-abandoned outpost fort beyond the Wall. The moment they set foot south of the Wall they'd broken the truce Marcus had brokered. But that was the way of it. The war against the Picts never ended. You could defeat them a hundred times and still they'd keep coming.

Marcus unhooked his polished iron helmet from the pommel of his saddle and settled it over his head. The blackened leather padding that lined the interior instantly deadened the screams, the bitter-sweet scent of old sweat comfortingly familiar. His mind focused on the disposition of his forces, the layout of the settlement and any potential weaknesses in his plan. He felt no fear – a leader couldn't afford such distractions – only that familiar, almost breathless sense of anticipation that preceded battle.

'Stay close to me,' he growled into the darkness. 'And remember, I want prisoners.'

He nudged his mount forward and sensed movement all around him as his squadrons followed suit. A rough and poorly maintained wooden palisade encircled Alona, with entrances to the north and south. By now Caradoc and his hundred cavalry veterans would be converging on the northern gate. Marcus would lead two hundred more up the Epiacum road.

No trumpet calls or glorious charge. Instead, the riders advanced in an almost leisurely arcing trot that brought the column to the road out of sight of the village. Luko, Marcus's *draconarius*, bearer of the dragon standard, rode a pace and a half behind his left flank, and Marcus curbed Storm, his midnight-black Andalusian stallion, to allow the standard-bearer to close. He felt a shudder of expectation run through the horse as he drew his long sword from its scabbard with its familiar metallic hiss.

Storm responded by increasing his pace and Marcus let him have his head. The sound of hundreds of hooves echoed from the hard-packed road surface, but the Picts inside these walls would hear nothing but the crackle of flames and the screams of their victims.

The gates hung open, the bodies of those who'd been cut down while fleeing mere patches of deeper darkness on the roadway. He quickened the pace to a canter. This was the time of greatest danger. If his scouts had missed a single guard the horsemen would be met by a wall of spears.

As he swept through the gate a pair of shadowy figures rose from where they'd been stripping a body. The closest picked something up from the road and Marcus saw the glint of an iron spear point in the light from a burning building. Too late. Storm was already inside the point and Marcus brought his heavy cavalry sword round in a smooth, practised swing. The leather grip cushioned the jarring impact, but his fingers sensed the edge bite into flesh and the point grate across bone.

His victim went down with a howl of agony and dark liquid spurted high from the falling body. He angled Storm towards the second shadow as it darted towards a house to the left. Before he could strike a whooping figure passed him and skewered the man in the spine with the point of his long ash spear.

'Janus, you crazy bastard,' he rasped. 'Get back in position.'

The column had split into three as it entered the settlement. A pair of squadrons broke right and left across the patchwork of rutted fields and vegetable patches inside the palisade, to envelop the houses like the horns of a charging bull. Marcus took his remaining hundred men straight up the main street towards the glimmer of the flames.

The Picts had herded the inhabitants of Alona into the forum, where they could be butchered at their leisure, but not before they'd been tortured into revealing the location of any hidden valuables. A dozen bodies already lay scattered around a fire where reaping knives and a blacksmith's tongs glowed a fearsome red.

Every face turned at the clatter of hooves as Marcus's horsemen rode into the open space: he registered expressions of fear, astonishment, defiance and relief. The Roman cavalry outnumbered the raiders by five to one, but that didn't make the Picts any less dangerous. A few fled northwards only to be met by a new wall of bright iron as Caradoc entered the Magna gate with his squadrons. The others abandoned their captives and clustered in a defensive huddle that bristled with thrusting spears as the cavalrymen moved to surround them.

'I want them alive,' Marcus reminded his officers. 'Every last one.'

A single Pict, a seasoned warrior draped in wolfskins, remained by the fire. He held a young woman in a white shift with her back against his chest and the blade of his long, curved knife touching the pale white skin of her throat. Stark terror contorted a face that might normally have shone with extraordinary beauty. Before them, a man who must be her husband knelt with his hands bound behind his back.

Marcus walked his horse from the encircling riders and approached the Picts.

'Throw down your spears and I will spare your lives.' He used the

Pictish tongue which every frontier soldier learned before he was allowed on his first patrol.

The big man met his gaze and spat. Without taking his eyes from Marcus he drew the knife across the pale flesh of the girl's slim neck. For a moment it seemed nothing had happened before a terrible gurgling cry rent the air and a dark stain sheeted the front of the white dress.

Marcus sighed and turned Storm away. 'Take them.'

It was daylight by the time the last of the Picts had been subdued and they sat in a sullen, battered huddle under the spears of their captors, each man's hands securely bound at the wrist. Fifty-six, if he'd counted correctly. Most were young men, their wispy beards more ambition than reality, but a scattering had the look of experienced warriors. They wore their hair in a curious style, an intricate topknot Marcus hadn't previously encountered. Stinking, matted furs or filthy, oft-patched plaid tunics offered scant protection against the chill air. Cloth *braccae* encased their legs to the calf and some of the older men had boots of felt or leather, but most went barefoot. It had required six men to subdue the big warrior with the knife and Caradoc had suffered a fearsome slash across the ribs in following his commander's order to take the man alive.

'How is he?' Marcus asked Zeno, the unit's *medicus*, as he worked on the injured decurion's wounds.

'He'll live.' The doctor cheerfully ignored Caradoc's groans as he stitched the gash. 'If it doesn't mortify he'll be back in the saddle before the turn of the year.'

Seven Picts had died in the fighting, which Marcus counted an acceptable price. A number of the others had suffered broken bones and other injuries, but they were mostly whole. A pile of confiscated weapons lay nearby and Marcus picked up a broad-bladed Pictish sword. It was an unwieldy weapon, rust-pitted and notched, but it would do.

'Bring them to the big oak,' he ordered Luko. 'And tell those vultures,' he pointed towards the hovering band of villagers who'd armed themselves with whatever edged or blunt weapon came most easily to hand, 'the first man to harm any of my prisoners will take his place. And Luko?'

'Yes, lord?'

Marcus nodded towards the prisoners. 'Choose five of the most dangerous-looking bastards and keep them apart with that big savage.'

He regretted what must be done, but his orders from Eboracum were clear. The Pictish raids had become too frequent and their warriors' confidence a sign of growing threat. A message must be sent. One that could not be ignored.

The oak, gnarled and twisted, towered over the other trees at the forest's edge, topped by a vast canopy of skeletal branches and with a trunk the circumference of a roundhouse. It had been the settlement's gathering place long before the Romans arrived to give Alona a semblance of civilization and a name. Ragged strips of cloth fluttered in the lower branches and little copper coins glittered within cracks in the bark, evidence the tree still inspired a certain awe in the superstitious and the gullible.

Dismounted cavalrymen escorted the prisoners from the gate as the villagers hissed and cursed. Some of the wrathful men, including Velanos, the settlement's leader, waved knives and reaping hooks, but none dared risk Marcus's wrath. The Picts remained untouched.

A large fire had been set close by the stump of a mature tree felled years earlier. The tethered prisoners eyed the flames uneasily as they were herded into a group close by.

'Strip them,' Marcus ordered. The cavalrymen went to work cutting away the Picts' clothing with knives to the hoots of the villagers, which quickly turned to jeers and taunting as the prisoners' nether parts reacted to the touch of the chill morning air. Picts. The Painted Ones, as the frontier soldiers had called them since the time of Marcus's father's father's father. His men used the name for any warrior north of the Wall, but Marcus knew that among themselves many of those considered southern Picts retained their old tribal identities: Novantae, Selgovae, Votadini and Damnonii.

The origin of the title became obvious when the men were naked. Most of them wore facial tattoos, intricate patterns of dotted lines and unreadable symbols. But the story of their lives and the accomplishments that gave them status and fame among their people was written upon their chests, backs and arms. All of the younger men sported the mask of a stylized fox above their left breast, indicating their clan. More dotted patterns decorated them according to rank, courage, raids completed and enemies killed or outwitted, different designs and other animals: the hare, the wolf, the horse, the boar, the hawk and the eagle. The veteran fighters wore a veritable menagerie, but it was the warrior who had cut the girl's throat who drew his attention. Scarcely an inch of his heavily muscled flesh was left bare of symbol or pattern. Fine warriors, fearless and merciless, but today they would be taught that Rome still had teeth.

As the prisoners were stripped, five of Marcus's men threw plaited ropes across a sturdy branch perhaps ten feet above the ground. A great moan went up as the younger Picts noticed the nooses that adorned the ropes' ends. The big warrior snarled at his comrades to be silent, to show courage, and as the cavalrymen hustled the five veterans towards the branch he turned to Marcus with loathing written across his swarthy features.

'We are not afraid to die, Roman,' he spat. 'And be sure that your death will be a hundred times more painful and prolonged.'

Marcus watched as the nooses were placed around the necks of the doomed men and the ropes slowly tightened, raising them on to their toes as they began to struggle for breath.

'We will see how brave you are in a moment.' He turned to address the main group of prisoners. 'This is the fate you all deserve.' He raised a hand and the cavalrymen on the ends of the ropes hauled so that the Picts were lifted a few inches off the ground, the rough hemp nooses cutting into their necks, constricting their throats and forcing their tongues from their mouths. The dying men wriggled and twisted like hooked fish, faces livid and contorted. Desperate cawing sounds accompanied their agony, encouraging a growl of approval from the watching villagers. 'But I am minded to be merciful,' Marcus continued impassively. 'One man brought you here. One man blinded you with lies of treasure and plunder. One man encouraged you to kill.' He nodded to Luko. 'Secure him to the tree.'

They'd discovered that under a grown man's weight ordinary nails quickly tore through the flesh of his wrists and ankles, which made it an untidy business. Marcus's armourer had solved the dilemma by forging nails with flat two-inch heads. The Pict didn't make a sound as the nails were hammered through his flesh into the oak, piercing skin and shattering bones, though he bit his lip so hard blood ran down his chin.

'This is the Pict who led the attack on your village,' Marcus called to Velanos. 'He is responsible for the destruction of your property and the death of your loved ones. Do with him as you will.'

'Murderer!' The husband of the butchered girl dashed forward with a howl of rage and anguish and a reaping knife in his hand. He reached for the big warrior's groin. Marcus turned away as an agonized shriek tore the still air and a dozen other villagers rushed past him to take their revenge.

Who would it be? He studied the prisoners as they watched their leader die. A face drew his attention. He might be kin to Janus. 'You,' he pointed to a young man of about twenty who stood shaking with fear and cold, his bound hands covering his groin. 'Come here.'

Terror had drained all the strength from the Pict's legs and one of Marcus's troopers had to support him across the glade.

'Who is your lord?' Marcus spoke quietly, using the tip of the Pictish sword to raise the man's chin so he could look into his pale, bewildered features.

'Lord?' The wide eyes darted from side to side in search of an unlikely avenue of escape.

'Who rules your tribe?' Marcus persisted.

'Our chief is called Keother.'

'And to whom does this Keother pay tribute?'

'I do not know, lord,' the young man whispered.

Marcus nodded slowly. 'Then I wish you to carry a message to Keother.'

'A message?'

'Yes. Take him across there,' Marcus pointed to a spot on the edge of the clearing and the cavalryman dragged the young man aside. Marcus strode purposefully to the tree stump. 'Bring the first one forward,' he ordered.

Two troopers chose a prisoner from the huddled group and man-handled him towards the stump. A low growl went up from the remaining captives, only to be stifled instantly as the ring of spear points surrounding them tightened. When the troopers reached the stump one held the prisoner's shoulders while the other dragged the bound man's arms onto the flat surface.

The terrified Pict looked up into Marcus's eyes and Marcus felt a momentary pang of regret before he steeled himself to do what no leader could avoid.

'This is Rome's mercy.' He raised the sword and brought the edge down on the outstretched arms just above the wrist. The prisoner shrieked in agony and disbelief and a great howl erupted from his penned tribesfolk.

The cavalryman tossed the severed hands aside and dragged the uncomprehending Pict to the fire, where his screams reached a new pitch as Luko stemmed the spurting blood with a glowing iron. The stink of burning flesh and loosened bowels filled the air. Another pris-oner was dragged to the stump. Sickened by what had been forced upon him, Marcus threw the sword to the nearest of his troopers and stepped away. 'Let every man play his part,' he said.

An hour later he stood amid a sea of severed hands, his breath mist-ing the morning air and the metallic stench of the slaughterhouse filling his nostrils. A groaning line of hunched, shivering men, bound to each other by the neck, waited nearby, each consumed by his own personal agony and the certainty of a future without hope. Only one Pict remained unharmed. Marcus called the waiting prisoner to him. His face was as white as a December snowfield.

'What is your name?'

'I am Melcho,' the prisoner replied with a fearful glance at his mutilated comrades.

'You understand the message you are to carry to Keother, Melcho?'

'I . . . I think so, lord.'

'You will lead these men back to your village – I will give you an escort as far as the Wall – and you will inform Keother this is what happens when he breaks his king's oath. If there is a next time his warriors will return without their eyes and tongues.'

The man swallowed, barely able to nod his agreement.

'And Melcho?'

'Lord?'

'Never venture south of the Wall again.'

'No, lord.' The young Pict was about to turn away, but he hesitated, lip trembling. 'Who shall I say sent the message?'

Marcus gazed across the gore-spattered clearing to the dangling bodies of the Pictish warriors and the bloody mess that was all that remained of their leader.

'My name is Marcus Flavius Victor and men fear me. I am Lord of the Wall.'

EARTH

I

Hunnum (Halton Chesters)

An empire does not just die: first it fades, then it crumbles. Who had said that? Was it his father or his blood-father? Marcus couldn't remember which, but there was no denying the truth of it.

Yes, the truth of it was abundantly clear in the decaying barrack rooms of the fort, the missing paving slabs in the courtyard and the roofs where thatch had long ago replaced the terracotta tiles of two or three generations earlier. He'd used the broken slabs and fallen tiles to fill in gaps where the original stone had fallen from the outer walls. With a pang of conscience, he'd replaced some of the slabs with the last of the pagan altars his predecessors had set up to the gods they worshipped. Minerva, Mars and Jupiter had served them well. Now Marcus liked to believe they were content to fulfil a different role keeping his men's feet from the mud. A soldier could live comfortably enough beside his horse in a barrack block, however draughty, but he needed good solid walls to fight behind, and Marcus couldn't afford to properly repair both.

Hunnum, his home and his refuge for the last ten years. Base of the First Pannonian Wing of Sabinus since the time of Septimius Severus,

13

though none of the present Ala Sabiniana had ever trod the earth of Pannonia, and they neither knew, nor cared, who Sabinus had been. The fort lay on the crest of a hill, straddling the Wall and surrounded by the many hundreds of *iugera* of good grazing land that was the prime requirement of a cavalry *ala*. To north and south the country undulated into the distance in a gently flowing succession of peaks and troughs. Hunnum had always been a curiosity on the frontier. It was built, if the dedication stones were to be believed, by the Sixth legion at the same time Hadrianus Augustus ordered the construction of the Wall. But what made it unique was the extension added by some long-dead commander to create more space for horses and men, and which gave it the shape of a cavalry trooper's boot lying on its side.

Marcus took a moment to savour the sights and sounds and scents, revelling in the familiarity of it. Smoke from the bread ovens still hung in the air of the chill morning, competing with the permanent reek of horse dung that marked any cavalry fort. Gofanon, the unit's armourer, sat hunched over his anvil in his workshop trying to salvage a batch of faulty blades foisted on them by Eboracum, and the rhythmic clang of his hammer echoed from the walls. On the far side of the courtyard, beyond the pig pens, two boys, the sons of Marcus's troopers, flailed at each other with wooden practice swords in preparation for the day they would join their fathers in the saddle.

'Do you think they'll repair?' Marcus called as he walked past the armourer.

'I'd have a better idea if me and my lads hadn't spent every spare moment knocking out your toys for the last week.' Gofanon didn't look up or pause in his work. 'But I reckon the blades will be ready by the time you get back.'

Hunnum had been sited to provide protection for Porta Aquilonis, the gate which carried the Great North Road through the Wall. Turn south and that road would take a man over rolling uplands, across countless rivers and streams, through valley and pasture and rich forest all the way to Londinium. To the north it had once bustled with carts and pack animals conveying supplies to the outlying frontier forts, and couriers destined for the long-abandoned outer turf wall a hundred miles further on. Now it was used only by Marcus's cavalry patrols and the engineering gangs who kept it in decent repair as far as the ruins of Habitancum, an old scouting base a day's march away. Good hunting country even now, by God's favour, because Marcus ensured his officers took only what they needed for the table and left the deer alone during the calving season. The rivers teemed with trout and grayling, and great, slab-sided salmon provided a generous bounty in spring and autumn, along with the geese and thrushes the huntsmen netted in their thousands.

Luko sat patiently in the saddle with the *draco* resting on his right shoulder. Beside him, Claudius, Marcus's stable boy, was clinging on to Storm. The horse skittered restlessly with suppressed energy and the boy's lean, ten-year-old features were set in a frown of concentration.

'Don't worry, Claudius.' Marcus took the reins from the boy's hands with a smile. 'I'll bring him back to you soon enough.'

As he mounted, a young officer approached from the *principia*, the fort's headquarters building. 'Demetrius,' Marcus greeted his deputy commander. 'You know your orders. Keep the barbarians from the gate at all costs.'

'That would be easier if you'd left me enough people to man the watchtowers, never mind the walls.' Demetrius accompanied the words with a wry look. 'But I'll use every man, including the clerks and the kitchen slaves. The boys from the settlement can earn their place for a change by taking their turn on the ramparts.'

'Good,' Marcus nodded, 'and Demetrius?' He leaned from the saddle. 'At need you may call on a century from the garrison at Corstopitum.' Demetrius gave a little whistle. Corstopitum was the main supply base for the central Wall garrisons, a substantial township in the valley two miles south of Hunnum. The soldiers who defended it were legionaries from the Sixth Victrix at Eboracum. 'I've told the tribune that, at least for now, the integrity of the frontier takes precedence over his precious stores. He may be reluctant, but . . .'

'He knows better than to cross you,' Demetrius laughed. 'I won't ask unless they're lining up in front of the gate.' He took a step back and saluted. 'I'll do my best, prefect.'

'I know you will, Demetrius. I wouldn't have left you with so few men if I didn't trust you to cope. If it's any consolation I don't think you have to worry.' He glanced at the dark, lowering clouds with their promise of snow. 'Only a fool would be out and about in this weather.'

Demetrius pursed his lips. 'And yet you'll be gone for a month, lord?'

'My inspection tour is long overdue.' Marcus ignored the veiled rebuke and smiled. 'And I'm called to a meeting with the *dux Britanniarum* at Segedunum. A good hunter never misses a chance to take out two ducks with one cast.'

'Then I wish you Fortun—' Demetrius grinned at his mistake. 'I mean may God watch over you, lord.'

Marcus shook his head. 'One day you're going to say that to the wrong person, boy. Fare well.'

'And you, lord.'

Marcus nudged Storm towards the south gate past the granaries and the hospital. Outside the gate houses, shops, workshops and taverns lined the road, along with a *mansio* guest house built to host visiting dignitaries, but which now housed Hunnum's brothel. Like the fort, the stone houses had seen better days and some had been replaced entirely by wooden structures. Marcus heard an excited female voice calling his name from the brothel.

The bulk of the regiment had preceded them and little clumps of the village's residents lined the main street to watch apprehensively as the fort's prefect rode to join his men on the heath to the east of the village. These soldiers were their protectors, the only thing that stood between them and a Pictish war axe. Most of the older men were former auxiliaries who'd served with the troopers of the Ala Sabiniana before settling in the village to eke out their retirement with their families. The others were the wives and children of serving soldiers, and their slaves. Young or old, most of the faces wore the pinched look that went with acute hunger, and many of them didn't hide their resentment about their empty bellies.

Marcus grimaced as he recognized a bearded face among the crowd and he reined in Storm as the man stepped out to meet him. 'Liberalis,' Marcus nodded. 'I hope I see you well?'

'They tell me you're going to be away for a while? Weeks even?' Liberalis spoke with the authority of the head of the village's administrative council. He farmed a tract of land among the low hills to the south, but the tanning works that gave his clothing its all-pervading, pungent aroma of stale urine provided his main income. To Marcus's certain knowledge he also had a lucrative sideline selling off the mounds of horse shit the fort's hundreds of mounts and remounts produced to local farmers. Nominally he was subject to the prefect's authority, but he'd served with Marcus's father and it suited Marcus to treat him, for the most part, as an equal.

'Then I hope the Picts don't have as efficient an intelligence department as you do, *curator*,' Marcus answered cheerfully. 'Otherwise they might be paying you a visit.'

'You're stripping the fort bare?' For all his status Liberalis didn't dare venture a direct criticism, but his meaning was clear enough.

'Demetrius is a steady man.' Marcus ignored the puffed-out cheeks and shake of the head. 'And Justus down at Corstopitum has a standing order to supply him with a century of legionaries at the first sign of trouble.'

'Even if he obeys – and he'll find a reason not to – Justus will spend an hour making up his mind what to do. By the time they get here we'll all be dead.'

Marcus studied the men grouped behind the elder. 'Then perhaps you and the other veterans should scrape the rust off your swords, give them a proper edge and put in some practice,' he said. 'I hear training sessions aren't too well attended?'

He saw a nerve twitch in the other man's cheek. The frontier veterans' discharge diploma contained an agreement that they maintain their skills at arms and fitness ready for a return to the ranks in the event of an emergency. It was Liberalis's responsibility to ensure they kept to their part of the bargain, but Marcus knew barely one man in three did so. He made to turn Storm away, but Liberalis decided he wasn't finished.

'Your men haven't received their *stipendium* for months. We can't be expected to extend credit to their families indefinitely.'

'I'm aware of that.' Marcus's words were measured and restrained, but Liberalis detected a dangerous glint in the dark eyes that made him hesitate.

'I . . .'

'I'll see you receive your money, Liberalis. As you always have in the past. Today you will organize a donative of food and clothing in my name and you will double their credit until I return.' The other man opened his mouth to protest, but Marcus continued relentlessly. 'Because if you do not, I will begin an investigation into certain tax irregularities involving food being sold to the quartermaster at Corstopitum instead of being handed directly to the garrison as it should be by law. Is that understood?'

Liberalis nodded mutely and turned quickly away.

'That stopped the cheeky bastard's gob,' Luko chuckled as they rode away. 'Has he really been flogging off our rations?'

'I have no idea,' Marcus admitted. 'But wouldn't you if you were in his position?'

Their route took them past neglected mausolea that lined both sides of the road, one or two of them impressive monuments which contained the remains of the fort's previous commanders and their families. Beyond them lay the carefully tended graves of the settlement's Christian cemetery, each burial marked by a whitewashed boulder brought from the stream that fed Hunnum's water supply.

The three hundred men of Ala Sabiniana waited in parade formation for their commander's inspection on a flat, bare plateau to the east of the road. Even the birds seemed to have paused for breath in an abnormal silence that deepened as Marcus and his standard-bearer approached. They took up position beside the regiment's senior decurion and the prefect's trumpeter.

Marcus choked back an oath when he recognized the officer. 'I

18

thought I told you to stay in barracks, you old fool.' He glared at Caradoc. 'You still have a hole in you I could ride this horse through.'

'Begging the prefect's pardon,' the decurion grimaced. 'But the *medicus* said I was fit to ride.'

'Did he say how far?'

'We'll just have to see, won't we, sir.'

'All right,' Marcus allowed his tone to soften. 'Return to your squadron, decurion.' In truth he'd been pleased to see the grizzled old soldier back in the saddle. Caradoc was the most experienced trooper in the regiment and he would need every veteran who could wield a sword before this expedition ran its course. Caradoc saluted and turned away with a wink. Marcus stifled a laugh. He waited until the decurion had taken his place in front of the rightmost squadron before allowing his gaze to slide across the ten compact squares of riders, each nominally thirty men strong.

Clouds of steam rose in the chill air above the animals, the only sound the chink of horse brass, the thump of hooves pawing the frozen earth, and the snorting of beasts energized by their riders' palpable sense of anticipation. Every trooper wore a woollen cloak that had once been green, but was now so faded, patched and mended it resembled muddy plaid. Beneath the cloak, over a padded leather tunic, a vest of linked iron rings or scales covered his body from neck and upper arms to knees. Like their cloaks the mail had been mended so often it was akin to the farmer's mattock which he boasted had 'lasted a lifetime', he'd only changed the shaft three times and the head once. Heavy winter breeches of different patterns clad their legs and each had been issued with a new pair of stout boots made by the unit's cobbler from leather unwillingly supplied at a discount by Liberalis. Pot helmets of various designs encased their skulls, many of the metal helms on their fourth or fifth owner and with the dents and scars to show for it.

But Marcus didn't need them to look pretty. He needed them to be able to fight. For all its hard wear, their battered armour showed not a speck of rust. They had two other things in common. One was the round shield every man carried, freshly embossed with the unit's emblem of a red eagle, wings outstretched and gaping beak screaming its defiance. The other was the glitter of the iron points that topped their nine-foot ash spears, polished at great effort to a mirrored sheen. They carried three days' rations in a leather bag on one side of the saddle and three days' fodder for their horse on the other. Horse soldiers, an elite and immensely proud of that fact, Marcus had trained them so they were equally at home on foot, either in attack or defence.

Only the elaborate decoration of the iron helmet he wore differentiated Marcus from his soldiers. Sheathed with silver and studded with garnets, it had a long nose guard, hinged cheekpieces that strapped together beneath his chin, and a broad neck protector. Bands of iron ran from brow to nape and ear to ear to reinforce the dome, and leather and wool padded the interior for greater comfort. For all its beauty Marcus disliked the helmet. In battle it marked him out as a target for any ambitious Pict seeking plunder and fame. But his blood-father had taught him that a commander had to be more than a leader. He must also be a symbol: the visible manifestation of calm, order and authority among the chaos. The helmet was an expression of power.

He edged Storm a little closer to the still formations.

'You look well, Pannonians.' His strong voice carried across the parade ground. He knew the opening would amuse them. Apart from one or two exotic exceptions every man had been born on the island of Britannia and counted himself a Briton. Half of them were the descendants of auxiliaries who'd manned the Wall over the centuries. Pannonians, yes, but also Tungrians, Batavians, Asturians and Thracians. He had two Picts, the brothers Janus and Julius, twins, though instantly identifiable by their contrasting characters, taken captive as children and as happy to slit the throats of their brethren as any other. One African, Senecio, who was shy about his origins, but seemed to have been born in the saddle. He could put an arrow through a mouse's eyeball at sixty paces from a horse at full gallop, which was all Marcus cared about. Zeno, the *medicus*, was Greek, with a history that was much more interesting than he cared to admit.

Marcus also had five or six deserters from the Sixth Legion Victrix, who'd enlisted under assumed names. Their past didn't concern him, only that they would sooner fight than preen, and preferred the more relaxed discipline of the *limitanei* frontier troops to the iron hand and wooden rod of the regulars, the *comitatenses*. The rest were Marcus's Brigantian tribesfolk, raised to service in the Roman cavalry for countless generations.

'I am glad you have looked out your ceremonial finery for our meeting with the *dux Britanniarum* at Segedunum,' he continued, to a ripple of laughter. 'But our jaunt has a more serious purpose. You will have heard that we will be in the saddle for some weeks as I embark on my long-delayed inspection tour of the Wall garrisons. What, you ask, in the dead of winter, with sparse grazing and ice soon thick on the ponds? Well there is a reason for our haste. Perhaps it is a whisper on the wind, or just a stirring in the air, but I have a feeling we will be busy come the spring.' A growl of appreciation. They all understood the resurgent power in the north. 'Regiment will prepare to advance,' he called.

He waited until the decurions had turned their squadrons towards the *via militaris* before he urged Storm into motion.

'Ride, brothers,' he ordered. 'Ride for Segedunum.'

II

A blanket of dense, low cloud the colour of piss-stained wool hung above the Ala Sabiniana as the long column of horsemen rode east on the supply road that ran parallel to the Wall. From the thick haze an almost imperceptible drizzle drifted down that clung to everything it touched and made Marcus glad of his thick, lanolin-coated cloak. As he rode, part of his mind was on his surroundings and the incredible structure for which Rome held him responsible. Between the road and the Wall lay a system of what had once been impressive banks and ditches. When it was first dug it would have been an immense physical scar of raw earth and Marcus had long pondered why the labour of so many thousands of men had been expended to create a barrier that appeared, to a soldier's eye at least, to be of little practical value. It could never have been manned and even with the usual ingenious additions of palisade, sharpened stakes and thorn bushes wouldn't have delayed a determined enemy for long. The banks remained, steep grass-covered mounds, but the ditch had been filled in long, long ago, and in most places it was now little more than a shallow depression in the landscape.

'This is a fine country.' Zeno, riding at his side, broke Marcus's reverie. He looked southwards over a patchwork of grey, green, gold and brown that swelled and undulated like the waves of a gently rolling sea. 'It shouldn't be at war. You should be on your estate, lord, growing crops and breeding sons.'

Marcus turned in the saddle to follow his gaze and winced at a sudden pain in his chest. 'We've always been at war. Besides,' he said, 'I have a son. Not much of a son,' he added almost to himself. He and Bren shared the same blood, but little else: a sickly child whose birth had cost Marcus the only woman he'd ever truly loved. If the rumour he'd heard was true perhaps they no longer even shared as much. 'But there is still plenty of time for more sons.'

The *medicus* noticed the reaction to the old wound. 'You should let me look at that.'

'Don't fuss over me,' Marcus growled. Zeno was dressed and armed in the same fashion as his comrades and could fight as well as the best of them. His helmet hung from the pommel of his saddle and he rode with the butt of his long ash spear in the leg of his boot. He was tall and thin, with curly raven hair, a small, expressive mouth and skin that seemed to glow with health whatever his circumstances.

'It's your funeral, lord,' the *medicus* agreed. 'But, as I was saying, a man should have children early. Not as early as a woman, of course, women should bear children early and often, if they survive.' He smiled as a thought came to him. 'God should have said that. Sow thy seed early and often lest thy seed run dry. What age are you now, lord? Forty?'

'Thirty-seven. It's just land,' Marcus steered the conversation back to less provocative territory. 'Field and forest, pasture, moor, mountain and bog. Some of it is good. Some of it isn't. Didn't they have land like this in Greece?'

'In Greece the earth only seems to produce stones.' Zeno frowned at some troubling memory. 'And vines, of course, and sometimes olive trees. But I often wonder whether the Persians salted the land wherever they touched it. Asia was different, at least the parts I saw outside Constantinopolis. But it was a different type of green, especially in the north. More verdant, but less comforting, you might say.'

Marcus smiled. Zeno liked to tell anyone who would listen that God had come to him in a dream and told him his healing powers would be of more value to the brave heroes stemming the barbarian tide in the north than in the fleshpots of the Empire's eastern capital. The truth was a little different.

They continued at a leisurely walk and after an hour in the saddle the familiar outline of the fort at Vindobala appeared on the ridge line to their left. As always, Marcus felt a stirring in his blood at the sight of the tall corner towers and the grey ramparts once lime-washed to give the stronghold its name – White Walls. This was where he had made the painful, frustrated transition from boy to youth and he knew every worn step and paving slab of those ramparts. A hundred and seventy paces north to south, and a hundred and twenty east to west, the fort straddled the Wall and its gateways had once formed a major crossing point for trade between the frontier tribes in time of peace. A horn blared in the distance, sounding high and tinny, and armed men appeared to line the walls.

'Arrius's people are alert enough.'

'For once,' Luko grunted.

Marcus called Senecio from the ranks. 'Ride to the fort and tell them there will be no inspection today, but that we will be back within the week.'

'No inspection today, lord.' Senecio's skin was so dark it had a purple tinge and the deep brown eyes never betrayed emotion, but he could outride any man in the unit. He spun his horse and urged the animal diagonally across the slope at a flashy gallop over humps and hollows that marked a long-abandoned settlement. When he was halfway, a hare broke from under his mount's hooves. Before it covered twenty jinking paces, Senecio had unslung the bow from his back, notched an arrow and loosed it to pin the fleeing animal through the body. Still at full gallop and with the bow in his left hand, he stooped from the saddle to pick up the carcass by the arrow that impaled it.

'One of these days he'll break his neck doing that.' Zeno shook his head.

'What was Constantinopolis like?'

Zeno frowned at the unexpected return to the conversation of an hour earlier. 'You have seen Rome, lord?' he said eventually.

'No, but I've visited Londinium.' Marcus's nose wrinkled at the memory of the sewer stink that had hung in the air thick enough to chew. 'There were too many people and I didn't much like their habits.'

'Well Constantinopolis is like neither,' Zeno assured him. 'It makes Londinium look like a squalid country hamlet and is to Rome what the Empress Maria is to some ancient, toothless crone. Arcadius's Great Palace is clad in gold and precious stones and is not one palace, but four, aye and barracks and baths and beautiful gardens by the dozen, each as broad as your parade ground. The entirety of it would swallow up the Palatine, the Capitoline, and everything in between.' Marcus had little notion of the exact dimensions Zeno was describing, but he had heard enough of the Palatine and Capitoline to appreciate the scale. And Zeno was only getting into his stride. 'The great palace is only one of many: every aristocrat has a mansion worthy of the name. Magnificent churches by the score. Shaded courtyards where any may partake of cool water fed from underground cisterns. The Mese, that is to say the main thoroughfare through the city, is four miles in length and wide enough to carry five wagons in line abreast, flanked by columned basilicas, and passes through no less than five forums, each of which rivals the Forum Romanum, before it reaches the Golden Gate . . .'

'This Golden Gate must be set into great walls,' Marcus interrupted. 'How do the walls of Constantinopolis compare with this?' He pointed to his left where the outline of a turret rose above the leaden-grey line of the Wall on the horizon. Three times the height of a man and three paces in width at the base, every stone of the Wall had been quarried and set in place centuries earlier by the men of three Roman legions. It stretched to east and west as far as the eye could reach and was the greatest feat of construction in the western Empire.

Zeno frowned. The question gave him pause for good reason. This would call for diplomacy.

'As I understand it our Wall runs for more than seventy miles and stretches from sea to sea, a feat which is surely unmatched in all the world.' The Greek accompanied the words with a smile of transparent insincerity. At barely twice the height of the spear he carried, Marcus's vaunted Wall was little higher than the pens Zeno's forebears constructed in Boeotia to keep the wolves from their cattle. For Zeno, the Wall was less of a barrier than a dividing line between civilization and barbarism. The Picts could cross at will in any one of a hundred places. The only thing that kept them from doing so was Marcus's combination of diplomacy, bribery and the kind of bloody example he had set at Alona. Yet the events at Alona were the exception rather than the norm. Along most of the Wall, north and south, families lived and farmed peacefully, sometimes within sight of the rampart. 'The walls of Constantinopolis encompass a mere ten miles,' the Greek confessed, 'though much of their length is also protected by the sea.'

'And yet they must be taller, surely?' Marcus accompanied his question with a hint of wry amusement that told Zeno his stratagem had been in vain.

'In truth, lord,' Zeno laughed, 'the walls of Constantinopolis do not rise, they soar, to twenty times and more the height of this battered little rampart of yours. So high that they seem to touch the clouds and it is a miracle they are not topped by snow in winter like the Taurus mountains. Too high by far for any siege ladder. Nova Roma is impregnable to siege, yet before I left the city Emperor Arcadius, may God protect him, had ordered his engineers to draw up plans for an even greater fortification.'

'And all the while,' Marcus growled, 'we must defend the north with the wind whistling through the cracks in our barrack walls and the arse torn out of our breeches.'

'The world has ever been ill divided, lord,' the *medicus* acknowledged. 'In my enthusiasm I may have painted an overly complimentary picture of Constantinopolis. True, it is a physical paradise, but the people are prone to arrogance and vanity, particularly the women, who flaunt their charms in a most un-Christian manner. Corruption, conspiracy and betrayal are woven into their souls like strands of silken thread. Arcadius's palace is a festering political cesspit where the weak are devoured and the strong grow fat on their flesh. Arcadius was led by his nether parts by his wife Eudoxia, whose poisonous influence pervaded all Nova Roma. She alienated the common folk and Rome by raising one of her eunuchs to the position of consul, and both she and the Emperor are held in thrall by the power of the Goths and the Ostrogoths who inhabit the fringes of the eastern Empire. Arcadius likes to call them his watchdogs, but in truth they are the wolves waiting in the bushes outside a sheep-fold. That is the reality of Constantinopolis, lord.'

'I have plenty of experience of wolves outside the sheepfold.' Marcus stared northwards.

'And the province has much to thank for your success in dealing with them.'

Marcus turned in the saddle and pinned him with his dark eyes. 'Do not think your oily flattery deceives me, Greek.' He tempered the threat with a laugh. 'If only the festering political cesspit was as easy to deal with as a few thousand Picts.'

They rode on in silence for a long time. The river in the valley below grew broader and eventually Marcus caught the familiar tang of salt on the breeze. Quite soon the fort at Pons Aelius came into view, and the wide, stone bridge that gave it its name.

'What happened to the wife?'

'She died,' Zeno said, keeping his eyes on the horizon ahead.

She slipped between the huts like a wraith until she reached the centre of the compound where the largest building stood. Two guards flanked the doorway, but they acknowledged neither her presence nor her existence. She might have been invisible, but for the fact that she could sense the fear that clung to them like a fog. She passed between them and pushed the door, which was unbarred as she had ordered, slipping into the darkened interior. Here too the scent of fear hung thick in the air. Around her, still as death, a dozen guards feigned sleep. Any one of them could have killed her, but the power of her reputation and the hostages she held from their families kept them

27

frozen in position. Untroubled by the stygian gloom she strode confidently towards the room at the rear and drew the curtain aside. The remains of a fire glowed in the hearth to provide just enough light to see the bed and the mound of furs, but she would have located it even in the pitch dark by the animal snoring. She reached beneath her dress and withdrew a wooden tube with a stopper at one end and a mouthpiece at the other. The furs moved and she stepped forward to be confronted by a naked girl-child who smiled at the sight of her and rolled clear of the bed. A twitch of the head sent the child away. She approached closer, and now she could see him. A face that might have been carved with an axe, all harsh lines and flat planes. Rumpled silver hair and a pointed beard of the same colour. He had his head thrown back and his mouth open. She carefully removed the stopper and put the mouthpiece to her lips. She waited for the right moment and blew a cloud of dust directly into his mouth just as he drew in a breath. He choked and his eyes flew open. She saw the moment when, in his mind, his hand went to the sword he always kept beside the bed, and the realization that it could never be. The dust was a compound of dried mushroom that brought instant temporary paralysis, though he still retained the ability to cry out.

'You,' he hissed. 'Guards, to me. Guards!'

She stood back and watched until he understood how helpless he was and the cries faded. But he was not completely cowed.

'I am Lucti, High King of the Caledonian Picts, and I swear by the spear of Beli Mawr that I will have my revenge. Begone, witch.'

She smiled. 'You are an old man and your time is past.' She pulled a narrow, pointed dagger from a scabbard at her waist and Lucti gasped. 'But you have one more service you can do for your people.'

She placed a hand on his chin and made three deft strokes with the knife, rejoicing in his howls of terror and pain. When she was done, she showed him the dagger with his left eye gleaming like an obscene jewel on the point.

'This is only the beginning.'

III

Segedunum (Wallsend)

'Halt the column and have Caradoc make a final inspection of weapons and armour,' Marcus told Luko. 'Tell him I want to make an impression when we ride in.'

Luko rode off to pass on the orders. Marcus turned to study the fort on the flat ground above the river and to turn over in his mind the encounter that lay ahead.

Segedunum was the Wall's end and the most easterly fort. The grey-brown waters of the River Tinan curved in a great arc below the stone ramparts towards the sea two or three miles distant. The Wall abutted Segedunum's western flank just below the main gate, and continued beyond the fort for a further four hundred paces at a sharp angle, from the south-eastern tower to where it reached the river. On its parapet, just above the tideline, a colossal figure stood facing seawards. Between the Wall and the river, the dilapidated ruins of what had once been a thriving civilian settlement straggled along the northern bank. Tumbled stone cloaked with emerald moss, ochre roof tiles, cracked and scattered, weed-choked doorways and walls and windows draped with fronds of ivy. The earthen bank that had protected the settlement

29

from seaborne raiders had crumbled into the outer ditch leaving a shallow depression that wouldn't have checked the stride of an infant. Despite the dilapidation, a few of the buildings showed signs of habitation and thankfully the bathhouse was one of them. Smoke from the furnace drifted in the still air across what had been the forum.

Marcus's eye drifted to four substantial merchant ships moored at a wooden jetty below the fort. He gave a grunt of satisfaction at the sight. It was better than he dared hope. At least he shouldn't be delayed any longer than necessary. On the far side of the river a train of carts moved ponderously along the road from Pons Aelius to Arbeia, the port and granary that supplied the eastern forts of the wall. Small, heavily laden craft used the incoming tide to help carry them upriver against the current.

Unlike at Hunnum, the families of Segedunum's depleted garrison lived with their protectors behind the fort's walls. However, many of them had been evicted to accommodate the soldiers who had arrived on the four ships with their illustrious visitor. Those who remained lined the Via Decumana and watched from between the barrack blocks as the squadrons of Marcus's cavalry regiment made their entrance. Caradoc led with the first squadron, three abreast, looking neither to right nor left, the hooves of their mounts clattering on the cobbles. Marcus and his escort rode in the centre of the column and he watched with satisfaction as the leading riders peeled effortlessly into the street on the right as they approached the *principia*.

A delegation of senior officers had assembled on a wooden podium in front of the building to watch them pass. Seated on what could only be called a throne at the front of the group, a shrunken figure in a voluminous, richly decorated cloak viewed the passing riders through narrowed eyes, his slumped posture as much as his malevolent expression proclaiming his distaste for the proceedings.

As Marcus approached, the bald head lifted and the eyes settled on him. A flicker of a smile touched the thin lips, but it contained no hint of welcome from Julius Postumus Dulcitius, *dux Britanniarum*, military commander of north Britain, and Marcus's superior at least in name. Marcus twitched his reins and Storm wheeled left in instant response to take position beside the podium next to the fort's hospital. His escort followed to form up in the roadway beyond as the remainder of the Ala Sabiniana passed at the trot to follow the leading squadrons along the Via Singularis and out of the north gate.

'You have not lost your taste for the ceremonial I see, prefect,' Dulcitius called. 'But one would expect nothing less from the illustrious Marcus Flavius Victor, Lord of the Wall and Defender of the North. That is what you call yourself these days, is it not, Marcus?'

'Lord of the Wall is the title bestowed upon my father by your predecessor, and passed on to me on his death.' Marcus held Dulcitius's gaze. Was there a reaction to the word 'father'? If so, it was subtle enough to pass almost unnoticed. Nearly twenty years now, but he was a patient man. 'I bear it with pride,' he continued. 'As for the other, I fear you are mistaken. No man can dictate what the world calls him. I have never sought nor encouraged the use of those words, but surely you would not deny it to the soldiers I command, the garrisons of the Wall, the true defenders of the north?'

'Of course.' Dulcitius could barely keep the sneer from his lips. 'Your ragtag army. Fine horsemen, I have no doubt. I commend them for their bearing, but surely you could have found some dye for their cloaks. And their mail? You should have your armourer flogged.' He waved a hand that encompassed the elegantly uniformed officers around him. Marcus noticed that Cassius, the commandant of Segedunum, at least had the grace to look uncomfortable, but the others, officers of the Sixth legion based at Eboracum, were clearly enjoying his predicament. 'This is what real soldiers look like,' Dulcitius continued. 'A fine turnout indicates good discipline and without discipline any command will swiftly disintegrate into as foul a rabble as the Saxons and the Picts. Isn't that right, Hostilius?'

'I fear it is so,' a dark-visaged young officer to his left agreed. 'But what do you expect of frontier gate guards?'

Marcus ignored the insult, but he marked Hostilius for the future. He could have pointed out that the only decent swords and chain armour to appear north of Eboracum in the past five years did so in the scabbards and on the backs of the men of the Sixth, but he knew he'd be wasting his breath.

Dulcitius studied him, perfectly aware of the effect his words had achieved. 'Stilicho would have told you that, if you'd been prepared to listen to him, but he always did find you too prone to enthusiasm.'

Marcus suppressed a snort of disdain at the mention of their former commander. Dulcitius intended his words to goad, but all they did was evoke warm memories of a man almost as important in Marcus's life as his father and his blood-father. Three years earlier Flavius Stilicho had rushed together an army to aid Britannia in its time of trial. He had driven back a barbarian federation of Picts, Saxons from Germania, and Scotti from Hibernia, with enough slaughter to ensure a fragile, if occasionally fractious, peace. Marcus had fought at Stilicho's side. Dulcitius had been awarded command of one of the general's legions as a result of his status, and spoke of him as a friend and an equal, but Stilicho had branded him 'Old Slowbody' for his caution.

'You find something amusing, prefect?' Dulcitius asked.

'No, lord, I was merely reflecting on your insightful assessment of my character. It's true I have been impetuous in the past, but I hope one day to match the glories of your own illustrious career.'

Someone at the rear of the group stifled a laugh and even the officers of the Sixth struggled to hide their mirth. Dulcitius knew he was being mocked, but also that continuing the discussion would only make the fact more obvious.

'Very well.' He waved a dismissive bejewelled hand. 'Immediately you have seen to your men's welfare you will join me in the *principia*. Before we discuss this "inspection tour" of yours there is someone you should meet. You are not the only visitor to Segedunum today, nor the most important. We have another guest. A barbarian. Your presence will make him feel quite at home.'

Barbarian? Yes, the Pict was a barbarian. But he was also a king, his lineage apparent in the way he carried himself and the aura of unconscious dignity that surrounded him. A band of gleaming gold encircled his brow, hair the colour of a raven's wing hung to his shoulders and his long, pointed beard was the same obsidian black, but shot with streaks of silver. Deep-set, inquisitive eyes looked out from beneath heavy brows and he had a long, thin nose and a curiously feminine mouth. A cloak of fine plaid cloth hung from his shoulders over a tunic of dark green, pinned at the right shoulder with a circular brooch. Around his neck he wore a heavy chain of linked silver rings and his belt was inlaid with the same precious metal. A king and a fighter. He carried no sword – to show their peaceful intent no man in the room bore arms – but something about the way his hand hovered close to where the pommel would have sat told Marcus he was familiar with the weight of a blade.

Cassius, the fort's commander, escorted the king to an ornate chair on the opposite side of the room. Seven more Picts accompanied their ruler. Three grey-bearded elders, their finery covered by long cloaks, moved in behind him, and two lean, iron-muscled warriors, their faces and torsos almost obscured by tattoos that proclaimed their rank and their valour, flanked him to right and left, arms folded across their chests. A boy of about ten, dark-haired and richly dressed, attended the king.

In contrast, the seventh man seemed to blend with his surroundings. Short and lean, he had sharp, pinched features and the wary eyes of a hunted fox, the effect enhanced by the russet-brown cloak he wore. The Picts surveyed the Roman contingent with undisguised suspicion and Marcus saw the eyes of the small man narrow slightly as they drifted past him.

As pagans, the Picts were unlikely to appreciate Christian symbolism, so instead of crosses, unit standards of the Fourth Lingonum and busts of various former emperors adorned the walls, obscuring paintings of saints and martyrs. A few – Marcus had an inkling one bore the features of the centuries dead Septimius Severus – had clearly been dragged from storerooms and spoil tips for the purpose. The statues seemed to have a perverse fascination for the Pictish noblemen. They studied them intently as the unnatural silence stretched out like a taut bowstring. Eventually, a rustle of cloth and a murmur of voices announced the arrival of Dulcitius, who limped through the ranks of his advisers to take his seat opposite the Pictish king. His sour features twisted into what might just have been construed as a smile of welcome and he waved a languid hand to summon an interpreter to stand at his side.

'Tell the king that I – that Rome – is pleased to welcome him to our fortress of Segedunum and that this meeting is a symbol of the unity that exists between the Empire and his people. Any request he chooses to make will be met with all the benevolence our long history of friendship merits.'

The interpreter was a tall man with a long nose and the supercilious, self-satisfied air Marcus knew well from his dealings with the clerks at Eboracum. He bowed to Dulcitius and relayed his words in a sing-song address of which Marcus recognized one word in every six.

The king listened with an expression that grew more perplexed with every passing second. When the interpreter lapsed into silence, the Pict looked to his closest adviser, who shrugged before they conducted a short whispered exchange. Eventually the king nodded and made his reply. Rather than repeat the words aloud the interpreter whispered into Dulcitius's ear.

Dulcitius turned to Marcus. 'This,' he nodded towards the Picts, 'is King Gefrin of the Votadini. Somewhat predictably he has come here to ask me for more silver to add to that which my profligate treasurer has seen fit to supply him in the past. It seems no amount is enough to keep him to his treaty obligations. If I agree to his wishes that silver will have to come from the portion I have allocated for this foolishness you plan. What do you have to say to that, my impetuous Lord of the Wall?'

Marcus felt the king's eyes on him. He turned and bowed, receiving a nod of acknowledgement in return. 'With your permission, I have some questions for our illustrious ally.' Dulcitius sniffed his assent. Marcus addressed the king in the Pictish tongue in an exchange that developed into a prolonged conversation which clearly irritated their host.

Marcus listened to the king's final words with a smile. 'Firstly,' he said, 'his name is not Gefrin. Din Gefrin is his fortress and the stronghold and sanctuary of the southern Votadini.' A nerve twitched in Dulcitius's cheek and he darted a poisonous glance at his interpreter. 'This is King Coel, their ruler. Civilis, your treasurer, refused to treat with King Coel, choosing instead to negotiate with King Luddoc of Caer Eidinn, who rules the northern clans of the Votadini. I told Civilis a dozen times that the money was wasted. Luddoc has been giving the Picts free passage over the Bodotria for years and encouraging them to fight for the territory of his enemies the Selgovae. Instead, the Selgovae have pushed them back east, greedy for land and slaves. This leaves King Coel with a choice. If we pay him the silver he will guarantee no Pict sets foot on his lands south of Great Cheviot. In effect he will defend one fourth of the Wall for us. He also pledges that no Saxon ship will be welcomed into his ports and harbours, which means fewer opportunities for them to outflank us by sea.'

Dulcitius stared at the king, but the expressionless features told him nothing. 'Can he be trusted?'

Marcus hesitated. He knew that any silver Coel received meant less for him. He needed that silver.

'For now,' he admitted reluctantly.

'Now?'

'He's a king.' Marcus didn't hide his irritation. 'His policy will be dictated by the ebb and flow of power among his enemies and his allies. As Pictish strength grows and ours weakens he may require further encouragement. In any case, he offers hostages to back up his words. One of these noblemen and his youngest son.'

'How long, do you think?' Dulcitius persisted.

'One year, maybe two.'

'Two years,' Dulcitius whispered. 'What cannot be achieved in two years?' He stood and bent his neck in a perfunctory bow towards the king. 'Tell King Coel I must retire to deliberate with my officers. He asks a great deal . . .'

Marcus made the announcement. King Coel's lips twitched in what might have been an ironic smile before he nodded his assent. They watched Dulcitius limp out and Marcus heard him declare that the interpreter would spend the rest of his service filling in latrine pits.

'You are the Lord of the Wall.' Marcus turned at the softly spoken words to find King Coel standing at his shoulder. 'Marcus Flavius Victor.'

The two were of a similar height, though Marcus was broader at the shoulders. Their eyes locked for a moment, each seeking out the measure of the man within, before Marcus allowed himself a smile. 'I did not know my name had travelled so far north.'

'Oh, much further, I assure you,' King Coel said. 'Who has not heard of the "message" you sent Keother. Fifty useless mouths to feed – not to mention their families – in the dead of winter. He cannot even sell them as slaves. Take away a man's hands and you take away his worth and his pride, but of course you understand that.' A servant handed Coel a silver cup and he took a sip of the contents. 'I hear he has promised a similar fate for you, with the added refinement that you will end your days drowning slowly in one of his shit pits.'

'Then let him send fifty more of his warriors to fulfil his vow and see where it gets him.' King Coel flinched at the sudden injection of savagery into the other man's voice. His words had been intended as a test of Marcus Flavius Victor's mettle and the results were more than satisfactory.

'Your commander seemed hesitant,' Coel diverted the conversation to more suitable ground. 'I thought the offer to provide security for this part of the frontier – for that is what it was – was a very fair one, particularly with the addition of valuable hostages to ensure I keep my part of the bargain.'

'Julius Dulcitius believes caution is an essential part of the negotiating process,' Marcus said as if the outcome was of indifference to him. 'He will keep you waiting until he believes he has bored you into submission, then offer half what you have asked for.'

Suspicion shadowed the deep-set eyes. 'You are very candid, Roman.'

'You were right. The offer is a good one. But Dulcitius is a politician.

36

He will posture for effect because he thinks it impresses those around him.'

'Then he is a fool.'

'Yes, he is a fool. And you are not. Which is why you will win in the end, lord.'

One of King Coel's advisers approached. Marcus bowed his farewell and wandered off to stare at the mouldering bust of Septimius Severus. A noble head, bearded and with a thatch of thick curls; most of the nose was missing, but lapis lazuli gave the eyes a piercing quality.

He sensed a presence close behind and the words were spoken so softly he barely registered them.

'The Wall's end, at dusk.'

IV

Marcus hugged his cloak tighter against the chill east wind. Extreme cold seemed to make the knife point embedded between his ribs throb like a living thing, but he welcomed the pain as a reminder that he was alive. Another inch and he would have been bare bones two decades since.

He stood by the bank of the Tinan at the Wall's end, the spur that cut a diagonal from the south-eastern angle of Segedunum to the river. To the east the dull grey of the waters took on a darker sheen as the light began to fade.

As he waited, his thoughts turned to the two men who had made him who he was, his father and his blood-father. Brenus had brought him up as his own, but there had always been signs of another distant presence in Marcus's life: small, exotic gifts, odd, apparently pointless exercises to conduct, books he'd had to be beaten into reading. It was only much later he'd learned that Brenus, recently widowed, had married his mother, a royal lady of the Brigantes, while she was still carrying Marcus in her womb.

The gifts apart, his had been a typical Brigantian childhood, a young hawk flying free among the woods and the streams and the fields until the day his father had handed him a spear and he knew he would be a warrior.

Everything changed the day the god came.

Of course, they were not supposed to talk of gods, there was only one God who lived in his heaven. But when Marcus looked upon the tall figure armoured all in gold, with a plume of scarlet on his helmet, and mounted on a great black horse that seemed to breathe clouds of smoke, he knew he was seeing something more than a mere mortal. He remembered the god speaking to his mother and father, then calling him to his side. Piercing eyes seemed to reach into the very centre of his being. Whatever the god saw must have pleased him, because the stern features softened. 'You'll do,' he'd said, which seemed inadequate for such a moment. 'When the time comes bring him to me,' he'd called to Brenus. It was Marcus's last moment of childhood. From that day on he carried a sword and rode at Brenus's shoulder, learning the arts of war and the trials of leadership, the son of two fathers and the product of both.

The sound of footsteps from the direction of the fort alerted him and his fingers closed on his sword hilt, though he knew danger was unlikely.

'Your presence here was . . . unexpected,' he greeted the newcomer.

'The king insisted.' The face was lost in the shadow of a hooded cloak, but Marcus sensed an ironic smile behind the words. 'He is a man who appreciates my talents.' Though the words 'as do you' were left unspoken, Marcus heard them clearly enough.

'And rightly so.' Marcus understood how much the other man thrived upon flattery. 'Yours is a remarkable gift. I take it Dulcitius allowed King Coel to add another illustrious chapter to the annals of the Votadini?'

'Naturally,' the spy snorted. 'The king outwitted his clumsy Roman opponents in negotiation and came away with twice as much silver as he expected. Dulcitius even gave him a gift of twenty amphorae of the finest wine, an ornate bowl his wife will use as a pot to piss in, and a red cloak, such as your officers wear, that will soon adorn the back of his horse.'

'But not twice as much silver as he asked for, I hope? I have a use for the remainder of that treasure.'

'When the Sand Lizard looked down his long nose and offered a fourth of what was asked, with conditions attached, King Coel smiled and walked from the negotiating chamber.' Marcus laughed at the nickname which suited the reptilian Dulcitius so perfectly. 'Dulcitius spluttered and fumed, but they say he turned pale when he was informed the Votadini were saddling their horses. He sent the prefect himself to plead with the king and persuade him to return. Coel expected to have to pledge his sword arm to Rome for at least two years, but the Lizard gave him what he wanted in return for one.'

Marcus stifled a groan at the latest evidence of Dulcitius's arrogance and blindness. Coel was only promising to do what was in his interests in any case, as long as Luddoc continued to allow safe passage for the invaders through his lands. Likewise, it was in the Roman interest to provide him with the means, but Dulcitius had brokered a poor bargain. 'And the hostages?'

'Oh, Coel was happy to part with them. Drust, who stood at his right shoulder,' Marcus recalled a bearded elder with narrow, untrustworthy eyes, 'has been working to undermine him for a year past, though he believes Coel is unaware of the fact. Coel lamented that he must part with his most trusted adviser and argued until Dulcitius believed he had won a great victory. The other is the boy who travelled with us. He dresses as a prince, but whether he is truly Coel's son, who knows? In any case, Coel has many other sons and the loss of one will not trouble him too much.'

'So he has little reason to keep to his bargain?'

'I believe he intends to,' the spy said. 'He has ambitions of his own, ambitions in the north. For that he needs more mounted warriors, which your silver will no doubt help provide. He would have liked to ask Dulcitius for a Roman stallion to improve his herds, but he knows Rome has forbidden trade in horses with tribes beyond the frontier. Of course, his ambitions would be more achievable with the help of a host of experienced cavalry.'

'And where is he to find a host of cavalry north of the Wall?' Marcus didn't have to be told the answer. He pictured the country beyond Great Cheviot and the River Tuedd, lush pasture, good grazing and rich dark soil that provided a fine annual harvest if the weather was kind. Lands that could have been created for cavalry. No wonder Coel coveted them when he considered his scattered kingdom of remote hilltop fortresses and wind-battered fishing villages. If he could persuade Dulcitius that it was in the Roman interest to send Marcus and his men north, with his gods' favour the Celt had a chance of uniting the Votadini and ruling as far as Caer Eidinn and the Bodotria.

'Perhaps the question is not whether he *will* keep his bargain, but whether he is *able* to,' the informant continued. 'The Picts of the High Lands grow stronger with every passing year. For the moment they are keeping Corvus and his Selgovae busy, but who knows what may happen in the spring. It's possible that Luddoc, too, will feel the need to flex his muscles, for he and Coel share the same ambition. Coel does not have the strength to fight off both the Caledonian Picts and his Votadinus cousin in Caer Eidinn. He would have to come to an accommodation, and the most attractive accommodation would be with the Picts.'

Marcus looked up at the ancient statue towering above them, staring out to sea with sightless eyes as if daring any pirate or invader to enter his realm. The monument must have been set up by the builders of this final section of the Wall as a tribute to its founder. The identity was impossible to tell now because the features had been obscured by countless years of erosion by wind, rain and salt, leaving a jawless mask of pitted horror and an armour-clad torso with a single arm. He'd always believed it to depict Hadrianus Augustus, the creator of the Wall.

Countless generations had gazed upon the decaying countenance of the nameless emperor, but what had really changed since it first stood here in all its marble glory? The enemy still lay in the north and the Romans had to strain every sinew to keep them there.

'So you will carry news of Coel's great triumph to his clans?'

'In the morning,' the spy confirmed. That was his great talent. To listen and remember every word spoken between powerful men after hour upon hour of conversation and negotiation, and have the facility to repeat it word for word. Coel would ensure news was carried from tribe to tribe to the edge of his lands and beyond, safe in the knowledge that the spy would embellish and exaggerate his powers with every telling.

Marcus's right hand caressed the sword hilt as he stared towards the deepening gloom in the east. 'It is in my interest that you overestimate Dulcitius's weakness.'

'Will that not dull the lustre of my king's triumph?'

'Not if it is done with subtlety.' Marcus pulled a leather purse from under his cloak and weighed it in his hand. 'I will make it worth your while.'

Instinctively the spy reached out to take the purse, but just as swiftly the grasping fingers withdrew. 'You tempt me, lord, but it would not do. Coel appreciates my gift, but that does not mean he trusts me entirely. My skin is delicate and I would wish it to stay that way, so keep your money, lord. There may be a day when I need it . . . and the sanctuary you have promised.'

'Your farm in the hills south of Luguvalium is waiting,' Marcus assured him. 'But first there is more work to do. When you have done Coel's bidding, you will carry word beyond his borders, to the north and the west?'

'He will demand it,' the spy acknowledged. 'What use is the news of a great triumph if his enemies do not hear it? Fortunately, though they all believe I am a spy, they still welcome me into their halls as long as I have information to give. Sometimes they even pay me for it.'

'Then I have a further piece of information for you to carry. This information is for the ears of kings, do you understand?' He stepped in close so he could smell the wine on the spy's breath and even the decayed emperor towering above could not hear what passed between them.

'Is this true?' The spy sounded appalled.

'There is truth in it.' Marcus allowed himself a wry smile. 'And what man can foretell his future from one day to the next? On your life, only those I have named are to know.'

'Of course, lord, but . . .'

'No buts and no regrets.' Marcus clasped the spy's shoulder with a force that made the other man wince. 'When you have completed this task, come to me. You will know where. No more looking over your shoulder for the glint of the knife. You will never have to venture north of the Wall again.'

V

Marcus bit back a cry of agony as the point of the thin metal probe forced its way between the rib bones over his heart. He'd lived to regret refusing Zeno's offer of a draught of wine spiked with powdered opium which would have rendered him senseless during the surgery. He lay on his back and sweat filled his eyes as the *medicus* hunched over him. Zeno twisted the probe into a new position, while an orderly dabbed at his brow with a cloth. Marcus tried to concentrate on his breathing, but every movement of the iron point brought a new, barely endurable level of suffering.

'Christ's bones, are you a doctor or a butcher?'

'We'll find out in a moment.' Zeno paused in his work and turned to his orderly. 'Bring me the small forceps.'

The man stepped away and Marcus's mind flickered as he relived the moment the *medicus* had unrolled the leather pouch containing his instruments. Scalpels and bone saws, needle probes, hooks and long spoons, but for some reason he couldn't recall any forceps. Weapons of war he understood – sword and spear, knife and axe, their purposes and the horror they could inflict on a human body – but not this cold, inhuman array of instruments of torture. Another bolt of pain jolted Marcus and Zeno used his free hand to hold him down as he arched his back.

'What is it, anyway?'

Marcus allowed a few seconds to pass until the sparse little room stopped spinning. He had a feeling the *medicus*'s question formed part of some internal debate, but he chose to answer it in any case.

'Knife point,' he groaned. 'The very tip of one of those long, thin blades the Picts carry. Punched through a set of ring mail, but it snapped when he twisted it.'

'Good. It's arrows that are the real bastard, with those hooked barbs. You weren't wearing a leather jerkin or a vest.'

'They lured us into an ambush. I was lucky to be able to grab the mail. How did you know?'

'Because you'd have been food for the maggots long since if the knife had driven leather or cloth into the wound. It would have mortified within days and you'd have been dead within a week. Christus!' the *medicus* growled in frustration and stepped back, shaking his head.

'What is it?' Marcus demanded.

Zeno wiped the blood from his hands with a cloth. 'It's buried too deep. If I probe any further to get it out, I'll probably kill you.'

'And if you leave it?'

The Greek shrugged. 'More of what you've been suffering . . . and it'll probably kill you anyway.'

'Then get it out.'

Zeno shook his head. 'Better to leave well alone.'

It was only then they became aware of a new presence in the room. A tall warrior rested with one shoulder against the door frame, polished mail glittering in the lamplight and a helmet almost as ornate as Marcus's held languidly in one hand. Tangled russet hair fell in waves past a long, pale neck to the mail-clad shoulders. Deep in the wide-set dark eyes lurked a hint of mischief, and perhaps something more dangerous than mischief. A handsome warrior, and one not to be taken lightly, but, when you looked closely, handsome wasn't the word you were looking for.

'Who invited you?'

'You know how I've always enjoyed watching you suffer,' the newcomer grinned.

'My lady Valeria.' Zeno bowed and received a graceful nod of the tawny head in reply.

'Save it for later,' Marcus growled, 'and patch me up before this wildcat devours me. She never could resist the scent of blood.'

They waited until Zeno and his assistant had packed up their instruments and left.

'I didn't think to see you so soon.' Marcus studied his half-sister. The shadow on her face told him her mission had taken a toll, no matter how much she tried to conceal it. How could he not know? Nine years younger and born of the same mother, she'd attached herself to him once she was old enough to crawl and no matter how often he pushed her away she always came back for more. He'd shown her how to climb trees to gather sparrowhawk chicks and rubbed away the pain when she fell out of the branches. When she thought she could swim, he pulled her spluttering from the river before she drowned. His friends had resented her presence, but Valeria wasn't like other girls. She didn't cry and she had no fear. He'd put the first sword in her hand and their parents had encouraged it. 'The women of the Brigantes have been warriors since the time of Cartimandua and before,' their mother said. When she came of age it seemed only natural that she should join him in the saddle. They'd fought together and bled together, and she'd saved his life more than once. She could outride everyone in the regiment bar Senecio and Marcus himself, and outfight most of them.

'Dulcitius offered me passage on his ship. We arrived yesterday.'

'You have news?'

'I would have come to you earlier, Marcus, but you were with Dulcitius, then Zeno insisted you needed treatment . . .'

Her tone told him what he needed to know, but the question had to be asked. 'What happened at Grabant?'

'You knew most of it before I left.' She shook her head. 'A large Saxon raiding party managed to slip past our patrols and land on the coast east of the settlement. Nobody expected them to venture so far inland, they never have in the past . . .'

'They know how weak we are.'

46

'What defenders there were on mother's estate were overwhelmed and the people had nowhere to flee. The Saxons sought plunder and slaves. They butchered anyone foolish enough to resist and took the rest. I spoke to a family who managed to find a hiding place nearby. They saw Venutia – mother – and little Bren carried away along with the rest, shackled and led off to the shore . . .'

His world seemed to take a sudden lurch, as if the floor had collapsed under him. They had taken his son. His first blood. A moment of self-loathing threatened to overwhelm him. It was his fault. He had never forgiven Bren for the fact of his birth eight years earlier, a birthing that had killed his mother, Julia. To compound his enmity, the boy had grown up fragile and sickly. With each passing year the feeling multiplied, so that in the end he could not stand the sight of his own son. He had abandoned Bren to Venutia. Now he would never see him again. Gradually, Valeria's voice pushed back the cloud of anguish that enveloped him. '. . . we followed their trail, but of course they were long gone, apart from one. A stray boy who could not hold his beer and had become separated from the rest. I put him to the question, Marcus. I know where they have taken them.'

'Definitely Saxons, not Jutes or Angles?'

'Saxons.' Valeria's voice quickened. 'Their leader calls himself king of some settlement fifteen miles upstream from the estuary of a river called the Albis. He leads fewer than a hundred warriors. Give me your letter of authority and I can have three ships ready to sail from Eboracum as soon as we are able to fill them.'

'She will never have survived the voyage,' Marcus said. 'And if she did, she could be anywhere. Sold at the block in any slave market in Saxonia.'

The dark eyes widened in disbelief. 'You cannot know that. In any case, Bren—'

'The Saxons are sea wolves, we are not.' Anger and sorrow harshened Marcus's tone and he ignored the dangerous hiss that escaped his sister's lips. 'They would be fighting on their own ground while we are three hundred miles and more away from home. Three hundred miles of sea with the winter gales in our face and the waves pouring over the sides. We don't even know where this river mouth is. In any case I am committed—'

'Now we get to it.' Valeria's lips twisted in a snarl. 'Now we discover why my brave brother is willing to abandon his own mother and his son to a pack of rabid Saxon dogs. So, what is it? What is the real reason for this inspection of yours?' Her anger was like a fire fed by a gale, a living thing that whirled and surged and spat flame. 'It isn't to check the masonry. You have engineers to do that. Nor the mettle of the men, who know their lives depend on their alertness and are more frightened of you than the Picts in any case.'

'I am pledged to Dulcitius—'

'You owe that slimy toad nothing.'

She waited while Marcus pulled a tunic over his wounded chest and they walked to the door together.

'Mother . . . ?'

'You were right,' Valeria said, her voice now flat and cold. 'She will not survive the voyage. She is already dying. But then you didn't know that, did you, Marcus Flavius Victor? Your mother and your own son sold into slavery? May God forgive you, Marcus, because you can be sure I will not. I hope this is all worth the sacrifice.'

They stepped out of the doorway. On a path beside the river below them one of Valeria's bodyguard stood holding a rope attached to the neck of a bare-chested, fair-haired youth of about fifteen.

'Who's that?' Marcus demanded.

'The boy we captured.'

'I thought you put him to the question?'

'He's not the bravest Saxon we've ever met.' A snort of scorn escaped Valeria. 'He told me everything I needed to know before we heated the first knife. He's quite decorative. I'm going to keep him as a slave.'

'Give him to me,' Marcus nodded at the captive, 'and I'll send him screaming to his gods in a manner worthy of those who took our mother.'

'No, Marcus,' she said, and he knew her well enough to see she

48

would not be shifted. 'He is mine. Perhaps if I treat him with kindness God will see fit to do the same for Bren.'

'You've gone soft, sister.' Marcus spat towards the boy.

'But not you, Marcus. Is what I heard about Alona true? I always knew you were a hard man but I never thought of you as cruel.'

He glared at her, but was saved from the ill-judged remark that was on the end of his tongue by the arrival of a messenger.

'Lord Dulcitius requires you to attend him immediately.'

Marcus exchanged a glance with his sister.

'Do not take him lightly, Marcus,' Valeria warned. 'He means you ill.'

VI

He noticed the guards as he entered the chamber. Eight stalwart legionaries, two to each wall of the largest room in Segedunum's *praetorium*. Veterans every one, judging by their battered features, and very unlike the decorative officers with which Dulcitius normally liked to surround himself. Each fully armed and armoured. Not that unusual in a frontier fort, it was true, but a suspicious man would think it a little excessive given how many infantry and cavalry currently occupied Segedunum.

Dulcitius sat hunched over a brazier in the centre of the room, warming his hands over the glowing embers, fingers like hooked claws clutching at the heat.

'Prefect Victor of the First Ala Sabiniana, lord,' the orderly announced.

The *dux Britanniarum* looked up with a doleful smile of welcome. 'Three hundred-odd years in this benighted ice house of a country and they still haven't managed to work out how to heat a room this size.' A rasping cough accompanied the words. 'But of course, you natives barely notice the cold.'

'I hope I see you well, Dulcitius?' Marcus ignored the implied insult. 'How can I be of service?'

'No titles? No respect for age? Is this what we have come to?' Dulcitius might have been talking to himself. 'The cold chills my very soul, my hands are not fit to hold a sword, and my legs will barely carry me,' a smirk dusted the thin lips, 'but my heart beats strong for Rome.'

A jug of wine sat on a table close to Dulcitius with four silver cups on a tray beside it. Marcus helped himself to a cup and filled it to the brim, sipping the wine – surprisingly fine – before taking a seat uninvited on a couch opposite the other man. 'And all Britannia is grateful for it,' he replied with mock gravity.

'And your own health?'

The lack of interest in the other man's voice told Marcus what he already knew. Dulcitius was as acquainted with his injuries as he was himself.

'A warrior will never be allowed to forget his past battles,' he shrugged.

Marcus watched the other man, but Dulcitius sat with his features angled towards the fire so it was impossible to read his eyes or his expression.

'As you are aware, my diplomacy has bought us a respite here in the east. King Coel guarantees to hold off any Pictish incursions. Which brings us to the question of your own efforts at diplomacy.' Dulcitius's tone betrayed a hint of smugness and Marcus sensed a heightening of tension in the room. Hands straying inadvertently towards sword hilts.

'My diplomacy, as you call it, has kept the Picts from the Wall, apart from the occasional minor raid, for two years. Swords and silver save soldiers' lives. Your agreement with Coel is living proof of that.'

'Cutting off men's hands?'

Marcus could see the trap now, a clumsy deadfall that almost made him laugh aloud. Did Dulcitius really believe he was such a fool?

'You told me to send the Picts a message. I gave Keother fifty useless mouths to feed. Every time he sees one of those cripples, he'll be reminded what will happen if his men ever dare to cross the Wall again. Would you rather I had returned them whole? An invitation to bring their swords against us whenever it pleased them?'

'Fifty men without any hands.' Dulcitius stared at his own, turning them unhurriedly in the glow of the fire. 'Yes, a potent message. But what happened to the others? What happened to their leaders?'

'Five I hanged – slowly.' Marcus had no doubt Dulcitius knew every detail of the Picts' demise, but he would not make it easy for him. 'The sixth I gave to the villagers whose kin he'd just butchered.'

'Gave? I understood there was a much more novel aspect to his end.'

So here it was.

'First I had him nailed to a tree.'

'In effect, you crucified this man.'

'I had him nailed to the tree,' Marcus allowed anger to seep into his voice, 'and he died screaming as the villagers cut him into small pieces to feed to their pigs.'

'You see,' Dulcitius continued as if Marcus hadn't spoken, 'the Emperor Theodosius – may God bless his name – denounced the practice of crucifixion as a heresy, a mere parody of our lord Christ's death, and he prohibited its use throughout the Empire, east and west. His son, Honorius – may he also be blessed – has naturally adopted his father's decrees with enthusiasm. Those who continue to use it as a method of execution are therefore heretics, and subject to the punishment outlined in the Edict of Thessalonica.'

'Let me guess,' Marcus said. 'A nice short period of exile somewhere warm?'

'Oh, it's certainly warm, my dear Marcus. The punishment for heresy is death by burning.'

An unnatural stillness fell across the room. The guards were ready now, hunting dogs waiting for the command.

'I didn't crucify him.'

'No? I have twenty witnesses who say you did. Would you like to hear from one of them?'

Marcus allowed himself time to think. 'If I prove he's lying will you cut his throat?'

Dulcitius called an order and Marcus poured himself another cup of wine. He studied the painted plaster on the walls. The pictures told him the room Dulcitius had commandeered was used for more than one function, which might be useful. He turned as two legionaries hustled another man into the room and marched him to stand shaking in front of Dulcitius. Velanos, the *curator* of Alona.

Velanos's eyes widened in terror when he recognized Marcus.

Marcus took another sip of his wine and gestured to the newcomer. 'Come here.' He laid down his cup and picked up an oil lamp from the same table. 'You say I crucified the big Pict?'

'Y-y-yes, lord.'

'Like this?' He raised the oil lamp so the flame lit a wall painting that had been hidden in the shadows. The room must function as Cassius's private chapel, because the painting showed a depiction of the Crucifixion. A bearded Christ hung from a rough-hewn timber cross, an expression of pained boredom on his face and a yellow glow round his head. His arms were extended horizontally and his hands nailed through the palms to the wood, legs and feet close together and secured through the ankles by two more large nails.

Velanos studied the painting for a long moment, a frown of concentration on his thin features. Eventually, he said: 'Why no, lord.'

'What?' Dulcitius spluttered.

'Tell him,' Marcus said.

'It was more like this, lord.' Velanos spread his legs and threw his arms upwards at an angle, making an inexact approximation of the letter X.

'You said the Pict was crucified.' Dulcitius's face had turned a violent shade of purple, Marcus was pleased to see.

'I said he was nailed to a tree.' Indignation overcame Velanos's fear. 'The soldier said, "He was crucified then, like our lord?". So I says I wasn't entirely sure what crucified meant. And he says "like a cross". Well it was like a certain kind of cross, so I says yes, he was crucified. Then, when they brought me here, this soldier says to make sure I say he was crucified and that's what I did.'

'Get out of here,' Dulcitius raged. 'Before I have *you* crucified.'

Marcus returned to his seat opposite Dulcitius. 'You see,' he said. 'There are no heretics to trouble you here. Only loyal, God-loving

Roman Christians. No court in the land would convict me. Not that it would have got that far anyway.'

'No? I could have you arrested here and now on my authority as commander of the north.'

'And some accident might befall me on the way to Eboracum?'

'Only God knows our fate,' Dulcitius said with false piety. 'Treacherous seas and slippery decks are a dangerous combination.'

'That would be a pity.'

'Yes, it would.'

'Not least because if I die in suspicious circumstances certain trusted friends of mine have been paid to ensure you join me within the month.' Dulcitius shifted in his seat at this new and unwelcome development. 'Given the catalogue of sins I could lay at your door, I doubt you will get any kind of welcome at the Gates of Heaven,' Marcus continued. 'And then there are your sons. Were you aware they've been in conversation with a young man from Londinium, a prosperous merchant, who thinks we no longer receive value for money from our increasingly onerous taxes? His name is Gratianus and his solution is a parting of the ways with Rome – you're sweating, Dulcitius, perhaps you should move away from the brazier. They were careless enough to put their names to a letter which fortunately fell into my hands. Fortunately, because we both know that such discussions would raise the question of their allegiance had it reached, say, the governor in Londinium. He would be honour bound to send it to Emperor Honorius by the first ship. A pity if a family with such a bright future should fall victim to the strangling rope.'

They sat for a moment, each considering the implications of what had been said. 'Thank you for bringing the matter to my attention.' Dulcitius's complexion had turned pale, but he managed a smile that succeeded in being both ingratiating and false. 'I'm sure their conversations were perfectly innocent. In any case everything we have said here is entirely hypothetical. Now, perhaps we should move on to the subject of what happens to the remaining silver now that the barbarian has had his share.'

Marcus rose from his seat. 'I don't think we need worry about the silver, do you? I'll send men to collect it when I've completed my inspection of the fort and my discussions with Cassius. He's curiously reluctant to part with the cavalry I need.'

'Cavalry?' Dulcitius stared at him. The Fourth Lingonum consisted of three hundred infantry and a hundred and twenty cavalry, the latter of whom were indispensable for patrolling beyond the frontier. Naturally, Cassius would hoard his veteran horsemen like gold coins.

'Perhaps I could persuade you to write a direct order transferring them to me for the duration of my inspection,' Marcus continued. 'I would be in your debt.'

Almost in a daze, Dulcitius reached for a writing tablet.

'How many?'

'All of them.'

VII

Valeria looked down at the face of the man below her. She concentrated on counting the beads of sweat on his brow as she struggled against the intense heat building up at her very core. It was all about the timing. Slowly, slowly. She moved her hips in a languid rhythm, each small change of pressure introducing a new sensation so her whole body seemed to be sending her different messages. A tiny gasp escaped her partner's lips at a subtle inner contraction and his eyes widened.

'Bitch,' he grimaced.

She grinned and shifted her weight a little. Make him wait.

A hand reached up and two long fingers grasped her erect nipple and twisted, sending a surge of liquid pleasure from her breast to her lower belly. At the same time the hips beneath her own began to pulse in a more intense tempo. She could feel the power surging through the slim body and she shifted slightly to make the best possible use of it.

'Bastard.' She raked her long nails across his chest.

She'd missed their irregular clandestine couplings during her enforced absence in the south. It had been difficult to arrange, but she'd finally found a room and a time convenient to both. There'd be precious few such opportunities in the coming weeks.

'Now.' She closed her eyes and ground her lower body against his, throwing her head back and arching her spine to achieve the greatest pleasure. He returned her efforts with more of his own and she felt a hand against her groin, stroking and touching in a way that seemed to make her soar. Something exploded in her head and she lost all semblance of control in a paroxysm of ecstasy that seemed to go on for ever before she slumped, utterly spent, across the equally drained body on the bed.

She felt his fingers stroking her back.

'I hate to think where you learned those tricks,' she murmured. 'But I'm glad you did.'

'As a medical man I consider it my duty to know as much as possible about the human body,' Zeno said. 'There are girls in Constantinopolis who are trained in the arts of giving pleasure and they were happy to indulge my interest.' This was surprisingly candid for her lover, who seldom spoke to her of his time in the east, though she knew he had discussed it with Marcus. His arrival at Hunnum had been accompanied by a troop of guards, which he'd blithely shrugged off as an indication of his former status. What he hadn't known at the time was that they'd carried a letter which their commander had delivered in private to Marcus. In many ways the scroll was an astonishing document, stamped as it was with the twin seals of Arcadius, Emperor of the East, and Honorius, Emperor of the West. It announced that Zeno, *medicus* and former dietician to the Emperor of the East, was hereby exiled for life to the furthest ends of the Empire. The letter concluded with the suggestion that Zeno's exile should be of short duration and terminated with a painful accident at the prefect of the Ala Sabiniana's earliest convenience. Valeria had convinced Marcus that Zeno was of more value to the Ala Sabiniana alive than dead, so he had reason to be grateful to her.

'I'm sure they were.' He gasped as she wriggled her body free of him and rolled over onto her side.

'Do you think anyone knows about us?'

'Some suspect.' She snuggled closer. 'Some think they know. But nobody is certain, and as long as we are discreet that is the way it will stay.'

'Your brother?'

'If my brother so much as suspected we were doing this, my beautiful, athletic friend,' she stroked the hairs on his stomach in a way that sent a shiver through him, 'do you think you would still be alive?'

'Who is Niall of the Nine Hostages?'

She sat up and her breasts were so close and so enticing he had to curb the urge to reach out for them.

'Are you a spy, Zeno?' Her eyes seemed to search out the very heart of him. 'Is that why you were run out of Constantinopolis with an Emperor's execution warrant pinned to your cloak?'

'I was inquisitive, it's true,' Zeno admitted. 'It has ever been a fault of mine. That is one reason, but there were others.'

'Why do you ask about Niall?'

'Because some men say that he is the true reason for this mad, midwinter inspection tour.'

'Some?'

'One of Dulcitius's clerks has piles. He is very grateful for the ointment I gave him. He said Dulcitius gave your brother a great hoard of silver to carry to this Niall as a bribe. They say your brother has had word Niall plans a raid on Luguvalium in the spring. When he arrives, he will find Marcus and a substantial force already in residence and the negotiations will take place. Could that be true?'

'It's possible.' She wrapped the blanket about herself against the evening chill. 'Niall came from Hibernia three years ago and created a kingdom for himself on Mona. He's getting old, he must be forty now, and every ship that sets sail from Hibernia could contain a potential rival. A truce would give him the opportunity to consolidate what he's won since in Ordovicia and Demetia without any interference from our *limitanei* cohorts east of the Severn.'

'You know a great deal about military strategy,' Zeno said admiringly.

'You mean for a woman?'

'No, I don't mean that at all,' Zeno assured her. 'You are learned in ways I will never understand and I am blessed every day I am with you.'

'Marcus is right,' Valeria flipped her body so she was astride him again, shrugging aside the blanket. 'You are a flatterer and not to be trusted.'

'So you are the daughter of a Brigantian princess?'

She smiled down at him. 'And as such I expect to be obeyed.'

'A poor Greek *medicus* is at your service.'

'So I see.' She exhaled a long breath. 'Then let us make use of what time we have. Opportunities will be few on the march.'

VIII

The transport ships which had brought Dulcitius and his escort to Segedunum were tied up across the river at Arbeia's wharf to take on cargo for the trip south. Traders who had arrived with King Coel had sold the Roman commander and his retinue pairs of ferocious, long-limbed hunting dogs, piles of furs of indeterminate origin and forty Pictish and Selgovae slaves. Marcus and Valeria accompanied Dulcitius through the fort's granaries and warehouses along the road south of the river. As they passed the slave pens Marcus ran an eye over the captives and guessed that Dulcitius had been cheated for the second time. A few had the look of genuine Pictish warriors, but for the most part they were scrawny, old or sick, probably Coel's own slaves who weren't worth keeping.

They were a sullen, cowed group and Marcus would have immediately forgotten them had it not been for a skinny figure standing shivering in a loincloth who tried to attract his attention.

'Lord! Lord, I beg of you—' the slave called. A soldier immediately silenced him with a spear butt in the belly before he could say more. Oddly, the man had called out in Latin, but Marcus wasn't inclined to concern himself with the welfare of a slave.

'If you will excuse me, lord,' Valeria murmured. She turned her horse towards the slave pen.

'Of course, my dear.' Dulcitius came as close as he ever would to a genuine smile. He and Marcus continued towards the harbour. 'Your sister is a charming woman, well-bred and excellent company. Handsome, too. She'd make a fine wife for someone of aristocratic rank.'

'Are you offering to take her off my hands?'

'I'm surprised you haven't already betrothed her to some tribune or tribal prince to secure an alliance.' Dulcitius was evidently pretending not to have heard. 'In fact, given your lack of scruples it surprises me you haven't married her off to some merchant or farmer in return for a year's supply of fodder.'

Marcus knew he was being goaded in retaliation for the chest of silver, counted and recounted, that now lay securely in the Ala Sabiniana's strongbox. He chose not to take offence. He had everything he wanted from Dulcitius, who had surprised him by complying so willingly with his request for Segedunum's cavalry. The tittle-tattle Valeria had brought back from Eboracum about the man's sons was a much more potent weapon than he'd realized, a fact worth bearing in mind for the future. Cassius had naturally been outraged at this potentially catastrophic diminution in the Fourth Lingonum's strength, but he'd had no choice but to accept Dulcitius's order. Segedunum's commander had even been pathetically grateful when Marcus offered to leave him twenty troopers he could use as messengers.

'Perhaps I should call Valeria back and you can make the suggestion yourself?'

Dulcitius's shrill cackle echoed from the warehouses they were passing. It was the first time Marcus had heard the man laugh. But the humour was of short duration.

'What's this nonsense I hear about Niall of the Nine Hostages?'

'I thought I'd surprise you, lord. Think of it as a gift.'

'Surprise me by conspiring with one of Britannia's most powerful and dangerous enemies?' Dulcitius feigned astonishment. 'It makes your heresy look almost trifling by comparison.'

'I believe we exonerated me on that front, lord.'

'Nonetheless . . .'

Marcus shrugged. 'I received intelligence that Niall intends to make a raid on Luguvalium in the spring with upwards of forty ships. I plan to be there waiting for him.'

They rode on to the jetty where a guard of honour from the auxiliary garrison at Arbeia formed two parallel lines in front of the waiting ship. At last, Dulcitius spoke. 'Very well, Marcus Flavius Victor. It will be as you suggest. But mark this,' he brought his face as close to Marcus as their fidgeting mounts would allow, 'betray my trust and I will destroy you.' The skeletal features broke into a smile. 'Letter or no letter.'

Dulcitius dismounted and Marcus watched as he limped through the lines of auxiliaries and up the ramp to the ship.

It had gone better than he expected.

Marcus heard the shouts before the slave pen came into sight. When he turned the corner, he saw that most of the slaves were ringing the outer reaches of the pen encouraging some kind of fight. His elevation allowed him to see the two protagonists circling each other on the frost-hardened ground in the centre of the stockade. One of them was an enormous tattooed Pict wielding a cavalry sword and the other the skinny slave who'd called out in Latin. The thin man held a short dagger clumsily in his left hand because his right was already bleeding.

'Stop this,' Marcus roared. 'Who in the name of Ch— Who gave this bastard a sword? Disarm him before he works out he'd be better off killing you and setting this rabble loose.'

The auxiliaries guarding the pen had been appreciating the one-sided contest as much as the slaves. Now they flinched from Marcus's wrath and darted wary glances to where Valeria sat her horse a few paces from the gate.

'I gave him the sword, brother.' Valeria's tone contained just enough deference to raise hackles of suspicion on the back of Marcus's neck.

'The slave is a Christian. He claims unscrupulous men sold him to the Picts and that he only wishes to join us and fight the barbarians. I knew you would expect him to prove himself first, so I arranged this contest.'

'Contest,' Marcus laughed. 'This isn't a contest, this is a slaughter. I knew you were cold, Valeria, but I never thought you'd send some poor runt out to have his guts spilled for your entertainment.'

'If he is killed it is no loss to us. Speak to him, brother,' Valeria said quietly.

Marcus's instinct was to turn away. Instead, he stifled a sigh and walked his horse to the gate. Two men held each of the fighters and a sheepish guard laid their weapons before Marcus. He recognized the sword as Valeria's by the old-fashioned Christ symbol embossed in silver on the hilt. He dismounted and picked up the dagger, testing the edge with his thumb.

'Bring the runt here,' he ordered.

The guards hustled their prisoner out of the pen and others shut the gate behind them. Up close he barely reached to Marcus's shoulder and his ribs projected from his flesh like the rotting spars of an ancient shipwreck. His only clothing consisted of a dirty cloth wrapped about his loins and his matted hair sprang from his head like a bush. The thatch was so infested with lice Marcus could see them moving among the springy curls. Caked dirt and a wispy beard all but obscured sharp, almost rat-like features made even more unlovable by a nose flattened in some previous altercation. By rights he should have been overawed, but startling blue eyes met Marcus's gaze with a wary but unflinching conviction.

'You claim to be a Christian, slave?'

'I *am* a Christian, lord.' The words emerged through lips cracked with thirst and cold. 'I was born into the Carvetii and my parents had me immersed in the River Itouna, south of Luguvalium, as our lord Jesus was baptized by Ioannes in the River Jordan. They named me Ninian.'

'Your name is irrelevant to me.' Marcus saw the man flinch at this expression of his lack of value. 'But my decurion there says you wish to join the Ala Sabiniana. Is that true?'

'Yes, lord,' the slave spoke in a rush as if uncertain he'd be permitted to finish his petition. 'Your fame has spread far beyond the Wall, even to the mists of the Graupian Mountains. Before my misfortune I learned that the Emperor Honorius, may God bless him, had sanctioned the enlistment of even lowly slaves, so there should be no barrier to my taking service with you.'

'And what do you have to offer in exchange for Rome's silver and a life of hunger, toil and danger?' Marcus didn't hide his scorn.

Ninian remained undaunted. 'I can read and write, lord, and I am versed in accounting, disciplines no military unit should be without, lord, as I'm sure you will agree? Does the great Vegetius not say, "The superintendents of the levies should select some recruits for their skill in writing and accounts"?'

The direct quotation from Rome's leading military tactician gave Marcus pause. Where did it come from? He looked across to Valeria who stared back with what he chose to interpret as a challenge. She thought she'd been terribly clever. Well, others could be clever too. 'Yes.' His eyes examined the thin body. 'But does Vegetius not also say that the young soldier should have a broad chest, muscular shoulders and strong arms? I need soldiers not clerks. You would not last a week and I don't have the bounty to spare for recruits who are going to die on me.'

'Then I will die anyway, lord.' Ninian glanced over his shoulder to where the hard-eyed Pictish warriors among the slaves watched the exchange with interest. 'You will note that these are Caledonian Picts who have no love for a Christian. I doubt I will last an hour on the ship. But if I am going to die, let me show you I can die with honour. Let me finish the fight with Lugotrix there. At least then,' he said with a sardonic twist of the lips, 'you might view my shade with a little more esteem.'

Marcus had a moment of regret, but stilled it as quickly as it came. The times had never been more dangerous and dangerous times required hard decisions. He could not afford any more of Valeria's strays on this mission. He picked up the sword and threw it to Lugotrix to a shout of acclamation from the penned slaves. The dagger he handed to Ninian. 'May God go with you.'

The slave weighed the blade in his hand with a look of sly calculation. They stood less than an arm's length apart and a single thrust would be all it took. 'You are very trusting, lord.'

'If you have any sense you'll run yourself onto his sword.'

'I'll bear that in mind, lord.' Ninian turned and the guards opened the gate to allow him to enter the pen, where he walked unhurriedly to stand in the shadow of his giant opponent. Lugotrix hawked and spat a gob of yellow phlegm at Ninian's feet. His fellow slaves shouted their approval, but the little Christian ignored them and looked to Marcus for the signal to begin the fight.

Valeria led her horse to her brother's side.

'Remember, this is all your doing.' Marcus stared at the mismatched combatants in the centre of the pen. It would be the work of moments. 'To the death,' he shouted.

The clamour rose as the two men faced each other. Lugotrix advanced with quick purposeful strides, cutting the air to left and right with the heavy blade. Ninian stood his ground, seemingly frozen to the earth, the hand with the dagger hanging useless by his side. 'Move, you fool,' Marcus growled.

When he came within striking distance, Lugotrix raised the sword two-handed and unleashed a mighty diagonal cut designed to slice Ninian from right shoulder to left hip. A butcher's blow that would turn the slave to bloody ruin in an instant, chopping bone and heart, cartilage and viscera. But the Pict might as well have been attacking a wisp of smoke. By the time the blade would have struck Ninian was no longer where the sword was aimed. In a single fluid movement he pirouetted to his right and then spun inwards to attack Lugotrix's exposed left flank. Marcus noticed the slave had somehow exchanged the dagger from his left hand to his seemingly injured right, giving him a more advantageous angle to strike. But Lugotrix was also fast. He reacted to the threat with the speed of a seasoned warrior, reversing his sword and whirling left with the blade at the level of Ninian's exposed neck.

Not fast enough.

Ninian dropped into a forward roll that brought him under the Pict's flailing sword and the dagger flashed as he emerged from the spin to thrust the point upwards into Lugotrix's unprotected groin.

Lugotrix screamed, a long shriek that split the cold air as the agony lanced through his lower body. The cry was repeated again and again as Ninian used all his strength to force the point still deeper, cutting vein and artery and up into the soft parts of his victim's belly. The sword dropped to the ground and Ninian darted away from the swaying Pict, the bloody dagger poised to strike again. Lugotrix's hands clutched at his groin, but his lifeblood spurted through his fingers in an unending stream to stain the dirt floor of the pen. He reached out towards his nemesis as if seeking some kind of absolution. Ninian made to take a step to meet him, but before he could move Lugotrix toppled forward to slam face first into the frozen dirt.

Ninian picked up Valeria's sword and spat on Lugotrix's prone body.

'Get him out of there before they tear him apart,' Marcus rasped.

A phalanx of guards ran into the pen and surrounded Ninian. The Picts surged towards them, but the swords of the auxiliaries kept the slaves at bay for long enough to hustle Ninian from the pen. When they were clear the slave fell to his knees and Marcus had to step back as Ninian coughed and sprayed vomit at his feet.

He allowed the kneeling man a moment to recover. 'Where did you learn to fight like that, slave?'

'A Christian among pagans learns the difference between life and death very quickly,' Ninian gasped. 'I was always fast, but a man who knows he'll have his balls in his mouth if he loses a fight has every incentive to become faster still.'

Marcus handed Valeria her sword. 'Remind me why we went to so much trouble to take on another stray?'

'He was a priest,' Valeria said quietly. 'A missionary to the Novantae.

I have often heard you lament we know too little of the western tribes. Ninian can change that. When Ninian converted their king, Runo, to the true faith it was counted as a miracle. He was destined for high rank in the church. Unfortunately, his bishop looked upon Ninian and saw a rival. If he could convert the Novantae, he said, he could convert the Caledonian Picts. A death sentence in all but name. Ninian decided he didn't want to die, but his bishop arranged to have him kidnapped and taken north in any case. In captivity a shaking fever overcame him that left him raving and frothing at the mouth. Rather than cut his throat the Picts included him in a batch of slaves traded to Coel. He believes God saved his life by assigning him the sickness and sending him here to serve you.'

'Why didn't you tell me he was a priest?'

'Would it have made a difference?'

'No.'

'So I told him he had to prove himself and he suggested the fight with Lugotrix. He said he would place himself in God's hands.'

Marcus laughed. 'God must have been in a generous mood today.'

'Yes, he must,' Valeria smiled.

'Have Zeno check him for any of those revolting diseases the Picts carry, then have him cleaned up and given a uniform. You can show him how to use a sword, though if he's as quick as he is with a knife that shouldn't be too difficult.' He had a sudden thought. 'But if I find out he can't ride I'll send him back to Coel as a gift.'

'He can ride,' she assured him.

'A priest.' Marcus closed his eyes. 'Just what we need.'

STONE

IX

Vindobala (Rudchester)

The first time Marcus set foot in the fort at Vindobala it had been a derelict ruin abandoned for almost a hundred years. He'd been just ten years old and knew nothing of strategy, but he guessed now the disuse resulted from a prolonged decline in Pictish activity. That period of relative calm on the frontier had ended by the time Marcus celebrated his fifth birthday. Once more, the Saxons and the Scotti had enticed the Picts south with promises of plunder and slaves. The Picts had swarmed over the Wall in such numbers that Marcus's father had been forced to send the family to Eboracum while he fought a pitiless war of ambush and retreat against the invaders. Only the coming of Count Theodosius had saved Britannia.

The great general had scoured the province of barbarians, hunting the scattered bands like rats as they struggled to carry off their plunder. When the cleansing was complete, he left orders to restore the security of the island. That meant the Wall must again become the formidable barrier it had once been.

Vindobala's ramparts survived, but the interior had crumbled to ruins. Marcus remembered a visit with his father, tiptoeing through the tumbled stonework, feet crunching on broken tiles and occasional pieces of smashed window glass, the remaining walls unstable and liable to fall on the careless or unwary.

'This is where your true education begins.' Brenus accompanied the words with the fox's smile Marcus had come to associate with aching muscles and a scrambled brain. 'What is a Roman officer's most important duty?'

Marcus almost blurted out 'To kill the enemy,' but he bit the words back. He thought for a moment and eventually came up with 'To command.'

'No,' Brenus shook his head. 'A Roman officer's first duty is to know how to build. With this,' he slapped a stone bedded in the wall beside him. 'If you live to be an officer you will spend one part of your life fighting and nine parts building, or supervising building, or checking someone else's building. You will build camps, you will build forts, you will build roads and you will build bridges. And everything you build will be expected to last for a thousand years. Do you understand, Marcus?'

'Yes, father.'

Brenus cuffed him gently around the head. 'No, you don't. Not yet. Not until you have built. Because with building you build strength, you build stamina, but above all, you build discipline. A century or a squadron that builds a road builds unity, it builds cohesion, it builds a brotherhood. If you want to command you have to be able to do everything better than any man in your unit. So this is where we start. You will stay here and you will learn, Marcus. You will learn to build. Build a fort. Build a command. Starting from now.'

And with that, he had walked away. Marcus had not seen his father again for two years.

He looked around at the masonry he'd carried, great blocks of sandstone and gritstone from the quarries that still punctuated the line of the Wall. At the mortar he had learned to mix to the perfect consistency by constant repetition, from lime, sand and water. His muscles had burned like fire. The skin on his fingers blistered, the blisters burst, the blood flowed, the skin returned and took on the texture of leather. He'd danced around the scaffolding with such ease and lack of fear that even humourless Gordianus had called him 'The Squirrel'. Shovels, spades, mattocks, trowels, hammers, saws and chisels, he learned to use them all. By the end he'd been able to look at the exterior of a wall and know what was happening inside it. Whether it was frost-blighted, whether the foundations were weak, whether the stone itself was crumbling. He understood how to make a joint to the finest of tolerances, to create a bevel the eye couldn't discern, and he had learned to hate the man who drove him to perfection every day, every week, every month, every year. Gordianus, master builder. Christ, how many times had he wished he could ram that chisel into Gordianus's throat? It was only now that he looked upon what they had created together that he appreciated what Gordianus had achieved. He had turned a ruin into a fortress, a boy into a craftsman, a fool into someone who could look a veteran auxiliary of ten years' service in the eye and tell him his work was a pile of shit. Marcus laughed out loud and grinned as the sound echoed round the walls. Christus, he'd been so young.

'Lord? Tribune Arrius respectfully requests an interview.'

Marcus turned. 'Caradoc. How is your wound?'

'The *medicus* says it is healing well, lord, but who would believe a Greek? I'll probably be dead by morning.'

'I was thinking about my father.'

'He was a great man, lord.' Caradoc managed a smile that showed two yellowing teeth in his upper jaw.

'Yes, he was, even when age began to slow him. I remember him as he was on the day he handed me my first sword: dark, bearded and scowling, a face God might have carved with an axe, and hard as the very stone that makes this wall.'

'The bravest warrior this island has ever known, saving your presence.'

For once Marcus accepted the flattery as his due. 'You fought with him through the good times and the bad. Through victory and defeat.'

Caradoc produced a laugh that spawned a twinge of pain and he put his hand to his injured side. 'By all the gods you do enjoy a victory, but it's the defeats you remember most. Your best mate's guts dragging behind him in the snow as he flees the skinning knives. Christus save us, I'll never forget those screams. And it might have been me but for your father. Would any other man have fed me bloody snow when my fingers were so blighted by frost that the tips turned black? Then it was spring, and what a spring. We slaughtered Saxons in the east, Scotti in the west and Picts in the north, and then, when Count Theodosius turned up, we did it all over again. I swear given time your father would have cleared all Britannia with his six squadrons of cavalry. We thought they'd gone for ever.'

'And then they came back.'

'And then they came back. Ten years later we had to do it all over again.'

'You were with him at Castra Exploratum.'

'I never left his side. He was the finest soldier I ever served with.' Caradoc's words rang with pride. 'He could read the land the way a priest reads a scroll. He could tell when a storm was just over the horizon and find the perfect place to shelter in a heartbeat. There wasn't a duck or a chicken within ten miles safe from him. We pushed them north until their backs were against the Wall and then we pushed them further.' The light in Caradoc's eyes faded. 'Then the greats among us decided we need go no further. Your father urged, then pleaded, then, by God, he wept. They are all there, he said, the barbarian chieftains we seek. Just one more charge and we will have them. At last they yielded and agreed that four *alae* would ride north to attack the fort . . . and you know what happened next.'

'I was in the *valetudinarium* in Eboracum with a piece of Pictish steel an inch from my heart, but I've heard it said Dulcitius took overall command?'

'I was but a man in a saddle,' Caradoc shrugged. 'We advanced in darkness, shoulder to shoulder, the lights of the fires within the walls of Castra Exploratum not a mile away. We were confident, because they had no idea we were coming for them. After all the fighting we'd done they didn't believe we would advance an inch further north than the Wall.'

'But you did.'

'Yes, we did and more fool us, because they were waiting for us. It cost your father his life. He was sixty summers old when he fell to a Pictish blade outside Castra Exploratum.'

'And no Dulcitius?'

'In Christ's name, lord, you must have asked me this a hundred times. I told you it was dark and then in the fight I got that dunt on the head that scrambled my brains. Someone was in overall command, but it wasn't Brenus. Dulcitius, maybe the general himself, or some other. There was always another officer to fuck things up, saving your presence.'

As always Marcus suspected Caradoc knew more than he was telling, but he would get no more.

'You said Arrius requested an interview.'

'They've had a runner. One of the Corn-tops took off north with his girlfriend to join the Picts.' Corn-tops was the Ala Sabiniana's derisive nickname for the mostly golden-haired soldiers of Vindobala's garrison, the First Frisians.

'Then he should let him run. It will do nobody any good to bring him back.'

'He's a centurion – they still use the old ranks here – and he encouraged his men to rise up and kill Arrius and the other senior officers. Arrius wants to set an example.'

Marcus cursed. 'The old fool thinks he's swatting a wasp, but he'll end up with a nest of angry hornets.'

X

Arrius and his wife Livilla insisted on inviting Marcus to dinner. It wasn't unexpected, but that didn't make it any more welcome. Marcus asked Valeria to accompany him as she had on previous occasions when he'd needed an escort.

The commander of Vindobala was an old-fashioned man and he prided himself on his old-fashioned ways. They dined reclining on low couches around a large square table set at the same height. Valeria tried unsuccessfully to hide a moment of astonishment at a setting she only recognized from crumbling mosaics and flaking wall paintings in the basilica at Eboracum. Livilla had provided her with a long green dress with a braided collar and sleeves. A seamstress altered it to fit her slimmer form, but after so long wearing a cavalry officer's armour she felt uneasy in its voluminous folds.

Livilla lay opposite and kept the conversation alive with the ease of a practised hostess, but there was a tension in the room that Valeria sensed had nothing to do with the forthcoming trial.

Marcus had reluctantly agreed to lend Arrius a troop of horsemen to hunt down the fugitive, but he'd urged the troop commander not to try too hard to find him. Unfortunately, the man's partner had turned her ankle in a ditch and the fool had stayed with her less than two miles north of the fort.

'We'll hold the trial outside the *praetorium*.' Arrius spoke in a ponderous, irritating drone that placed an unnecessary emphasis on every fourth word. 'I've asked Septimus to come over from Condercum to make up the numbers. I was hoping your cavalrymen could provide security for the proceedings.'

'You don't trust your own soldiers?' The question was more direct than Marcus had intended and he saw Arrius frown.

'I merely thought it was sensible. If you don't feel . . .'

'No, of course.' Marcus bowed his head in thanks as Livilla reached across to fill his cup. 'I'm surprised the men of his century are so willing to give evidence against him. In my experience soldiers tend to keep their mouths shut rather than inform on their tentmates, however obvious their guilt.'

'Oh, they weren't willing,' Arrius said with a tight smile. 'But I made it clear that if they didn't give evidence against Masavo they would all face trial for mutiny. If they were found guilty I would sentence the unit to decimation.'

Decimation was a punishment used in the distant past and so brutal very few legionary commanders had ever dared authorize it. Arrius was asking to have his throat cut in his bed for even threatening it. Marcus kept the opinion to himself, but Valeria put his thoughts into words.

'Decimation hasn't been carried out since the time of the Caesars,' she pointed out. 'Caesar himself threatened it, but even he didn't put the threat into practice. Surely you didn't mean it?'

'Of course I meant it.' Arrius shrugged off his wife's restraining arm. 'You cannot impose a sentence if you are not willing to carry it out, as that traitor Masavo will discover tomorrow.'

An hour later Marcus walked those same walls he trod as a boy, counting every pace as his nailed boots touched the slabs of the walkway. As he walked, he considered the coming trial, if it could be called a trial. He was no stranger to arbitration and the complexities of legal argument. They were central to the exercise of power as Brenus had taught it and added not only to his wealth, but his influence. Most of the tribunals decided relatively minor matters: village disputes over land and water rights, men accused of stealing their neighbour's timber or poaching in their woods, smallholders snarling at each other over a single *iugerum* of grazing. But some involved men who in times gone by would have called themselves kings, who now ruled substantial townships as *duoviri* where they would once have ruled tribes. They were wealthy men in their own right, and a wealthy man would pay well for a decision to go his way when the alternative was being held responsible for years of taxes owed by his *municipium*. Sadly, Masavo could have offered all the riches of the east and Marcus still wouldn't have argued in his favour.

Arrius was a fool, but for all his faults he was an effective officer. His men knew their duties well enough, a parade this afternoon had shown that. No sentries taking a sly nap on the battlements as Marcus had discovered at Condercum. The problem was that Arrius didn't respect them and they didn't respect him. They called him the Stag because so many of his fellow officers had placed antlers upon his brow.

Marcus smiled and shook his head. Memories stirred and he caught a faint hint of perfumed oil on the still air. As he entered the shadows at the top of a stairwell a cloaked figure detached herself from the darkness and fell into his arms.

The condemned man stood between two guards in the open square in front of the *praetorium*, heavy chains shackling his wrists and ankles. Not entirely condemned, it was true, because the proceedings had yet to begin, but the outcome was hardly in doubt. The First Frisians, three hundred strong, were formed up on three sides of the square in their best uniforms, but without their weapons. Two squadrons of Marcus's dismounted cavalry troopers created a wall of swords between the accused and his comrades. The air seemed alive with tension, the way it sometimes felt before a great thunderstorm. Marcus sat at

Arrius's left hand in a chair on the steps of the commander's house, with Septimus Iuventius, commander of the neighbouring fort at Condercum, to Arrius's right. They were flanked by the unit's standard-bearers and a clerk at the far end of the platform, ready to record the proceedings. On the opposite side of the square Valeria stood with Livilla on a balcony overlooking the parade.

'Send forward the first witness,' Arrius ordered.

A murmur ran round the courtyard as a tall, thin man dressed in a plain tunic and *braccae* emerged from the headquarters building across the open square. Arrius stiffened at the sound and Marcus could hear the unit's officers snarling at their men for silence. The soldier walked slowly across the hard-packed earth looking neither to right nor left and on legs that seemed reluctant to obey him. As he passed the chained prisoner something must have been said because the witness visibly flinched.

'If the accused speaks again without permission,' Arrius snapped, 'you have my orders to gag him for the duration of the proceedings.'

The witness continued his interminable slow march until he stood directly in front of the three officers. His fists were clenched so tightly Marcus could see the white of his knuckles and his legs shook.

'State your name and rank.' The order came from the clerk and seemed to startle the man.

'J-J-Julius Brocchus, infantryman, third rank, second century.'

'That is the century of the prisoner Masavo, is that correct?'

'Yes, sir.'

'And on the night of the fifteenth the prisoner entered your barrack block?'

Brocchus hesitated.

'Bear in mind that we already have your statement,' Arrius interrupted. 'Any deviation from that statement will have serious consequences. Do you understand?'

Brocchus mumbled something inaudible.

'Speak up, man,' Arrius said.

'I said yes, sir.'

'Then continue.'

'Masavo – the prisoner – has a room of his own in our block. He came out with a flask of wine and offered to share it with the lads. He was drunk, and angry. He said the commander had ordered him to cut our rations and that all leave had been stopped. He ranted for a while and then he said it.'

'He said what?' Arrius demanded.

'He said the whole century should get their weapons and take over the fort. He would kill you and your deputy and then we'd take all the supplies and everything of value from the fort and march north, where we'd be welcomed by the Picts.'

'He said you would be welcomed by the Picts?'

Brocchus lowered his head. 'Yes, lord.'

Arrius appeared perfectly satisfied with the witness, as Marcus thought he should be. In that first testimony he had enough evidence to condemn his man for mutiny and treason. But for Marcus something unsaid was even more damning. Masavo didn't only believe he'd have the support of his own century in this mutiny. He *knew* he could depend on the centurions of the other two centuries. Why else wouldn't he include them among those to be killed, or at least locked away?

One damning piece of testimony followed the other, from seven more witnesses, all members of Masavo's century. One of these men had decided he had more to gain by informing on Masavo than joining him. It was the betrayal all plotters risked. As soon as you came out into the open there was always the chance of some worm turning.

When the last witness had been led away, Arrius stood and addressed his cohort.

'You all heard what your comrades had to say.' His voice rang from the courtyard walls. 'The evidence is undeniable. Centurion Masavo is guilty of treason against the Empire and fomenting mutiny. We will proceed to sentence.'

A rustle of unease ran round the three hundred Frisians.

'I do not disagree.' A strident voice cut the silence and Marcus stifled a groan as Iuventius made his inevitable intervention. 'But whatever this man's crimes it is a central tenet of Roman justice that he also should have his say.'

Arrius spluttered and complained, but he knew he had no choice but to comply. He called Masavo forward.

The centurion shuffled towards the steps, each pace accompanied by the rattle of his chains. Yet he still managed to maintain a measure of dignity that seemed almost to ennoble him. He took his place in front of the judges and Marcus's heart sank at the look of calm acceptance that registered so clearly in the weary eyes.

Arrius glared at him and the sheer venom in his voice should have struck Masavo down there and then. 'Your guilt is clear, traitor. You would have killed me and mine and gone over to the enemy. Yet our love of justice is such that you now have the opportunity to show remorse.'

'I feel no remorse and I will show none,' Masavo said in a voice devoid of fear. 'True justice would have been done when you were lying dead in your bed, Rufus Arrius.' Arrius's face had turned such a bright shade of red Marcus wondered he didn't have a seizure. Better, perhaps, if in his rage he'd stood up and plunged a sword through the man's heart. 'And you should know,' the prisoner turned to stare at the eight men who had borne witness against him, 'that in one important particular my accusers lied. I had no intention of taking the First Frisians north to join our enemies. Do you think this is the only discontented garrison on the Wall? I would have sent detachments east and west and men from every fort would have flocked to join me. Because of him.' Marcus feigned amusement as Masavo's accusing finger pointed directly at him, but he said nothing, for now. 'Did you know,' Masavo continued, 'he has been stealing rations intended for this fort and others and diverting them to his precious horse soldiers. Even his horses eat better than we do.'

'A liar as well as a traitor,' Marcus sighed. 'Do we have to listen to this nonsense all day?'

'And when I had gathered enough men—'

At a signal from Arrius one of the guards took a cloth and rammed it into Masavo's mouth.

Not before time.

'Condemned by his own words.' Arrius didn't hide his satisfaction. 'If we are all agreed on his guilt I will pass sentence.' Marcus and Iuventius nodded their assent and the tribune rose to his feet. 'Gaius Masavo, centurion, second century of the First Frisian cohort, you are found guilty of treason and fomenting mutiny among your comrades. The only sentence appropriate for these crimes is death, but it is up to your commander to choose the manner of it. A quick death is more than you deserve and it is necessary that your century erase all the shame with which your continued existence contaminates them.'

From the corner of his eye Marcus saw an officer moving among the witnesses handing out wooden staves and he understood Arrius had planned this from the start.

'I sentence you to *fustuarium*.' A collective gasp ran through the assembled ranks that swiftly developed into a growl of anger only stilled when Marcus's cavalrymen took a step forward with their hands on their sword hilts. Marcus waved a hand to Valeria to take Livilla indoors. No one should witness this who didn't have to.

Fustuarium.

Was the man mad? Perhaps he was. They removed Masavo's gag and stripped away his clothing, cutting it away so he stood naked and helpless in his chains in the centre of the square. *Fustuarium.* It meant a soldier's crimes were so monstrous that he must be beaten to death by those closest to him. The men who testified against Masavo were hustled towards him by their officers. They held their wooden batons, sturdy elm pick handles, as if uncertain of their purpose, and their faces told conflicting stories. One or two showed grim purpose; they knew there was no way out but to do what must be done. Another mumbled to himself, nodding and beating his stave against his leg as if his own pain might absolve him of what was to come. The rest were slack-jawed and sickly pale and Marcus knew they would be the ones to prolong their centurion's agony because they could not bear to break bone or aim where the blow needed to be aimed. If Masavo was as clever as he appeared, he would have anticipated this and bribed one of them to strike a fatal blow in the first flurry.

The eight men surrounded their naked victim.

'Begin,' Arrius ordered. Not a man struck a blow. 'Hit home or you will replace him,' the First's commander cried. 'Decurions, take the name of any man who does not put his weight behind the strike.'

Masavo stood upright, his pride intact until the first blow in the ribs doubled him up. Another smashed into the side of his knee and he was down writhing in the dirt. His first cries of pain were forced from between gritted teeth that were smashed in the next instant to scatter in a spray of crimson. Now the beating began in earnest as if the sight of blood had removed the executioners' moral inhibitions the way a jug of sour wine did on the morning of a battle. The staves rose and fell in a terrible, relentless rhythm, each strike following the one before, hammering into flesh and bone. Masavo's cries were replaced by screams and eventually a single, prolonged animal shriek as he realized there would be no end to his agony.

'He paid Brocchus to give him a tap on the head, but it wouldn't have done,' Arrius said. 'An example is an example.'

Apart from the single blow that broke his jaw, they left Masavo's head intact. But the staves rained down on his chest, arms and legs with increasing force. Marcus heard ribs splinter and bones break and the awful rending crack, accompanied by a new volume to the screaming, of a thigh bone snapping. Minutes passed until the only sound was the dull, liquid thud of wood against smashed flesh and bone. Masavo gave a convulsive heave and a gout of blood exploded from his gaping mouth.

The executioners stepped back, steam rising from their sweating bodies. Arrius's *medicus* approached the prone body.

'Is he dead?' Arrius demanded.

The *medicus* shook his head.

'Finish it.'

Brocchus stepped forward and, with a terrible roar, brought his stave down in a blow that shattered Masavo's skull and scattered his brains across the packed earth.

XI

They concluded their inspection at a fortlet just to the west of Vindobala which marked Mile Fifteen of the Wall as measured from Segedunum. Eighty of these mile fortlets abutted the Wall with two smaller watch turrets between each. Marcus noted that the walls were in good repair, but, as with most of these buildings, the barrack blocks lay derelict, much of their stone used for repairs to the fort or the Wall itself. The fortlet measured perhaps twenty paces by thirty. A gate tower dominated the centre of the northern face, built into the Wall itself and linked to it by a paved walkway, but the gateway had been blocked in the distant past. In their own way, the arched gateways of the Wall were some of its most impressive works of construction. For all his experience rebuilding Vindobala Marcus knew he could never have created anything like it. How were the massive stones that made up the arch kept stable and in place until the triangular keystone was dropped into position? The gateways were one of the many things that intrigued Marcus about his Wall. Whoever had planned it had encouraged regular but tightly controlled access between north and south. Ironclad warriors of the old legions had no doubt poured through the gateway to invade the north, but the scale of the entrances and the rutted stones of the threshold were also evidence of substantial trade.

The fort would once have protected a permanent garrison of thirty auxiliaries, but those days were long gone. Now six men bedded down in an old storehouse and took turns at standing sentry on the battlements of the tower.

Marcus and Valeria climbed the tower while Arrius inspected the guard. When they reached the top of the steps Valeria looked across the northern battlements to where the boggy, featureless ground stretched away in a slight rise and shook her head.

'I can't imagine a duller posting.'

'It's true there's not much to see.' Marcus inspected a piece of timber from a pile stacked beneath an awning by the signal brazier. The wood and the moss that would fire it were tinder dry, more evidence that the small garrison took its job seriously. Nearby lay a pile of oily gorse that would send up a spectacular flare in the event of a night attack. 'But there's plenty of incentive to keep looking. We don't have enough soldiers to man them properly, so this is nothing but an over-sized signal post. If the Picts do attack it will be overrun and the garrison slaughtered by the time Arrius sees their signal smoke.'

'Given the state of the garrison, I doubt they can depend on any reinforcements from Vindobala whatever happens.' Valeria looked down into the courtyard where Arrius was berating an unfortunate auxiliary for some minor infraction.

Marcus nodded. 'The rot is set deep in the commander and his command. I've suggested that he transfer one of his centurions to Iuventius at Condercum, but neither man loved me for it. It's not a lot and I doubt it would make much difference, but what else can I do?'

'Perhaps it would help if you stopped debauching his wife?'

'Direct as ever, my dear sister.' Marcus stared at her. 'Was it so obvious?'

'I thought you were going to have each other on the dinner table.'

'Livilla says they have an arrangement,' Marcus said absently. 'But I doubt even old Arrius would have put up with that.'

'It's not good for morale.'

'Fucking?' He laughed. 'It's good for mine, I can assure you.'

'A superior officer having his way with a junior commander's wife,' Valeria said. 'You do not command only by your military authority, Marcus, but by your moral authority.'

Marcus placed a hand on his sword hilt. 'This is my moral authority.'

'If only everything was so simple.' She shook her head. 'How much of what Masavo said was true?'

Marcus had been heading towards the stairway, but now he stopped. 'So that's why you followed me up here?'

'I need to know, Marcus. Any one of us is only a heartbeat from Heaven. You never tell me anything unless I ask.'

'Some of it,' he admitted. 'I could blame Dulcitius for keeping us short of everything from weapons and armour to rations and boot leather. The reality is he has his own problems with supply from the Gaulish factories at Samarobriva and Aregenua. The silver he steals from me he uses to try to stop the Saxons and the Scotti. But my problem isn't the Saxons or the Scotti, it's those bastards out there.' He waved a hand to the north. 'I have three weapons against the Picts: fear, corruption and those horses down there. Our greatest strength is their greatest weakness, because they have very few cavalry. I call them Picts and we think of them as Picts. In fact, they are a loose federation of tribes riven by years of feuding, hatred and rivalry, forced together by fear of an even greater enemy. United, they will one day pour over the Wall in the company of the true Picts, so I keep them divided. I can never have enough silver and I can never have enough horses. It's more important to keep a horse fed than a man, but I steal and I hoard and I beg to keep the horse alive and the man in the saddle. Is it theft to keep back a trooper's pay so that you can bribe the quartermasters to put a sword in his hand, clothes on his back and food in his belly? If you're ever in my position you'll do the same.'

'All right,' she said. 'What about the rest of it? The garrisons who were ready to join him.'

'I don't know for certain,' Marcus admitted. 'But my instinct is that he was either lying or exaggerating. Soldiers have been complaining about poor food and poor pay and corrupt officers since Caesar's time and probably long before. Either way this inspection will allow us to test the mettle of those garrisons. He was right about one thing, though . . .'

'And what was that?'

'Resentment against Rome is growing, you can feel it everywhere you go. The legionaries of the Sixth haven't been paid for longer than the Wall garrisons. They're forced to steal from the local peasants and the peasants go hungry. They blame Rome, and who wouldn't? Rome takes more in taxes from Britannia every year, and every year Rome gives less back. The only thing keeping the people loyal is the knowledge that without the army the Saxons and the Scotti and the Picts will take everything they have, slaughter their menfolk and drag their women and children off in chains. But it doesn't have to be like that. Masavo would never have carried it off, but . . .'

She nodded thoughtfully. 'All it would need is a strong leader.'

'Precisely.' Marcus smiled. 'How fortunate for Rome that such a man doesn't exist in Britannia.'

'Isn't it.' He felt her eyes on him, but he didn't respond. Eventually she said: 'It's good to see you've recovered, brother, but sometimes you take too much upon yourself.'

'Perhaps you're right.' He hesitated for a moment. 'There is one thing you can help me with.'

'Yes?' A raised eyebrow accompanied the word. An acknowledgement of any kind of weakness was unusual.

'When Dulcitius tried to threaten me in Segedunum I told him I had a letter incriminating his sons. Twenty-four hours later he couldn't help crowing that he knew I didn't have it. Someone must have told him.'

'Could he have had your quarters searched?'

'No, I had the door guarded at all times. The only answer is that Dulcitius has an informant in the Ala Sabiniana. And it has to be someone close.'

He watched her consider the implications of what he'd said. Eventually she nodded. 'What do you want me to do?'

'Watch. Try to find out who watches me. Who follows me. Who has access to my papers when they shouldn't have.'

'All right,' Valeria agreed. 'I can do that.' She turned towards the stairs. 'There's just one thing.'

'What?'

'How do you know it's not me who is Dulcitius's spy?'

'I don't.' He laughed as she disappeared from view. 'A heartbeat from Heaven. I like that. So Zeno told you how bad my chest is? I really should cut his throat.'

XII

Marcus Flavius Victor laughed aloud as he cantered towards the vast army of Picts with the sun on his face and the fierce elixir of battle fever running through his veins. The Imperial forces were massively outnumbered, yet victory was certain. How could they possibly lose when he rode knee to knee with the greatest general the world had ever known?

Marcus nudged Storm ahead as the three lines of horsemen, each five hundred strong, thundered across the broken ground of marsh, field and meadow. The line was too loose. If the troopers struck the Picts as individuals instead of a solid block of meat and metal they would be torn from their saddles and slaughtered.

'Close up, close up.' Marcus heard Valeria's unmistakeable cry away to his left and it was taken up by other squadron commanders in the front rank. The terrain altered and high ground to the right forced the advancing cavalry into a more compact formation still. Half a mile ahead Marcus could see the Picts edging back into a funnel of land like the stopper in a wineskin. Behind them the ground opened out like the wineskin itself, almost an island but for that narrow neck between the two rivers. Still only an amorphous throng, perhaps six or seven thousand strong, but the gap was closing swiftly beneath the advancing hooves. Gradually he identified distinct groupings and Pictish war chiefs on horseback using the flats of their swords to hurry their warriors into position. Most would be armed with spears or the great single-headed war axe they could use with such deadly precision. A shaft as long as a man's arm and a heavy head with an edge as keen as any razor. Northern Picts for the most part, as they'd discovered from the few prisoners taken during the chase, but with a leavening of opportunists from the southern tribes, the Selgovae, Damnonii, Novantae and even the Votadini, Rome's notional allies.

The signaller on the right raised his curved trumpet to his lips and sounded the blaring invitation to charge. Marcus and every trooper in the three ranks put heels to their mounts and he felt Storm leap ahead beneath him. He forced himself to hold his spear lightly in his right fist, impetus would do the rest. A tight grip and a tense arm carried the danger of forcing your shoulder from the socket at the impact. Now the Picts filled his entire vision with painted flesh. Dancing spear points came at him with astonishing speed.

It shouldn't be like this. The battle seemed to pause as the thought sprang into his mind.

Something jarred his wrist. He sensed the spear point entering flesh and striking bone and released the shaft. His free hand automatically felt for his sword hilt. But his sword wasn't where it should be. Now he was flying. Had he been unhorsed? Killed? No, he soared above the battlefield like a hovering kestrel as if he had entered a different world. The world of the old gods.

He watched himself die.

'No, no.' Marcus heard himself scream the words. 'It wasn't like that. There was glory and eternal fame and—'

'Hush, brother.' He felt gentle hands on his brow and his pounding heart slowed. 'You have had a fever. It was only the fever.'

Marcus became aware he was lying naked beneath a sweat-damp sheet. He opened his eyes and stared blearily into his sister's concerned features.

'I dreamt . . .'

'Yes, we heard.'

Marcus became aware of Livilla washing cloths in a basin in the corner. Without a word she walked to the curtained doorway and left the room. Clearly, they'd been discussing him. He opened his mouth to voice his irritation, but the gravity in Valeria's eyes persuaded him to bite back the words. A chill ran through him.

'How long have I been here?'

'Three days.'

'Christus, save us.' He pulled himself upright, but his head spun and he knew if he tried to stand he'd only collapse.

'You're weak, Marcus, you need rest.'

'I've no time for rest.' He swallowed the sour bile that filled his mouth. 'Get Zeno to mix me something to get me back on my feet.'

Valeria shook her head in exasperation and walked out.

Three days. He'd lost three days – two and a half if he was being optimistic. Yes, he could make it back in the coming weeks, but there was so much to do.

Valeria returned with Zeno. The Greek carried a cup full of steaming liquid which he put to Marcus's mouth. Marcus almost choked on the thick, bitter-sweet potion. 'Drink it all, lord, then rest,' Zeno ordered.

Marcus gulped the remainder down. 'Why does everybody want me to rest? What do you think I've been doing for the last three days?' He tossed the cup to the *medicus* and wiped his hand across his mouth. The warmth of the liquid seemed to race through his veins and when it snapped into his head his mind cleared as quickly as mist touched by the sun on a midsummer morning. 'Leave us,' he snapped at Zeno, 'we have work to do.'

Zeno glanced at Valeria and she nodded. 'Who do you think has been doing all the work while you've been lying around?'

'Good,' he said. 'Then we should be able to move quickly. Come here, dear sister.' Marcus patted the bed beside him.

Reluctantly, she did as he suggested.

'You say I never tell you anything unless you ask,' he said quietly.

'Well, now I'm going to let you in on a secret. I want you to ride ahead with your squadron to Cilurnum.' Cilurnum was the next fort on his itinerary, home to the Second Asturum, who, like the Ala Sabiniana, were a specialist cavalry unit. 'When you reach there instruct Canalius to prepare ten squadrons for a week-long expedition north of the Wall, and to gather supplies and fodder to sustain the Ala Sabiniana for the same length of time.'

'He's not going to like that,' she frowned.

'I don't care if he likes it as long as he does it. That's why I'm sending you. He's like a puppy when you're around, all big wide eyes and his tongue hanging out. Remind him that we're all following Dulcitius's orders. If he complains, work your charm on him.'

Valeria had to stifle a laugh at the image. Canalius was notoriously ugly and the least romantic man on the entire Wall. 'So what's this secret?'

'That is the secret.'

'No, that's telling me to do something, the way you always do.'

'You women are never satisfied.' He managed a tired smile. 'Tell Arrius I want to see him in an hour – pass me that sealed packet.'

'Is this the secret?'

'In a way. And when I'm done with Arrius send me that priest. It's about time he earned his rations.'

Marcus spent the interval writing a set of orders which required painstaking drafting and diplomatic language that didn't come naturally to him, but no clerk could be allowed to set eyes on the contents. Later, as he lay in the darkness with one of Zeno's poultices over his heart and his head seemingly filled with hot coals, he relived every blow of Masavo's terrible death. Was it treason to turn against an Empire that had already abandoned you? It was a question still troubling him when Arrius bustled into the room.

'These are your sealed orders,' he told Vindobala's commander. 'You will open them when a messenger carrying a token from me arrives at Vindobala, and not before. Do you understand, Arrius?'

'Of course, but—'

'It may be ten days or two weeks, but you will wait. When you open them you will obey the instructions contained there without question and without hesitation, no matter how outlandish they seem.'

'I'm a soldier, prefect,' Arrius spluttered. 'Do not involve me in your silly intrigues.'

'Without question and without hesitation,' Marcus persisted. 'Until then you will keep the First Frisians at twelve-hour readiness for any eventuality.'

'You can't be serious,' Arrius almost laughed.

Marcus moved very close and Arrius shifted uncomfortably. 'I'll tell you how serious I am. If you disobey my orders on any level I will ensure you die the same monstrous death that poor benighted bastard Masavo suffered.' Arrius went deathly pale. 'Yes, Arrius.' Marcus's eyes bored into the other man's. 'I'm that serious.'

When he was alone, Marcus sat on the bed with his head down. He had a new pain in his chest he didn't like and he felt nauseous. A knock on the doorpost brought him back to his feet.

'Come,' he said.

Ninian, the former priest, entered with what someone had obviously told him was a true cavalryman's swagger. 'You sent for me, lord?'

'Do you still believe in God?'

IRON

XIII

Cilurnum (Chesters)

The Tinan river split into two separate flows a few miles west of Corstopitum, where the stream dubbed the North Tinan took a course directly north along a tree-choked valley, while the South Tinan continued westwards. Cilurnum guarded an important bridge that carried the *via militaris* over the North Tinan. Strategically, it was the keystone of the eastern defences and the sixth major fort on the line of the Wall. Twenty watch and gate towers dotted the walls and the terracotta-roofed barrack blocks were all in good repair.

Cilurnum's position and significance meant it had always merited a garrison of a full cavalry wing. The Second Asturum had their origins in the mountainous north of Hispania, but, like the Ala Sabiniana, the auxiliary cavalry unit had recruited locally for at least a century and their numbers were made up predominantly of native Britons.

Cilurnum's commander, Pompeius Canalius, however, was a Roman from the iron nails of his boots to the shock of black hair that shot up like a hedgepig's spikes from his round head. Small, deep-set eyes gave him a porcine appearance further emphasized by his blunt, upturned nose and almost non-existent chin. It was a face naturally disposed to belligerence, but Marcus had never witnessed it quite this angry.

Canalius was waiting outside Cilurnum's east gate ready to greet the Lord of the Wall. Valeria stood behind his right shoulder and a warning look told Marcus not to expect any form of welcome.

'Have you finally lost your mind entirely,' Canalius barked as Marcus led his men up the slope from the bridge to the fort. 'How do you think I'm going to replace these supplies at this time of the year?' He waved a hand to where a line of wagons straggled towards Cilurnum from the south. 'I've had to strip the country bare to find enough provisions and fodder for your men and mine to last out whatever madness you have in mind.'

Marcus could see no amount of bluster was going to placate Canalius, but sometimes a fractious mount responded better to being gentled rather than whipped. 'And you have my assurance that I wouldn't have made the request if it hadn't been forced upon me, Pompeius,' he said as he dismounted. 'Or made a demand I knew was near impossible unless I was certain of the mettle of the man I was asking to fulfil it.' Pompeius stared at him, unsure whether he was being flattered or mocked. 'But we should speak of this later, old friend.' Marcus clasped the other man's wrist. 'This chill has penetrated my very bones and you would indulge me if I could make use of your bathhouse so I can remember what it is to be warm again.'

Marcus's left hand strayed to rub the chain armour over his heart, a gesture that seemed to put a dent in Canalius's belligerence. 'Of course, prefect.' His expression softened. 'The waters will still retain some heat from this morning's immersion, but I will have the fires stoked and you will have your bath within the hour.'

Marcus nodded his thanks and allowed a trooper to take Storm's reins. Canalius led the way inside the fort and Marcus followed on the short walk to the commander's quarters. Soldiers worked industriously to prepare weapons and equipment outside barrack blocks designed to accommodate thirty troopers and their horses. One or two paused to look up with undisguised curiosity at the man responsible for this sudden flurry of activity. Valeria took step by his side. 'We expected you yesterday, Marcus.'

'I decided to stop off at Hunnum and pay Demetrius a surprise visit.'

'I'm sure he appreciated that,' Valeria laughed.

'I should have known better,' Marcus said wryly. 'He greeted me with a guard of honour that consisted of the armourer's assistant, Rufus the one-legged clerk, and four of the stupidest village boys armed with wooden swords.'

'You left him short-handed, I recall.'

'I did.' Marcus grinned. 'And didn't he remind me of it. But he still had a pair of eyes in every watchtower and two men at the gate. He'd even managed to persuade some of the villagers to help him mend that crumbling bit of masonry blocking the north gate. The bastards would have found an excuse to be somewhere else if *I'd* asked them.'

'Perhaps you don't have his charm. Still,' she gave him an appraising look, 'you managed to appease Canalius and I would never have believed that possible, apart from one thing.'

'What's that?'

'He thinks you're dying.'

When Marcus was installed in the rooms Canalius had prepared in the *praetorium*, Valeria appeared at his door carrying a flask of wine and two cups.

'We have slaves to do that,' he pointed out.

'I thought we should talk.'

'Things are that bad?'

Valeria took a seat at a table where a high window provided just enough light to see without an oil lamp and Marcus joined her after a moment. 'Canalius has reason for his anger, Marcus,' she said. 'It's easy to ask for enough supplies to keep seven hundred men in the saddle for a week, but not so easy to deliver them. His foragers have scoured the country and removed half the grain and fodder from the stores of every homestead that owes tax obligations to the fort. People will go hungry. Some may starve.'

Marcus caught the scent of cooking through the window. The fort's victuallers would be preparing supplies for the expedition. *Lucana* sausage by the scent of it, along with unleavened bread and *buccellatum*: iron-hard biscuits, 'jawbreakers', that were the soldiers' sustenance of last resort. 'Do you think they'd rather have full bellies ready for the moment the Picts kick in their doors and disembowel them so they can die watching their wives being raped and their children murdered? Going hungry is the price they occasionally pay for our protection. It's always been that way. The strong protect the weak, but only if the weak feed the strong.'

'But what if the strong also go hungry?' Valeria's lips pursed in irritation at having to state what was so obvious. 'Canalius has depleted his own stores to ensure his men are fed on the march. You know how difficult it is to replenish supplies in winter . . .'

'They'd be eating anyway, on the march or not.'

'Only last month he told you he'd struggle to get through the winter on full rations. You said he should disperse half his men and horses to outlying farms and the farmers would feed them. That can't happen now.'

'I'd forgotten about that.'

'No you hadn't, brother,' she insisted. 'You chose not to remember. Canalius's quartermaster reckons Cilurnum will be on half rations by February. Oh, you can dismiss it by saying two months of hunger never killed a man, but that's not the point. We know from Vindobala that the morale of these soldiers is close to breaking. They're owed months of back pay, which means they can't pay their own debts. The food they get is already poor and without money they can't supplement it with the usual small luxuries from the shops and markets. If the garrison goes hungry, so do their families. Fuel is short and winter means they have to go further to find it every year, which places them in greater danger from any roving band of Picts. Masavo is far from the only dissenter on this frontier. All it would take is one garrison to fail and this Wall will crumble and fall.'

'I won't let that happen.'

'Then what will you do?'

Marcus considered the question. 'When we get back, I'll persuade Justus at Corstopitum to release enough of that grain he's been hoarding to see Cilurnum through the winter, and the farmers too.'

She stared at him, wanting to believe, but knowing him too well to make the leap of faith required. 'This is your sister, Marcus, not some weak-minded auxiliary commander you can dazzle with your conjuror's tricks. How?'

Marcus hesitated. 'Because I know things that will put Justus's scrawny neck on a block. I only found out when you were at Grabant. He's not just stealing supplies from the garrisons, he's selling them to the Picts, and not just food, arms and armour too. I might just kill him myself, but that would deprive me of the pleasure of watching Dulcitius sentencing his old friend and fellow plotter to the block. Does that satisfy you?'

She gave it some thought before she nodded.

'Good,' he smiled. 'And Canalius really thinks I'm dying?'

'A cartload of spear points arrived from Corstopitum two days ago and every man in the fort heard one or other version of the story within the hour. Canalius is convinced it's true.'

'That's actually quite convenient.' He smiled at Valeria's bewildered frown. 'Because if he's angry now I suspect he'll want to kill me by the time we leave here.'

When Valeria left, Marcus called for a slave to accompany him to the bathhouse. He shook his head. So many lies even he sometimes couldn't remember where the falsity ended and the truth began. Still, she would thank him in the end.

If it worked.

Canalius was waiting for him at the bathhouse seated on a bench in the main pool, wreathed in steam and water up to his neck. More bear-like out of uniform than porcine, a thick pelt of black hair covered his chest and back. He had muscled shoulders broad as a yoke, and his face wore a myopic frown. The only light came from a pair of oil lamps

101

and the flickering shadows gave his mismatched features a nightmarish quality.

Marcus dismissed the slave and untied his robe. He heard Canalius's involuntary gasp at the sight of the raw, suppurating scar from Zeno's surgery, the surrounding flesh swollen and mottled with dark bruises.

'Your wound . . .'

'Looks much worse than it is,' Marcus assured him, but he couldn't disguise a sharp cry as the scalding water touched tender flesh. He lowered himself onto a bench and sat for a moment with his eyes closed. 'I thought it best we meet in privacy so that I can explain the situation to you without worrying about prying eyes and flapping ears.'

'I understand, but . . .' Canalius's tone took on a new belligerence. 'Your sister will have told you my concerns.'

'She did, and I accept them entirely,' Marcus met the aggression with conciliation.

'I must protest at what I believe is a dangerous misuse of resources and demand that the order be made in writing should you wish to persist with it.'

Canalius steeled himself for the inevitable explosion – the demand was an impertinence, and perhaps more than an impertinence, and both men knew it – but, surprisingly, none was forthcoming.

Marcus lay back and watched wisps of steam drift up to a ceiling decorated with a depiction of naked water nymphs cavorting with grinning dolphins. 'There are certain things even my sister does not know, Pompeius. What I am about to say must not be repeated outside these four walls. Not repeated to anyone. My head, perhaps both our heads, depends on it. Do I have your word on it?'

Canalius blinked. 'Of course, prefect, but I have to say I find this all very unconventional.'

'Is it likely I would embark on an inspection of the Wall forts in dead of winter without good reason?'

'We were surprised by the timing,' Canalius admitted.

'This is all part of a grand scheme set in motion by Dulcitius, our commander,' Marcus continued. 'I am following his orders, Pompeius, just as you must follow mine, without question. You and I are just gaming pieces on a board to be moved at his pleasure.'

'I had heard talk of some pact with Niall of the Nine Hostages . . .'

'Niall is part of it,' Marcus agreed, 'but only part. And what you have heard may be what you are meant to hear. I will reveal the truth of it before I leave for Brocolitia, but first we have another part of Dulcitius's mission to accomplish. He has been conducting secret negotiations with King Corvus of the Selgovae. If he can persuade Corvus that it's in his interests to act as a buffer between the Wall and the Caledonian Picts, as King Coel has agreed in the east, it will relieve pressure all along the Wall. Corvus isn't entirely opposed to the suggestion; after all it's only a return to the situation of the distant past, from which his tribe profited.'

'In the distant past, we had a strong Emperor,' Canalius pointed out. 'The Picts were half as numerous and they didn't have thousands of Scotti ready to fight at their side.'

'And Corvus is just as aware of those facts as we are, Pompeius.' Marcus ran a hand across the surface of the water, creating small waves that broke against the marble sides of the bath. 'Naturally he has concerns and conditions of his own. You have no doubt heard of this chest of silver I carry, these things are impossible to keep secret for long?'

Canalius nodded.

'Then you should know it is just one of two. The first is to test Corvus's resolve. He is cunning and unscrupulous and he has his own conception of honour, but Dulcitius believes being seen to accept Roman silver will bind him to us. He will also require assurances from us of support, should the Picts attack him in superior numbers . . .'

'Fight north of the Wall?' Canalius was appalled. 'With so few troops and untrustworthy barbarian allies at our backs? Even if Dulcitius were to bring the Sixth north . . .'

'Dulcitius is no fool,' Marcus insisted. 'In Constantine's day the province funded a Selgovae militia and provided support from the *arcani* based at the outlying forts at Fanum, Tarras, Habitancum and Bremenium. This is high strategy, Pompeius, and not for the likes of you and me.' He leaned across to pat Canalius's hairy shoulder. 'What is not in doubt is that I will travel north as Dulcitius's envoy as soon as our preparations are complete.'

Canalius frowned. The proposal raised so many questions, but one sprang to the front of his mind. 'What kind of envoy needs a small army to escort him to a peaceful negotiation?'

The answer was simple.

'The kind of envoy whose host would very much like to see him dead.'

XIV

Large though it was, Cilurnum could not accommodate all the troops gathered there, so Marcus's troopers had set up a tented encampment on flat ground outside the north wall. Marcus rose before dawn to break fast with his officers. After a simple meal of porridge sweetened with honey he watched as the cavalry wing broke camp with their usual efficiency. The only problem he faced was when he informed Valeria she was staying behind.

'You're leaving Canalius in charge.' She made no attempt to hide either her annoyance or the suspicion that had become second nature in dealings with her brother. 'He doesn't need me to hold his hand.'

'I don't doubt that, Valeria, but the simple fact is that where we are going you will be a liability, and a dangerous one at that.'

'Don't tell me you're frightened of that pig Corvus?'

'I'd be a fool not to be wary of him. He's a king who commands upwards of two thousand warriors and he hates my guts, with good reason. It'll be like juggling serpents with one hand tied behind my back. I don't need any other complications. You'll stay here and command the remaining squadrons in case Corvus decides to take advantage of the negotiations to make mischief.'

'Do you really think he'll remember me? It was a long time ago.'

Marcus shook his head. 'Valeria, you are one of the cleverest people I know, but sometimes you can be . . .' His voice trailed away.

It took a moment before she understood. 'You were going to say blind, weren't you?'

'Yes.'

'In that case, I suppose I have no option but to stay.' She frowned. 'Remind me, how much did he offer you for me?'

'About twice what you're worth.'

She matched his smile and punched him on the mailed shoulder. 'Then stay safe, brother. When you're juggling your vipers make sure one doesn't bite you on your backside.'

'If we're not back in four days give this to Canalius, with my apologies,' he handed her a leather scroll pouch, 'and bring your squadron to Brocolitia.'

The Ala Sabiniana and the Second Asturum formed up in squadron squares in front of Cilurnum's north gate, along with the three squadrons Marcus had borrowed from Segedunum. The cavalry from the Fourth Lingonum were expert scouts and couriers and that was the role Marcus intended for them. Close to seven hundred men in total and a sight to behold.

The harsh tones of the signallers' trumpets blared and the first squadrons of the Segedunum contingent moved out. The cavalrymen transformed seamlessly from square to column, riding two abreast up the long slope towards the ridge overlooking Cilurnum. Their route would carry them across a great eastern bow in the North Tinan and bring the column back to its banks three miles north. From his vantage point Marcus watched them pass. With him was the commander of the Asturians, a young, fresh-faced Carvetii nobleman named Sempronius. Behind them, Janus sat his mount, clutching the lead rein of one of the replacement horses which had a sturdy chest tied firmly to the pommels of its saddle.

They slipped into the centre of the column between two of Sempronius's squadrons. 'You may not be aware of it, sir, but my father served with your father,' Sempronius said. 'At the side of Magnus Maximus. I know we are meant to revile his name, but my father spoke of Maximus as a great man and a fine soldier.'

'And so he was, decurion.' Marcus felt the odd mix of exhilaration and not-quite shame that always accompanied the name. 'But, like Icarus, his ambitions overcame his judgement and he flew too close to the sun. Brenus also revered him, but it's not a name I'd mention too often in front of your superiors if you value your career.'

They topped the slope north of Cilurnum and the country opened out in front of them. Wave after wave of gently undulating hill and valley, forest, bog and pasture wreathed in the dispersing mist of a crisp winter's morning. Here and there the thicker smoke of a cooking fire pierced the haze, but settlements were rare on this part of the frontier. A peaceful, pastoral scene, but those gentle hills could hold any number of hidden dangers.

Marcus settled into the comfortable rhythm of the cavalry soldier destined for long hours in the saddle, an almost somnolent oneness of animal and man and nature; the bitter-sweet scent of horse sweat in his nostrils and the cold air biting his cheeks; hoofbeats, horse brass and the gentle snort of exhaled breath combining in perfect cadence; the ever-changing hills a blur of grey, green and brown, the mind at rest in the comfortable knowledge that trusted scouts and outriders were alert to any danger.

As the miles passed his attention wandered to that name once more. Three men symbolized the Rome of Marcus's lifetime. Three men had stepped forward in the times of greatest peril. Three men were hailed saviours of Britannia. Count Theodosius. Magnus Maximus. Flavius Stilicho. Two of them lived to wear the purple, the third might yet. Only one was reviled as a traitor and a usurper.

Maximus had been born in Hispania, the son of a Roman general, and nephew to Theodosius, on whose estate he'd been raised. He rose to become a favourite of the count, served in Africa and fought the Dacians on the Danuvius frontier, where he gained a reputation for recklessness. Acts of impulsive bravery against some of the most fearsome enemies of the Empire enhanced his repute, rather than diminished it. Theodosius had persuaded Gratian, then Emperor of the West, to send Maximus to Britannia as *magister militum*, military commander of all Rome's legions in the province. By chance, the new general's arrival in the province coincided with an eruption of savagery in the north as an alliance of Picts and Scotti poured over the Wall once more.

Marcus's father, Brenus, a man who knew every pasture, bog and forest south of the Wall, became Maximus's adviser and friend. Together they drove the Picts and Scotti back beyond the frontier. Marcus, already a veteran and a squadron commander at nineteen, had ridden with them and won the laurels and the *phalerae* he wore to this day. From Maximus, he learned the importance of strategy and the need to think beyond the moment. Brenus taught him the art of war, how to identify his enemy's every strength and every weakness, and the need to know every inch of the territory he fought over or was ever likely to.

The two men who had shaped his life. Both long dead now. One sacrificed to a Pictish blade and the other to the Emperor's executioners.

Their route brought them once more to the bank of the Tinan and they followed the river north. Marcus called a halt when they reached a broad area of flat ground nestling in a loop of the stream. 'We'll stop here to rest and water the horses,' he ordered. 'The men can eat once they've seen to their mounts. Then we'll cross the river and head east.'

'Yes, lord, but . . . ?'

'Always expect the unexpected, Sempronius,' Marcus smiled. 'That way the enemy will never surprise you. Corvus will have had scouts watching the road from Cilurnum. When we don't appear they will report back our absence and he will be confused. That's the way I want him.' The look of dejection on the young officer's face made him laugh. 'Don't worry, boy, it's not that I don't trust you. Think of it as a lesson in survival. There's an old herders' track through the hills. In less than an hour we should strike the Great North Road.'

Once they'd worked their way up the steep slope on the far bank, the terrain transformed into a series of gentle undulations of peat and heather that allowed rapid progress. Yet at mid-afternoon when they crossed the shoulder of the hill where they could look down into the next valley Marcus halted the column again and called Caradoc forward.

'You know where we are?'

'Of course, lord.' Caradoc grinned. Remarkably, long days in the saddle seemed to have some kind of mystical healing power for a man who'd spent half his life there. 'Weren't we here with your father many's a time? Your Great North Road is in the dip there hidden by the trees, and Bremenium lies a little to the north on the far side of the stream.'

'I want you to choose six of our best scouts and split them, north and south.'

'You smell Picts?' Caradoc's eyes gleamed.

'I can taste them,' Marcus said. 'If they're here, the buzzards will either be watching the road to the south, or that cut on the north side of this hill.'

'I know it,' Caradoc assured him.

'Once we know their positions for certain, we'll decide what to do. Sempronius?'

'Lord?'

'Tell the men to dismount and look to their horses. We might be here for some time. Make sure everyone knows that the first idiot who thinks it's a good idea to light a fire will end up roasting over it. And I don't want any undue noise. Is something wrong, boy?'

Sempronius hesitated. 'The prefect told me this was a simple delivery job. He, um . . .'

'Don't be shy, Sempronius. What did Canalius say?'

'He said any fool could make a success of it with a single squadron, lord.'

'He did?' Marcus laughed. 'Well, Sempronius, I have a feeling that you're about to learn that nothing is quite that simple when you're dealing with the Picts.'

The column broke up and gathered in their squadrons well back from the ridge so no man would be silhouetted against the skyline. Sempronius posted guards on the slope below and the hilltop to the north. Caradoc and his scouts needed no detailed instructions, they were well versed in the art of moving unseen and silent through the landscape. Marcus didn't expect any results before dusk, but Caradoc was back within the hour.

'You were right, lord,' the old soldier reported. 'Two hundred of them. Waiting for us like a pack of wolves above that cut through to the west. The old bastard must have reckoned on you trying to surprise him through the back door, only he chose the wrong one.' He nodded to the men scattered across the hilltop with their horses and grinned. 'Now I see why you thought you needed a small army for this diplomatic mission. If we'd walked into their trap with a couple of squadrons they'd have slaughtered us. Now we can slaughter them instead.'

'You'll find a flask of good wine tied to Storm's pommel; share it with the scouts, but be ready to move again on my orders,' Marcus said. So he'd been right about Corvus. It was no real surprise, double dealing came naturally to these people, and this one in particular. The important thing was that the devious bastard's balls now lay in the palm of his hand. All he needed to do was squeeze. But how to milk the most profit from it? 'And tell Sempronius to gather the squadron commanders.'

'The men? They should get ready?'

Marcus studied the sky and shook his head. 'Let them rest. There's plenty of time for what I have in mind.'

Marcus kept four squadrons in reserve as Sempronius led the remainder of the column into the growing dark. Silence was the key and his cavalrymen had used every device at their disposal to deaden the rattle and chink of their horse brass. The glitter of polished brass was another matter. With the ground frozen hard the men struggled to find mud or dirt to dull the ornaments that decorated their harness. When the last horseman had disappeared into the night, he wrapped himself in his cloak and lay down among the heather.

'Wake me before dawn,' he told Luko.

Sempronius watched the first blush of dawn touch the eastern skyline and touched the cross at his neck for reassurance. They'd spent the long hours of darkness in a hidden fold of low ground, every man fighting off the cold as best he could, but not having the freedom of movement to do anything much about it. Without Caradoc's leadership he doubted he'd have had the skill or nerve to make the nightmare blindfold journey across the hillside. A dozen streams had barred their path, none of them deep, but every one capable of breaking a horse's leg. Somehow the veteran, guided by some deep-seated instinct, found a safe path through and over them. When they'd reached their resting place, Caradoc explained what lay beyond Sempronius's sight.

The Picts were just over the next rise, strung out in scrubby woodland above a trackway flanked by yet another stream through the hills. Their attention would be focused upon the track where they'd been told Marcus and his paltry escort were likely to appear some time after dawn. They were so close that when Sempronius approached the brow of the hill to check on his sentries he could hear them talking among themselves, coughing and farting.

A little later Caradoc had led half the force in a long, curving march to the west. Sempronius touched the cross again and prayed the old man would be in position on time. Then he waited. As the first rays of the sun appeared between the hills he took a deep breath, placed his helmet over his head with numbed fingers and checked the draw of his sword. More interminable minutes of delay before there was enough light for the nearest squadron commander to make out the signal to mount. The adjacent squadrons took their lead from the first and formed up in two continuous lines across the heather, marsh and tussock grass. No spoken orders, every action taken in an unearthly silence broken only by the soft snorts of the horses and the jingle of an errant piece of brass.

Sempronius raised his arm and made the sign to advance at the walk and the two lines moved forward over the brow of the hill.

A bolt of exhilaration surged through him when he saw what lay below. Had there ever been such a moment? He felt like a hawk hovering above an unwary mouse. Hundreds of Picts lay among the scrubby trees that provided cover further down the gentle slope, their weapons by their sides or stacked in piles nearby. All he had to do was give the order and they would be swept away like chaff in an autumn gale.

A horn sounded from across the valley and the long line of Caradoc's cavalry crossed the brow of the hill, their spear points and armour glittering in the morning sun. The Picts below Sempronius exchanged panicked warnings and ran for their weapons. Not a warrior looked in the direction of the men waiting above. Every eye focused on the threat from the opposite side of the valley.

'Shall I sound the charge, decurion?' Sempronius's signaller asked.

Sempronius took a deep breath. The Picts were so close he could identify the designs of their tattoos.

'No,' he said. 'We have our orders. Just acknowledge Caradoc's signal.'

On the southern slope of the hill, Marcus heard an echo of the original trumpet call. He turned to the remaining squadrons of the Ala Sabiniana. 'Sound the advance.'

To Bremenium.

And Corvus.

SILVER

XV

Bremenium (High Rochester)

Marcus urged Storm across the river and halted to study the fort perched on top of the ridge. The severe lines of the walls and crumbling towers created an entirely alien effect in a landscape of rolling hills and gently snaking streams. Yet the worked grey stone so perfectly matched the outcrops projecting from the surrounding slopes and hummocks it gave the structure a reassuringly changeless quality. From a soldier's viewpoint the position could barely have been bettered. The walls dominated the terrain all around. Any force approaching from north or west would have a long, lung-bursting climb before they were within spear throw. At that point, a deep ditch barred their way, guarded by pointed stakes cunningly hidden in camouflaged pits. One word described Bremenium. Formidable.

And there it stood, abandoned and all but forgotten, except by the ravens nesting in the towers and the mice, voles and stoats that fought their own furtive little war among the gaps in the walls.

Until today.

Two lines of tattooed warriors armed with spears emerged from between the scorch-marked stones of the fort's gateway and took up station on either flank. Others appeared on top of the parapet to either side.

The thump of hoofbeats followed by the splash of disturbed water announced the arrival of the expected messenger from Sempronius. 'Everything is as you wished it, lord.'

'Thank you, Senecio.' Marcus didn't take his eyes off the gate.

At last another figure emerged, and even from this distance he stood out from the others.

'Squadrons will advance.' Marcus led the way up the slope with his signaller close by his right side.

He pulled Storm up just short of the gateway and paused while his horsemen moved from column to square behind him. The warrior who awaited him between the painted guard of honour ignored the ceremonials and studied his visitor with all the intensity of a weasel eyeing a stray leveret.

Marcus remained in the saddle and met the single-eyed stare. Corvus, king of the Selgovae, was an immense figure, not only in height, but in breadth and girth, and the bearskin cloak he wore against the cold only enhanced his bulk. A black beard peppered with grey hung to his chest and he had the battered features of a man who had run into one too many walls. To add to his fearsome aspect, a livid white scar which had turned the right eyeball to a red jelly ran from his cheek to the lank hair covering his forehead.

The remaining eye twitched to range over the cavalry squares. 'Our agreement was that you'd have an escort of only two squadrons.' Corvus had a voice to match his face, like an iron shovel spreading gravel.

'It was also agreed that you'd have only forty warriors.'

'And I kept to my part of the bargain.' The thick lips parted to show yellowing teeth and Corvus waved a hand at the men on the wall. 'How many do you count?'

Marcus nodded to his signaller and the man put his curved trumpet to his lips. 'It only takes a single blast to turn a lie into the truth.' Corvus's confident smile froze and Marcus allowed the silence to stretch before he spoke again. 'Two hundred warriors. In the valley to the north. More than enough to wipe out two squadrons, maybe even four, from ambush. Only they aren't the ambushers. One blast and you'll be carrying them home in pieces.'

'They'd be no loss, Awran and his useless bastards.' Corvus shook his head. 'You didn't think I'd come this far south, so close to the border with Coel's country, with an escort of forty men? And who would blame me for trying after what's gone between us, eh? Is she here?'

'I don't blame you for trying.' Marcus ignored the last question. 'What I can't work out is what you expected to gain from it.'

A sly glint appeared in the single eye. 'Keother has let it be known he would be very grateful to any man who brings him your head. And I've been having trouble with Keother. His people are like a wedge between the Selgovae and the west. I can't trade with the Novantae and the Anavionenses without his agreement, and I don't care to bend the knee to ask for that agreement.'

'Then trade with the Picts.'

'You know the Picts have nothing to trade. The reason they're moving south is that they're poor and they're hungry. And there are always more of them.' Corvus laughed. 'But enough of this pissing contest. We were friends once, we can be friends again. I've brought an amphora of your best Roman wine – I knew you wouldn't bring any, you miserable bastard – let's drink till we fall over, like the old days.' They hadn't been friends, not really, more cheerful rivals, young men with a love of women and fighting, but Marcus allowed himself a smile. It had been a short interval when the Selgovae found it expedient to ally themselves to Rome and Corvus hadn't yet murdered his way to a crown. The chances of resuming that relationship were about the same as of Corvus growing a new eye.

Corvus led him to the remains of a barrack block where a fire kept the chill at bay. By the time they reached it they'd agreed the Selgovae would make camp north of the fort and Marcus's troopers to the south. Each leader retained a guard of forty men and the only weapons allowed were the knives they needed for preparing food. Marcus surveyed his surroundings. The building remained more or less intact, but the last defenders had burned every bit of wood before they marched away, and the walls were blackened and cracked with the heat. Terracotta slates and the charred remnants of timber cots littered what was left of the tiled floor.

'Do you have a priest with you?'

'What?' Marcus couldn't hide his surprise.

'I'm thinking of becoming a Christian . . .'

'Jesus!'

'Yes, truly.' Corvus's voice took on an earnest tone. 'Runo of the Novantae is a Christian and you Romans give him an easy time of it. If I become a Christian maybe he'll be a bit keener on making an alliance and we can crack that bastard Keother between us like a nut.'

'Why don't you do it anyway?'

'He says he doesn't trust me.' The Selgova's face twisted into a troubled frown.

'You surprise me,' Marcus smiled.

They sat on the floor by the fire and Corvus produced two large wooden cups from a pack. A large amphora leaned against the wall of the barrack and one of Corvus's warriors brought it to them and filled the cups.

'We should discuss . . .'

'Plenty of time tomorrow.' Corvus raised the cup in his massive fist and drank deeply. 'For now, we should get drunk and talk about the old times. She's not here, is she?'

Valeria's face swam into Marcus's head. 'No,' he said.

'Probably for the best.'

'Certainly for the best.' Marcus raised his cup in salute and took a long drink.

Much later when the light had faded and the flickering oil lamps turned every corner into a shadowy haven for night nymphs and departed spirits, Corvus brought his face close so the single eye seemed to be boring into the Roman's head.

'You shouldn't have done it.'

'Done what?'

'You know what.' Corvus wasn't drunk, but the wine had made him edgy and that could be dangerous. Marcus momentarily wished he hadn't relinquished his sword. He knew the power in those arms and he wriggled just out of their reach on the pretext of stoking the fire. 'You shouldn't have taken my eye.'

'It was a mistake.' That at least was the honest truth. He'd been trying to slit Corvus's throat, but the Selgova had ducked into the blade. 'You shouldn't have tried to kidnap her.' Valeria had been barely conscious and kidnap was a polite word for what had been about to happen.

'I offered you treasure for her.'

'You did,' Marcus agreed. 'More treasure than you actually had.'

'But you turned me down. What choice did I have? She was the one for me.'

'She didn't think so.'

'I know you, Marcus Flavius Victor.' The single eye narrowed. 'Why would you let any woman have a choice?'

'She's not just any woman.'

'She's not, is she?' Corvus laughed and Marcus sensed the tension ease from him. 'Is she still as beautiful? Or has she got fat like me?'

'Even more beautiful,' Marcus said. 'Slim as a prefect's sword and cleverer and more dangerous than both of us put together.'

They watched the flames for a long moment.

'The Caledonian Picts have a new leader,' Corvus said.

The words were innocuous enough, but Marcus sensed there was more to them than the simple facts communicated.

'What's the name of this new king?' He tried to sound unconcerned.

Corvus laughed, unconvinced. 'She is not a king,' he whispered. 'She's a queen. And she's cleverer and more dangerous than both of us put together.' The Selgova reached across with a grin to punch him on the arm and Marcus realized he hadn't moved far enough. It was like being hit by a charging bull.

Later, Corvus's commanders and Marcus's officers joined them for a feast. Wary at first, but as the wine flowed they began to talk of tribes they'd encountered and men they'd fought, the way soldiers did. A gathering of warriors perfectly at home in each other's company.

Marcus outlasted all but the most hard-headed, though by the end his mind was cloudy and the oil lamps little but golden orbs in the smoky atmosphere. His hand never left his dagger, even when Corvus collapsed into his furs like a heart-pierced deer. Sempronius lay snoring wrapped in a blanket. Caradoc could barely string two words together, but somehow managed to have a conversation with Awran, a warrior who'd had one ear removed by a sword or an axe.

It was difficult not to forget that not four hours ago Corvus had been planning to kill them.

Trust no one.

But it wasn't always quite so easy.

And there was something important he'd learned today, something hidden in the deepest recesses of his wine-dulled brain. Yes, that was it.

A queen. The Picts were ruled by a queen.

XVI

'You have the silver?'

'Of course,' Marcus smiled. 'We have an agreement.'

'But not here?'

'Of course not.' *Do you take me for an idiot?*

Still Corvus wasn't satisfied. 'No hostages to make sure I keep my part of the bargain? You trust me?'

'You'd only give me some orphan boy in pretty clothes and call him a prince. And no, I don't trust you.' Marcus stared into the Selgova's single eye. 'But you can be sure that if you play false I'll kill you. Some day you'll eat broth made with the wrong kind of mushroom and take a week to die.' The threat was mere ritual, and both men knew it, just as they knew it must be uttered, but Marcus continued. 'Or maybe I'll be merciful and you'll never see the knife point that sticks you behind the ear.'

Corvus sighed. 'It's not getting any easier, keeping the Picts honest. I could take you to a valley just south of the Bodotria and at night you'd see the flames of a thousand Pictish campfires, and a glow beyond it that spoke of ten thousand more. They've had two poor harvests and they can already see the bones sticking out of their bairns' flesh. If there's a third, all the silver in Britannia won't stop them coming south.'

'You spoke of a queen?'

'Briga.' Corvus laughed but there was little mirth in the sound. 'A she-wolf with a face to make your head spin. When you look at her all your brains drop into your belly. She sent an embassy inviting me to a feast and an exchange of gifts at the boundary stone on Soutra Hill. Who was there but Luddoc of the Votadini, looking near as wary as I was, and with reason. Briga had her predecessor Lucti skinned alive for our entertainment. Then his relatives proved their loyalty by riding their horses over him until he was nothing but a smear in the heather. Not that it saved them, because Briga had their throats cut during the feast. It almost put me off my meat.' Corvus cast Marcus a sideways glance. 'Pray you never meet Briga.'

Marcus sent a messenger down to the Ala Sabiniana's camp and Janus appeared an hour later, leading his pack horse and with a squadron for escort. The young soldier hefted the chest from the horse's saddle and placed it before Corvus.

The big man licked his lips and smiled at Marcus. 'Get him to open it.'

Marcus nodded. Janus pulled a Pictish dagger from his belt and used the point to work the lock until it clicked. He pulled open the lid and Corvus whistled as he saw the gleaming metal nestling inside. He reached for a piece of what had once been a large platter. Dulcitius's armourer had cut an ancient dinner set into pieces of more or less similar weight. Once a bribe like this would have been paid in coins, but these days not even a barbarian would accept silver coinage. The Empire's mints had been using less and less of the precious metal for years. As Marcus knew to his cost, many coins were just a bronze core with a thin surface veneer of silver and worth a tenth of their face value. Corvus hefted the silver in his enormous fist. 'With just half of this I could probably buy Briga off for six months and save myself some trouble,' he chuckled.

'Or Keother,' Marcus acknowledged. 'But perhaps I can be of some assistance in the matter of Keother?'

Corvus glanced up with a wary look in the deep-set eyes. 'You're offering to do me a favour?'

'It just happens that in this instance our interests may align.' Marcus shrugged as if it was no matter. 'You tell me Keother has been muttering dark threats against the Lord of the Wall. For a man in my position that can't go unchallenged. But if you'd rather . . .'

'No,' Corvus said quickly. 'Tell me what you have in mind?'

'You'll know the location of every settlement and farmstead Keother's folk have built on the fringes of your land? Where he hoards his supplies and has hidden his granaries?'

'Of course,' the Selgova growled, 'and not just the fringes. He's moved into the hills south of the Tivyet source along the old Roman road to Tarras. Poor grazing, every acre barely capable of supporting two cows, but poor or not it is my land by all the gods. Awran is your man. He knows that valley well.'

'What if some wicked Roman from south of the Wall were to destroy Keother's granaries and burn his farms and their winter supplies?'

'He couldn't feed his people through the winter.' A dawning realization on Corvus's battered features. 'He'd have to beg for help.' He laughed at the thought. 'And he wouldn't get it from me. But that would take time. No, they'd have to move quickly if they're not to starve. He'd be forced to take his people back to Briga with his tail between his legs. By Taranis's balls, Marcus Flavius Victor, you know how to make an enemy.'

'So you'll give me Awran for a day and a night?'

'I'll send for him now.'

When the message had been passed Corvus stood on the parapet staring westward with a broad grin on his face. 'I never thought I'd see the day I'd be glad I didn't manage to kill you.'

'I told you there would be nothing but profit if we worked together.'

'You did,' Corvus said. Marcus caught the look that accompanied the words, so what followed wasn't unexpected. 'What if I'd said your sister was the price of our agreement?'

Marcus turned to meet the Selgova's gaze. 'We'll never know, will we?'

123

XVII

Janus worked his frozen fingers against the shaft of his spear to try to get some feeling back into them. By Fib's hairy arsehole, it was cold tonight.

'On the right, two hundred paces ahead,' Awran whispered.

It took a moment before Janus identified the faint chink of light from a cracked or broken piece of wattle. A farmstead, the most northerly of six in this part of the valley if the Selgova was to be believed. With luck, each would have its own granary and storehouse bulging with provisions for the winter and ripe for the plucking. The farms were scattered across sloping ground above the little stream, with their paddocks and byres close to the hillside where the beasts would enjoy more shelter. Their fields occupied a narrow shelf on the far side of the river. This was the third settlement Janus's warriors had raided tonight so every man was well versed in his duty. A convoy of heavily laden captured wagons followed them half a mile to the rear.

They approached warily, but Janus expected no surprises. Caradoc's squadron had created a shield across the far north of the valley where Keother and his bodyguard garrisoned a small fort perched on a raised spur. Not even a mouse would pass unnoticed through the screen of veteran riders. All they had to worry about was the people in the houses.

He waved the second and third troops ahead to take care of the other farmsteads and whispered to his ten men to converge on the closest. Light flickered in the doorway. The shadows of four or five people slipped away towards the western hills, but Janus ignored them. He began to relax. If the women fled it would give their menfolk one less reason to fight. A sharp cry of fear echoed in the darkness, confirmation the flanking troop was alert to any strays.

Yet danger there was and a heartbeat later he had reason to curse his momentary complacency. From the corner of his eye he noticed a blur of movement and the glint of firelight on a blade. He wrestled his horse round to meet the threat, but he was already too late. The attacker covered ten paces in the space of three heartbeats. A savage howl from a snarling gape of a mouth and the sword swept in a great arc towards his exposed side. Janus twisted away in a futile attempt to avoid the blow, vaguely aware of a shout and the clatter of hooves on the frost-hardened ground. In the same instant an unseen power plucked the shadowy figure from the earth and launched it backwards accompanied by a bubbling cry of agony.

'Torches,' Janus shouted. 'Let's have some light.'

One of his men clicked flint and iron three times before a spark lit the pitch-soaked cloth of a torch. In the circle of flickering light, Janus's brother withdrew his spear from the guts of a shuddering figure lying a few paces away.

'In Jesus's name, Julius, we said no killing or raping. The prefect wants them hating Keother, not us.'

'No killing unless we were threatened,' his brother pointed out. 'That bastard was about to cut you in half. I'd have thought you'd be a bit more grateful.'

An old man and a boy appeared at the door of the house and stared in horror at the dying man. The boy held a long-handled Pictish axe.

'You'd best drop that if you don't want to end up the same way,' Janus called in the boy's own tongue. 'We won't harm anyone who lays down their weapons. All we're after is your supplies. Tell him, grandad.'

After a whispered exchange the pale-faced boy dropped the axe. One of the cavalrymen dismounted and retrieved the weapon and the sword that had fallen from the now dead man's fingers. He handed the sword to Janus.

'Not a bad weapon.' The cavalryman examined the sword. 'But better for him if he'd left it in its scabbard.'

'If you take away our food you might as well kill us now, like poor Breth.' Tears ran down the old man's cheeks and he cried out as spear-wielding riders herded a group of women and children into the torchlight.

'You'll have to take that up with Keother,' Janus dismissed his plea. 'Keother brought this upon you, so Keother must feed you for the winter.'

'He's right about one thing.' Julius surveyed the shivering captives. 'If we leave them like this most of them will be dead by the time they reach Keother.'

'All right.' Janus acknowledged the sense in his brother's words. 'Pass word to the others.' He turned back to the elder. 'You have to the count of a hundred to gather warm clothing and blankets. No food and no concealed weapons. You understand me, old man? No food or weapons or maybe you'll all end up like him.' He pointed to Breth's body. 'And make sure you choose a warm blanket for yourself. We'll be taking the tunic and breeks from every grown male.'

'You'll not be taking my breeks.' A figure burst from the hut into the torchlight and ran flailing at Janus. The cavalryman easily danced his mount clear and the Pict tumbled onto the frozen ground with the Roman troopers grinning down at him. It took a moment before Janus realized his attacker had no hands.

'It's one of the Alona cripples,' Julius laughed. 'Who is he?' he asked the old man.

'My son, Drosten, son of Ciniath. You people destroyed him.'

'Fight me.' Drosten struggled to his feet. He lashed out with the truncated stumps, but the effort only made the auxiliaries howl all the louder. 'Fight me.' He was weeping now. 'Kill me.'

'I'll tell you what, cripple,' Janus said evenly. 'Catch this and I'll fight you.' He tossed the sword so it fell between Drosten's outstretched arms. Janus nudged his horse so that its haunches tumbled the mutilated Pict back to the ground. 'Time's a-wasting, grandad,' he called to the elder. 'Boy? Pick this man up and keep him out of trouble. We'll take the sword.' A whiff of excrement tickled his nostrils. 'But he can keep his breeks. Christ's name but he stinks.'

He heard the creak of wagon wheels in the darkness. At last.

'Let the people get what they need and then shepherd them a mile up the valley,' he ordered his brother. A first faint glow in the sky to the north announced that they'd spent enough time on this. A second glow followed the first, then several more in quick succession till the entire northern sky glowed red as Keother's farmsteads burned. The flames would alert the Pictish war chief, but Janus trusted Caradoc to keep Keother and his warriors out of the way until he and the other squadrons were able to shepherd the wagons and their precious supplies clear of any potential retaliation. He waited until his men hustled the refugee Picts into the darkness and the only sound was the ravings of the handless man and the soft whistle of the wind through the trees.

'The carts are all loaded, decurion.'

'Good, give me the torch.' Janus dismounted and went to the roundhouse. The outer thatch would be too damp to burn quickly so he pulled back the leather curtain and walked inside. His eyes took in the stools by the fire, the shelves, beds and chests. He gave the place a cursory check, in case the family had left any valuables, but he didn't expect to find anything. There'd been an iron pot on the hook over the fire that he'd seen one of the women carrying away concealed beneath a blanket. Any food would have been removed by his scavengers, men well versed in the art of plunder. Familiar sights and scents stirred a long-forgotten memory and it was with a vague feeling of regret that he put the flaming brand against the inner thatch.

They reached the rallying place Marcus had chosen just after dawn the next day, but the Roman commander made it clear they wouldn't be together for long.

'We'll split up here,' Marcus told Janus. 'You'll take your squadron and escort twenty carts directly to Borcovicium. I'll join you there in two days.'

'Of course, lord.' Janus saluted. They'd harvested more than fifty wagon loads of provisions from the Picts and sacks of grain and fodder hung from every saddle. Only Caradoc remained absent, maintaining his defensive screen between the raiding parties and Keother's country. So far the Pict had made no move to retaliate.

Still, Janus didn't hide his surprise at the unexpected order. 'I know,' Marcus said. 'It would make sense to accompany you to the fort and return to Cilurnum by the *via militaris*, but I have my own reasons for staying north of the Wall. We'll be safe enough. Keother has been put in his place and Corvus has returned to his hills. A couple of hours won't make much difference. You have the Pictish clothing and war gear?'

'Of course, lord.' Janus nodded.

'Keep it safe and keep it hidden,' Marcus said cryptically. 'We'll need it later.'

The young Pict grinned. He had no idea what Marcus planned, but he could smell mischief in the air and there was nothing Janus and his brother liked better than mischief. Which was what Marcus was counting on.

A blare of trumpets announced the arrival of the main column at Cilurnum just before dark. They made their approach by the north road and word soon attracted many of the occupants to the ramparts. At first the defenders greeted the new arrivals with a puzzled silence, but that changed as the garrison realized the significance of the carts and wagons. A cheer rose up that quickly grew to a roar of acclamation that had every man in the column grinning.

Valeria met them at the gate and Marcus's sister embraced him as if she'd never expected to see him again. 'Careful, decurion,' Marcus smiled. 'People will talk.'

She watched as the long line of carts rumbled through the fort's north gate. 'How did this come about?' she said in wonder. 'Enough supplies to see the garrison through the winter.'

'And to feed every farm and settlement within five miles of Cilurnum, with some to spare,' Marcus assured her.

'I know you can be generous, brother,' she laughed. 'But it's not like you to play the great benefactor unless there is something to be gained. You persuaded Corvus to part with all this? He must have had the harvest to end all harvests.'

'We came to an agreement,' he said, happy to avoid providing any awkward detail.

'And Justus?'

A moment of confusion before Marcus remembered his tale about the commander of Corstopitum's imagined perfidy. 'Justus can wait for another day,' he assured her. 'His time will come.'

'Here comes a relieved man,' Valeria said. Canalius bustled towards them accompanied by his clerk.

'Do you have that scroll I gave you?' Marcus said quietly to his sister.

'Of course.' She reached beneath her cloak. 'I suspected you'd want it.'

'So you've survived, prefect,' Cilurnum's commander hailed Marcus. 'You haven't taken too much out of yourself, I hope?' Concern didn't sit naturally on Canalius's porcine features, but he made a decent show of it. 'And you have performed a miracle. I had thought to be chewing on my belt ere the spring, but Christ be thanked every man will have a full belly. And the civilians?'

'There will be enough for them too,' Marcus assured him. 'Though I will trouble you for a few wagons of fodder for my horses if there is enough to spare.'

'Of course,' Canalius said. 'It's the least I can do for our benefactor. You will be leaving us soon, I fear?'

'We will be on the road for Brocolitia at first light tomorrow,' Marcus admitted, to Canalius's obvious relief. 'But before I go,' he tapped the leather scroll case against the palm of his left hand, 'there is another matter we must discuss. Let us find a place to talk in private.'

Canalius eyed him suspiciously, but he followed Marcus to the *praetorium*. 'It grieves me to give you this.' Marcus handed over the leather scroll case. 'But, as you'll see, I have little choice.'

Canalius plucked at the straps and withdrew the roll of parchment.

His brow furrowed as he read the words and his eyes bulged as their import sank into his brain.

To the commander of the fort. You will relinquish all the cavalry under your orders to accompany Marcus Flavius Victor, Lord of the Wall.

Julius Postumus Dulcitius, dux Britanniarum

The order had been transcribed by Dulcitius's clerk and intended only for the eyes of Cassius at Segedunum. When Dulcitius had scratched out the original on his wax tablet it contained considerably more detail, but it had occurred to Marcus that, with a few minor adjustments, it might come in useful at some future date.

'You know what this says?' Canalius had gone pale.

'Of course,' Marcus said. 'It was dictated in my presence.'

'But . . . all my cavalry? Every man?'

'I'll take Sempronius and the troopers who accompanied me to Bremenium – they were very impressive, Pompeius, you should be proud – plus another two squadrons. That will leave you about two hundred men, more than enough to hold Cilurnum now that I've bought Corvus off. You won't starve, I've made sure of that. I thought you'd be more grateful?'

Canalius stared at the parchment. 'Something of this magnitude. I should ask for confirmation.'

'Dulcitius is in Eboracum.' Marcus took him by the shoulders. 'By the time you have word back from him all will be lost. We have one chance, Pompeius. One chance to destroy the power of the Picts. How do you think our great commander will react if you rob him of his chance of glory?'

'I don't know. Cilurnum . . .'

'Will be safe, while I lead your cavalry to glory in your name, Pompeius. This is the great secret, my friend. Dulcitius commands me to join the Novantae, drive Keother from the southern hills and push the Pictish army and their new queen back into the Bodotria.'

FIRE

XVIII

Brocolitia (Carrawburgh)

'I hate this place.'

Marcus took his time to respond. The approach to Brocolitia from Cilurnum was much the same as any other in the central section of the frontier. After a steep climb the supply road flattened out along the ridge south of the Wall, with the ground sloping away to the left. Bleak, it was true, with the sleet driving into your face, and whatever view hidden by the drifting mists, but unremarkable for all that. Of course, Valeria wasn't passing judgement on the weather or the topography.

'Surely our God isn't frightened of an outdated superstition?'

Valeria glanced sharply at her brother. She knew his faith was less certain than her own and she didn't like the hint of mockery in his tone. 'There is only one God,' she reminded him. 'You should have hounded her out years ago. Tullius has been itching to take a whip to her for long enough.'

Marcus laughed. 'Tullius is the tribune in charge of the First Batavians and under my command. He does what he's told. In any case I'd like to see him try.'

'She's a sorceress. A witch. And the shrine is an insult to God.'

133

'Calista has a facility for conjuror's tricks,' he acknowledged. 'She can make a man think a coin has come out of his ear or hatch a mouse from a hen's egg. But it's not sorcery, merely harmless sleight of hand.'

'A witch.' She glared at him. 'Who can turn men's minds.'

'So can you when it suits you, sister.' Marcus ignored the gasp of outrage and his voice took on a new edge. 'She's my witch and it suits me for the moment that she continues to act as the keeper of the sanctuary, despite the opposition of Tullius and his fanatics. Coventina's Well has been drawing people here since before Hadrian built this Wall. Even now, when it has long lost whatever power it may have had, men come from a day's ride away and more . . .'

'To worship . . .'

'Not to worship.' Marcus shook the water droplets from the hood of his cloak. 'Emperor Honorius would never allow that. It is a curiosity. A repository of bits and pieces crafted by men long dead: fragments of altars, stones so worn who knows what they once showed, chipped frescoes and pieces of rusty iron Calista couldn't sell when she fished them from the well. Rubbish. Yet even Christians are curious about the past. You'd be surprised who visits Calista. And perhaps she does have a certain magic. She has a knack for making people at ease. They listen to her stories and they drink wine and breathe perfume-scented smoke and they talk. And sometimes they say things Calista believes I might be interested in.'

'She's your spy?'

'A man in my position can never have too many spies.'

By now they could see the walls of the fort in the distance and Marcus heard the faint blare of a trumpet. Like Hunnum, Brocolitia was another distinctive landmark on the Wall. Every other major fort, apart from one, had been built to straddle the rampart, with gates to north and south. Brocolitia, garrisoned by Tullius Nepos and his First Batavians, was built directly abutting the Wall and without a northern gate. As Gordianus, the master builder, had explained it, Brocolitia was a later addition to the Wall's defences, constructed after it spanned the isthmus to fill a strategic gap the engineers had failed to identify during their original survey. This also explained its curious position midway between Cilurnum and Borcovicium and barely an hour's easy ride from each. Coventina's Well wasn't the only pagan curiosity in Brocolitia. Not far away lay a ruined temple dedicated to Mithras, the soldiers' god. Marcus knew that tonight some of his soldiers would visit the place to pay tribute, but he would pretend not to notice. He'd crept into the temple a few years previously and remembered stone benches lining the walls and three stone altars tumbled down among the debris beside the sacrificial pit. Of the massive sculpted relief of Mithras killing the bull only a small fragment remained, but for all that the temple still retained a power he couldn't explain and the locals kept well clear of the ruins.

Caradoc cantered up to join them at the head of the column. 'Shall I have the men water their horses in the stream while you carry out your inspection, lord?' the decurion asked.

'No, we'll make camp on the flat ground on the far side of the settlement.' Marcus ignored the glances of surprise. 'Borcovicium can wait another day.' He turned to Valeria. 'As you suggested, Tullius has a unique set of problems to deal with. We'll do this properly.'

The fort's commander emerged from the southern gate followed by a small guard of honour to greet his visitor with the ceremony he would expect. Marcus turned aside from the column, but he didn't dismount.

'I mean no disrespect, Tullius, but I must see the men settled before I call on you.'

The tribune frowned. 'You plan to take the column through the village?'

'You don't think it right that the people are witness to such an impressive display of military might when the Picts are getting restless?' Marcus waved a hand at the long column of riders passing steadily behind him. 'Surely they will be happy to see us.'

'Restless?' The frown turned to outright concern. 'We've heard nothing, but . . .'

'Yes?'

'There have been mutterings among the villagers. Threats.'

'Threats against who?' Marcus growled.

'Against the witch.'

'We've had this discussion before, Tullius. She is no witch, just a harmless collector of old stones.'

'That's not what the people believe.'

'So it's your Christians?'

'We are all Christians here, prefect,' Tullius said primly. 'They've always been wary of her, but recently that has changed to outright hatred. Anyone visiting the well is berated and sometimes the women throw stones. They haven't harmed her, they wouldn't dare when they know she's under your protection. But they're getting braver by the day.'

'Something like this does not suddenly happen by chance.' Marcus turned to stare at the civilian settlement to the west of the fort. 'Someone has been stirring them up.'

'There was a travelling priest,' Tullius admitted. 'A most holy man. He preached a sermon in the forum calling down God's wrath upon the barbarians north of the Wall. Every man must be ready to take up arms against them or face eternal damnation . . .'

'I'm beginning to like your priest.'

'He also said that the presence of the shrine in our pious community was an abomination and a direct challenge to God. The woman should be whipped from the settlement and the sanctuary torn down stone by stone.'

'Then again, maybe you should have hanged him from the nearest tree.'

Tullius noticed the cavalrymen spreading across the gently rising heathland beyond the settlement and the tents being erected in their tidy rows. 'You're staying overnight, prefect. I thought . . . If I'd known I would have had quarters prepared for you.'

'There's no need to put yourself to any trouble,' Marcus assured him cheerfully. 'I'll sleep with the regiment. By the sounds of things, it's just as well I'm staying.' A gust of wind blew sleet directly in their faces.

'Now get out of this cold or your toes will turn black. I'll be back within the hour and I'll want to see your supply tallies.'

The tail of the column had passed through the settlement and Marcus and his escort followed them. Villagers crowded the street on either side, but this was no guard of honour. Tension hung in the air so thick you could almost taste it and sullen anger etched almost every face. Some of the riders called out to people they knew, but the only answer was pursed lips or a turned back. Even the children glared.

'You'd think we'd shat in their well,' Luko muttered.

Marcus recognized Ninian's thin, bearded face at the centre of one group, but, though their eyes met, neither acknowledged the connection. By the time they reached the temporary camp, Marcus's headquarters tent had already been erected and Valeria was sitting at a collapsible campaign desk writing with a metal stylus on a thin sheet of wood. 'A section of Sempronius's troopers left their cooking pots behind in Cilurnum. They need replacing. I've made out the order in your name.' She showed him the sheet with its neat, close-spaced lines of ink. 'And these are the ration returns you asked for.' She pointed to another pile of the thin wooden tablets on the desk.

Marcus ignored the returns. If Valeria had checked them they were in order. 'Send the requisition to Tullius's quartermaster. We'll replace them from his stores and take the cost out of their wages. And have Sempronius prepare the negligent section for a night patrol north of the Wall. Tell them I've had word that Keother is out there looking for revenge.'

'Is that true?'

'Of course not, but a night freezing their arses off and chasing shadows while they're wondering if they'll still have their bollocks in the morning is the least the bastards deserve.'

'You're testy today, brother.' Valeria rose to give him the chair. 'Is your wound bothering you?'

His hand automatically touched his mailed chest. 'It never stops reminding me it's there,' he admitted.

'Perhaps I should ask Zeno to check it?'

'No time for that.' Marcus drew the heavy mail over his head with a noticeable wince. 'I want to see Tullius while it's still light.' A servant entered with a bucket of steaming water. Marcus tested it with a finger and then dashed more over his face. He unlaced the leather jerkin that padded his body against the sharp edges of the mail, and removed his shirt and threw it to one side.

'I'll do it,' Valeria said as he reached for the cloth that hung over the side of the bucket. She sponged his back and chest, taking special care around the puckered red flesh of the scar. It was something she'd done a score of times before, as natural as breathing. 'A wash and a clean shirt? Tullius should be honoured.'

Marcus cleared his throat. 'It's possible I may not be back tonight.'

'Yes?'

'Who knows how long it will take with Tullius. The man never knows when to stop talking.'

'Of course,' she grinned.

'Don't be—'

'I'm your sister, not your keeper, Marcus. It's not as if the lady is married.'

'You knew?'

'Everybody in the regiment knows, Marcus.'

'Well then.'

Valeria smiled. She had her own reasons to be pleased her brother wouldn't be sleeping in the camp tonight.

It wasn't against the law to be a pagan in Honorius's armies, but neither was it encouraged. Imperial edict denied pagans the right to openly worship their own gods, and banned the sacrifice of any animal, living or dead. Anyone who claimed to read the entrails of a chicken was guilty of treason. Anyone who allowed his house or estate to be used for a sacrificial ceremony would automatically have the property confiscated. Marcus had been born into a household that held the old gods dear. Brenus, his father, regarded adherence to the Christian faith as a weakness and for many years would not promote a Christian to captain one of his cavalry squadrons. In contrast, Marcus's blood-father had been a devout follower of Christ and it was through his influence that Marcus had been baptized at the age of ten, with the blessing of Brenus, who by then understood nothing would stem the Christian tide. Yet a pragmatic man could be a soldier of Christ and still have a respect for the ways of the past. The power of the old gods had waned and all but disappeared. How many fallen altars to Mars or Jupiter now paved a courtyard or held up a section of the Wall? Yet there were pockets on the frontier where that power could still be felt, and Brocolitia was one of them.

He'd spent a dull afternoon going through the motions of the inspection with Tullius and pretending to be fascinated by his supply manifests. Brocolitia was an infantry post, and infantry had no part in Marcus's plans. At least not yet.

No, he'd come here for an entirely different purpose.

The building he sought was to the north of the settlement, not far from the Wall. By the time he'd shared the obligatory feast with Tullius it was almost full dark as they walked through the outskirts of the settlement. Two of his bodyguard led the way with lit torches and two more brought up the rear. A prudent man couldn't take too many chances. Judging by the warmth of the welcome there was little love for Marcus Flavius Victor here. A cold night, with the hard-packed earth already slippery beneath his boots, and a clear sky that heralded a heavy morning frost.

At last the bulk of the house loomed in front of them. In reality, much more than a house. It was built of stone, unlike most of the other structures in the settlement, which were constructed of wood, and had a thatched roof. The building was much larger than any of its neighbours, perhaps twelve or fifteen paces on each side. A larger entrance on the western flank had been bricked up and passage was now through a small doorway set into the brick.

'I want two men on guard here all night, changed every two hours,' he told his guards. 'And make sure they all know I'm not to be disturbed unless the Picts are hammering at Brocolitia's gates.'

'Yes, lord,' the men grinned.

Marcus pushed the door open and stepped inside. Into total darkness.

He stood perfectly still and listened. Silence, apart from a soft muttering from outside as his guards discussed who was to take the first stint. A faint rustle raised the hairs on the back of his neck. Gradually his other senses added to the picture. A musty scent in his nostrils that spoke of age and decay and dust. Damp, too, in the chill air around him. He was in a void. A great single chamber. He reached out a groping hand. Nothing. Where would it come from? Could he take a step forward? No. Who knew what traps awaited him in the darkness? The dull ache in his chest grew as the tension stretched out like an over-taut bowstring. More rustling, but was it to the left, or the right? Behind him?

Something flew out of the darkness with a sharp cry, a hard body slammed into his, fingers clawed for his throat, and a long leg tried to trip him. He attempted to stay upright, but his attacker was too subtle and he collapsed to the slippery flagstones below, hot breath singing in his ear.

'Christ's bones, you're an insatiable bitch.'

'Do not say that name here,' she whispered. 'Take me. Take me now.'

How could any man refuse such a plea?

Much later they lay on her bed on a balcony reached from a steep ladder and warmed by a brazier on the floor below. A flickering oil lamp lit their surroundings with an eerie glow and Calista used its light to trace the wound in his chest with the long nail of her right forefinger.

'They told me you were dying.'

'Do you believe them?' He didn't ask who. Like him she kept her informants' identity to herself.

'Not now.'

'You might have killed me,' Marcus murmured. 'I sent word. Why didn't you have a lamp on?'

'I wanted to surprise you. It aroused me, waiting in the darkness. The door opening, and the scent of that oil you're wearing. You seemed to enjoy it.' She slipped a hand between his legs and he felt himself begin to harden.

'Once I worked out no one was going to murder me.'

It was like making love to a whirlwind. That lithe, hard little body with the small breasts, first under, then over, offering this, then that, nothing withheld, nothing refused, raking nails and nibbling teeth, grinding hips and an all-encompassing heat, the taste of bitter honey in his mouth and the scent of her on his beard. How to describe their relationship, if it could be called such? Not love, it was much too barbed for that, too many hidden thorns. Lust? Oh yes, there was lust, but it wasn't just that. They liked each other and each liked what the other had to offer. They enjoyed each other, that was it, in bed and out.

'What are you thinking?'

'I was wondering why I keep coming back here.'

'Because I tell you things, and because of this.' Her hand was back and he felt a shiver of anticipation.

Below them in the gloom lay the sacred well dedicated to Coventina, a Celtic goddess of great antiquity, Calista's charge and, sometimes, burden. In her own way, Valeria had been right, the keeper of the shrine was a witch, certainly a priestess, the font of the knowledge of ages and the possessor of a vast accumulation of lore which could have dangerous applications. A villager who stole a small ring from the shrine had died of convulsions, his skin pocked with boils and his insides running out of his nether parts.

The well was set in the centre of the floor and measured two paces by two. Calista claimed it was bottomless, but Marcus knew she'd sometimes lived on what she dredged up from its depths. This place had once been a temple, though its grandeur had long since faded. A dozen stone altars still lined the walls, dedicated to the goddess by Batavians and Germans, Frisians and Gauls. Village whispers conjured up tales of human sacrifice and cannibalism and rumour had it

141

that the well also contained a great treasure amassed over the ages. Calista had only laughed when he'd asked her about it, and said that if any man wanted it all he had to do was swim down until he found it.

'Again,' she whispered, turning onto her knees and presenting herself to him. She looked over her shoulder down the length of a tawny flank, the dark eyes gleaming. 'Let me feel all of your power.'

XIX

'They've always hated me,' Calista said. 'That dog's turd Tullius tries to make life as difficult for me as he can without it becoming too obvious. Even if I'm first to the market, there's nothing for Calista. "Sorry, lady, this is a Christian town and this is Christian food." I survive because those who come here bring offerings for the priestess as well as for the goddess. But now it's getting worse. We had a priest here last week, a stunted weasel of a man. He preached to them and told them I was a stain on their little community. Five minutes in here with a brazier and a glowing knife and I'd teach him all about stains. Their *little community* wouldn't exist if it wasn't for the Well of Coventina.'

'Maybe it's time to give this up.' He nodded to the well and the altars.

'You want me to be your concubine?'

'No,' he said. 'That would never work for us. You would be like a hawk in a gilded cage. But I think you sense that your time here is coming to an end. The fanatics are becoming braver. I can't protect you for ever. I have a house in Corstopitum. I could set you up there. You could live the life you pleased.'

'This is the life that pleases me.' She almost spat the words. 'Without Coventina I am just a little woman in a little house. A nobody. No,' her

143

voice calmed. 'I thank you for your kind thoughts, Marcus, but it appears you don't know me at all.' Calista turned away, her face hidden in the shadows. 'And yet, I do not know how long I can stay in Brocolitia. I have seen it in the well. Coventina's power here is fading.'

'Where would you go if you had the choice?'

She hesitated. 'I had a vision of a mountain, shaped like a crouching lion, overlooking a narrow sea with more mountains in the far distance. A new well and a new power. It cannot lie within Britannia, perhaps my destiny is in the north?' Marcus didn't answer, and she continued. 'I have news for you,' she whispered. 'Two Picts came by night to pay their respects to Coventina. They spoke of a new power from beyond the Bodotria. A queen. Her name is Briga and she is both dangerous and cunning. She despises weakness and gelds any warrior who shows fear.'

'I know of her,' Marcus said.

'Briga will be a formidable enemy, Marcus. Do not underestimate her.'

'I don't underestimate Briga,' he said carefully. 'But however powerful she is, she will want more. What queen would refuse the services of a seer and the support of a goddess of Coventina's influence?'

'You want me to go to her?' Calista didn't hide her disbelief. 'What can Briga have to do with the lion mountain and a new well?'

'I don't know,' Marcus admitted. 'But she could be a stepping stone towards it. I too don't lack influence. Perhaps I can help you fulfil your destiny?'

She stared at him, long and hard. 'This is not a decision that can be taken lightly or quickly.'

A muffled thud from above stifled Marcus's reply. Moments later smoke began to seep through the thatch and billow about them. He saw Calista's eyes widen in terror and a light filled the room that had nothing to do with the oil lamp on its stand beside the cot.

'Fire!' Marcus drew her tight against him and rolled off the bed onto the floor of the platform. Already flames were flickering their way greedily across the underside of the thatch and licking at the joists. Their clothing was strewn across the floor and they quickly gathered it up and crawled towards the ladder. 'How in the name of Christ did it catch so quickly?'

He helped Calista to the floor below and they dragged on their clothes as Marcus took a few heartbeats to consider their situation. Was there a chance to save anything? He had water from the well, but nothing immediately to hand to carry it. By now pieces of burning thatch had fallen to set the bed alight and as the fire spread swiftly across the roof more fluttered round to burn on the stone floor around them. If anything, the smoke was worse than the flames: it filled the entire upper part of the room and soon it would overwhelm them.

'There's nothing we can do,' he coughed. 'Is there anything you want to save?'

'Everything of true value is stone and water.' Her voice was almost a cackle and he could tell she was close to hysteria. 'And the roof will fix. But I put a curse on whoever did this. Men will die screaming for the attack on the goddess.'

'Come.' He hustled her towards the door.

They paused on the threshold for one final look at their surroundings before Marcus lifted the locking bar and hauled at the door handle. The door didn't budge. He tried again. It was stuck fast.

'Marcus?' Calista pleaded.

The handle was a simple wooden bracket and he pulled again using a strength driven by rising panic. It splintered with a sharp crack and came away in his hand.

Marcus battered at the door with his fists. Where were the guards he'd set? A thrill of outright fear ran through him as he realized his own men might be in league with whoever had fired the roof. He searched for an alternative escape route, but the temple was a place of private reflection and worship. It had no windows.

'Help,' he shouted. 'Get this door open, we're trapped.'

Calista took up his cry as Marcus put his shoulder to the door. Smoke filled their nostrils and made their eyes water. The flames

145

above were a dull glow in the murk, but Marcus could already feel the heat on his shoulders. Another attempt at the door almost broke his shoulder and convinced him strength alone wouldn't be enough to save them. He struggled for breath and drew Calista close. She was sobbing with terror. Think! The smoke seemed to have him by the throat and it was tightening its grip.

'Help.' In his mind it was a hail that could be heard in the encampment. The reality was a dull croak.

But it was echoed from beyond the door, where someone was hammering at the timbers.

The hammering increased and suddenly the door burst in followed by four uniforms. Rough hands grabbed Marcus by the shoulder and dragged him through the door.

'No, the woman—'

But Calista was ahead of him between two others. Out into the blessed darkness where he sucked in chill air that was as welcome as a fine wine. His chest and throat felt as if they were on fire, and he vowed he would never take that air for granted again. He shrugged himself free and crouched, hacking up gobbets of phlegm.

When he looked up, he saw a ring of faces illuminated by the light of the flames. Men, women and children; the flickering shadows distorted their features but he knew what they were thinking. This was God's work and that gave them satisfaction and proved that they had been right to want to drive the witch from their midst.

Marcus pushed himself to his feet. 'Get me Tullius,' he rasped.

But Tullius was already here, watching appalled from the edge of the crowd as part of the temple's roof caved in and sparks drifted high into the night air.

'This isn't the games, tribune,' Marcus croaked. 'I want these bastards putting the fire out, not gawping at the entertainment. This is what happens when you're too soft. If this place is still burning at dawn I'll string twenty of them from the fort walls.'

The civilians heard Marcus's threat and they believed it. Within a few minutes a bucket chain had formed from the nearby stream and men brought ladders so they could pour the water onto the flames. It was a vain attempt, but Marcus would not let the temple burn. He saw Valeria comforting Calista, the priestess's face a deathly white and her singed hair wild and unkempt. He had little doubt one of the ladders had been used earlier for a different purpose.

Valeria saw him and left Calista to be cared for by Zeno.

'Pitch,' he said, as she approached.

'Pitch?'

'They poured it onto the thatch and let it soak deep before they threw a torch to light it. Where are my guards?'

'Doing their best to put out the fire.' She pointed to the top of the ladders.

'If any of them had anything to do with this I'll personally tear out his guts and feed them to him.'

She shook her head. 'Someone simulated a fight and lured them away. By the time they returned to their post the shrine was on fire and the door had been jammed shut.'

'Whoever did this wanted her dead.' He nodded to Calista.

Valeria gave him a pained look.

'What makes you so certain it was only her they wanted dead?'

As dawn broke the ruins continued to smoulder, but the walls of the shrine were largely undamaged and the flames had finally been extinguished. Tullius Nepos had worked all night directing the firefighting efforts; his narrow features shone with sweat, despite the cold, and he was pale with exhaustion, apart from a streak of soot across his forehead.

'I want them found, Tullius,' Marcus said. 'I want them found and I want an example made.'

'I understand, prefect.'

'Someone will know. They all appeared quickly enough to see the show. Don't be too gentle. A glowing poker can save a lot of time. But throw a bit of money around too.' He saw Calista with Zeno staring at her burned-out home and walked away from Tullius, calling over his shoulder. 'And take a couple of hostages for her safety and find Calista a temporary place in the village. If one hair on her head is harmed, they'll have more to fear from me than any Pict.'

'Is she hurt?' he asked Zeno.

'Just shocked,' the *medicus* said. 'And a little singed.'

Calista managed a wan smile, but Marcus saw she was close to the end of her strength.

'We'll get you some food and find you somewhere to rest. Somewhere safe,' he assured her. He nodded to Zeno and the Greek left them alone.

'Then what will happen to me?' She was close to tears. 'I've lost everything.'

'Nothing that can't be replaced.' A roof beam crashed down throwing up a new cloud of sparks and Calista winced. He lowered his voice. 'We talked of the future last night. Will you go north?'

'What choice do I have?' she demanded. 'I can't stay here. If they can burn me out despite your protection, they are capable of anything. Britannia holds nothing for me. Your all-encompassing Christian beliefs are the chains that bind you. Your very thoughts are the prisoners of your faith. If you were the man I thought you were, Marcus, you would cast off those bonds and come with me.'

'I have work to do here,' Marcus said. 'But I will provide you what help I can. A pass to allow you north of the Wall, supplies for your journey, a wagon for whatever treasures you can recover from the well.'

'Coventina's treasures remain where they are,' Calista's voice took on a new strength. 'And let it be known I place a curse on any Christian who taints the well with their presence. This place is the past. Out there,' she pointed north, 'lies my future. And you, Marcus? I want none of your help. You don't own me, and you never have.'

XX

'There, Brenine,' Nechtan called.

Briga watched the ragged band appear out of the mist, from the wall of her palace complex in the great fort above the valley of the upper Tuedd. She'd been informed of their coming, and the reason for it, days earlier. The mounted group at the front would be Keother and his personal guard; she almost laughed at the thought. A personal guard of twenty warriors. Her own numbered forty mounted spearmen and could be doubled or even trebled at will from the host spread out across the valley before her. Even more warriors waited among the flatlands between the hills and the Bodotria, the great firth that separated north Pictland from the south. Soon, of course, there would be only one Pictland, but those who inhabited the south of it were not yet aware of that.

A shambling figure made his ungainly way towards her, forcing a path through the crowd of warriors who waited eagerly to do her bidding. Short and stunted, with wild hair and a beard that almost entirely covered his face, he wore a jerkin of uncured wolfskin and one leg was shorter than the other. When he came within five paces he went down on one knee before her.

'Are they hungry, Blaid?' Briga demanded.

'Yes, my Brenine, they are hungry.'

'Then prepare the pit.'

The stunted man forced his way to his feet with a grunt of pain and stumbled back the way he'd come.

Briga had learned long ago that a woman could not just match the ways of men, but must outdo them. She had chosen ruthlessness, ambition and fear as her pieces in the game of power, and, of course, strength, which was the sum total of those traits. Her first husband had been a young warrior of great lineage who brought with him a war band matching his status. She had allowed him to use her body, seduced his mind, coerced his followers and finally placed a thin-bladed dagger behind his right ear and pushed. She had liked Lenart.

More husbands followed, each warier than his predecessor, but she had outwitted them all. Each brought his war band and still greater power. When the royal succession was in doubt it had always been her people's fashion to choose a new ruler from the female line; why not take the natural next step? So the time came when she did not need a husband and she was Queen Briga, the Blood Taker, Briga, the She-Wolf, ruler of a dozen different tribes and tribute-taker from a hundred settlements and fortresses. But it was not enough. Even if it had been enough, two poor harvests and the Scotti who pressed her western borders would have changed that. The mountains could not feed her people, so she must move from the mountains to the plain.

It had been her intention to create an alliance with Lucti, but he had been such a weak man, like all the other men she had known, she had no choice but to kill him. She took no pleasure from the way he died, but to instill fear and obedience it was necessary to inflict horror and suffering and pain. Those who had watched Lucti die had learned respect, and respect was the first step to submission. Their time, too, would come. The only person she trusted was Nechtan, her cousin and commander of her warriors. He was a hard, humourless bullwhip of a man, who had won the respect of the tribal chiefs by his fighting prowess. As yet he had shown none of the ambition that had proved so fatal to his predecessors.

Briga had chosen this position with care. Secure at the centre of her host, she retained the freedom to move the entire army south, south-east, or south-west, at her pleasure. Each choice would take her to the Roman Wall, but the final decision could only be made after further thought and with further knowledge. For the moment she was still without that knowledge, but she had all the pieces in place to secure it.

To the east lay the lands of the Votadini, who had taken Roman silver from the first day the legions laid one stone of the Wall on top of another. They were a numerous people, farmers and fishermen for the most part, raiders when the mood took them, but only truly warlike when they were required to defend what was theirs. Luddoc of Caer Eidinn believed he was cunning, but he feared her and dared not interfere with her plans. To reinforce his caution she had returned five Votadini cattle thieves alive, but without their skins, and had received an entire herd from Luddoc in acknowledgement of the message the doomed men conveyed.

Corvus and his Selgovae were her southern neighbours. She had reacted to her spies' news of his pact with the Romans with a bolt of fury that did not bode well for King Corvus. Yet his was a fractured land, and a fractured people who would need careful husbandry, and perhaps that would save him. Corvus posed no immediate threat. One way or the other the Selgovae would come within her power, or be destroyed.

Keother led his warriors through the makeshift villages and temporary farmsteads of Briga's domain and wondered at the sheer numbers she'd brought together in this one place. Small herds of bony cattle and flocks of scrawny sheep grazed on the sparse grass in the open meadows between the settlements, guarded by ragged bands of children. Black-haired pigs rooted for acorns and beech nuts among the leaf mould in patches of forest. He was aware of the hungry families in his wake, stumbling beneath the weight of their few remaining possessions, but he paid them little heed. Briga would see to their needs in return for the services of his warriors.

His men asked at a hut for the queen's location and a crooked finger pointed in the direction of a distant height.

Keother had considered this moment and its implications during the two-day journey north. Thus far, the name Briga had only been a rumour, a mythical night-stalker whose presence in the hills scared children. A shape-shifter who could appear and disappear at will. News of her arrival south of the Bodotria had filtered through to his valley, but caused no immediate concern. Time would tell if the event heralded opportunity or threat.

Then the Romans had come to his valley with fire and sword and Keother lost what little real power he possessed. He'd raged and cursed and threatened to take his warriors south, but soon he understood that he had no choice. Without food, these families would starve over the winter, and the men of his bodyguard had relatives among them. If he did nothing, they would simply take their people in search of food, and the last of his strength would drain away with them.

A long hogback mountain loomed to his right, ringed with banks and ditches and with a palisade at its highest point, and he turned his horse to climb the narrow track that led to it.

'Tell Ciniath to keep his people here and wait for instructions,' he called to the captain of his bodyguard. 'I'll have food sent for them.'

He urged his mount up the hill, followed by the men of his guard. Groups of warriors camped beside the track studied their progress with detached interest and Keother realized, with a shiver of anticipation, that his arrival was expected.

His mind turned to the coming meeting. What would she look like, this queen? Old Lucti had worn few outward trappings of his status apart from a golden circlet in his hair and a chain of silver at his neck. But Briga was a queen. Keother saw this as the key to the restoration of his fortunes. She was a woman, a woman without a man, and, beautiful or ugly, he intended to charm her. In Keother's experience there were two kinds of women – at least the women who mattered – women who could be taken and women who needed to be seduced. It didn't occur to him that Briga might not be impressed by him. He brought with him a warrior band wielding twenty spears, all horsed, and every man with an iron sword at his waist. His courage was unquestioned and no one could call him ill-favoured or lacking strength. No hint of an old man's grey touched his dark hair or his beard. She would welcome such a man and perhaps make him one of her captains. Who knew where that road might lead? A woman needed a man and it was a short step from a woman's esteem to her bed.

He passed through the outer stone wall at the head of his men. Warriors in their hundreds now to each flank. A type he recognized, rough, feral men who lived their lives in the open, ever ready to lash out with fist or knife, and with scars to prove it. Merciless men who would stick a blade through a fellow's guts and laugh as they watched him die. Killers. The air reeked with the stench of their leavings, the acrid sweat of their matted fur tunics, and their filth-caked bodies. They huddled around their fires sharpening sword edges and spear points and mending clothes and equipment.

The gate swung open as Keother approached the inner palisade. A chill ran down his spine as he watched a wooden chair appear to float out towards him until he noticed it had human legs and was actually being carried by either a small child or a midget. The chair was followed by a procession of creatures – the only word that fitted them – who staggered and danced and in one case actually crawled to form two lines outside the gate. Near paralysed in astonishment he counted two midgets, a giant with a face carved from granite and eyes that never stilled, a broad variety of cripples including a boy with no legs, a naked woman with a body that would haunt a man's dreams and the wizened features of an aged crone, a man with no face whose lidless eyes were like staring into the very heart of madness, and a blind girl with a face that would break your heart, who danced and crooned and whirled as if this was the most joyous day of her existence.

And Briga.

Queen Briga.

'Is it not customary to dismount when one greets a queen?'

The soft voice jolted Keother out of his lethargy and he leapt from the saddle like a scalded cat. He heard the creak of leather and a series of dull thuds as his men followed suit. Servants appeared and led the horses away.

'I apologize . . .' He hesitated, unsure how to address her. In truth, his mind had stopped and his breath caught in his throat the moment she'd appeared from behind her collection of monstrosities. Queen Briga was tall and slim and made taller still by her hair, which had been coated with lime-wash and sculpted so it looked like a sunburst erupting from her head. White powder coated her face, apart from her eyes, which stared out from a band of midnight black, and her lips, which had been painted the colour of fresh blood. But the mask couldn't disguise features of such perfection she might have been the sister of the beautiful mad girl who danced to her side as she almost flowed onto the wooden seat. Her body was enveloped in a long cloak of green plaid and Keother teased himself with the notion that beneath it she was naked.

'You may address me as Brenine.'

'I apologize, Brenine.' He belatedly remembered to go down on one knee.

'And how may I address you?'

'I am Keother, Lord Keother.'

She tilted her head to one side. Keother had the odd experience of being returned to his childhood and caught stealing an apple from the winter store.

'And what, *Lord* Keother, are you a lord of?'

The legless boy giggled.

Keother shifted uncomfortably. 'I have lands to the south-west.' He tried to sound more confident than he felt. 'Good grazing by the river and fine pasture on the lower slopes of the hills. My stronghold—'

'Has recently been occupied by Corvus of the Selgovae after the Romans evicted you from your valley,' Briga interrupted. 'Which explains your presence, but not *why* you are here. Why are you here, Lord Keother?'

'I am here to pledge my sword to you, Brenine.' Keother felt he was

now on more confident ground. 'And the swords and spears of my followers. I have brought you twenty warriors who will take the oath
beside me.'

'Twenty warriors,' Briga sounded impressed. 'No doubt every one as
brave as a wolf and as strong as a bear, but . . .' She frowned and turned
to the crooning girl. 'Did we not hear that the great Lord Keother
could call on at least *eighty* warriors, Scara?' The girl's rapturous
expression remained unchanged. 'Do you want her, Lord Keother?'
Briga's hand stretched out to cup the closer of Scara's breasts and the
crooning instantly reached a higher note. 'She would like that. Scara
enjoys a lusty warrior. She would rut with you on the earth before me
and think nothing of it. But to return to your warriors, Lord Keother.
You have pledged the services of twenty, but it appears you have robbed
me of the swords of a further sixty. How could that be?'

XXI

Her question shocked Keother into silence. How had she come by all this information? What answer could he give her? He resisted the temptation to tell her that the eighty swords were a figment of someone's imagination or an exaggeration of his own to magnify his prowess. He was beginning to understand just how Queen Briga came by her throne and how dangerous it would be to take her lightly. He could feel a worm of fear beginning to twist in his lower stomach.

'Lost your tongue, Lord Keother? How many of the sixty you sent to Alona are still alive?'

'Twenty,' he said.

'Only twenty? Then let us see these twenty mighty warriors. Bring them before us.'

'Not warriors,' he spat, allowing his anger to get the better of him. 'Cripples.'

'As you can see,' Briga waved a hand at her attendants and the cloak slipped aside to reveal a perfectly shaped breast. 'I can make use of cripples, too.' Without warning her voice took on an altogether different authority. 'Send for them.'

Keother looked to his men. They'd heard every word of the discussion and they shuffled uneasily under his gaze. 'One of you find

Drosten and tell him to bring the cripples up.' He turned back to face Briga. 'My people need food.'

'Yes.' Queen Briga took no apparent offence at the abrupt demand. 'I understood that as well as your warriors you had brought more hungry mouths to deplete my granaries. Still,' she summoned one of the midgets with a twitch of her finger, 'the fault is not theirs. See that Lord Keother's people are fed and find them somewhere to build their huts. The long slope behind Calum Cruithne's war band will do.'

Somewhere close by a wolf howled and Keother's hand fell to his sword hilt. The eerie cry was taken up by a second, then a third wolf. Keother heard one of his men curse, or perhaps it was a prayer. He turned to Briga. 'What . . . ?'

'My pets,' she smiled. 'Perhaps I will show you them later.' She pointed to the second midget. 'Bring food for Lord Keother and his warriors.'

Cowed servants appeared with roundels of flat bread, salted mutton and cups filled with some brew that smelled of apples. Keother accepted a cup and a wooden plate, but hesitated before touching the food.

Queen Briga noticed his wariness and smiled. She rose from her chair and came close enough for him to smell the sharp, but pleasurably female tang of her unwashed body. 'Are you not hungry, lord? I would have thought you would be ravenous after such a long journey.' She reached out and broke off a piece of the bread and nibbled it between perfect white teeth. 'Eat,' she commanded his warriors. 'You need not fear I will poison you. I require your sword arms to be strong for what is soon to come.'

She returned to her seat. Keother relaxed a little and crammed a large chunk of bread into his mouth.

In the valley below, Drosten sat with his family steeped in a haze of misery and exhaustion, hunger gnawing at his vitals and tormented by the spear points of agony that pulsed through his stumps. It had been like this since the Romans killed Breth. His brother's body must still be lying where it had fallen beside the burned-out ruins of their home. Poor Breth who had seemed reborn with his father's sword in his hand, only to be cut down a dozen heartbeats later. Drosten tried to imagine his brother's stolid features, but the only image that appeared was of crows pecking out the dead man's eyes and wolves and foxes gnawing at his flesh.

If they had expected sympathy or aid from Keother they were doomed to disappointment. What food the war chief had was reserved for his warriors and he made it clear that if they could not keep up with the horsemen they would be left to die. Drosten had done what he could for his wife Duna and the baby, but it was little enough, and only the fact that he had a friend among Keother's guard kept them alive. It was with intense relief they'd emerged from the mist to see the huts and farms of Briga's host spread out across the valley before them.

Relief for his family, but what did the future hold for a man with no hands? Slaves appeared with baskets of bread and wooden pails of water and began to distribute them among Keother's people. Ciniath accepted two loaves and divided them among the family. Duna broke up her portion and fed the pieces into Drosten's mouth.

'Feed yourself, woman,' he growled, but the bread tasted good and gradually the gnawing in his guts faded.

'Drosten?' He looked up into the face of Melcho, who had kept them from starving on the march. Fate had decreed that Melcho had kept his hands and though Drosten knew Melcho felt guilty about his good fortune, he still resented him for it. Melcho could hold a sword and was now also a member of Keother's elite. 'Collect your people' – at least Melcho would not call his former comrades cripples – 'and follow me up the hill.' His face creased into a frown. 'You're going to see the queen.'

Duna let out a gasp and Drosten felt a bolt of fear lance through him. Ciniath, a man who seldom allowed his emotions to show, stepped forward and drew his son to his feet, enveloping him in his arms. Drosten felt the warmth of tears against his cheek.

'Go well, Drosten,' Ciniath said, but there was a finality to his words that told its own story.

Drosten went a little way up the slope and called out the names of the men who had suffered with him at Alona. Far fewer now, of course. The others had thrown themselves in the river, died of hunger when their families abandoned them, screamed their way to the next world when their wounds mortified, or simply pined away. Gradually they gathered in front of him, clothed, for the most part, in filthy rags, faces etched with pain and mirroring his own lack of hope. The hair of one or two of them had turned pure white. None would meet his gaze, nor the gaze of any other. Drosten understood perfectly. They preferred to be alone in their desolation.

'Follow me,' he said. 'The queen has asked for us.'

He turned to set off up the hill before the inevitable question, but one man stumbled to his side.

'Why would the queen want us?' he whispered.

A derisive snort escaped Drosten. 'Look around you,' he said. 'She is gathering an army, an army that will consume every grain of barley and mouthful of meat she can collect. What would you do with twenty useless mouths?'

The man's eyes darted to right and left. 'Should we run?'

Drosten turned to look out over the forests and pastures that surrounded the hill. 'The only thing that awaits us out there is starvation and a slow death,' he sighed. 'At least this way it will be quick.'

When they reached the inner palisade Drosten searched for Keother, but his lord didn't even acknowledge the newcomers. Beyond him a tall figure in a green cloak rose to her feet and Drosten felt a mix of awe and dread at his first sight of Queen Briga.

'Come forward.' Her voice was surprisingly gentle. 'Advance and kneel before your queen.'

There was a rustle of consternation from behind him, but Drosten didn't hesitate. If he was going to die, he would die a man. He straightened his back and marched forward to kneel directly in front of the queen with his eyes on the bare patch of earth beneath him.

He heard a rustle of cloth and a pair of intricately patterned leather shoes appeared. A soft hand took his chin and raised it and he found himself staring into piercing blue eyes that seemed to bore into his soul, made all the more startling by the dark band from which they gazed.

'Your name?' The words were as soft as a caress and in that moment they were the only two people on the hill.

'Drosten, lady.' If he died now those eyes and that voice would be the last thing he remembered.

'Show me your arms.' Drosten lifted his stumps and she reached down to stroke them with her fingers. 'Who did this to you, Drosten?'

'A Roman, lady.' The words caught in Drosten's throat. 'Who laughed as he took my hands.'

'Do you know his name, this Roman?'

'He boasted of it. Marcus Flavius Victor. He called himself the Lord of the Wall.'

The gently moving fingers seemed to contain some sort of elixir that ran up his useless arms and into his heart.

'What was it like,' Briga's voice took on a new intensity. 'What was it like when he took your hands?'

Drosten found it difficult to breathe, but Briga was patient even as the silence lengthened. Eventually he was able to speak. 'First came the helplessness and humiliation as we were held bound and naked. Then the fear as we watched our friends being dragged one by one to the sword. Fear replaced by terror when finally they came for you and you knew there was no escape. Pain such as no man should have to endure when the blade fell for the first time. A shock that made your heart stop. A new level of pain at the second blow, and the third, that finally cut through flesh, and sinew and bone. Disbelief. An emptiness like death. Then the searing agony as the glowing iron touched torn flesh. Death would have been an escape.'

'And now?'

Drosten felt a tear run down his cheek into his matted beard. 'Now, if I die I have felt the power and gazed upon the face of Queen Briga.'

'Who do you blame?'

He felt a moment of understanding as if a flame ignited inside his head. Now he knew why he was here. The name she wanted. 'Keother. I blame Keother for the loss of my hands.'

A chorus of agreement and for the first time he became aware of the men kneeling in a line to his right and left. From all around came a murmur of angry voices, the product of a crowd much larger than before.

Briga stepped back. 'You cannot fight,' she called to the mutilated men. 'But you can run. You are my gifts from the gods. You will be Briga's messengers in battle and out. And should you die in battle you will have a place of honour among the fallen. Serve me well and you will be rewarded. Betray me and you will die. Lord Keother?' Keother had listened to the exchange with growing dread. If he'd had a means of escape, he would have fled the hill as fast as his horse could carry him. But suddenly he was surrounded by warriors, and not those who'd followed him here. His sword and dagger were removed and rough hands took his arms.

'Please . . .'

'Lord Keother, your foolishness has cost me the services of sixty brave warriors. Do you still wish to serve me?'

'Yes, lady.' His head nodded so hard he felt his neck crack.

'Then I will provide you with the opportunity to atone.' Briga smiled. 'Should you succeed you will become a captain in my army and sit at my right-hand side. Bring him.'

Keother was hustled through the gates into the stronghold in the wake of the queen and her gaggle of repulsive acolytes. Hundreds of hard-eyed warriors watched them pass and some joined the procession.

Their destination was a ruin at the centre of the hill. Another wolf howl split the air and Keother felt a growing realization and terror. Warm liquid ran down his legs and his captors laughed at the acrid scent of piss and fear.

Through the ruined walls, and his reeling mind registered that this must be a former Roman fort of some kind. At its heart lay a curious structure perhaps three paces by three and with a haphazardly repaired wall that stood a sword length high. Queen Briga took up a position on the far side of the walls, close enough to see into the interior.

'Bring forward my messengers,' she said. 'So they may witness Briga's justice.' Drosten and his tribesfolk were ushered forward to a position where they too could see over the walls into the pit. 'Now, the Lord Keother.'

Keother's guards pushed him forward to the edge of the wall and his heart died inside him. Three lean grey shapes paced the bottom of a six-foot pit and when they saw him one launched itself at the wall, its jaws snapping and flecks of foam flying from the bared fangs.

'These are my pets,' Briga announced. 'Fenrir, Geri and Freki. To show your loyalty to me you must face them. Bring his sword.'

Keother felt a sudden and unexpected blaze of hope and even a surge of savage elation. With his sword he had a chance. Now he would show the bitch he could fight. One against three, but a man with a heavy blade fighting for his life would surely prevail.

'And yet,' Briga's voice pierced his thoughts like a knife point. 'How to make the contest more equal? Take his feet.'

For a moment, Keother's mind refused to believe what he'd just heard. Then the giant stepped forward. He was holding a hand axe. The guards held him down and though Keother struggled with all his strength the giant pinned down his right leg. A bolt of agony ran through him from his foot to his brain. More blows, but by now the pain was just a single, all-consuming entity. He tried to retreat into darkness, but his mind wouldn't allow it. Someone placed an object in his right hand and his fingers closed on his sword hilt.

'Lower him down.' The voice seemed to come from another world. 'Gently now. Be sure to hold on to your sword, Lord Keother. Remember you are a warrior.'

Keother managed to keep the wolf snapping at his face at bay for a few moments, while the others ripped gobbets of flesh from his bleeding wounds, but when the fangs eventually closed on his throat, he thanked the gods for his release as the darkness closed in.

Briga watched until the wolves were sated. She searched the faces around the pit until she found the features she wanted. She summoned her dwarf. 'Bring me the one who was Chosen.'

ICE

XXII

Borcovicium (Housesteads)

Marcus had more than one reason for his visit to Borcovicium. Firstly, it was probably the most run down of all the Wall's occupied forts. Its proximity to Brocolitia, and to Aesica, four miles further west, meant previous Wall commanders, including Brenus, had seen little reason to invest their precious resources in rebuilding its walls and barrack blocks. Vindolanda, a reserve and supply depot whose soldiers could easily have dealt with any problems on this section of the Wall, also lay less than two miles south, though infuriatingly it remained under the direct command of Eboracum.

While he was at Segedunum, Marcus had discussed the fort's future with Dulcitius and they'd agreed he should make the final decision whether Borcovicium should continue to be garrisoned or abandoned for good. That would mean a more detailed study of the defences than normal, because Marcus knew he would be called on to justify whatever decision he made. He didn't intend to give Dulcitius the chance to add another nail to his cross.

The second reason might, or might not, be linked to the first. Clarian Apollo, the fort's commander, had written him a string of messages complaining about the German mercenaries who'd been foisted on him by Eboracum. Rome had been employing barbarians as soldiers since the time of Augustus. Strategically and economically the investment in manpower made sense. At the most basic level, if they were fighting *for* Rome, they couldn't be fighting *against* Rome. Their use was carefully regulated in auxiliary formations and had the added advantage of drawing their homelands closer, politically and militarily, to the Empire, often to the extent that they were entirely absorbed. Every fort along the Wall had been garrisoned at one time by an auxiliary cohort, and, in most cases, still was.

The Germans were different.

Auxiliary units, like the Frisians, Gauls, Batavians and the First Tungrians, who made up the bulk of Borcovicium's garrison, were subject to Roman laws and Roman discipline, commanded in many cases by Roman officers, wore Roman armour, carried Roman weapons and fought beside the legions as an integral part of the Roman army. When they completed two and a half decades' service they were entitled to Roman citizenship, twenty-five *iugera* of good land to farm, a pair of oxen to plough it and sufficient grain to plant it, and immunity from the *capitatio* – poll tax – for themselves and their wives.

The German mercenaries weren't a military unit, as such, they were a barbarian war band, whose effectiveness depended on the ability of their leaders, and who lived day to day according to their own customs and traditions. They were paid an annual stipend in gold or silver and at the end of their twelve months they could walk away, even in the midst of a battle, and no man would think it anything but normal. In Marcus's experience they were fearless warriors who were content as long as they were well fed and given regular opportunities to spill blood. If the second requirement wasn't fulfilled, they had a tendency to spill each other's or anyone's who came near. In battle they could be depended on to attack any force weaker than their own or to hold a position as long as it didn't look as if it was going to be overrun. Civilians tended to be terrified of them. A few of the bands had a reputation for slipping off to raid the nearest settlement if they were bored, but

Marcus had found them decent enough comrades and fierce fighters. They even worshipped their own gods. For the moment, the edicts which denied pagans in Roman auxiliary units the right to make sacrifices and worship at stone altars didn't extend to the Germans who sometimes fought beside them.

'Germans' was an all-encompassing title which took in at least a dozen different tribes from east of the Rhenus who shared, more or less, a similar language that Marcus likened to a dog barking. They included Vandals, Goths, Alamanni, Chatti, Cherusci, Longobardi and, he remembered with a pain that felt like a knife to his heart, the Saxons who had abducted his own son.

He called Valeria to the head of the column. 'Does your pet Saxon speak a decent Latin yet, or do you still have to keep tugging his leash?' He saw the shadow of suspicion that fell over her face. 'I'm not going to harm him, Valeria. It just happens he might be useful to me.'

'How?' she demanded, still not entirely trusting him.

'It seems to me there is something amiss with these complaints of Apollo's. He says his Germans are lazy, treacherous and mutinous, but in my experience once you give a mercenary your money he will fight for you to the death, even if the person he's fighting against happens to be his brother. I doubt they'll speak to me, but perhaps your lapdog can find out why his countrymen are causing Apollo so much trouble. What does he call himself?'

'Leof.'

'Then get him up here, I want to talk to him.'

Marcus explained the situation to Leof and the boy immediately agreed to be of service. At first acquaintance the Saxon was an open-faced, guileless youth, but the blue eyes were sharp and he immediately understood what was required. He was clearly devoted to Valeria and accepted his captivity, if it could be called that, with cheerful equanimity.

'Where is your home, Leof?'

'We live near a settlement called Treva, lord, a township on the north bank of the Albis River. It is a good place, with fertile earth and fine hunting, and a man could be content there, but we Saxons have ever been wanderers. Always there is more land or more plunder round the next bend.'

'Will my son be kept there, do you think?'

A frown creased Leof's handsome features. This was dangerous territory for a slave. He looked to Valeria for reassurance, but she was deep in conversation with Zeno. Eventually he decided he had no choice but to answer. 'That would depend, lord,' he said carefully.

'On what?'

'My people are slave takers, and the most likely fate of a boy of eight would be as a household slave, if he was fortunate, or in the fields chasing crows from the crops, if he was not. But that is not certain. If he was known to be of noble blood – I understand your son is learned for his age – then it is possible he might be taken into a wealthy household as a foster child, to replace some family's loss,' he produced a wry smile, 'perhaps even mine. If that is the case he would be treated as a son, educated in Saxon ways and tutored in Saxon arms. He would have opportunities, even as an outsider, to prosper and advance. I hope that eases the pain of your loss, lord. I know it would be of comfort to my father.'

'I'm sure you are a credit to him.' Marcus forced the words past the lump in his throat. He made a decision. 'Tell your decurion you are no longer her slave, but one of my soldiers. She is to issue you with a sword and mail and find you a place in her squadron.'

Leof's face split into a huge grin. 'Thank you, lord.'

Borcovicium held a central position in the Wall defences and it would once have been an important place, but over the centuries its significance had waned. It had been built on a hillside that sloped from west to east, in a shallow saddle between two of the highest sectors of the Wall, and had fine visibility to both north and south. To the north lay the barren moss Marcus had crossed to attack Keother's valley, and in that mass of bog and hill country lay the key to Borcovicium's decline. No Pictish commander would willingly use it as a passage to attack the

Wall when much easier routes lay to the east and the west. Marcus had been reading the reports of Borcovicium's officers for years and they could be summed up in two sentences. *No enemy sighted. Patrol returned without casualties.* The defenders of Borcovicium were more likely to die of boredom than from a Pictish spear.

Marcus led his long column of horse soldiers over the rise and halted for a moment to study the fort below. The Wall at this point followed the highest ground and met the rampart of the fort at a sharp angle which was oddly untidy to the military eye. A haze of smoke from forges and cooking fires hung over the familiar, orderly pattern of barrack blocks, granaries, and the headquarters and office buildings without which no fortress could function. The roofs were a mixture of thatch and tile, but he could tell from his elevated position that perhaps a quarter of the barrack blocks had no cover at all. When it was built Borcovicium had been one of the largest forts on the Wall, bigger even than Cilurnum, and designed to hold a garrison of eight hundred men. The walls still encompassed the same space, but the latest manpower returns showed a complement of two hundred auxiliary infantry, nominally Tungrian, and a hundred German mercenaries. Barely enough to man the parapets. Even from this distance he could see where areas of the eastern and southern ramparts had collapsed to form piles of rubble, and more than one of the towers was kept upright only by timber supports.

On the lower ground to the south, inside a great ditch, had once been a substantial civilian settlement, but all that remained were a few grassy mounds where the twenty wagons he'd sent ahead with Janus were laid out in a defensive square.

He gave a grunt of satisfaction and nudged Storm into motion.

From the way Clarian Apollo simpered and fussed around Valeria it was clear he considered himself to have the singular charms of the Greek god from which his family had taken their name. Equally clearly, Valeria was as immune to those charms as if the fort commander himself had been a marble statue. He had a long nose, a narrow, angular face and protruding teeth that reminded Marcus of his horse. Still, Marcus was sipping at one of the finest wines he'd ever tasted; being welcomed by a rich man desperate to ingratiate himself had its compensations.

'As I was saying, prefect, the damage you have mentioned is superficial and can be repaired by the simple application of material and manpower.'

'Then why haven't you applied it, Clarian?' Marcus demanded. 'If anything the outer wall of the fort is in a worse state than when I was here two years ago. The west tower only remains standing because the prevailing wind happens to be in the right direction.'

'Please,' Apollo appealed to Valeria, who met his plea with a tight smile, 'do not think I have been idle. What stone and mortar we have has been used to keep the Wall itself from collapsing. Believe me, the section above the east culvert is a constant strain on not only my resources, but my health. We have dismantled two of the watch turrets between here and Aesica for building material. You cannot but agree that the Wall must be my primary concern?'

'No,' Marcus admitted; the instructions from Eboracum were clear enough. 'I can't fault you on that front, but the matter of the fort itself will not go away.' Apollo grimaced as if he had an attack of the gripes. In these days of constant contraction of the army, the prospects of an officer who lost his post, whether through his own negligence or not, were far from bright, even for someone so well off and well connected. 'What about water? How is your supply?' It was an unnecessary question and earned him a sharp look from Valeria, who might not appreciate the attentions of Borcovicium's commander, but could never be called cruel. As a result of the surrounding terrain, Borcovicium was one of the few forts on the Wall which didn't have an aqueduct to provide a regular water supply. The garrison depended on the very irregular flow of a nearby stream and the contents of dozens of stone-lined tanks that collected rainwater from the roofs of the fort buildings. The frontier was blessed with an apparently infinite amount of rainfall, but it still required constant balancing to ease the men's thirst, wash their clothes, and, as the stink that invariably hung over the fort hinted, to flush the latrines.

'The recent frosts have made it difficult,' Apollo admitted. 'Of course,' he allowed a hint of vinegar to sharpen his tone, 'it has not helped that we've had your supply column and their horses as our guests for the past day or so. As for your regiments . . .'

'They already have orders to set up camp by the lake at the bottom of the hill. They will not trouble your water tanks. And Janus and his wagons will be gone before nightfall, you have my word on it.' Marcus exchanged a glance with Valeria. 'Let us be frank with each other, Clarian. I do not believe you are telling me the whole story.'

'It's these damned Germans.' Apollo rapped his cup on the table. 'They don't know one end of a mattock from the other and they won't obey my orders. If they'd been auxiliaries, I'd have had them in irons, or worse, but . . . well, prefect, you know how it is with these people. They're barbarians. If I tell them to dig a ditch, they just look at me. If I say, "Repair that wall," it's the same. At first I put them on guard duty so I could use the auxiliaries to repair the place, but every time I inspected them they were asleep. They lounge around plaiting each other's hair and beards, sharpening their swords and scratching their arses. They're just another hundred mouths to feed.'

'And have you been feeding them?' The question came from Valeria.

'Not for the past two weeks,' Apollo admitted. 'Their chief, the one with a name like a mouthful of Tungrian vomit, laughed in my face one day when I told him I'd had enough of their idleness. I stopped their rations and—'

'Wasn't that dangerous,' Marcus said. 'A hundred disgruntled fighting men inside your walls?'

'Oh, they're loyal enough,' Apollo frowned. 'And they buy what they need from the stores at Vindolanda. They just won't work and I need builders, not warriors.'

'What do you think?' Marcus asked Valeria as they walked back to their horses in the dusk.

171

She considered for a moment. 'I think you need a commander here who understands how to lead men.'

'Will you do it?'

He was only partly joking and Valeria knew it, but she didn't pursue the point. 'I've given Leof half a dozen wineskins and told him to befriend the German chief. When do you want to talk to him?'

'In the morning, if he hasn't had his throat cut by then.'

She laughed and mounted her horse. 'Aren't you coming?'

'I need to see Janus and give him his orders for tomorrow. Once we've resupplied, he'll be escorting the wagons to Banna.'

She nodded and rode off through the south gate and down the hill towards the cavalry encampment, where the lights of oil lamps were beginning to appear one by one through the gloom.

Marcus walked out of the fort past the gate guards and across the slope to where the wagons were parked.

Janus was waiting for him. 'I've never been so glad to see you, lord,' the Pict said. 'This is as miserable a fornicating place as I've ever set eyes on. All that space inside the walls and not a barrack room to lay our heads. Only the horses are allowed to drink from the stream. What water we get from the fort tastes like their piss, even when we mix it with our posca. In fact I think it is their piss.'

Marcus smiled. Posca was the rough wine his soldiers received as part of their daily rations. The rainwater in the tanks must be foul indeed to make it taste any worse. 'I'll have the tribune send out some proper wine to take away the taste, but first tell me your status.'

'All present and accounted for.' Janus straightened. 'We made our way here as ordered, without incident. One of the wagons broke a wheel, but it was soon mended.'

'Then I want you on your way before dawn.' He ignored the grunt of disappointment; no cavalryman wanted to be tied to a column of lumbering wagons if he could help it, and Janus had done more than his share. Marcus led the young Pict away from the wagons where they couldn't be overheard. 'But before you go you'll need to choose a new escort. An escort of fifty men.' Janus whistled. An escort of fifty troopers was ridiculously large for a few carts filled with grain and fodder. 'They have to be men you trust to keep their mouths shut. Be certain, because your life may depend on it.' Now he had the other man's attention. 'You'll escort the wagons westwards and park up below the quarry crags halfway between Aesica and Banna. You know the place I mean?'

'Of course, lord.' Janus didn't hide his puzzlement.

'You'll have to be careful, because if you're seen by any patrols from Aesica this will all come to nothing.'

'This, lord?'

'When you reach your camp, you'll dress those fifty trusted troopers in the Pictish clothes you took from Keother's folk, arm them with Pictish weapons, and at nightfall you'll double back east. There's a mining settlement on the river two miles south of Aesica. It's a poor place, maybe twenty or thirty houses, a hundred souls all told. I want you to raid it.'

'You want us to raid our own people, lord?'

'That's right, Janus, I want you to raid our own people. Make as much noise as you can, burn a few houses, and rough up one or two of the men if you have to. I want them frightened, but nobody dies.' He gave the last three words special emphasis and Janus nodded.

'Nobody dies.'

'Only you and Julius will speak. You'll call out your orders in your own tongue. The only words the people hear will be Pictish words and all they'll see is Pictish warriors.'

Understanding dawned on Janus's stolid features. 'We're Picts.'

'That's right, you're Picts, and Janus?'

'Yes, lord?'

'Make sure those houses burn brightly. It's important the commander at Aesica can see them.'

XXIII

'I don't like the look of this, lord.' Zeno studied the wound on Marcus's chest. The scar was surrounded by a circle of swollen red flesh and Marcus could feel it throbbing as if it had a life of its own. 'There's none of the noble pus I would have expected and I fear the onset of mortification. Perhaps it would be best if you rest up for a day or two?'

'He's right, Marcus,' Valeria said from the far side of the tent. 'You look pale as death and you move like an old man. What difference would two days make?'

'Christ's bones,' Marcus growled. 'The pair of you will have me in my grave by Saint Agnes's feast. How many times do I have to tell you I have no need of rest? What I need is for you,' he glared at Zeno, 'to slap on a poultice and keep me on my feet.'

'A poultice is not just something you *slap on*,' Zeno snapped back. 'It needs careful preparation and the wrong poultice can do more damage than good. I can put together something that will draw out the heat, and hopefully the more harmful humours with it. Dried garlic, a mix of spice oils and the right herbs should do it. I used the last of the moss on Ninian's ribs, but I can get more from the *valetudinarium* up at the fort.'

'How long will it take?'

Zeno frowned. 'Two hours?'

'I don't have two hours to waste.' Marcus eased himself off the bed and reached for his tunic. 'Is your Saxon ready?' he asked Valeria.

'He's waiting outside.' A wry smile flickered across Valeria's lips. 'A little frayed at the edges. He wouldn't wake up until we dipped him in the lake. We had to break the ice first. I don't think he appreciated it.'

'Hand me my cloak.' Valeria draped the thick plaid over her brother's shoulders. 'I'll be back in two hours or so. Then you can slap on your poultice.'

'Of course, lord,' Zeno bowed. 'No doubt it will feel as if it's burning a hole in you,' he muttered, 'but you can be sure it will be doing you good.'

Leof was waiting outside the tent with a mournful expression and the defeated look of a whipped dog. His face had a curious yellowish tinge.

'You spoke to the Germans last night?'

'All night, lord.' Leof swallowed at the memory. 'They were very grateful for your gift of wine and insisted I share a barrel of their ale by way of thanks.'

'I appreciate your sacrifice,' Marcus smiled. 'And what did you get out of them?'

'They're not happy, lord.'

'I know that already.'

'They think the fort's commander is a fool. He demands that they dig holes as if they're slaves. They're proud men, lord, and none prouder than their chief, Ramios, who brought them here from Trupea with promises of glory and gold. Why would a proud man demean himself by digging a hole? There was no mention of holes when he made his mark in Eboracum.'

'Then what do they want?'

'He wouldn't tell me. He says he will speak only to the Lord of the Wall.'

'To me?'

'Yes, lord. He speaks Latin better than I do.'

'Very well, arrange it.' Marcus looked to Valeria and she nodded her agreement. 'But I will only meet him in private. Borcovicium's commander can know nothing of this for now. First tell me about this proud warrior chief Ramios.'

Marcus took a hunting bow and a quiver of arrows and rode out to a forest beyond the *via militaris* to the east of Borcovicium, but when he reached the trees he left both the bow and his escort behind. Ramios might have been a brother to the Frisian auxiliaries who garrisoned Vindobala, but there was something wilder about him, something of the hawk, especially in the pale ice-blue eyes, that made him a very different and much more dangerous species. He stood as tall as Marcus, and even in the freezing weather he wore a sleeveless leather jerkin that showed off heavy muscular arms. Dirty blond hair fell in waves to his shoulders and a long moustache drooped to the level of his square chin. Iron rings decorated each of his fingers and Marcus guessed they must signify some great deed their owner had performed, in the same way Roman *phalerae* recorded a man's bravery. They would also protect Ramios's hands in a fight and make his fists a remarkably potent weapon.

They studied each other for a while, each taking the measure of the man before him. It was Marcus who broke the silence.

'You wished to speak with me, Jarl Ramios? Well, I am here.'

Jarl. Ramios liked that. His narrow eyes creased and he nodded his appreciation. Leof had explained that a jarl was a German prince, the son of a king, even if that king might only be the ruler of a dozen huts and a stockade full of cattle. Ramios was neither, but he appreciated the flattery and the acceptance of his status as an equal.

'We will see no deer today.' Ramios's Latin was formal and stilted, but perfectly comprehensible. 'They will be in the valleys.' He sniffed the air. 'There is a storm coming, I think. Perhaps snow. They will seek what shelter they can.'

'The grazing is better, too.' Marcus bent and plucked a blade of rough grass, rubbing it between his fingers before casting it aside. 'But we did not come here to talk of deer.'

'No,' the other man agreed solemnly. He looked away and Marcus knew he was choosing his words with care. For a man like this words were like silver coins and not to be spent imprudently. The wrong expression might cast doubt on his courage or his authority, or worse, be construed as an insult that might be the catalyst for another in reply. 'You know the tribune of Borcovicium well?'

'He commands with my authority.'

Ramios's lips twitched. So the Roman wasn't going to make it easy for him. Marcus Flavius Victor was living up to his reputation. 'We offered our swords to Rome, instead he wants us to pick up shovels.'

Marcus shrugged. 'It is no dishonour for a Roman soldier to pick up a shovel or rebuild a wall. They are proud of these skills, and justifiably so. Without diggers and builders there would be no Wall and likely I would be speaking Pictish now. Digging and building have made Romans the masters of the world.'

'And yet the masters of the world now call on a jarl of the Cherusci to help them defend their frontier.' Ramios looked to Marcus for a reply, but the Roman remained silent. 'We are warriors, not builders,' he continued. 'We took Rome's silver at Eboracum because the *dux Britanniarum* asked us to kill Picts for him. But Tribune Apollo will not even send us out on patrol where we might use *our* skills to seek out the Picts his men can never find and who are no doubt spying on him even now.' He shook his head. 'I have made my mark and given my word that my people would serve Rome for twelve Roman months. I will not go back on that word. But we will not dig.'

Marcus wondered at the foolishness of whoever had allowed Ramios and his warriors to be sent to Borcovicium, where their chances of killing a Pict were about the same as those of killing an elephant. He considered his options. He couldn't simply leave things as they were. There had already been fights between the Germans and the auxiliaries who thought they were being given favourable treatment. One would inevitably result in a killing and the garrison would end up butchering each other. Ramios would not go back on his word, but Marcus, though it would cost him dearly with Dulcitius, could release him from it. But perhaps there was a third possibility?

'Can your men ride?'

Ramios frowned. 'Of course,' he said. 'Not in the Roman fashion with a saddle, and if we fight on horseback we would fight our own way, but yes, give them a horse and they can all ride.'

'And you want to fight.'

'Yes.' There was a fierceness to Ramios's voice that hadn't been there earlier. 'We want to fight.'

'Very well.' Marcus paused. He must choose his next words as carefully as Ramios had chosen his earlier. Two paths would soon offer themselves and he had to make sure Ramios and his men would follow him down whichever of those paths he chose, or was forced to take. 'You must understand that I cannot say now how or when I can make this happen. First, I must find suitable replacements for you, men who are prepared to dig as well as fight. Are we clear, Jarl Ramios?'

'We are clear, Lord of the Wall.'

'When that time comes, I will supply you with horses and send for you.'

'And we will answer your call without the waste of a moment.'

Marcus held the other man's gaze. 'There is another condition, perhaps a more important one.'

The blue eyes narrowed. 'Yes?'

'When I send for you I will release you from your obligation to the *dux Britanniarum*. From that moment onward you will serve Marcus Flavius Victor, not Julius Postumus Dulcitius.'

Ramios went very still. This was different territory entirely. He was placing his honour in Marcus's hands and, quite possibly, his neck in a noose. Did the Lord of the Wall have the authority to override the orders of the *dux Britanniarum*? Certainly there was no doubt Marcus, the man, had the personal authority, but did he have the power? It was a matter of trust.

Ramios held out his hand. 'We will kill many Picts together?'

'You will kill who I tell you to kill, Jarl Ramios.'

They stared at each other, but the right hand remained rock steady. Marcus took it in his own and shook it in the Roman fashion.

He didn't yet know how he would make it happen, but he had added another hundred horse soldiers to his growing army.

XXIV

How was he to solve the dilemma of removing Borcovicium's German mercenaries from Clarian Apollo's already depleted garrison? When facing any problem of this kind, Marcus's thoughts always turned first to his two fathers.

Brenus had been his father, the man who had raised and guided him.

Magnus Flavius Maximus was his blood-father.

Maximus. Soldier. General. Governor. Emperor.

Eventually, men called him usurper, but they would not have called him that if he had not been betrayed and murdered. Marcus preferred to believe his father was the usurped. Robbed by weaker men of the opportunity to return Rome to its true greatness.

Maximus had served in Britannia as a junior officer in the years before the Great Conspiracy, which was when he and Marcus's mother had become lovers. Later, he'd been sent away, but he had never forgotten his son. Marcus had been brought up and educated, not as the son of Brigantian royalty, but as a Roman nobleman. He learned to read and write in Latin and Greek. Books appeared. Herodotus, Cicero, Seneca. Tacitus's *Histories* and his *Agricola*, with its tales of the taming of Britannia. Suetonius's *Lives of the Caesars*. Caesar himself and the *Gallic Wars*, and Plutarch.

Meanwhile, Brenus made sure he also learned to fight. He spent hours every day wielding a wooden sword and a practice spear and taking many a cracked head or a rap over the knuckles when his skills failed to live up to those of his opponents, Brenus's armourer and some of his most experienced fighters. Brenus used hunts to instill tactical knowledge and understanding.

'See how we use the terrain to funnel our prey into the trap,' he said one day, as they beat the forest to force a herd of deer towards a line of nets. 'They flee from a danger we create towards a greater danger that is invisible to them. Once they reach a certain point there is no hope, even for those unentangled.' Yet that was not the only lesson Marcus learned that day. From their haul, Brenus ordered that a buck and ten of the younger hinds should be set free. 'If we kill them all, where will next season's calves come from? Those animals are the guarantors of meat for your tables and the tables of your sons and grandsons. Destroy all life and all you leave is a desert.'

Maximus must have returned from his journeys at one point, because he had appeared at Grabant with all the pomp and trappings of a Roman general. That was the day Marcus learned his true lineage. He remembered his confusion and bewilderment, and something not far short of hatred at his mother and Brenus for deceiving him. For depriving him of the upbringing and the father who was rightfully his. He had wanted to go away with Maximus, but the general told Marcus he would serve him best by staying with Brenus. He would be a warrior from that day forth. Then Maximus was gone once more.

Marcus had become a man riding at Brenus's side as they hunted Pictish raiding parties and resolved petty squabbles between tribal chiefs. At fifteen he bloodied his sword in earnest for the first time, plunging the blade into a Pictish spearman about to cut a child's throat. As a reward, his father had given him his first woman, a little tear-stained orphan from some long-forgotten settlement. He'd kept her for a year until she'd died from the bloody flux.

That was the year the Scots and the Picts swarmed over the Wall and all Britannia was at peril. Brenus did what he could for his people – Marcus recalled a tearful farewell from his mother – and went out to hunt Picts in earnest. They had no answer to the speed, guile and flexibility of the Brigantes' cavalry tactics and Marcus's head filled with whooping chases through the trees, Picts scattering like chickens across the high moors, mere fodder for Brenus's spears. Yet for all their success Brenus knew his raids were mere pinpricks on the hide of a Pictish bull that rampaged at will over the provinces of Britannia. He needed help, or the Picts would put down roots.

Help came in the form of Magnus Maximus.

Appointed *magister militum*, supreme general of the island's forces, Maximus arrived in Britannia with a full legion, the Twenty-second Primigenia, around which he intended to form an army. When Brenus rode south to offer his services to the *magister*, he took Marcus with him.

Had there ever been a prouder moment than the day General Magnus Maximus appointed Brenus a prefect, commander of the First Ala Brigantum, and made Marcus a decurion, and leader of the Second Squadron? Maximus had called Marcus to his quarters in the great city of Londinium and personally handed him the *phalerae* of his new rank. 'I have things to say to you, my son, important things, but they must wait till this business is done,' he said. 'For the moment, I ask you to accept that I cannot recognize you for what you are. Our relationship must remain entirely between us, but one day that will change.'

For the first time, Marcus was able to get to properly know his true father. Maximus often appointed his son's squadron as his personal bodyguard and they would share a tent in the evenings as the army marched north. It turned out Rome was not the unified all-encompassing, all-knowing Empire Marcus had been brought up to believe in.

'A single Empire is like a horse,' Maximus told him. 'It needs a single guiding hand, not two pulling in different directions. Gratian was wrong when he gave his uncle power in the East, and Valens died for it at Adrianopolis. Wrong to replace him with Theodosius, God love him, who is too honest for his own good. Augustus ruled without a co-Emperor, so did Vespasian, until he tired of the work, and so did Trajan and Marcus Aurelius. No good ever comes of sharing power.'

What he'd heard troubled and confused the young Marcus. 'I don't understand, father. Why would any man deliberately give away even part of his power?'

'No.' His blood-father's eyes had brightened. 'That means you do understand, Marcus. You understand the contradiction between taking or being handed power and having the capacity to wield it. If you do not have the capacity to wield it, do you deserve to keep it?'

'No, father. Power is nothing without strength, Brenus taught me that. If you do not have strength then someone who has will come along and take away your power.'

'Yet the Emperor has both power and strength,' Maximus pointed out. 'He has his loyal generals and his legions, who are the beating heart of that power. All he has to do is have the courage to wield them. So where is the flaw?'

Marcus considered for a moment, thinking of everything Brenus had taught him about authority and command, the need for control and discipline, the fact that men would only follow a true leader, and . . . suddenly Gordianus the master builder's face swam into his vision and he understood. A wall could look strong and invulnerable on the outside, but if the core was weak it would eventually fall.

'The flaw is at the very heart of the Empire,' he whispered. 'The flaw is in the man.'

His father had smiled. 'We will talk about this further another day, Marcus.'

Often, as the legions advanced and Brenus's troopers patrolled ahead, they would see the sudden flare of blazing homes in their rear where a Pictish raiding party had infiltrated to spread chaos and confusion. Maximus raged at these assaults on lands he had already assured Rome had been liberated.

Winter came, but despite a heavy snowfall Maximus still insisted on inspecting and encouraging his troops. One evening, Marcus's squadron was escorting the general back to the main camp at dusk when a blizzard forced them to take shelter in an abandoned farmstead. Marcus's shirt had been soaked by the melting snow and he removed it to dry it before a fire his troopers had built. They'd been there less than an hour when Maximus, ever restless, noticed a blaze which could only be another farm burning off to the west.

Before anyone could react, the general roared an order to take to the saddle and Marcus barely had time to haul his mail over his bare torso and throw on a cloak before he joined the others.

'It's time we taught these beasts from the north a lesson,' Maximus called over his shoulder.

Marcus argued for caution, but he argued in vain. As they drew closer to the glow of the burning farm he tried once more.

'Lord,' Marcus called, 'we don't know how many there are or even if they're still around. They could be long gone by now.'

'Do not question my orders, decurion,' Maximus snapped, his anger palpable. 'I heard a scream. Roman citizens are dying a few minutes' ride away and I will not abandon them.'

Marcus had heard nothing, but he kicked his mount through the billowing snow after his father. 'Caradoc,' he called to his senior trooper, 'take your section and stick to the general like a second skin. At the first sign of trouble get him out of here.'

'The silly bastard is going to get us all killed,' Caradoc muttered as he rode past.

Marcus picked up speed and led the remainder of the squadron past Maximus, who at least had the sense to slow his mount and let his bodyguard take the lead. By now the burning farm was visible through a dense wood ahead, the light of the flames magnified by the wintry landscape. 'Can anyone see any sign of life?' he called.

'Nothing, decurion,' announced a trooper called Perig who had the sharpest eyes of any of them.

A farm track led through the trees and Marcus's heart sank. Any prudent commander would avoid such a direct approach, but he knew Maximus in this mood wouldn't countenance a time-wasting detour.

'First and second sections to me.' Marcus nudged his horse into a canter and within moments they surged twenty or thirty paces ahead of the main group. 'Draw swords.'

They were halfway through the wood when a shadowy mass erupted simultaneously from the undergrowth on either flank, howling like so many hungry wolves. A glint of metal darted at his eyes and Marcus slapped away a spear point as he urged his horse forward. Another came from his left and he felt it glance from his mail and rip through his cloak. Men were roaring insults at each other and he heard the butcher's block *thunk* of a sword edge meeting flesh with lethal force. Where was Maximus? He prayed Caradoc had managed to turn the general – his father – back before the ambush. Shouted orders from a distance. At least someone in the squadron had the sense to take control.

A sudden lurch and his horse was falling. He rolled from the dropping shoulder as he'd practised so many times before and he was on his feet almost before he hit the ground. His helmet was gone, but he still gripped his sword. Two of the dark shadows closed on him with incredible speed. He managed to parry one blow, but something slammed into his back with enough force to catapult him into his attackers. A horse, his reeling mind told him, you've been hit by one of your own horses. One of the men was down and Marcus hacked at where the eyes should be, his efforts rewarded by a satisfying howl. He turned back to meet the second man only to be punched in the chest with astonishing force. An icy bolt of agony lanced through him following the shock of the blow, and his racing mind told him his mail had been pierced. A bearded face snarled into his, the warrior's howl of triumph accompanied by a spray of spittle. A new measure of agony as his killer

185

twisted the thin-bladed knife to work it deeper. The sharp metallic snap as the thin blade broke. A pair of bone-white eyes in the gloom widened in puzzlement, followed by a moment of resolution as the broken dagger was pulled back to ram into Marcus's throat. Oddly, the eyes parted, one abandoning the other, and Marcus felt himself bathed in warmth. The sharp *smack* of the sword edge splitting his attacker's skull in two seemed to come much later.

'Is he dead?' Another day, who knows when, but even though his eyes were closed he could tell it was daylight. The voice seemed to come from far away, but it belonged to Brenus.

'Not yet.' Maximus, terse and defensive.

'You should never have—'

'That's in the past,' the *magister militum* of Britannia snapped. 'It will do none of us any good to rake over old coals.'

Marcus wished his two fathers would stop arguing and leave him in peace to die.

XXV

Janus studied the settlement below from the edge of the wood. Smoke and sparks belched from the smelting works at the far end of the valley a mile south of the Wall fort at Aesica. Closer to him a neat row of two-storey thatched houses and shops lined either side of the street, each with its garden to the rear and a small enclosure for chickens or goats. Pigs snuffled and grunted among the rubbish heaps and steaming piles of manure and down by the river the village's cattle occupied a fenced stockade. Marcus had reckoned on a hundred souls all told, but either he'd been ill-informed or the population had increased rapidly in recent times, because Janus calculated at least double, many of them living in rough, possibly temporary houses that scattered the rising ground between the village proper and the iron works.

'What do you think?' his brother Julius asked from the hollow beside him.

'I think the Lord of the Wall has sold us a pig, and an ugly one at that.'

The two hand-picked squadrons who'd accompanied them were hidden in another wood a mile distant, ready to don their Pictish war gear as darkness fell. The cavalrymen had been chosen either for their ability to pass as Picts or their ruthlessness, combined with a facility for keeping their mouths shut. Of course, such a combination pretty well guaranteed that many of them were no saints. Having seen Barcum, as the inhabitants called it, Janus decided that was the least of his problems.

'Maybe we should look somewhere else?' As so often, Julius turned his brother's thoughts into words.

'We don't have time, and this is the only village worth a name that could be seen burning from Aesica. It's here or not at all.'

'If we don't go through with it we'd be as well heading north and taking our chances with the relatives,' Julius snorted.

'So we go through with it.' Janus turned his attention back to the village. 'We'll come in from the south, burn those houses beside the street and get back out as quick as we go in. The smelters' houses are hardly worth burning anyway. We leave them alone.'

'Safer that way,' Julius agreed.

They slipped back into the cover of the trees.

Three hours later they led their little column of men up the valley, picking their way through the rocks beside the river rather than using the track that served Barcum from the much larger settlements beside the River Tinan. Despite the freezing night, Janus and Julius had removed their tunics and rode bare-chested. The twins had known nothing but Roman ways since they'd been taken at the age of ten, but they were oddly proud of their warrior heritage and had taken to tattooing the record of their deeds on their flesh in the Pictish fashion. A snarling wolf and a screaming eagle shared Janus's chest, among a whirling vortex of symmetrical patterns created by a single snake and artfully stylized combinations of beast, man and reptile. They carried Pictish war axes in slings across their backs and Pictish swords hung at their waists.

The others were clothed in the war gear looted from Keother's valley and every man wore a sword, but pitch torches replaced the spears they would normally have held, and spare torches were thrust haphazardly into their belts. White eyes glared from faces blackened by soot in which the brothers had traced similar Pictish symbols to those that adorned their own chests. Anything that identified them as soldiers of the Ala Sabiniana had been left behind in the wood.

'Remember,' Janus said to his brother. 'Nobody dies.'

An owl screeched nearby and Janus's horse shuffled under him. A hungry owl, because the winter was a barren time for all creatures. All creatures except a man with a sword.

Fifty men with swords approached Barcum on the grassy slope beside the stream.

They rode in pairs and the final duo carried between them a small iron pot attached to their saddles by two leather ropes. In the pot glowed the embers of one of the fires on which they'd earlier cooked the day's meal. All it would take to make the cinders catch again was to add a few wisps of dried moss. When the flames touched the pitch the torches would burn, and when the torches burned they would be quickly followed by the houses of Barcum.

Janus halted them when he could see the faint glow of an oil lamp through a faulty shutter. The glimmer stirred a memory of the raid on Keother's valley and the man they'd been forced to kill. He'd felt nothing that night. Would have slaughtered them all because they were the enemy. The families who worked and lived and loved beneath these thatched roofs weren't the enemy, they were Roman citizens whose lives were about to be destroyed by Roman soldiers. Janus wasn't a man inclined to deep thought or doubt; as a rule he enjoyed making sport of civilians, protected by his sword and his status. Yet there was something troubling about tonight. Still, the Lord of the Wall would have considered all of this. Marcus Flavius Victor had decided Barcum must be harried and Janus had learned never to doubt his commander's judgement.

'We go in and out fast, but make sure the houses burn properly,' he called out. 'There's no point in being here if we don't do the job right.'

'And nobody dies,' Julius added.

'Nobody dies.' The cinder pot flared and within moments the night was illuminated by scores of flaming torches. Janus urged his horse forward into the unsuspecting village. He'd assigned men to specific houses and his was in the centre of the right-hand row. The first torches arched onto roofs thick with generations of thatch. One or two caught, but as he'd feared a number simply scorched the thick upper layer of damp reeds. This initial phase was meant to be carried out in strict silence, but circumstances decreed a change of tactics. Janus flung himself from his horse and kicked in the door of the house he'd chosen. A single room, starkly lit by the flames of the torch. A ring of frightened faces staring from the cots where they'd been sleeping peacefully a heartbeat before. A man rose with a shout of protest and Julius stepped past his brother and kicked him in the stomach. A woman screamed. Five children, three boys and two older girls. 'Out,' Janus roared. The terrified family didn't understand the Pictish word, but the sentiment was unmistakable. The woman helped her husband to his feet and supported him past Julius – who was already piling any-thing flammable in the centre of the room – followed by her howling brood. Janus put his torch to some likely-looking wall hangings while Julius jabbed his against the inner thatch at its lowest point. As the flames caught, they looked at each other and Janus nodded. Enough. Julius set light to the heap of clothing and furniture and they turned to leave. Somewhere close by a baby cried.

'Shit.'

'Get out,' Janus ordered his brother. 'Make sure the others are doing their jobs.'

He fought his way towards the sound past the crackling bonfire of the family's furniture and belongings. In the farthest corner of the room sat a tiny cot, forgotten by the mother in her terror. Perhaps she thought the eldest girl would look after the babe? He picked up the tiny bundle and looked into a wrinkled angry red face, cursing as his hand touched something wet, soft and warm. With the babe beneath his arm he fled the burning house.

The family stood in a confused huddle in the centre of the street. Janus thrust the baby in the mother's arms and received a look of puz-zled shock in return. Around him Barcum burned.

A few stunned villagers milled about in the open roadway between the houses, but most had fled into the sanctuary of darkness. No organized resistance yet, but that couldn't last. Some clustered around still forms lying in the dust and he prayed they were only battered and bruised. Over the crackle of burning buildings he could hear Julius roaring in Pictish.

At the far end of the village some fool had set three or four of the iron smelters' huts ablaze. Not family houses as it turned out, more of a barracks for the hard men who laboured in the iron works. Men who now swarmed from the huts with heavy hammers and mattocks to protect what little was theirs.

'Julius,' he called in Pictish, 'round up the troopers and get them ready to leave. We've done enough.'

He rode up the street to make sure all his men had heard the order. Someone appeared from between two houses and lunged at Janus with what he took for a spear. He swung his sword at his attacker's head, intending to use the flat of the blade, but he heard a scream as he passed and when he looked the edge shone bright with blood. A stone glanced from his shoulder with enough force to make him cry out. Time to go.

He was breathing hard when he reached Julius.

'Christus save us,' his brother said. He counted the men with Janus. 'Where the fuck are Gellius and Avidius?' Two riders rode up and he nodded. 'All present and accounted for, the stupid bastards. Let's get out of this festering shithole and back to civilization. Your ugly pig turned out to be a fucking wildcat.'

FOG

XXVI

Aesica (Great Chesters)

The twin tyrannies of time and distance weighed on Marcus's shoulders like two sides of a yoke hung with the stones that made up the Wall. Soon he would come to a crossroads where there could be no turning back. A decision must be made. Left or right? In some ways it didn't matter which he chose. Either path could lead to triumph or disaster, and disaster meant his own death and the deaths of many of the men who followed him. On the other hand, it would be the most important moment of his life. Did he want his name to be remembered with honour and pride, or tarnished by shame and ignominy?

He'd solved the problem of Ramios and the German mercenaries by persuading his former deputy at Vindolanda to transfer fifty men to Borcovicium and hand over a hundred remounts on which the Germans now rode. They'd taken time to accustom themselves to the big Roman horses, but eventually their efforts had lived up to Ramios's promise. Marcus had no misgivings about their ability to fight, but how they would behave in battle was another question.

He glanced at his sister, riding to his left-hand side. They had skirted the high crags, where the Wall hugged the brink of the cliff like a lover and the vistas over lake and forest and stream stretched far into the north. Ahead lay Aesica, on the high moor, just beyond the small fort-let that marked the forty-second mile of their journey west. Was it time to tell her? Of course, she deserved to know. Perhaps he should have divulged his intentions all those months ago when the little worm began to squirm inside his head, with its whispers of opportunity and potential. Before he'd taken the first faltering steps towards this great, all or nothing gamble in which the collateral was all of their lives. He wanted to tell her. Perhaps, with the cold iron in his chest becoming ever more palpable, needed to, if only to share the burden.

But something always stopped him. Now was never the time. That sharp stab of fear at the thought of revealing the inner thoughts that had brought them to this point. Worse, of trying to justify the decisions he'd made and the acts he had caused to be carried out in his name. The risks he'd taken with the lives not just of the hundreds of soldiers around them, but the countless thousands north and south of the Wall. Would she applaud what he'd done? No, what he called confidence, she would see as arrogance. His determination might be interpreted as recklessness. All his clever stratagems as conspiracy. He could not face that. Not yet.

His thoughts returned to his father. Magnus Maximus must have confronted these same dilemmas. Even when Marcus had been lying delirious in his sickbed in Eboracum, Maximus's mind must have already been turning to what lay ahead. Perhaps he had even set events in motion.

While Marcus lay helpless Maximus and Brenus had cleansed Britannia of the Picts in a great merciless sweep through the northern hills. They'd smashed the enemy's strength between the hammer of Brenus's cavalry and the anvil of the Sixth legion. The Pictish king had escaped, along with scattered bands led by his surviving nobles, but Brenus didn't give them a moment's respite. By the time they slipped over the Wall near Petriana they were exhausted and demoralized. But Brenus was not finished with the Picts. His scouts tracked them down to the abandoned Roman fort at Castra Exploratum. The entire leadership of the barbarian north lay unsuspecting within the tumbled walls less than an hour's march north of the Wall.

Maximus had set up his headquarters at Luguvalium. Brenus, who had based his troops at nearby Petriana, was in favour of an immediate advance. Destroy the Pictish nobility and Britannia could breathe easy for a generation. He knew the ground as he knew the palm of his hand. If Julius Dulcitius's Sixth marched an hour before dusk Brenus would pledge to bring them to a position from which they could surround Castra Exploratum at full dark. When they attacked at dawn not a man would escape.

Dulcitius refused to move. His troops were tired. He had no mandate to operate beyond the edge of the Empire without Imperial decree. Brenus raged. Magnus Maximus was the *magister militum* of Britannia, the only decree that mattered was his. Give him even four cohorts of cavalry and he would be back in a day with Lucti's head on his spear. Maximus had eventually agreed, for Brenus set out the next day, but here Caradoc's memory lost its way. Ask him once, and he'd say Brenus had overall command. Ask him a day later and Maximus, perhaps tired of Dulcitius's gloating, told him that, though his troops would not cross the frontier, an expedition of this importance should be led by a general.

Whatever the final decision, Brenus and his cavalry had converged on Castra Exploratum at the dark of the moon. And walked into a Pictish trap. 'We were betrayed,' Caradoc said. Picts had fallen from the trees on unsuspecting cavalrymen, dashed in their hundreds from hidden valleys and the nearby river bed. The ambushers became the ambushed. 'We fought for our very lives,' Caradoc remembered. 'But even that would not have been enough without Brenus's sacrifice. He led a force to break the ring of Picts. We escaped, but Brenus fell, never to rise again.'

By now Marcus was close to recovery and Maximus called him to his side when he made his headquarters for a time at Eboracum. He walked in marble halls at the heels of his father and witnessed the wielding of political power at first hand. Learned the true nature of Maximus's ambition.

Maximus spoke in guarded terms of the Emperor Gratian's failings, which, it appeared, had brought the Empire to the brink of actual collapse. Rome needed a leader of strength, experience and conviction. It was only gradually that Marcus understood that leader was to be his father.

Messages arrived regularly from Rome demanding the return of Maximus's legions. Maximus replied with a letter exaggerating his problems in Britannia and begging a further six months to deal with them. Gratian agreed to three, and imposed a substantial tax increase on Britannia for the privilege. Gratian's ultimatum ran out in July. In June, Maximus marched on Londinium with the Sixth and Twenty-second legions, where his army and the populace hailed him Flavius Magnus Maximus Augustus, Emperor of Rome. An Emperor stranded on an island at the edge of his Empire, while his rival still lived and ruled at its heart. An Emperor with strength, but not yet the power to wield it. Marcus had pleaded to ride at his father's side, to share the risks and the potential spoils; instead, Maximus sent him to take command at Vindolanda.

XXVII

Valeria was first to notice the smoke as they breasted the rise on the undulating line of the Wall.

'Look, Marcus,' she called.

Marcus followed her gaze. Perhaps a mile and a half to the south-west and just below Aesica, a heavy smudge of grey hung over the treetops of a forested valley.

'Trouble,' he echoed her thought. He turned Storm down the slope. 'The first four squadrons with me,' he ordered. 'Caradoc, continue to the fort with the rest and set up camp beside the stream.'

They rode diagonally across the springy turf until they reached the track that linked Aesica with the valley below. 'There's a small settlement not far down from here,' he recalled. 'The stream feeds a smelting works and a couple of water mills.'

'Picts, do you think?'

'Most likely,' he admitted. 'I thought I'd taught the bastards a lesson. Not Keother's people, that's certain. Maybe this Briga wants to let me know I don't frighten her. A raid so close to the fort is certainly sending someone a message. Then again,' he shrugged, 'maybe one of Corvus's chiefs thinks he has a point to prove?'

The acrid scent of burning hung heavy among the trees and smoke drifted lethargically through the network of skeletal branches above. The first building they reached was the smelting works, surprisingly untouched, and beyond it the burned-out ruins of the settlement. At least six or seven houses had been reduced to blackened timbers standing like a grim guard of honour on each side of the street. Soldiers from Aesica's garrison mingled with the villagers as they rooted among the ashes of their homes for any possessions that had escaped the flames. A grey-haired officer stood in the centre of the street surveying the smoking wreckage around him and dictating orders to a clerk. Four or five cloth bundles lay at his feet and a shriek rent the air that felt like a nail being run across Marcus's skull as a small body was brought out to join them. He couldn't tell whether it was a boy or a girl, but the child would be of a similar age to Bren and he had to suppress a surge of panic at not knowing where his son was, or even if he was still alive. Valeria jumped from the saddle and ran to comfort the grieving mother and Marcus nudged Storm to where the officer stood.

'Is there anything we can do to help,' he asked Claudius Dexter, commander of the First Asturians, who garrisoned Aesica. They'd never been friends and Dexter had never hidden his resentment at Marcus, a mere tribesman in his eyes, being handed a title he'd always believed should be his.

'You can hunt down the animals who did this so I can hang them from Aesica's walls and watch them rot.' Dexter could barely speak for anger.

'How many did you lose?'

'Six that we know of, but there would be a lot more if Arcadius here, who manages the mine and the smelting works, hadn't rallied his men to come to the aid of the village.' He waved forward a brutish-looking man with a black beard and a torso like a tree trunk.

Marcus surveyed the damage and wondered at the timing of Arcadius's aid, but that wasn't his concern. 'Did you get a good look at the raiding party?' He expected Arcadius's manners to match his looks, but the mine manager stepped forward with a bow. 'Yes, lord. A hundred and more black-faced Picts . . .'

'Someone found this after the Picts had fled.' Dexter held out a war axe that unmistakably belonged to one of the Pictish tribes.

'What about the raiders,' Marcus asked. 'Did you kill or capture any of them?'

Arcadius shook his head. 'We must have left a few with scars to remember us by, but we killed none, though we lost two of our own. I wondered . . . ?'

'I'll make sure their families are compensated,' Marcus assured him, to the big man's obvious surprise. 'Have you checked the area for tracks?' Marcus addressed the question to Dexter.

'Yes. They came into the valley from the west, but must have been in more of a hurry to get back, because they crossed back over the Wall not a mile from the fort.'

'Your sentries didn't see them?'

'You know we don't have the people to man every turret, Marcus. By that time the sentries on Aesica's parapet would have been attracted by the flames from Barcum. We tracked them for a couple of miles into the moss country, but they were good. Very good. We lost them on a stony crag and never found the trail again.'

'I have men who are experts,' Marcus said, thinking of one man in particular who had some questions to answer. 'I promise you, Claudius, that we will find who did this.'

'There is one more thing.' Claudius stooped and lifted back two of the blankets from the dead. 'Marcellus, the local silversmith.' A plump, surprised face above a ragged tear of red flesh. 'And his wife.' She might have been her husband's twin. He pulled the blanket lower to show the woman's hands. Two fingers on each hand had been roughly amputated.

'She must have been wearing rings,' Marcus frowned.

'We think it's more than that,' Dexter said. 'Marcellus kept his silver well hidden, but when we searched his house it had been dug up from beneath the floor. It seems the raiders tortured his wife to make him give it up.'

A shadow fell across Marcus's face. 'Someone will pay for this.'

Luko led Storm up the hill towards Aesica as Marcus accompanied Claudius Dexter back to his fortress. 'Nothing like this has happened here for years.' The auxiliary commander's grizzled features mirrored the despondency in his voice.

'Don't blame yourself, Claudius,' Marcus said. 'There was nothing you could do to stop this. The Picts have been quiet because they've been building up their strength, but there comes a time when the young men have to test that strength. This was a raid by warriors of little or no experience. Look at the way they allowed themselves to be bested by a gang of iron miners. Have you ever seen a raid so poorly planned and poorly executed?'

'You're right,' Dexter admitted. 'It wasn't like any murder raid I've ever seen. I wondered that they didn't slaughter half the village and more.' They walked on for a few more paces. 'You say that the Picts are building up their strength; there can only be one reason for that.'

The statement contained a question and Marcus took his time before he answered it. 'Can I depend on your discretion?'

'Of course, prefect.'

'Two and a half years ago we both helped chase the Picts back across the Wall. We defeated them, but we couldn't destroy their power, as Maximus once did. The result is the constant threat of raids like this. What if I could do what Maximus did and destroy the power of the Picts for a generation? Provide Britannia with twenty years of peace.'

Dexter froze for a moment. 'How would you do that?'

'I can't tell you the detail. Not yet. But the whole world appears to know I'm gathering cavalry for a certain purpose. Those hundred and twenty cavalry under your command at Aesica could make a difference.'

Dexter let out a bark of laughter that startled the men around them. 'I received a letter not two days since, from Tribune Justus at Corstopitum, saying that he'd heard rumours about you and advising me not, under any circumstances, to let you have any of my troops. Not an order, obviously. Justus's authority comes direct from Eboracum, but you are the Lord of the Wall and my superior in the command chain. But enough to make a man think. After all, the post and the men in it are under my charge.'

'So?'

Aesica's commander allowed the silence to stretch for another few paces as he turned the matter over in his mind. 'Bring me the heads of the Picts who did this and you will have your cavalry.'

By the time they reached the fort, the majority of Marcus's assorted band of riders had set up camp in their various regiments on the long, gentle slope beside the stream east of Aesica. At the centre he saw some of the units already lined up for resupply from the wagons he'd sent in advance with Janus. Valeria, who'd ridden ahead from Barcum, met him as he approached the camp. 'I thought you said you were sending the supplies to Banna?'

'We were running low,' he said. Was there anything she missed?

'Just as well you did. We can last another week with what remains in the wagons,' she said. 'But the quartermasters are worried about fodder for the horses. The grazing up here is poor. Still, we should be able to refill the wagons when we reach Luguvalium. When did you say you expected to meet Niall of the Nine Hostages?'

'I didn't.'

She stared at him with fire in her eyes and he immediately had reason to regret his abrupt reply.

'I've had enough of your smoke and mirrors and clever word tricks, Marcus,' she snapped. 'We march from fort to fort leaving confusion and distrust in our wake. It's like trying to see through thick fog. You know something's not right out there, but you have no idea what it is. Take this raid . . .'

'What about it?'

'It stinks worse than a week-old corpse. Show me the Pict who would have attacked a settlement like Barcum with so few warriors. Show me the Pict who wouldn't have slaughtered all of those villagers in their beds. I spoke to a woman whose baby had been left in one of the houses. A Pict rescued it. He handed it back to her when he'd

203

more likely have thrown it in the well. Show me the Pict who would do that.'

'I hope to show you those very Picts by sunset.' Marcus was careful not to react to her fury. 'Or at dawn tomorrow by the latest. I'm sending Janus and his two squadrons out after them within the hour.'

He called Janus to his headquarters tent a few minutes later and ordered the place cleared so they could speak alone.

'I thought we agreed there'd be no dead?' Marcus kept his voice low; a tent in the centre of a thronging military camp was no place to be bellowing secrets.

'I'm sorry, lord.' Janus could barely meet his eyes. 'We ended up in the shit up to our necks and had to fight our way out. Those iron smelters and miners were tough bastards. From what I could see anybody who got killed was killed by accident. There was this kid—'

'What about the silversmith and his wife?'

The young cavalryman shot him a look of bewilderment. 'I don't know anything about a silversmith, lord.'

Marcus told him what he knew, short and sharp so Janus winced at every second word. 'If even a whisper of this ever gets out my neck will be in a noose, your head will be on a spike and the Ala Sabiniana won't exist, but worse than that my carefully put together plan will come to nothing.'

'Those bastards,' Janus raged. 'When I find out who—'

'We can't bring back the dead, but you will bring back that silversmith's treasure, do you understand me, decurion? You will take your squadrons out beyond the Wall, find those raiders and return with some heads, preferably Picts.'

'Lord!' Janus saluted.

'Because if you don't, it might be wise to stay out there.'

Janus led his fifty chastened and dog-tired troopers from Aesica's north gate in the early afternoon. They returned the following morning with two empty saddles and three dead bodies, visibly affected by their experience.

The fort's commander and the prefect of the Ala Sabiniana were there to greet them. Janus dropped a small iron-bound chest at their feet. 'I apologize for bringing so few of the enemy back, lords,' the young Pict said. He went to one of the bodies and lifted the head by a bush of dark hair. A boy, Marcus saw, and by the slight figures the others would be the same, probably herd boys the patrol had stumbled on. His face was covered with soot and marked with Pictish symbols similar to those described by Barcum's villagers.

'Aren't they a little young to be warriors?' Dexter frowned.

'They teach them to kill early in the High Lands,' Marcus assured him. 'We had five or six no older than that at Alona. A young viper's bite can be as deadly as an old one's.'

'We had to hunt far and wide to find them,' Janus explained. 'When we finally caught up with them they fought like wildcats. We were just getting the better of them when another band appeared and came to their aid and we had to ride for it.' He pointed to the empty saddles. 'Sadly, we lost troopers Gellius and Avidius.' Janus gave Marcus what might be called a significant look. 'Two of the more enterprising members of the squadron. And,' his voice turned brittle, 'Trooper Julius is missing.'

XXVIII

Eboracum (York)

'He what?'

'It is all true, Lord Dulcitius. We've had whispers from frontier forts all over the north. The Ala First Herculaea rode north from Epiacum two days ago, leaving a garrison of fewer than fifty men.'

They were in the great palace overlooking the river at Eboracum. It had been built by Constantine and more recently restored by Count Theodosius, but it was showing its age. Still, even in winter, Dulcitius preferred the great draughty marble-clad rooms to the relatively cramped quarters he could have had in the fortress on the hill overlooking the far bank. With its long, statue-lined corridors it had a grandeur from a bygone era no man could afford to reproduce now unless he had an Emperor's purse. Even the upkeep was difficult, because there were so few craftsmen remaining who still had the skills, and Dulcitius preferred not to pay to bring them from the mainland. The result was a faded, decaying splendour like an aged beauty whose wrinkles showed through her badly applied face powder.

'Cavalry, always cavalry.' Dulcitius chewed his thin lip. 'How many saddles, Senaculus?'

'Two hundred for certain,' his clerk said. 'But there are also suggestions that the Numerus Defensorum are on the move from Braboniacum. The Numerus Exploratorum at Lavatris and the Numerus Directorum at Verteris could supply another two hundred between them.'

'But these are my men.' Outrage made Dulcitius's voice shake. 'He has taken my men.'

'Apparently the orders were issued in your name.'

'I'll have his head for this.'

'Yes, lord,' Senaculus said carefully, 'but perhaps we should be asking ourselves why Marcus Flavius Victor thinks he needs quite so many mounted troops? These soldiers are in addition to the three hundred he rode with from Hunnum, and those he added at Segedunum, and who knows where else along the line of the Wall. The Asturians at Cilurnum would add another three or four hundred to his strength if Canalius was foolish enough to part with them.'

Dulcitius made a rapid calculation and came to a result that rang a warning bell in his head. 'By now he may have as many as fifteen hundred horse. What could he need that many cavalry for?'

Senaculus shuffled through the scrolls on his desk until he found the report he wanted. 'One of our agents north of the Wall heard a rumour of some kind of meeting between a Roman officer and King Corvus of the Selgovae. Could that be of significance?'

'Corvus? From what I've heard of that unscrupulous barbarian anything is possible. Unless . . .'

'Yes, lord?'

Dulcitius was finding it difficult to breathe. 'Unless . . .' he choked, 'unless Victor has made common cause with our enemies. Look.' He dragged a long roll of linked papyrus from the shelf behind his desk. 'He has stripped the Wall of cavalry for perhaps half its length. The entire centre section is wide open to attack. How could I not have seen this before?' He pounded his fist against the desk and beads of sweat appeared on his forehead. 'If Corvus attacks now he could be halfway here by the time we heard about it.'

'Yes, but the infantry garrisons—'

'The infantry garrisons are static,' Dulcitius pointed out the obvious through clenched teeth. 'Their entire purpose is defence. They won't move against a powerful enemy force unless they can somehow combine. Look at the gap between Vindobala and Brocolitia, almost twelve miles.'

'But that still doesn't explain why he needs so many cavalry,' the clerk said. 'What does he gain by leaving Corvus free to ravage the northern settlements?'

Dulcitius stared at him. The answer was nothing. Therefore it was no answer at all. What was he missing? The clerk was right. This was not a question of what Corvus could gain, but of what Marcus Flavius Victor could gain. He studied the map again with new eyes.

'Christus save us.'

'What is it, lord?'

'All these years I have underestimated Victor's arrogance, ambition and greed. Truly he is his father's son.'

'Brenus?'

'Not Brenus, fool,' Dulcitius spat. 'Brenus was just a beast with a sword, little better than the barbarians beyond the Wall. A mind much more subtle spawned this. Magnus Maximus, the usurper, was our Lord of the Wall's natural father, as I should have remembered. I should have had Victor killed years ago when I had the chance.'

'But what is he doing?'

'Marcus Flavius Victor is bidding to become the King of all Britannia and I am all that stands in his way. Look again.' He traced the line of the Wall on the map. 'Here is the gap he has created. And here the lands of the Selgovae. Victor has stripped the Wall garrisons of any mobile force with the capability of filling the gap. But it is not just Corvus we must fear. To achieve his goal, Victor needs more than one ally.'

At last Senaculus saw it. The great amorphous mass of tribal settlements to the north of Corvus.

'The Picts,' he whispered. 'The Lord of the Wall has allied himself with the Picts, may Heaven preserve us.'

'Niall of the Nine Hostages has always been nothing more than a deceit; the magician's feather designed to draw the eye while the other hand is busy placing the dove, or in this case the dagger, in the silken cloth. It all makes sense. Now I understand why Victor urged me to bring in my outposts from the west and consolidate my strength here. See how he moves his troops from east to west, building up his strength every step of the way. Londinium is his goal. He believes we have no choice but to advance north to meet the Pictish attack, while he slithers down the coast under the protection of the mountains like the serpent he is.'

'But even with fifteen hundred riders, how can he possibly take Londinium, with its permanent garrison, great walls and towers?' the clerk asked.

Dulcitius remembered how Victor taunted him with a letter linking his sons to a conspirator – what was his name – yes, Gratianus, like the late emperor. He had dismissed that letter as a trick. But what if it was real? Victor had certainly known the name Gratianus. How could he have come into possession of such a message unless he had contact with the man who wrote it? These were days of increasing detachment from Rome. A prominent merchant could have the means and the contacts to pave the way to a takeover of power by someone with the military strength to enforce it. The Lord of the Wall might well be a brute, but he had the ability to be charming, persuasive or threatening as he chose. He was also a liar of enormous ability. He would use one or all of these attributes to coerce every garrison along the way into supporting him. And if that didn't work, he would simply buy them. Hadn't Dulcitius himself provided him with the means? By the time he reached Londinium his army could be two or three times the size.

'Shall I summon your commanders, lord?'

'Of course.' Dulcitius slapped the table. 'He believes I will have no option but to go north and face the Picts, but there are other possibilities. I can let them ravage what little there is to ravage and move west with the legion to meet him. The larger fortresses can look after themselves, the smaller would have to take their chances.' He turned back to the clerk. 'There is time yet, I believe, to make my decision.' With his finger he drew out three sides of a triangle on the map. 'Even with his cavalry, Marcus will take three days to reach Mamucium. The Sixth, on the other hand, can be there in one and a half. It is just a question of choosing where to meet him. I do believe I could have Victor's head within the week. For the moment we will consolidate all our forces here in Eboracum. Call in all our outposts.' He studied the map again. Was he missing something? It was possible. 'And tell tribune Geta to await my orders. I have a special job for him.'

'There is also something I neglected to mention, lord,' Senaculus said.

'Yes?'

'I have had word from no less than three sources that the Lord of the Wall may be dying. Some question of an old wound.'

Dulcitius smiled for the first time. 'Then perhaps God will intervene to save us the effort.'

DECAY

XXIX

Banna (Birdoswald)

Marcus shivered as a drop of rain fell from the seam of the tent and trickled down the back of his neck. His head was filled with the drumming rattle on the leather panels. Runnels of water gurgled and snaked their way across the turf floor despite the trenches his engineers had dug to channel the flood towards the stream a hundred paces down the slope. They'd chosen the position with the usual care. A Roman military camp must be easily defensible, as dry underfoot as humanly possible, and close to a stream large enough to water every inhabitant, whether human or horse. Yet a day earlier, with frost still dusting the sward, who could have foreseen this deluge that had turned the entire slope into a muddy swamp which grew more so with every tramping foot and passing minute?

Worse, the damp seemed to penetrate his very bones and seep into his soul so he found it difficult to breathe and struggled to control a dry, choking cough that racked his body. All this merely to reinforce the perception of his original mission. Banna itself, and neighbouring Camboglana to the west, were garrisoned by infantry units and of little genuine interest to him. He tried without success to make sense of the

213

returns and inventories the fort's commander had supplied as evidence of Banna's preparedness, then shook his head. The only thing that truly mattered was that he'd left Aesica with the cavalry contingent of the First Asturians. Another hundred and twenty precious riders added to his growing host.

Marcus pushed himself to his feet and his head began to spin; before he knew what was happening he was on his knees staring at the muddy grass. He tried to crawl to his cot, but all the strength had gone from his arms and legs. Christus, what was happening to him?

A gust of wind as the tent flap flew back and Valeria was crouched over him. 'Marcus? Luko!' she called, 'help me get the prefect onto his cot. Then find the *medicus* and get him here, quickly. Speak to no one.'

Rough hands lifted him by the shoulders and half carried, half dragged him to the cot. Someone pulled a blanket over him. He knew it was Valeria, but his whole world seemed to be hurtling past like a galloping horse and he couldn't focus on any single thing. The blanket made no difference; by now the cold was as much part of him as the blood in his veins.

A new voice, and he knew he should be worried when he heard something close to panic in Zeno's tone. 'Jesus, Mary and Joseph, I told him this could happen, why didn't the stupid bastard listen to me. We need to get him somewhere warm and dry before he rots away from the inside.'

Now, now, Zeno, his mind chided. Remember I'm your commanding officer. Valeria, tell him.

'He insisted on sleeping outside the fort walls. He wouldn't say why.'

'Well if we don't get him into Banna and a room with a fire, he'll be sleeping outside the walls for a lot longer than he reckoned, with six feet of damp earth to keep him company.'

Banna, what was it about Banna? Someone had warned him about Banna, but it was lost in that whirling vortex of his brain and he didn't have the strength to chase it down. Shivering. So cold. Now the spinning became too much and he felt hot bile rising in his throat. Something cawed like a carrion crow challenging a rival.

'Quick, help me get him on his side before he chokes on his own vomit.' More movement and a retching heave that eased whatever was happening inside him. 'Christus, my new boots.'

'If we move him into Banna the men will see how badly ill he is.'

'If we don't move him he'll die. Do you want that?'

'No.' For some reason the conviction in the word eased Marcus's mind, and the feeling spread to his sickness-ridden body. 'He may be the most devious, infuriating bastard south of the Wall, but he's still my brother.'

A different scent in his nostrils, not the mix of damp leather, wet grass and bog myrtle of the camp ground. Dry and musty, the bitter-sweet smell of decaying papyrus. He realized he'd been here before. He was in the guest quarters at Banna where Arelius Verinus, tribune of the First Dacians, kept his library. It had been two years ago and Arelius had loaned him his precious copy of Vegetius's *De Militari* which he'd never returned. For some reason that bothered him more than his condition. The damp chill he remembered still infused his inner body, but someone seemed to be roasting his flesh. A fire, of course they would have set a fire to warm him. Still, it wasn't unpleasant and he allowed himself to sink again, back into . . . panic.

Remember.

Fire and blood and death. A man who uses the loyalty of his soldiers to win himself a province and then an Empire.

'No.' A hand on his brow. 'Not me. Not me. Maximus.'

'Stay still, lord.' Zeno's comforting tone. He has something to say to Zeno, but he can't recall what it is. Perhaps it was: Am I dying?

If he was dying it would all have been for nothing, all his schemes and his stratagems, the lies and the intrigues, all the death and heart-ache he'd spread along the way, all the friends lost for ever. And worse. Panic replaced by terror now. He had left Britannia naked and helpless before the wrath of Briga and her Picts. He fought his way up from the

215

deep pit where whatever drugs Zeno administered had consigned him. He opened his eyes. Zeno was preparing something close by his side and Marcus's hand closed over his wrist like a claw.

'Valeria,' he whispered. 'Get me Valeria.'

Valeria's face swam into his vision. Had it been a minute or an hour?

'I should have known by now.' His voice was a wheezing croak.

'Lie back, brother,' she whispered. 'What should you have known?'

'There should have been a sign.'

'A sign of what?'

'You need to know it all.'

'Another time, Marcus. You are too sick.'

'No.' He forced himself up. 'You must know or it's all for nothing. Everything I have done is for one aim. If I die . . .'

'You're not going to die. Lie back and I will tell *you* what I already know. I know you have been gathering an army for some purpose. The Ala Herculaea arrived this afternoon from Epiacum. Another two hundred veteran cavalry ready to do the Lord of the Wall's bidding. We had messages today from two more units I knew nothing about . . .'

Marcus lay back and closed his eyes. So Julius Pastor, the Herculaea's commander, had answered his call. 'What messages?'

'The Numerus Exploratorum and the Numerus Directorum say they await your orders. Why did you deceive me, Marcus? Your own sister. Why didn't you trust me? Did you think I would try to stop you? Well you would have been right and now we can end the pretence. You thought you could use this fast-riding cavalry force of yours to move on Londinium, just as your father did.' Marcus lurched upwards, but she pushed him back on the bed. 'Yes, I know about Maximus. I've always known.' She shook her head. 'I understand why you would want to do that, brother. We are all sick of the corruption and neglect. The Empire is rotten to its very heart and Londinium, for all its riches, or perhaps because of them, is the pus at the heart of Britannia. If any man is capable of cleansing Britannia, it is you. But you can't do it alone. You have to make your peace with Dulcitius . . .'

If Marcus had the strength he would have risen and shaken her for harbouring such nonsense, but Valeria wasn't finished.

'I know you think the Picts won't attack until the spring, but you have opened the door to them. I won't allow you to risk the slaughter of our people and the burning of their farms and settlements because of your ambition, no matter how unselfish that ambition is. I will not let you risk civil war.'

Marcus listened, horrified, to his sister's monologue. Had his subterfuge been so effective that it now threatened to nullify his carefully assembled plans? If he couldn't find the energy Valeria would scatter all the precious building stones he had worked so hard to place in position. 'No,' he managed. 'You don't understand. It was all for Briga.'

'Queen Briga?'

'Some water please.' She nodded to someone out of sight and Zeno appeared with a cup. 'Raise me up,' Marcus demanded.

'I warned you that you were going to kill yourself, lord,' the *medicus* whispered as he placed a folded blanket under his shoulders.

'All for Briga,' Marcus repeated. 'I had word the Picts had a new ruler, and that they were building up their strength for an invasion in the coming spring.' He took a sip of the water. Every word was an effort, but he must tell the story. 'I only discovered it was a woman, and the calibre of that woman, when I met Corvus. The Picts could attack anywhere they chose and we would never have enough troops in one place to stop them. Our only hope was to encourage an attack on our terms. For the plan to work the Picts must be lured to attack before *they* are ready, and at a point where the route of their advance south would be enforced by the terrain.' A coughing fit interrupted his words, but he pushed away the restraining hands. 'No, I must finish this, even if it kills me. To achieve this I needed to take a risk. A very enormous risk. I knew Dulcitius would never countenance them, so he could not be allowed to know my plans. I would leave the gateway to Britannia unguarded. Not seem to be unguarded – the ruler I'd been warned of would never be deceived by mere trickery – but actually and entirely unguarded. So I stripped the central section of the Wall of all its mobile and most dangerous defenders. Now the gate is open and Briga is invited to walk through it into the field. But at the same time I have built up my own mobile forces so that I can be in a position to move in sufficient strength to stop her and destroy her army at a place of my own choosing.'

'Always meet your enemy on ground of your own choosing,' Valeria repeated her father Brenus's mantra. Yet Marcus sensed scepticism, and something very close to anger. 'But stripping the central section of the Wall of cavalry means you left Demetrius at Hunnum as a tasty morsel for the Picts to snap up on the way through, and the garrison at Corstopitum, perhaps those at Vindobala too. I would have believed much of you, Marcus, but not that you would sacrifice your friends for an opportunity at glory.'

'This is not about glory.' Valeria was not the only one who was angry now and anger gave him renewed strength. 'It is about saving Britannia and destroying the power of the Picts. No one will be sacrificed' – it wasn't quite true, the farmers and settlers living just to the south of the Wall would be fortunate to survive the Picts' initial surge, but that was a small price to pay – 'certainly not Demetrius. I gave him orders to retreat to Corstopitum, with Liberalis and the villagers of Hunnum, at the first sign of a Pictish scout. Arrius at Vindobala will join them. Briga will be carrying enough supplies not to worry about having to take Corstopitum. It is my calculation that she'll bypass it, especially if she sees it's strongly defended.'

'Let's be clear, brother, everything depends on your calculations.'

'Lord, you should rest now.'

'Enough of your mothering, Zeno, if you can't keep quiet leave us. And make sure you forget everything you've heard. Yes,' Marcus turned his attention back to Valeria. 'Everything depends on my calculations. There is an old saying "Time is my enemy's enemy", but that's not true in this case. Time is *my* enemy. I need to know exactly when Briga moves so I can be in place to meet her.'

'Meet her where?' Valeria demanded. 'And what if she doesn't move at all? Dulcitius will reach the same conclusion I did and he'll either come after you or inform the Emperor that you're a traitor.'

'I'll get to where, and as for Dulcitius he will have his part to play in this drama of ours.'

'Not ours, brother,' she snapped. 'Yours.'

'Very well, mine. Briga will want to take the bait because *she* believes precisely what you did.'

'If she's as clever as you say, she may not,' Valeria warned. 'Never underestimate a clever woman.'

'She'll believe it because she's been hearing the same tales from her spies. A different tale from every one. Apart from her most trusted sources, who will tell her what she believes to be, and what appears to be, the truth. That Marcus Flavius Victor is a traitor and enemy of Rome who plans to march on Londinium and take Britannia for himself.'

Valeria was quiet for a time and the only sound was the rasp of Marcus's laboured breathing.

'Why didn't you tell me this before, Marcus? Didn't you trust me?'

'Because I needed you to appear as confused as everyone else. There are spies among us, Valeria. Dulcitius has his spy, Briga certainly has hers. Zeno here may well have been sent here to spy for the Emperor —'

'But lord,' Zeno protested, 'he also sent an order suggesting you killed me. He is babbling, lady.'

'True, but think on it. A genuine *medicus*. Would I really decline the opportunity to add such a treasure to my regiment? And if I cut your throat as the Emperor urged, he would just have sent someone else. No, Valeria, if these spies had witnessed you actively supporting me with all your usual energy their masters would have no doubt that I was *up to something*. How much better to keep you wondering what that something was, and by extension them?'

'And what if I thought your plan was an act of egotistic madness that risked destroying all of Britannia for no good reason other than the glory of Marcus Flavius Victor?'

'Yes,' he admitted. 'What then?' He met her gaze and held it, an unsparing contest of will, or a search for a truth that would certainly be painful, possibly even deadly? They would never know the answer. He managed a smile. 'Now you know why we must leave for Petriana tomorrow, even if you have to tie me to the saddle. The die is thrown. There is no turning back now.'

'What do you hope to gain by visiting Petriana? Why not just turn south now?'

'Because I'm looking for a sign.'

XXX

A long night, tormented in mind, but the ravages of body soothed by whatever concoction the *medicus* had administered after his exhausting talk with Valeria. At one point Marcus distinctly heard Zeno telling him it could end now, all he had to do was ask. Ah, Zeno, my faithful accomplice, what would Valeria do to you if she knew you had been deliberately poisoning me for the last fifty miles to maintain the pretence of my near-death illness? This last crisis had no part in the plan and came very near to killing me, but I trust you to resurrect your Lord of the Wall. Was it worth the risk? Was it really necessary, this one deception among so many others? Who could tell? But Briga would undoubtedly fear the reputation of Marcus Flavius Victor, so any evidence of weakness in the man would only increase her confidence. He wanted her to feel confident.

Another presence, not so benevolent, but strangely he felt no fear. A hand on his brow to test the heat of his fever, a moment's hesitation before the prick of the knife point against the big artery in his throat. Was this the moment? Did it all end here in a warm bed in a musty room filled with decaying scrolls? It seemed not, for after a few heartbeats the knife was removed and the presence faded. Death did not require his company tonight.

He woke the next day with a starkly bright, low winter sun slanting in to illuminate the room so every colour seemed brighter and more vivid. Weakened, but not to the extent that he couldn't get out of bed. He put a hand to his throat. Had he dreamed it? He thought not and a tiny scratch provided evidence he was correct. He searched for any memory of a scent or any other hint that might identify the intruder but could find none. Someone from the fort, or from the column? An investigation might provide an answer, but he had no time for an investigation.

He dressed as quickly as his enfeebled state allowed and was pulling on his boots when Valeria burst through the door and marched to the open window. 'Is this the sign you were looking for, Marcus?'

He struggled to his feet and walked on hesitant legs to where she stood. The fort's guest room was on the first storey of the commander's house and the windows gave it a view across the barracks and store-houses and the north wall to the barbarian country beyond. 'Where?' he demanded.

'There,' she pointed. 'A little to the east of the gate tower.'

He looked again. On the rising ground beyond the Wall, perhaps five hundred paces from the fort, someone had set up a wooden cross. A chill ran through him as he recognized the object hanging from the horizontal beam.

'Well?'

'Make sure Janus goes nowhere near it. In fact make sure no one goes anywhere near it until I've had a chance to investigate.'

'You think it's Julius?'

'Wouldn't you?'

'I'm coming with you.'

'Suit yourself,' he sighed. 'It may not be pretty.'

It wasn't pretty.

They'd tortured him very thoroughly indeed before they'd killed him and nailed him to the cross. Most of his extremities had been removed, nose, ears, eyes and, of course, those parts that had made him a man. They must have left the tongue until last, because presumably the purpose of the torture was to make him reveal every-thing he knew. Briga would have known just how proud he'd been of that tongue. The rest, the burns and the bruises and the broken bones, would have been the prelude to let him know what was to come.

'It's not Julius.' Valeria didn't sound entirely certain.

'No, it's not.' Not Julius, but a message all the same.

'Do you know him?'

'No.' Another lie, but the spy would forgive him that, anonymity had been his way of life. He'd been so certain of his invulnerability. Had he been careless? Or betrayed? Perhaps he'd overstretched himself. Marcus tried to remember the dead man's part in the web he'd woven. He should have been with Corvus, not anywhere near the Pictish queen. None of that mattered now. What mattered was that Marcus had told him only what he'd needed to know. Nothing he'd screamed out would alter what Briga believed. Unless he'd been a better spy than Marcus gave him credit for? A pity. He'd genuinely liked the man. Now he would never see that farm in the hills south of Luguvalium.

Julius crouched in the shadow of the rampart and waited for his moment. Any encounter with the queen of the Picts must be approached with caution, and he preferred to make his move when her face took on a certain expression. It wasn't easy to detect, and to misread it might be fatal. Just a slight twitch of the lips, a faint, ethereal air of self-satisfied amusement, like a cat who'd just trapped a blackbird beneath its paws and was contemplating that first bite. Judge your moment poorly and you'd spend all day dying like that poor bastard yesterday. Julius was bare-chested in the Pictish fashion, wore his long hair in a topknot and carried the same axe he'd wielded in the raid at Barcum. He'd arrived at the camp with Coel's contingent and though his tattoos were of an unusual style no man would challenge him. He was a Pict among Picts, who spoke the Pictish tongue with the same melodic fluency as every warrior around him. This was far from his first visit to the Pictish camp. He'd long felt a oneness with his tribesfolk in the north and it was natural enough that he should slip away occasionally to mingle with them by their campfires. Far from condemning it, Marcus had encouraged him to test the mood of his enemies.

His first sight of Briga, well before she'd killed Lucti and replaced him as the Picts' supreme leader, had impressed him, and after watching her from afar it occurred to him that a closer relationship might be profitable. A risk, of course – he'd heard what Briga did to anyone who failed or betrayed her – but one he judged worth taking. And a risk too far, it appeared, when she'd ordered him strung up by the ankles beside a roaring fire, so close the flames singed his eyebrows and blistered the end of his nose. But he'd choked back his fears and laughed in the face of her threats and she'd liked that. She'd promised him land and riches if he was willing to provide information on the Lord of the Wall's activities. Since that's what he'd planned all along, he was happy to oblige her. He guessed the numbers who followed her must have more than doubled since that first meeting. Judging by some of the banners he'd seen as he approached the camp they were about to swell even further. What he was witnessing now explained their presence.

Corvus of the Selgovae, massive in his matted bearskin coat, swaggered forward through a crowd of warriors to meet the queen, paused just long enough to allow himself to believe he'd kept his self-respect and went down on one knee.

'Welcome, lord king.' Briga rose from her throne and held out a hand. Today the cloak was a bright, vibrant yellow and beneath it she wore a blouse and skirt of deep vermilion, belted at the waist with the largest silver chain Julius had ever seen. Together, the blouse and skirt combined to give her the appearance of a tall, flickering torch, enhanced by the starburst of lime-wash that surrounded her head. With a wary glance at Fenrir, Geri and Freki, who lay at her feet, Corvus took the outstretched fingers as he pulled himself to his feet, avoiding the piercing eyes in their dark band.

The Selgova ruler towered like a cliff of granite over the slim figure of the Pictish queen, but no man who saw the encounter could be in any doubt who was the leader and who the led. Corvus had faced a choice of sitting at Queen Briga's side and participating in the banquet she planned or being one of the morsels in the pot, and Corvus, for all his manly bluster, was no fool. 'I have summoned you here,' Briga continued, 'to take your place among my commanders and your brave warriors to be part of my host, what have you to say?'

Julius grinned as he saw the reply stick like a fish bone in proud Corvus's craw. It took three attempts before the bone became unstuck. 'I . . . I . . . I Corvus, king of the Selgovae, pledge my services to Briga, Brenine of the northern Pictish peoples, scourge of the cursed Romans and their southern puppets, protector of the weak, slayer of the unfaithful.'

Briga smiled and signalled to a bearded midget who stepped forward and opened the lid of a wooden box he carried. With a ceremonial flourish, she reached in and drew a golden torc from its depths, so large and magnificently worked that it drew a gasp from those who saw it. Corvus bowed his head almost to the waist and she placed the ring of gold around his broad neck.

'This is the mark of my favour,' Briga said. 'But you should know, Corvus of the Selgovae, that should you play me false I will take it back along with the head above it. I made the same vow to Luddoc of the Votadini not an hour since. Do you remember Lucti, Corvus?' Corvus nodded. 'Good.'

She raised her voice so that it carried across the wide bowl of the hilltop. 'Soon we will move south,' Briga said. 'Soon all of you will bathe in the blood of the Romans and their southerner allies. When will your warriors be ready to move, Corvus of the Selgovae?'

'We are ready now, Brenine, as you instructed. But surely we cannot march until after the spring planting?'

Briga laughed. 'By the time spring comes you will be drinking Roman wine from golden cups amid the ashes of Londinium with the sweet scent of rotting corpses in your nostrils. Soon, Corvus, perhaps within days.'

'If that is your will, Brenine, favoured of the gods.'

As if the words were a signal a figure on a shaggy pony appeared in the fortress gateway and rode to where Briga and Corvus stood. A murmur of surprise ran through the great throng on the hilltop as the cloaked and hooded rider approached the queen. Briga stood motionless as the hood was pulled back.

'A sign,' she cried. 'A sign from the Otherworld.'

'I have news for you, Brenine,' said Calista, keeper of Coventina's shrine. 'Britannia lies defenceless before the Queen of the Picts and the faithful who follow her. The gods have opened the gates and lured the Lord of the Wall south. The guards have abandoned their posts. The way is open.'

DUST

XXXI

Petriana (Stanwix, Carlisle)

Marcus's life changed for ever on the day Brenus rode from Petriana to his fate at Castra Exploratum. Two years later he was Lord of the Wall, in overall command of all the fortresses and soldiers from Luguvalium to Segedunum, and the son of the man who ruled all Britannia. He wanted to shout his new status from the walls of every fort, but Maximus counselled patience. Better for his son to make his own mark on the world than at the tail of his father's cloak. There was also the not unimportant obstacle that an obstinate few in Britannia had still to accept Maximus's elevation to the purple. He must consolidate his position as master of the province before he considered his next move.

'You will aid me best by holding the Wall and keeping the Picts quiet while I go about my business here,' he said. 'I would trust no other man to take command of my frontier forces.'

As Marcus carried out his father's bidding, disquieting rumours filtered from the south. Of villages and settlements ravaged, not by Saxons or Frisians, but by legionaries under the command of the new Emperor's officers. At first Marcus dismissed them as mere stories, but they became too persistent not to have some basis in fact. Detail emerged, of mass executions of those who wouldn't renounce Gratian, and entire communities of pagans burned alive in their homes. He'd written to Maximus to tell him of the rumoured atrocities, but the Emperor's clerks replied that there was no foundation to the accounts. Marcus should concern himself with the security of the Wall.

Marcus sent regular messages pleading to be allowed to take his place at his father's side. When would he ever be needed if not now, at the moment Maximus risked everything? But Maximus would not waver. His son's time would come. For now he needed a steady hand he could trust in Britannia. He was stripping the province of the Twenty-second and almost half the men of the Sixth, as well as the auxiliary garrisons of most of the forts of the interior. Dulcitius, who would also remain in the province, would require careful watching and Marcus should write regularly to update his father on the legate's actions.

From that point, news of the Emperor's progress reached the frontier only in snatches. Maximus had landed safely with his army in Gaul. There had been a great battle near Lutetia Parisiorum and Gratian was defeated. A month later Gratian was dead and Magnus Maximus unstoppable as he marched on Rome. Then came the first setback. Theodosius in Constantinopolis let it be known he supported Gratian's half-brother and any attack on Valentinian would be regarded as an attack on himself. Thwarted for the moment, Maximus halted his army on Valentinian's doorstep at Mediolanum and waited. His patience was rewarded. Soon, Theodosius must have sent emissaries because within six months Maximus was hailed Augustus and recognized as Valentinian's co-Emperor in the West. Meanwhile, Marcus's letters to his father were acknowledged in a clerkly hand, but never fully answered.

He had waited impatiently for the message that would summon him to Augusta Treverorum in Gaul, where Maximus set up his capital. Dreamed of the day he would take his place at his father's side, command his armies and lead them to victory. Who knew what glory awaited the son of the Emperor Flavius Magnus Maximus Augustus?

In the dream his father would place the purple on his shoulders and name him his heir, for the day when he could no longer rule himself.

The message never came.

For a time Maximus reigned virtually unchallenged, but suddenly the news from Gaul took on a new and worrying tone. Maximus had made enemies as a result of his harshness against holy men he regarded as heretics. A famous bishop had been accused of making magic and executed. Maximus's young co-Emperor Valentinian, now sixteen, was plotting against him. Maximus must have reacted to the threat, because a year later Theodosius felt obliged to join Valentinian for the invasion of his co-Emperor's territory. Now it was Maximus on the run, his armies brought to battle, his generals defeated and their Emperor forced into hiding. Exposed. Executed. His father was dead.

And so was his son, Flavius Victor.

Marcus's mind reeled from the shock of it. A brother? And not just a brother. Flavius Victor had been executed because he was Maximus's heir. He had stood in Marcus's rightful place at his father's side and been decorated with the honours Marcus should have worn. And his reward had been the strangling rope.

For a time, Marcus was left wondering if that was also to be his fate. Yet the anonymity he'd so despised proved to be his salvation. It was as if he'd never been born. Marcus came to believe his father had deliberately kept his existence a secret to save his life.

Petriana had once been the mightiest stronghold on the Wall, the great bastion of the western ramparts, but the rise of nearby Luguvalium as an administrative and military centre had first diminished its importance, then nullified it altogether. It had originally been named Uxelodunum – the High Fort – but its garrison, the eight hundred-strong cavalry wing Ala Petriana, had been in residence for so long they eventually gave their name to the fort itself. Half a day's ride from Banna, it stood on a steep rise in the gentle crook of the Itouna river, where Ninian claimed to have been baptized, perhaps twelve miles

from the coast and the Wall's sea defences. If the purpose of his expedition had been as he'd originally claimed, Marcus would naturally have
continued to Luguvalium, clearly visible across the river. The *centurio
regionarius* there, the officer who had overall responsibility for the
coastal forts, would have had reports of Marcus's approach and be
wondering why he'd halted at the abandoned fort. Marcus had his own
reasons for staying away. They would sleep here among the ruins
where the man he'd called father had set out to fight his final battle.

Marcus still felt weak from the fever that felled him at Banna, but
Zeno had produced a tonic which slowly restored his strength. His
mind remained sharp and it was his mind that plagued him with
doubt. Despite all his efforts he'd never quite managed to unmask
Dulcitius's spy. Valeria had taken all the morsels of information he'd
allowed to become known and concluded Marcus was preparing to
march on Londinium and take Britannia for himself. If Dulcitius's
agent was as well placed as he suspected, how could the *dux
Britanniarum* come to anything but the same conclusion? The question now was what Dulcitius would do about it. As Marcus saw it, the
other man was faced with three choices. He could march north immediately with the Sixth to meet Briga's expected invasion. In this scenario
the likely outcome was that he'd be hugely outnumbered and, unless
he was capable of some feat of generalship he'd never shown in the
past, annihilated. Alternatively, he could take the legion west to where
the Numerus Exploratorum and Numerus Directorum waited for
Marcus's orders, persuade them to join him, and then march to intercept Marcus. Either of these movements paved the way to a potential
disaster. For Marcus's great plan to work, Dulcitius had to stay precisely where he was until the last moment.

Frustration chewed at his soul like a hungry rat. If Briga didn't take
the bait he was finished. Dulcitius would destroy him. Unless . . .

No, he couldn't even think that. Not yet.

She must take the bait. He'd expected confirmation at Banna; instead
Briga had sent him the tortured corpse. Had he misread the message?
He'd believed it was a simple confirmation that his agent had been

unmasked. What if it was actually the death of his plans and his hopes? If Briga had read his mind, how simple would it be to send a force to contain him while her warriors ravaged all of Britannia? Marcus Flavius Victor, a gambler and a fool who'd allowed himself to be outwitted by a barbarian: a Roman province destroyed. A strangling rope would be the best of it, if the shame and ignominy didn't kill him first.

All he could do was wait. And hope.

To pass the time, he called his senior commanders to join him at a feast amid the ruins of Petriana. Faithful Caradoc, Janus, still bemused and concerned at his brother's disappearance, Sempronius, the young Carvetius who led the Second Asturians, Julius Pastor of the Ala Herculaea, and the tribunes of the lesser units. Valeria knew she would have been welcome, but she'd been watching her brother closely and had a premonition of what might occur. Luko, Ninian and six of their comrades stood watch in the shadows outside the circle of firelight, silhouetted by torches that had been set in the crumbling walls of what had once been the *principia*.

It was a simple enough affair: fresh venison flushed from the woods along the line of the march, oysters carried in barrels of salt water on the supply wagons, cured pork, dried fish, and a dish of eggs. Marcus had ordered a double ration of wine for the men and he urged his officers to indulge themselves from the jugs liberally distributed by the servants.

'Enjoy this night, because it might be the last on which we can feast so well,' he told them. 'When we next move, we may have to do so at speed and there will be no time for ceremony.'

This brought some curious glances. By now every one of them must be aware Marcus's expedition was much more than an inspection tour, but they were soldiers, used to hard service and unheralded changes of course. None had dared, or cared, to question their commander's intent. But here was evidence the uncertainty was coming to an end. To what purpose? Why had the Lord of the Wall gathered together such an enormous assembly of horse soldiers? They'd all heard the rumours about a possible assault on the north, or an ambush on an

Irish pirate, or an incursion against the Novantae in the west. Marcus understood their hunger for certainty, but for now he didn't choose to indulge it. They would know in good time. When he knew himself.

'If you had a mind to do it,' Sempronius laughed, a combination of drink and tiredness making him more carefree than usual, 'with this number of horse and the quality of the men who mount them you could take all of Britannia. We'd follow you through the very gates of Hades, lord.'

A murmur of approval told Marcus that Sempronius wasn't the only officer who'd come to the conclusion. He grunted what might have been his appreciation and poured another cup of wine. 'Sing us the song of Brenus,' he called to Caradoc. The veteran only stared at him. His guests sensed a change in atmosphere, but Marcus was oblivious to it. He was aware that his weakness seemed to have made the wine more potent than usual. A sunsprite danced in his head and his confidence in the success of his enterprise increased with every swallow. 'Sing, old man,' he roared. 'Or have you forgotten the words?'

'I have not forgotten the words,' Caradoc glared.

He cleared his throat and began a melodic, low-pitched chant that picked up the rhythm of the verse as the hooves of a horse increase in tempo from a trot to a canter, a canter to a gallop. Individual words echoed from the ancient walls as clear and sharp as if they'd been etched in marble. The faces of the young men around the fire turned grave as they understood the song's message, but their eyes shone bright with pride.

'A mighty man, his years well spent
Once sat among us
His valour and his fame
Familiar as his glorious name
Faster to the fight than to the feast
Quicker to the raid than to the wake
Wielder of blades, Maker of widows
Comrade to all was mighty Brenus.'

234

Valeria appeared from among the ruins and hung back unnoticed amid the flickering shadows, staring at her brother as if she was trying to read his mind.

A cry that might have been joy or lament and Luko took up the second verse from the shadows.

'Did Brenus shrink when others flinched?
Not he, beloved of the Brigantes
Pictish blood it must be shed
This night beyond the Wall
Lucti awaits with shining sword
Brave Berth with raisèd spear
Invincible Brude that giant man
Blasts out his mighty roar
No honours today for the kings of the Picts,
Nor glory ever more
It's the will of the gods
They must follow their fates
To the halls of Beli Mawr.'

There was more. Brenus's plea to his Roman commanders for more troops. Their refusal. His march through the darkness to seek out his hereditary enemies, men of great valour whose deeds he recalled along the way. The endless wait in the darkness. The flickering torches in the distance. Betrayal and ambush. Marcus was aware of a disturbance somewhere close by, but he was so mesmerized by the elegy to Brenus he barely registered it.

'To me, my horse lords
To me, my warrior heroes
What is life to men like us
When glory calls our name
Hold steady now and fear no foe
To flinch will bring us shame

A final charge
A final blow
A reddened blade
Eternal rest beneath the shade.'

As the words pulsed through his mind, Marcus rode at his father's side. He was there for that last charge that broke the enemy's line. The savage butchery that held the gap open so that his warriors might escape to fight again. He cried as the sword pierced Brenus beneath the right arm. Felt the flicker of his final heartbeat.

'Marcus?' He looked up, bewildered, into Valeria's concerned eyes. Another figure hovered behind her in the distinctive yellow cloak of an Imperial messenger. 'From Dulcitius.'

XXXII

It was as if an icy hand clutched his heart. He stared at the courier, thinking that if he concentrated hard enough the spectre might disappear. But the messenger remained. A young man, weary and travel-stained, nervous – he must be aware of the contents of the polished leather scroll case he clutched in his right hand – but resolute. Marcus struggled to his feet, spilling wine from his cup as he rose. 'You have a message for me?' A fool's question and one that brought a blink of surprise from Valeria.

The courier stepped forward and placed the scroll case in Marcus's hand. Two leather straps and buckles held it closed and a wax seal impressed with the *dux Britanniarum*'s symbol of a fist holding a sword showed it hadn't been opened. 'I am to stay until an answer is composed, if there is one.'

'Get him food and drink,' Marcus signalled to Ninian. And more quietly, 'Make sure he doesn't leave without my say so.' He reached to break the seal, but Valeria placed a warning hand on his arm. Of course . . . 'If you will excuse us,' he bowed to his officers. 'Imperial business. Please continue with the feast.'

He walked into the darkness and Valeria plucked a torch from the wall as she followed him. When they were in the roadway outside the building, Marcus worked at the fastenings and broke the seal. Valeria held the torch steady as he unrolled the parchment scroll and he peered at the contents.

'Christus,' he whispered.

'Dulcitius has named you as a traitor to Rome?'

'You knew?'

'I guessed,' she corrected him. 'He's not as foolish as you think, Marcus. He knows he cannot move against you until he has condemned you.'

'I'm to hand myself into the custody of the *centurio regionarius* at Luguvalium, who will provide me with an escort to Eboracum, where Marcus Flavius Victor will face trial for treason, mutiny, encouraging insurrection, colluding with the enemy and betrayal of the Emperor's trust. The only thing he's missed out is that I eat Christian babies and drink the blood of virgins.' He stared at his sister. 'He means to kill me.'

'There's still a chance,' she urged him. 'Go with the courier. Ride through the night and tell Dulcitius your *real* plan. Beg his forgiveness for not making him part of it, but persuade him that it can still work.'

'You don't understand.' He could feel the heat building in his head, but he tried to keep his voice steady. 'There is no *real* plan. Not until Briga makes her move. Without Briga he can prove each and every one of those charges he's laid against me.'

'Then what?' she demanded. 'Will you hand yourself over to Emeritus at Luguvalium? All you would be doing is delaying the inevitable. Run? Where to? Seek sanctuary in Britannia and Dulcitius will hunt you down. If you managed to reach Gaul you'd be condemned out of your own mouth the first time you were stopped at a *mansio*. The only place to escape Rome is to go north, and I doubt you can depend on much comfort from the Picts.' He imagined he could see the agile mind working away behind the dark eyes. 'There is one possibility,' she said quietly.

'Yes.' Had she seen it?

'We could take ship to Saxonia. Just you, I and Leof, and seek out little Bren.'

He pretended to consider the notion for a moment. 'There is another way.'

She shook her head. 'No.'

'Does honour and reputation mean nothing to you?' The harsh voice came from the doorway behind them. Caradoc stepped into the torchlight. 'I've watched him every step of the way as he blundered into this foolishness.' He directed the words at Valeria. 'It has been festering in his mind for near a year. Do you really believe Britannia will fall into your hands like a ripe plum? Do you think Dulcitius and the Sixth will be frightened of a few hundred miserable horse soldiers, or that the people of Londinium will be impressed by them?'

'He's right, Marcus.'

'No. He's an old fool who never learned to keep his mouth shut.'

'They will eat you alive,' Caradoc persisted. 'And even if they don't, men will sing of you, not as a hero like Brenus, but as a traitor, a usurper and an arrogant fool. Just like your father.'

'My father was a great Emperor.' Marcus fought the urge to take the older man by the throat. 'He won Britannia, and Gaul, and he would have won Rome if he had not been betrayed. He would have made the Empire one again and driven back the Goths and their German allies. If Magnus Maximus was still Emperor he would have sent me an army and I would have pushed the Picts back into the northern sea and all of this island would have been his . . .'

'Your father used your mother, he used Brenus and he used you. He didn't give a dog's turd about Britannia except as a convenient stepping-stone to the purple. He stripped this island's defences bare and his arrogance and his greed would have handed it all to the Picts if it hadn't been for you and Dulcitius. You saved Britannia from the Picts, Marcus, not your father. Have you ever asked yourself why he didn't take you with him?'

'Because he trusted me to hold the Wall, and that's what I did.'

'No, it was because you were an embarrassment to him. He had a Roman son, what did he need of a Brigantian stable boy who thought the ability to read a sentence in Greek and count more than ten made him an aristocrat?'

'No, Marcus!'

Marcus didn't even know the dagger was in his hand until the point was at Caradoc's throat.

'You would kill me then, rather than acknowledge the truth?' In his anger Caradoc barely registered the sting of the blade. 'Truly you are your father's son. Greed and ambition drive you to take Britannia for yourself, and what then? Will you be content or will you also be blinded by the glitter of an Emperor's gold wreath of laurel? Will you march on Rome and end your days in a damp Gaulish cell listening for the footsteps of the executioner bringing your strangling rope? Perhaps you will. After all you even abandoned your own son to the Saxons.'

One push. One push was all it would take. 'Give me a single reason why I shouldn't kill you, old man?'

Caradoc shrugged, wincing as the point dug a little deeper into his throat. 'I didn't kill you when I had the chance.'

'So it was you.' Marcus remembered the night in Banna during his delirium. The voice in his ear and the point of the dagger pricking his throat. Realization slowly dawned on him. 'You've been Dulcitius's spy all along.'

'What was I to do?' Caradoc was careful to avoid Valeria's eye. 'I could not just stand back and watch you destroy, not just your reputation, but your father's.'

'You despised Maximus.'

'Not Maximus, fool. Brenus.'

Marcus took a step back and withdrew the knife from Caradoc's throat. 'Brenus? Then why would you work for Dulcitius when Dulcitius betrayed Brenus?'

'Dulcitius didn't betray Brenus, Maximus did.'

In the long silence that followed Marcus tried to reconcile what he knew with what he'd just been told. He turned to Valeria seeking help, but she only stared back at him. 'How?' he said. 'Why?'

'Brenus knew what Maximus intended, just as I knew what you intended—'

Valeria would have intervened, but Marcus held up a hand. 'Let him speak.'

'He believed he'd persuaded Maximus to abandon his plans to take Britannia, but Maximus was only biding his time. I heard him discussing it with General Andragathius not a mile from here. If Brenus would not support them, he must be removed. I told your father, but he wouldn't listen. He placed too much value on Maximus's honour. When Brenus argued for an attack on the Picts at Castra Exploratum, Maximus saw his opportunity. I think Brenus knew he would die that night.'

'Why didn't you tell me?'

'Would you have believed me if I had?'

The answer was no.

'You need to tell him, Marcus,' Valeria said.

'Tell him what?' Caradoc looked from the one to the other.

Marcus shook his head. 'No, it's too soon. Keep him from the others. I'll decide what to do with him in the morning.'

'Whatever happens this is no time for division, Marcus,' she warned him. 'Or for lashing out in anger. Even if Maximus did kill Brenus it changes nothing. I don't remember Brenus as a father, only as an officer. Yes,' she said with a flourish of her arm at the armour she wore, 'he created this, but he did not create me. That was mother, and the brother who loved and cared for me. Who picked me up when I fell from the apple tree and saved me from the river when I thought I could swim. Brenus is just an indistinct face, like a wall painting seen through a veil. And what was Maximus to you, brother? Caradoc is right. He could have recognized you at any point. Instead he left you in Britannia while he went in search of an Empire with the boy he did call son. And when he did win the great prize, what did he do? He left you here to rot . . .'

'I—'

Valeria put a hand to her brother's lips.

'But Caradoc is wrong about one thing. You are not your father's son. You are your own man, and I do not believe for a single moment that you are motivated by ambition or greed. Oh,' she puffed out her cheeks, 'you can be arrogant and insufferable and pig-headed, but when you talk of taking Britannia I know that you are only doing what you believe is right. If that is your decision I will ride at your side, and if you will it, I believe the old man will, too, once he knows the whole story. But for now?'

'For now we wait.'

'We wait and we pray.'

'And Valeria . . .'

'Yes?'

'If we get out of this alive, I swear by my immortal soul that one day we will go to Saxonia. We will find Bren. And we will free him.'

XXXIII

Was it true? Was everything he believed a lie? Had the life of Marcus Flavius Victor, Lord of the Wall, been nothing but an invention? A self-indulgent illusion he had created to protect himself from the reality that, whatever the accident of his birth, he had always tried to live up to the values of the wrong father? Caradoc, God rot his soul, had opened his eyes. Magnus Maximus had been like the butterflies he'd chased through the meadows as a child, a wisp darting here and there, sometimes golden, sometimes fiery, sometimes saintly white, but always just beyond his reach. Maximus had been part of *his* life, but he had never, and would never have had, any part to play in his father's. Nothing would change that. It was almost laughable. He had dreamed of the purple, and now the only future he could hope for was to avoid the scarlet reality of a cut throat. Worse, he had placed the men he led and everything he loved in peril. And all he could do was wait, utterly helpless, the plaything of decisions being made beyond his reach and beyond his sway.

It all depended on Briga. If Briga moved south, everything would fall into place. That still might mean he would lead every man in the cavalry camps around Petriana to their deaths, but at least they would be dying for a purpose. But what if Briga didn't take the bait?

In that case, he reasoned, he probably faced two choices. Valeria had meant well, but he would not run merely to delay the inevitable. No, he must either fall on his sword and save what remained of his honour and his command. Or he must accept the gift the Fates seemed to be conspiring to present to him. Londinium. Britannia. And who knew what happened next. Maximus had decided he could not hold Britannia without holding Gaul, and he couldn't hold Gaul without Italia. Would his son be any different?

Marcus hadn't been quite as open with Valeria as she believed. This had always been a possibility he'd planned for, though he'd never expected to have to use that part of the plan. Caradoc was right, Londinium would be a tough nut to crack with, as the veteran so rightly pointed out, a few hundred miserable horse soldiers. To that end, Marcus had been in secret correspondence with certain important city merchants, and through them the high-ranking officials on the *ordo*. These men controlled the local militia and the public services and claimed great influence over the military commander. They resented the Imperial officials who lorded it over them from the palace by the river, imposed rules that restricted their trade, and taxes that reduced their profits, and all with little or no return from Rome. If a certain set of circumstances combined, they had agreed to open the gates to Marcus Flavius Victor and hail him as their saviour. If Briga failed him, that was the route he resolved to take.

But to make the final decision he had to have information.

Ninian entered the tent with a set of fresh ration returns. 'What have you done with the courier?' he asked the former priest.

'He's in the first tent inside the gate. But he's getting a bit restive.'

'Well he won't be going anywhere soon. Tell him I'm still working on my reply to Dulcitius.'

For the fourth time that morning he climbed the stairs of the surviving northern gate tower and gazed out over the landscape of marsh and meadow to the north. Senecio was taking a turn on guard, crouched beneath the remains of the parapet away from the cutting north wind. 'Have you seen anything?'

'It would help if I knew what I was looking for, lord.' The African blew on his hands and rubbed them together to warm them.

'You'll know when you see it.'

'And it will definitely be in the north?'

'More likely east of north.' Marcus gave his voice a confidence he didn't feel. What if it never came at all? He stayed in the tower staring at the distant horizon till his eyes began to blur.

'How do you feel today?' Zeno was waiting for him when he returned to his tent among the ruins.

'As if a bull has stamped on my head.' Marcus ran his hands across his scalp. 'What was in that concoction you gave me?'

'I should have warned you that the potion doesn't mix well with wine, lord.' The *medicus* drew back Marcus's tunic to study the wound in his chest.

'But it escaped your attention?'

'Indeed, lord. But may I congratulate you on a remarkable recovery. Since we stopped the hellebore treatment your body heals like the tender flesh of a man in the first flush of youth.'

'Did you get everything you wanted in Luguvalium?'

'I couldn't have done better if old Asclepius had supplied me himself.' Zeno grinned. 'But the quartermaster said *Centurio* Emeritus was surprised you hadn't paid him a visit?'

'Wasn't Asclepius a pagan god?' Marcus ignored the hint of a question in the Greek's last statement.

'He was, lord, but in the world of medicine you take help from wherever it is offered.'

'Well, Zeno,' Marcus said, 'I have a feeling that you're going to need all the help you can get. If you take a walk down to the wagon park by the river you'll find two hundred mules that the Ala Herculaea very kindly collected for me. When we leave here we'll be travelling fast so there will be no wagons. Take as many men as you need and load twenty mules up with every bandage, poultice and potion you have.'

Zeno stared at him. 'Are we expecting plague and pestilence, lord?'

'No, *medicus*,' Marcus said with grave formality, 'you should do everything you can to prepare for war.'

Valeria burst into the tent less than an hour later. 'So your mind is made up? You've told Zeno to prepare for war?'

Marcus packed the last of his personal equipment in his saddle bags. 'Whatever happens that's what we're going to get, so yes.'

'The only thing that awaits you in Londinium, Marcus, is death.'

'Perhaps,' he acknowledged, 'but forward is the only way I know. I can't go back, Valeria. I can't run. No more than you could.'

'Don't make me part of your absurd schemes.' She shook her head. 'I follow you because I have to, not because I want to.'

'Is everything ready?'

'The column is waiting for your order, but we can't keep them in their ranks all day.'

'An hour,' he said. 'If we hear nothing in one hour we begin the march south for Londinium and we don't look back.'

Marcus stood outside the southern gate of Petriana's ruins and watched the sun inch its way across a sky of pristine egg-shell blue. On the flat ground beside the river his haphazardly gathered regiments stood by their mounts in neat squares waiting for their orders to mount. The Ala Sabiniana, three hundred strong, Sempronius's Second Asturians, of similar numbers and hardened now by their long days in the saddle, the Ala Herculaea recovered from their ride from Epiacum, and four squadrons each of the Fourth Lingonum, Fourth Gauls and Aesica's First Asturians. A disordered mass of shaggy-coated riders already in the saddle brought a wry smile to his face despite his troubles. Ramios's Germans, who had proved they could ride as well as fight. Close to fifteen hundred of the finest cavalry soldiers in the world and all ready for his command. He knew he should make a decision now, but when it came to it he found himself gripped by the same paralysis he'd scorned in so many others. Once given, the order couldn't be reversed and at the speed he intended to travel the chances of word reaching him on the march were minimal.

246

He could feel the others watching him. Valeria would follow him in the name of their shared bloodline, Luko, out of blind faith, Caradoc, forgiven for now, to atone for his lack of trust in his lord, and Janus, kept close since the loss of his brother, purely for the love of a fight. He glanced at the sun and let out a long, shuddering breath. It must be now.

He opened his mouth to give the order.

'Lord,' a voice cried urgently from the top of the crumbling ramparts. Senecio. 'Lord, you must see this.'

Marcus ran back through the gates. Senecio pointed to the northern wall and he dashed through the broken-down barrack blocks and up the steps with Valeria in his wake. Nothing to the north. He turned his attention to east of north. Janus appeared beside him and saw it first. 'There.' His shout faded to a whisper: 'It can't be . . .'

Marcus saw him now. A shambling figure leading a lame horse at a half-run emerged from a fold in the ground about five hundred paces away. 'No,' he called a warning. But Janus was already down the stairway and tearing at the timbers of the gate.

'Bring Storm,' Marcus ordered Luko. Valeria called for her horse. By the time their mounts arrived Janus had almost reached the stumbling figure and as Marcus mounted he saw the young Pict take the other man in his arms. Two heartbeats later he launched into an enormous head butt and the pair fell struggling to the ground. Marcus spurred Storm towards the two men and leapt from his horse to drag the wrestling figures apart.

'You bastard,' Janus spat at the man below him.

'Hello, lord.' Julius's cocky grin was slightly marred by the swelling above his right eye.

'What's going on, Marcus?' Valeria demanded.

'Where have you been?' Marcus growled. 'I expected you two days ago.'

'What?' Janus stared at him.

'Our lady friend was enjoying my company so much I had trouble getting away.' Julius ignored his brother's gasp of astonishment and struggled to his feet. 'I had to wait until her attention was elsewhere and make a run for it.' He patted his horse's flank. 'I nearly rode this poor beast into the ground and he went lame on me an hour ago. It was touch and go who was carrying who by the end.' The smile grew wider and Marcus felt a shiver run down his spine. 'She did it, lord. She took the bait.'

XXXIV

It was a moment before Marcus could breathe.

'Stand the men down,' he told Valeria. 'And have the senior officers gather in the *principia*. Your brother has done us a great service, Janus, you owe him an apology, but perhaps he'll settle for one decent swing at you?' The brothers grinned at each other. 'Julius, you will take command of the First squadron.' He heard Caradoc's hiss of disappointment. 'Decurion Caradoc will be joining my command group.' He turned back to Valeria, forestalling the question that was already on her lips. 'I'll need him because I have a special job for you. Come, we have much to do and not enough time to do it.'

They gathered in the ruins of the *principia*. Twenty men – the regimental commanders younger than the veterans who led their squadrons – with their pot helmets held under their arms, arrayed in a circle around Marcus, who crouched over a patch of earth in the centre of what had been the courtyard. Ramios stood out among the shining armour in his tattered leather jerkin.

'You believed you were to follow me to Londinium, plunder and glory.' Marcus smiled and let his gaze slide over the ring of men. 'And I thank you for your unquestioning loyalty. However, it turns out I have a much more entertaining mission for you. You will have noticed that our progress over the past three weeks has been somewhat ponderous and my dispositions sometimes puzzling . . .'

'Puzzling?' Sempronius's deputy grunted. 'We thought you'd gone off your head.'

'Well,' Marcus waited until the laughter had subsided, 'it turns out all the diversions, the odd additions to our numbers, and the enemies I've made along the way, have had a purpose. By the next full moon every man in this room will either be a hero . . . or dead.' That quietened them. 'Comrades, we are going to destroy the Picts, once and for all.'

'And how are we going to do that?' The unexpectedly soft voice belonged to Valeria.

'Like this.' He drew his dagger from his belt and drew a line in the dirt. 'Our Wall,' he said, 'and beyond it,' he scratched a circle above the line, 'the Picts, the enemy. Like you, the Pictish queen believes that I have ambitions far above my status. Her spies whisper that the Lord of the Wall has stripped the garrisons of their finest soldiers and the way south lies open, between Cilurnum, here, and Vindobala, here; and that he means to march on Londinium.' He allowed time for the import of his words to be grasped. 'This is all true, apart from the last,' he continued. 'But it is also what I wanted Queen Briga to believe. I too have my spies, and those spies tell me that Queen Briga will soon march from her viper's nest in the hills and will cross the Wall within a week, here,' he stabbed the dagger into the earth, 'somewhere near Corstopitum.'

'That means we have left our comrades garrisoning those forts to die.' Sempronius didn't like it and he didn't care who knew it. 'She will destroy every stronghold that stands in her way.'

'No,' Marcus assured him. 'Briga is not interested in burning forts. She has promised her people plunder and riches, and plunder and riches lie in the south. She is well enough supplied, for now. Corstopitum and Cilurnum have nothing she needs and by the time she reaches the Wall their garrisons will have been strengthened beyond measure. She will bypass them' – he exchanged a glance with

Valeria, who knew how optimistic the hope was, then picked up the dagger and drew a line through the Wall and deep into the interior of Britannia – 'and be drawn towards the glitter of gold. The towns of southern Britannia and their treasures lie defenceless before her, unless . . .'

'Unless we stop her.'

'Yes, sister. Unless we stop her.'

'Which brings us back to my original question. How?'

'Briga's Picts are mainly infantry.' Marcus met their eyes as he spoke. 'They can march perhaps fifteen miles a day at most, but probably many fewer. We are cavalry and if I will it, we can cover three or four times that distance—'

'And kill our horses,' said Julius Pastor, commander of First Herculaea.

'What does it matter if we get to kill Picts?' The guttural Latin of Ramios sounded like a challenge and Marcus moved swiftly to head off any reply.

'I hope it will not come to that,' he said. 'We are here. This,' he drew a line parallel to the Pictish advance, 'is the spine of Britannia, the mountains which Briga will believe protect her right flank. What she doesn't know is that they will also cover us as we ride south to here, where we turn east, through the Verteris Gap, to Lavatris, then north to intercept the Pictish advance.'

'Where?' The question was on every man's lips, but it was Valeria, once more, who asked it.

'Longovicium.' The name drew a murmur from the assembled soldiers. Most of them knew the infantry fortress on the Great North Road between Eboracum and Corstopitum. Marcus's eyes gleamed. 'Briga will avoid the coast where our garrisons are strongest and hug the mountains. You've all travelled these hills and valleys. Every hump and hollow in the terrain will combine to bring her to us at Longovicium.' It was by no means a certainty, but he had to believe that. 'And at Longovicium we will stop her,' he stabbed the dagger into the earth with savage force, 'and destroy her.'

251

'How many Picts do we expect to meet?' Someone asked the question he'd hoped to avoid for a while yet.

'Julius?'

'Briga's warriors alone number seven thousand, with more joining her from north of the Bodotria every day. Corvus, the oath-breaking bastard, has promised two thousand spears. Luddoc of the northern Votadini will bring three thousand, including five hundred horse, and his southern cousin Coel –'

'So much for your diplomacy, brother,' Valeria murmured.

'– the same, though these last three will need to strip every farm of men between fourteen and fifty to fill their ranks. Expect fifteen thousand all told, but it could be more. There are rumours that the Damnonii are also ready to join her.'

'It would be easier if we invade Pictland and leave them to get on with plundering Britannia,' Janus laughed.

'Fifteen hundred against fifteen thousand.' Sempronius shook his head. 'With the greatest respect, you are a fine soldier, lord, and the men who ride with us are Britannia's best, but even you cannot defeat those odds.'

'Not fifteen hundred, Sempronius, more like eighteen hundred by the time we reach Longovicium.' Marcus held his gaze. 'We'll be picking up the mounted elements of the Numerus Defensorum at Braboniacum, and others along the way, a hundred more at least from the Numerus Directorum at Verteris, and the same for the Numerus Exploratorum at Lavatris. And you're forgetting the Sixth legion at Eboracum. If we can combine with the Sixth, the infantry will pin the Picts in place and the cavalry will be the blade that carves them up. You heard Julius. Many of those we face will not be warriors, but old men and farmers. Believe me, we can win, and that is what you must all convince your men. We can win and we will win.'

'For Rome!' Sempronius's response was echoed by the circle of men. Marcus shook his head.

'Not for Rome,' he said. 'We do this for Britannia. So our wives can sleep safe in their beds and our children can grow up without having to fear the beasts from the north. We'll rest the men and the horses tonight, but be ready to be in the saddle at first light.' He dismissed the officers and turned to Caradoc. 'Something's troubling you, old man. You're too quiet.'

'I was just wondering if you haven't been too clever for your own good, lord.' Caradoc, uncharacteristically hesitant, rubbed the scratch on his throat where Marcus's dagger had left its mark. 'What makes you think the Sixth legion will rush to join you? The message from Dulcitius shows he gobbled up that story you concocted the way a blackbird swallows a big old worm. He's going to take an awful lot of convincing to change his mind.'

'Oddly enough,' Valeria said, 'I was thinking the same thing.'

'Good,' Marcus smiled. 'Because you're the one who's going to do the convincing.'

'What?'

'It makes sense, sister,' Marcus said. 'He likes you, he told me so himself, but more importantly he trusts you. Take your squadron, Dulcitius's courier and as many remounts as you think you need. It should take you two days to reach Eboracum. Say a day to rest up and persuade Dulcitius that if he wants to save Britannia and his reputation he should join me. How long for the Sixth to march from Eboracum to Longovicium?'

She stared at him, working the problem over in her mind. 'It depends if Dulcitius has consolidated his entire strength at Eboracum. Who knows, maybe he's already marching north to fill the gap you've left. Or more likely he's ordered the Sixth west to intercept your advance on Londinium.'

'But if not?'

She laid her helmet on the ground and went to the rough map he'd drawn in the earth, trampled but still decipherable. Her long fingers traced a line north. 'From Eboracum to Isurium on the north road, a day's march for the Sixth. They reach Cataractonium on the second day, Morbium on the third . . .'

'Picking up their garrisons on the way,' Marcus suggested.

'Maybe, but he won't strip them bare. From Morbium to Vinovium is only half a day, but he'd be sensible to take the chance to rest. Then another fifteen miles of hard marching to reach Longovicium late afternoon on the fifth day.'

'So eight days, depending on how long it takes to persuade Dulcitius.'

'*If* I can persuade Dulcitius,' she corrected him. 'You're asking a man you deliberately deceived to trust you, a man who wants you dead. How long for Briga to reach Longovicium, assuming she even takes the road you want her to?'

'Oh, she'll take that road,' he said with more confidence than he felt. 'Good marching all the way on a well-found road. Plenty of water. Abandoned settlements to plunder and burn. If Julius is right, she'll reach the fort at just about the same time you do.'

Valeria picked up her helmet and turned to leave, but she hesitated in the doorway. 'And what will you be doing while I'm convincing Dulcitius?'

'I'll be preparing a welcome for Briga she'll never forget.'

When he was alone Marcus stood for a while contemplating the multi-layered deception he'd spent so much time constructing. So many pieces that must still fall into place for it to succeed.

'Lord?' Julius stood in the doorway watching him.

'Yes?'

'There's one thing I forgot to tell you.' Marcus imagined a shadow fluttering through the air towards him and shivered as if a knife point had just run up his spine. 'The keeper of Coventina's Shrine has joined Briga. She will ride at the queen's side.'

Calista.

XXXV

The male wolf's eyes never left her. It sat at Briga's right side occasionally emitting a soft growl from deep in its chest. The two females
lounged on her left, gnawing in turn on what looked suspiciously like
a human thigh bone. Like the wolf's, Briga's eyes were slanted and
glowed amber in the light from the fire and her stare made Calista
shiver, though she was careful not to show it. In the darkness behind
the queen, her human creatures rustled and whispered and humped
amid a pile of furs, seemingly oblivious to whatever else was happening in the tented leather pavilion. Briga's court had left the temporary
fortress at dawn with her confederation of Pictish tribes trailing in its
wake like a great murmuring swarm as they followed the twisting river
valley southwards. Impossible to know quite how far they'd travelled,
but Calista guessed that the rearguard of Briga's great army might well
be camped on the height the queen had occupied that very morning.
Briga and the van of the column had halted at the end of the first day
still in the north of Selgovae country, their tents spread along a feeder
stream of the Tuedd river, and a full week's march from the Wall.

And this was only part of the force she would bring against the
Romans. Corvus and his two thousand would join them the next day
at the place the Romans called Trimontium, and the contingents from

the Votadini at the Tivyet crossing the following morning. From there they would follow the Roman road that ran, straight as the flight of an arrow, to pierce the very heart of Britannia.

'Tell me again why you came to me.' Briga's voice was like a caress and the air in the pavilion seemed to quiver with the energy she exuded. Calista could feel it on her flesh as if a hundred thousand ants were marching across her skin.

'The goddess spoke to me in a dream.' She knew she must not deviate from her original story. Before she had left Brocolitia Marcus had approached her again with certain suggestions, and instructions should she choose to proceed with them. He hadn't been so foolish as to expect a commitment, only that she should enter Briga's camp with an open mind. She would not be entirely alone, he said, but it must be up to her what decision she made and whom she would trust. 'Coventina said the fire at the shrine was a sign she could not protect me there. The Christians had defiled the well so it was no longer truly hers. She bade me tip the altars into its depths and seek out the powerful one who would cherish her memory and restore her to her rightful place by wiping the Christians from this land.' Calista knew this last was no part of Marcus's design, but she would have her revenge on those who had ousted her. 'Coventina accompanies you in spirit: wherever water flows you will have the support and the kindness of the goddess.'

'That is of comfort,' Briga nodded. But the voice didn't match the words and Calista sat frozen under the gaze of the unblinking eyes. 'We are never far from water in these lands and the support of the gods is not to be lightly spurned. Your presence here is welcome. It has already allowed me to strengthen my hold over Corvus, Coel and Luddoc, who are as impressed by the support of the goddess as they are by the might of a queen. As for the Christians, I have little acquaintance with them; the last was a monk who preached to me about a man who did tricks with loaves and fishes. I had him baked into a loaf and fed to the eels. Coventina will have her wish. Any Christian who declines to worship her will be drowned in the nearest river and we will burn every Christian shrine.' Calista inclined her head in thanks.

'And you will see it all, because I believe I will keep you with me, Keeper of the Well. Will you ride into battle at Briga's side?'

'If it is the goddess's will.'

'It is my will. Perhaps I will make you one of my pets.' Her voice was almost a purr now and she waved an elegant hand to encompass the wolves and the piled furs. 'You will have noticed I am fond of pets.'

'I am no pet,' Calista's anger overcame her unease, 'not to man, nor woman, and no plaything either.'

'We shall see. What think you, Drosten, do you believe I should make the goddess's handmaiden one of my pets?'

A pale figure, tall and with a mane of shaggy hair, rose naked from the pile of furs, shrugging away the slim white arms that clutched at him. The male wolf growled, but Briga placed a hand on the animal's forehead and it went quiet.

'What do I care about gods and goddesses? What have they ever done for me?' the man growled. He would be handsome, Calista thought, if he hadn't been touched so closely by death that his face had aged half a lifetime more than his body. It was only when he stepped from the shadows that she noticed the truncated stumps of his arms and understood.

'The Romans left him with legs and eyes and a mouth, and, as you may notice, other things, so Drosten still has his uses,' Briga said. 'He carries messages, makes inquiries. What news of the spy, Drosten?'

Drosten rubbed the stump of his right arm against the hairy pelt of his chest. 'He disappeared an hour into the march. No one saw him go.'

'And the men who were watching him?'

'Nechtan took their eyes as you commanded, Brenine.'

Calista suppressed a shudder, but Briga smiled. 'Good.' The queen turned to Calista. 'He had been very useful to me, this spy, as have you. He provided an insight into the very heart and mind of the Lord of the Wall, but now what am I to think?'

Calista hesitated. What were her feelings for the Lord of the Wall? A long-standing affection, yes, perhaps something deeper, but love? No, certainly not love as she understood it. When it came to it, did she owe him anything? The answer again was no. In saving her life in the fire at Coventina's Well, he'd also saved his own. She could never be certain how much he'd sought to manipulate and use her. For now, her fortunes and her future lay with Briga, and, whatever it felt like, it was *not* a betrayal.

'Marcus Flavius Victor had his own pets,' she informed the queen. 'A pair of young Picts, twins, survivors of a raid on one of your villages. They were often his eyes and ears in the north, but who knows where their true allegiance lies.'

'Who knows indeed.' Briga allowed a long, significant silence to fill the hut. Calista noticed Drosten's eyes on her, cold and hard as any wolf's. 'I believed I could trust him because some of what he reported was confirmed by the messages you sent.'

'Any information I sent you was reported in good faith,' Calista held her ground. 'There are many reasons the spy may have vanished,' she said. 'You do not exactly provide a warm welcome, Brenine; perhaps fear of the consequences of staying within your reach drove him away.'

'No,' Briga shook her head. 'The spy was one of the few who did not fear me. He knew he had my admiration. Though it is true he witnessed the interrogation of one of the Lord of the Wall's agents who had infiltrated my camp with Corvus's Selgovae. He told us little of value, and that very quickly, but it did not ease his passing.'

'If he did not fear you, then perhaps he felt he could be of more value to you by returning to the Lord of the Wall and reporting his progress?'

'Perhaps,' Briga said. 'But you do not believe that.'

'It is one alternative,' Calista persisted; she was committed now. 'But there are other possibilities. Your attack on Britannia can be likened to the fox ready to make a dash into the lambing pen. The fox does not pounce at the first blood scent of a newborn lamb. First it sniffs for the presence of the shepherd boy's dog, or the boy himself. It listens for the sound of a threat, and it inspects its surroundings with every other sense. Yet no matter how cunning their kind, how many foxes end their days with their leg snared in a trap or their neck snapped, and their pelts nailed to a grain store door?'

Briga looked at her with new interest. 'Are you saying I should delay the attack?'

'No, Brenine,' Calista assured her. 'To falter now would damage your authority with the Votadini and the Selgovae. When will the opportunity arise again? The gate is open, the eyes of the most dangerous guard appear to be elsewhere. Britannia lies helpless and exposed before your wolves. All I urge is that you take nothing for granted where the Lord of the Wall is concerned.'

'I will ponder on what you have said. Perhaps the Lord of the Wall is not as clever as he seems. Yes, we may have a surprise for the Romans. Scara, a cloak for our wounded hero.' A slim girl with pale unseeing eyes appeared from the shadows, her flesh so translucent she might have been a wraith, and used a cloak to cover Drosten's nakedness. 'Escort the Keeper of the Shrine to her tent and return to me.'

Drosten and Calista walked through the encampment with the sun dipping behind the western hills and the ground beneath the trees dappled by sunspots and shadows. The Pict was silent until they reached the tent that had been provided for her. 'You feel satisfied that you did well,' he said. Calista could almost feel the heat of his suppressed anger. 'But I warn you not to be too complacent before Briga. Today the words you spoke pleased her, tomorrow . . .'

'Why are you here?' she asked him.

Drosten turned his eyes to the dying of the sun.

'For the same reason you are. I have nowhere else to go.'

XXXVI

Verteris (Brough-on-Stainmore)

The mile-and-a-half-long column of horsemen and mules was approaching the fort at Verteris in the late afternoon of the second day. Marcus
had maintained a moderate pace, twenty miles between sun-up and
making camp, content in the knowledge that he had at least three days
to spare over Briga and her advancing army of Picts. They'd collected
another two hundred cavalrymen from the Numerus Defensorum's
base at Braboniacum, bringing Marcus's cavalry contingent to just
under seventeen hundred horse.

Until now they'd always had the mountains of northern Britannia's
spine on their left hand, but at Verteris it appeared those heights had
been cloven by a giant sword and the way east lay open. The province's
rulers had recognized the strategic significance of the Verteris Gap
from the first day legionary engineers set eyes on it as they surveyed the
lands of the Carvetii and the Brigantes. A well maintained road ran
between west and east, with a fort at either end – Verteris and Lavatris –
that could communicate swiftly through a system of signal stations
sited at every mile marker. Tomorrow, if all went to plan, they would

take that road, and a day later, God willing, they'd be in a position to block the Pictish advance.

Yet so much still lay in the balance. During the ride south Marcus had tried to bury the question that was never far from his mind. Would the Sixth legion arrive in time? Would it arrive at all? Of all the imponderables that made up his plan, this was the greatest. Valeria would have reached Eboracum by now, but how would Dulcitius react? Would he even agree to meet her? But his every instinct told Marcus that the *dux Britanniarum* held a certain affection for his sister, and beneath that steely, unyielding exterior Valeria had the ability to charm if she set her mind to it. Just let her get into the same room and Dulcitius would certainly listen to her. For all his failings, Dulcitius had a finely honed instinct for survival, and, though Marcus had often mocked him, he was no fool. If he failed to move against the Picts it would be Julius Postumus Dulcitius whom Rome blamed for the ravaging of Britannia, perhaps even for the loss of the province entirely. Ultimately it would come down to the question of whether the certainty of seeing Marcus dead was of greater importance to him than fear of the Emperor's potential retribution. Put in those terms the decision might be closer than Marcus cared to think, and for the first time it occurred to him that he might have sent Valeria into real danger.

'Riders,' Luko called out, pointing to the east.

'It's the scouts.' Caradoc peered at the two specks approaching over the rumpled carpet of moorland north of the road. 'Senecio and one other. And they're in a hurry.'

Marcus ordered his signaller to halt the column and a trumpet blared out. An anxious foreboding swelled inside him as he watched the riders approach at the gallop, spray clouding the horses' legs as they crossed a shallow stream.

'Lord,' Senecio called breathlessly as he approached, followed by Ninian. 'You must see this.'

'What is it?' Marcus demanded.

'Trouble,' the former monk said. 'But Senecio's right, lord, best you judge it for yourself.'

Marcus didn't hesitate. 'First squadron to me.' He followed the two riders as they retraced their steps to a round-topped hill that gave them a view into the mouth of the Verteris Gap and the fort that guarded it.

'Shit,' Caradoc echoed the thought that entered Marcus's mind.

The east road ran between a pair of low hills and directly beneath Verteris's walls. Verteris occupied a commanding position on the high ground above a stream that snaked across the valley from the larger River Itouna to the south. Beyond the fort the road hugged the base of the northern mountains, but it was the space between the two hills that drew Marcus's attention. At least two lines of infantry barred his way in a well-chosen defensive position. On the slope to the left of the hills he could just make out the glitter of horse brass among the bushes. More disturbing even than the wall of soldiers were the numbers. Verteris was garrisoned by the Numerus Directorum, four centuries of auxiliary light infantry perhaps three hundred strong, plus a cavalry contingent of a hundred troopers. From his hilltop vantage point Marcus counted at least twice that many troops.

'What do you make of them?' he asked Caradoc.

'The front line is made up of auxiliaries,' the veteran cavalryman said. 'I can't be certain, but from the look of their shields I do believe the second line might be a cohort of our old friends from the Sixth legion, which means we're fu—'

'Which means we have a decision to make,' Marcus cut him off. 'The cavalry among the bushes to the left, I reckon them at fifty, which means there are at least another fifty somewhere?'

'If it was me, and they're here for the reason I think they're here, I'd put them in that grove of trees on the rise to the south of the camp.'

'So would I.' Marcus peered at the wooded hillside, but could make nothing of it. 'Why do you think they're here?'

'To stop you, of course.'

Marcus returned to studying the wall of infantry blocking the road ahead. This was the last thing he expected and the last thing he needed, but it had to be dealt with. 'Get back and tell Sempronius I want his Second Asturians in squadron squares, and align the Ala Sabiniana in the same formation on his left.'

'Christ's bones,' Caradoc hissed. 'You're not going to attack them?'

'Do you have a better idea? But first we'll talk – and give them something to think about. Fourth Lingonum and the First Asturians on the flanks, with the Gauls, Numerus Defensorum and the Ala Herculaea as a reserve in the rear.'

'What about those German maniacs?'

'Tell Ramios to keep them out of the way with the reserves.'

Marcus waited until the two *alae* and their flanking squadrons came up and he halted them out of sight of the defenders. He called Sempronius forward and the commander of the Second Asturians muttered a low curse as he recognized the motionless lines of soldiers.

'Yes, tribune,' Marcus said quietly. 'They're Romans and we have to be very careful not to make them dead Romans. That will take discipline. So make sure your men know that the first trooper who so much as twitches without permission will have me to reckon with. I hope to persuade them to join us, or at worst to let us pass unmolested.'

'What if they refuse?' The young soldier's hand strayed nervously towards his sword.

'They won't,' Marcus assured him. 'Their commander had orders to join me. It seems someone else has countermanded, or at least questioned, those orders. He'll be confused and that confusion will be passed on to his men. They don't want to kill us any more than we want to kill them.'

'But—'

'If anyone's going to die it's not going to be us,' Marcus snapped. 'Too much depends on it. The very future of this province.' He rode across the front of the two formations, raising his voice to call out as he went. 'We will advance at a walk. And you will behave as if you are on the parade ground for a governor's inspection. No nods or winks to anyone you know. No smiling or grinning. They're only infantry,' he allowed himself a smile of his own, 'which means they're frightened of cavalry, so they'll be tense. Tense is good. Your job today is to make sure they're just scared enough to do what I tell them, but not so frightened that anybody does something silly. You will do nothing to provoke and likewise you will not allow yourselves to be provoked. You are made of stone, and twice as cold. Listen for the command signals. Do not hesitate. You are Roman soldiers and your duty is to obey. Remember your orders and perhaps tonight we will share a cup of wine with our comrades down there.'

It shouldn't be like this. He'd known Rufius Clemens, who commanded Verteris, for half a lifetime. They'd fought together against Picts, Saxons and Scotti and had formed a bond that only existed between men whose blood had mingled on the battlefield. Clemens had agreed without question to allow his cavalry to ride with Marcus, even though the Lord of the Wall had offered no explanation. Clearly Dulcitius had undermined what faith Clemens had in his old comrade. Now Marcus must find a way to restore it.

'We could always bypass them through the mountains,' Caradoc suggested.

'No, they're here to stop us.' Marcus had already considered and rejected the possibility. 'If we take to the hills, Rufius will send his cavalry after us and some fool will die. Better this way. Signaller? Regiment will advance.'

A trumpet call rang out, its blaring tones echoed by the answering signals of the surrounding units, and the neat squares of riders set off at the walk. The twenty squadrons of the Ala Sabiniana and the Second Asturians, each squadron thirty riders strong, formed the centre, with the smaller units of the First Asturians and the Fourth Lingonum far out on the flanks. Clemens would hear the trumpet call, but he wouldn't be certain what to expect. Marcus calculated that the slow advance of eight hundred horsemen over the skyline would be as stunning as any cavalry charge. He wanted to create the impression of strength and a sense of mounting danger rather than an immediate threat. Soldiers tended to react to a threat with violence and that was the last thing he needed. As they breasted the hill he called Luko and Senecio to him and guided Storm at a canter towards the centre of the formation, where he took station at the head of his troops.

A ripple seemed to run through the static lines of infantrymen as the soldiers shuffled their feet and tightened their grip on shield and spear at the sight of the massed cavalry. They were formed up on the gently sloping ground to the west of the fort. Marcus admitted grudgingly that Clemens had chosen his position well. A stream anchored his right flank and one of the low hills his left. Neither constituted much of an obstacle for an attacker, but the positions were strengthened by the Numerus Directorum's cavalry contingents. If things went badly for him, the cavalry would provide cover and allow Clemens to fall back through the small settlement outside the fort gates and behind the safety of Verteris's stout stone walls.

Marcus's advancing squadrons moved steadily down the slope, occasionally losing sight of . . . no, not the enemy, he couldn't allow himself to believe that . . . rather, their misguided comrades, among the dips and troughs of the gently undulating terrain. This wasn't the battlefield he would have chosen, but if God was kind there would be no battle. Still, with each stride taking him closer to the moment, he had no definite idea how he would achieve a peaceful outcome, or of the circumstances that had driven Clemens to oppose him. It was unsettling to approach the confrontation like a blind man feeling his way forward through a forest. In previous battles he'd contemplated, the enemy had been obvious, his mind clear and his sword firm in his grip.

'Keep your positions,' he called over his shoulder. 'And remember, no one acts without my orders.'

They were on the flat now, with the wall of shields, perhaps four hundred paces across, clearly visible and filling the gap between the two hills to block the route to Verteris. Even at the walk, the restlessly twitching horses, bred to battle and with the scent of it in their nostrils, covered the ground surprisingly quickly. Five hundred paces. Four.

Three. The faces behind the shields visible now, eyes glaring from beneath the rims of their helmets. Clemens with his plumed helm in the centre of the front rank. The auxiliaries held their spears at rest, but that wouldn't last. The steady, unrelenting advance of the cavalry stretched the tension to breaking point, all the more as it was conducted in an almost unnerving silence. Two hundred paces. A rasping command from the ranks ahead and the spears came down to form a wall of glittering iron in front of the shields. Storm didn't break stride. A hundred paces. Marcus raised his hand and heard the rattle of horse brass as the advance halted. He waited a few moments, allowing his mind to settle, his eyes taking in the scene ahead. Caradoc had been right, the second rank was made up of legionaries from the Sixth, which meant that, yet again, Dulcitius had managed to surprise him.

Rufius Clemens stayed in position among the men of the Numerus Directorum. Marcus could almost feel his old friend's apprehension. The thought prompted a fierce smile that would have made Clemens more nervous still had he seen it. Perhaps he would have chosen this ground, after all, with its perfect flat approach and his enemy's flanking squadrons outnumbered two to one. All it would take was one blare of the trumpet and the First Lingonum and First Asturians would sweep those flanks clear for Julius Pastor and his Ala Herculaea to roll up the line from the south. Chaos. Panic. And then the cavalry would do what cavalry were made for, slaughter fleeing infantrymen as if they were so many sheep.

'Stay here,' he ordered Luko. 'Senecio.' The Numidian nudged his horse closer and Marcus issued a whispered order that made Senecio grin and unsling his bow. 'And don't miss.' With a final quick appraisal of the waiting auxiliaries he nudged Storm forward.

A faint jingle of metal greeted the movement and the line of spear points shimmered once more as the owners tightened their grip on ash shafts. Marcus had to remind himself to breathe, but he felt a growing confidence. Every fibre of his being told him he was in the right. If these men chose to stand in his way then they would have to reap the consequences. He walked the horse until its breastbone was almost touching the polished iron point of a spear held by a bewildered auxiliary.

When Storm was still, he pulled his ornate iron helmet from his head and ran his hand through his dark hair before his eyes settled on the face he'd been seeking.

XXXVII

'This is an odd welcome for an old friend, Rufius. An exercise, no doubt? And your garrison has been reinforced since I last visited Verteris, which is all to the good in these turbulent times. The only thing missing are the cavalry you pledged to me.'

An officer stepped from the ranks at Storm's left flank, his hand resting on his sword hilt. Rufius Clemens had the face of a boxer who'd lost one too many fights, but his expression said he was perfectly ready for another. Dark eyes glaring out from beneath heavy brows, a chin like a battering ram and a nose that had been broken more than once. He removed his helmet in turn and lifted his right hand in a perfunctory salute.

'You know how to make an entrance, Marcus, I'll give you that.' His eyes swept over the massed squares of horsemen a hundred paces away. 'If you hadn't stopped your lads where they are, I might have wondered if we'd had some kind of misunderstanding.'

'You know how cavalry like to put on a show,' Marcus said evenly. 'Especially when they have such an appreciative audience. Speaking of which,' he nodded to the two ranks of soldiers, 'what does this little display say about *our* understanding?'

'Well,' Rufius rubbed his stubbled chin, 'we might have a bit of a problem there, Marcus. On the one hand, here you are, an old and trusted friend . . .'

'I'm glad to hear it . . .'

'On the other there appears to be some doubt about your current status.'

Rufius's eyes shifted to his left. Marcus followed them to another Roman tribune standing behind the two lines. The face seemed familiar, but before he could place it, the officer brushed aside the soldiers in front of him and stepped out into the open.

'There is no doubt about the status of Marcus Flavius Victor,' the man called. 'He is a usurper and a traitor to Rome who intends to lead these men to Londinium and take the province for himself.' He made to draw his sword, but Rufius stepped in front of him and gripped his hand.

'So you see, Marcus, we have a slight problem here.' Verteris's commander frowned. 'I have Dulcitius's man – you'll remember Tribune Hostilius Geta, I'm sure – with a letter from the *dux Britanniarum* demanding your immediate arrest on account of the fact that you're the right hand of Satan himself. Then I have you arriving at my door with what appears to be your own private army. I'm a bit confused, to be honest.'

'Has he offered any evidence to back up these outrageous claims?' Marcus feigned disbelief.

'Not evidence as such,' Rufius admitted. 'But Dulcitius—'

'What more evidence do you need than what you see with your own eyes,' Hostilius Geta snarled. 'Why else would he have gathered a thousand horsemen?'

'Nearer two thousand,' Marcus said quietly. A modest exaggeration, but it made Rufius's frown deepen. 'Your flanks aren't quite as secure as you think they are, my old friend.'

'Ah . . .' Rufius's tongue ran over his lips and he studied the formation behind Marcus with more interest.

'Enough of this,' Geta said. 'You have your orders, arrest him.'

'I have a better idea.' Marcus allowed himself a smile. 'Why don't *you* arrest me? We'll see if you can back up your accusations with a sword.'

'No need for that,' Rufius countered rapidly. 'I don't know what you're up to, Marcus, but I know you well enough to believe you're no traitor. Something's happened to make Dulcitius think the opposite, but I'm sure you'll be able to persuade him if you meet face to face. Now Hostilius here has orders to take you back to Eboracum. If you agree to go with him, I'll be happy to come along with an escort to make sure there are no unfortunate accidents along the way. Your cavalry can either wait here and eat me out of house and home till we get back, or you can disperse them back to their own forts, which would suit me better. What do you think?'

Marcus pretended to consider the possibility. 'That sounds very reasonable, Rufius, but I don't have time to go with you and Hostilius to Eboracum. I'm needed elsewhere.' Rufius winced, and shook his head. Hostilius Geta's hand went back to his sword hilt and this time Verteris's commander didn't stop him. 'If you draw your sword, Hostilius,' Marcus continued, 'I have a bowman who can put an arrow through your eye at a hundred paces. Do you see the black cavalryman beside my signaller back there? I've never seen him miss. Good. Now I have your attention, let me explain what is happening here, Rufius. Have you not asked yourself why I'm here when Dulcitius believes I'm on my way to take Londinium?'

Rufius frowned. 'You wanted my horse soldiers.'

'But I could have just asked you to send them to Braboniacum or Mamucium. Did I need to bring every last one of my men, and all my supplies, half a day's march out of my way just to pick up a few score more?'

'Then why are you here?'

'I'm here because in a few days' time twenty thousand Picts are going to be pouring down the other side of these mountains.' Marcus's voice hardened. 'I'm here because if I don't stop them every farm and settlement and way station you are responsible for will soon be a smoking ruin.' He turned to Geta. 'Whatever orders you were given have been overtaken by events. By now the *dux Britanniarum* will have been given the news and be preparing the Sixth legion to meet me. But neither of us can do this alone, we must act in concert.'

'How do we know you're telling us the truth?' Geta demanded. 'The whole world knows you as a liar and a trickster.'

'I am no saint, brother.' Marcus ignored Rufius's grin. 'But any lying I have done in the past has been to protect this province. If you don't believe me, perhaps you will believe a man who was with the Picts less than a week ago.' He turned in the saddle and called out: 'Trooper Julius, to me!'

Julius left his squadron and cantered forward to Marcus's side. 'Lord?'

'These gentlemen don't believe the Picts are upon us, Julius.' Marcus nodded to Geta. 'Trooper Julius is a Pict himself, who can roam freely among his people. Perhaps he can convince you where I cannot. Where were you seven days ago?'

'I was in Queen Briga's camp in the upper Tuedd valley, lord, where she was taking the oaths of Corvus of the Selgovae, Luddoc of the northern Votadini and Coel of the southern branch of that tribe.' A hiss of disbelief escaped Rufius Clemens and a murmur ran through the ranks of auxiliaries within hearing range. 'If she marched when she intended, Briga and her forces will be halfway to the Wall by now.'

'Now do you believe me?' Marcus said.

'I have my orders,' Hostilius Geta choked out the words. 'And I intend to carry them out.'

'You think it's more important to arrest me than save Britannia?' Marcus didn't hide his scorn. 'Well I have two thousand veteran cavalry spoiling for a fight who may have something to say about that.'

Marcus studied the soldiers behind Geta. Those in the front rank who'd heard Julius had inevitably passed on his words to the men around them. Geta's legionaries in the second rank appeared more perplexed than before. Just how much loyalty did they owe their young officer? Part of the answer lay in the fact that, although he'd threatened arrest, he'd made no move yet to order his men to carry out the task.

Likely he was also unsure how the men of the Numerus Directorum would react. Marcus was known to be their commander's friend. Would they stand by while the legionaries manhandled a Roman officer, particularly after what they'd just heard? Perhaps more to the point, Geta was not a field officer. He served on the staff of the *dux Britanniarum* so he wasn't the regular commander of whichever cohort this was. Somewhere in those ranks was the centurion the men looked to for leadership, and, significantly – or so Marcus was beginning to hope – he'd made no move yet to support Geta's efforts.

'Tribune Clemens.' Verteris's commander stood two paces away, but Marcus shouted the words as if he was addressing his regiment on the parade ground. 'It would be presumptuous of me to request that I address your men, but if I was granted the honour,' Rufius gave him a look of amused resignation, 'I would ask them who they preferred to fight? Would it be their comrades here,' he swept an arm towards the silent, menacing squares of cavalry, 'who only wish free passage to the place of battle I have chosen? Or the twenty thousand Picts who will soon cross the Wall and bring murder, fire and rapine to the lands and peoples of Britannia?'

He nudged Storm to a walk and his voice rose still further as he traversed the line of men. 'We simple soldiers laugh at the scented southerners who look down their noses at us from the balconies of their villas and townhouses, but we understand it is our duty to protect them. We are all Roman citizens. Their way of life is our way of life.' He walked his mount back to where Rufius and Geta stood. 'It has been suggested that I have ambitions to rule Britannia, perhaps even to wear the purple. I pledge on my honour that this is false.' He drew his sword from its scabbard. 'And on my sword.' He flipped the blade so the pommel was pointing towards Rufius. 'If you believe it true, old friend, I give you leave to strike me down. But if you do not, I would ask you and these fine soldiers of yours to join me against the Picts.' A murmur ran through the long lines of men, that grew to a rumble and finally a great cheering clamour that engulfed both auxiliaries and legionaries. Geta took a step forward only to freeze as an arrow sprouted at his feet. He stared up at Marcus with a mix of fury and dazed wonder. 'We have looked on with frustration,' Marcus continued unrelentingly, 'as the Picts built up their power once more and we did not have the strength to move against them. At last God is bringing them to us. Are we to dismiss his gift? I say no.' He waited until the echo of his final word died in six hundred throats. 'I have nothing to offer you but the likelihood of death, and perhaps a place in history, but what soldier could ask for more?'

'What indeed?' Rufius Clemens said with a bemused half-smile. He nodded to one of his officers and the man shouted an order for the soldiers to return to the fort. Two legionaries escorted Hostilius Geta back to his unit. 'If I hadn't seen it with my own eyes, I wouldn't believe it. You just told six hundred men you were going to get them killed – including me – and they'd cheerfully follow you to the cemetery. Poor old Geta was only trying to follow orders.' Rufius patted Storm's flank. 'And I had no option but to go along with it. I had no idea how you were going to slip out of that one, Marcus.'

'Neither did I.'

'So what happens now? I thought it was only my cavalry you wanted.'

'I always knew you'd want to be in at the kill, Rufius, and now you have six hundred men instead of three hundred. You also have your artillery. That could all make a difference . . .'

'I was wondering about that, too. It's more than a month since you hinted you might be coming this way and want to borrow my cavalry. How did you . . . ?'

'It was just a matter of timing.' Marcus slid from the saddle. 'Briga was always going to attack in the spring, all she needed was a little encouragement to make her move before she was ready. But that's a story for another time, old friend. For now, get your men and Geta's legionary cohort ready to march at dawn.'

'March where?' Rufius demanded.

'Longovicium. It should take three days and you can pick up the Numerus Exploratorum at Lavatris on the way.'

'You won't hold twenty thousand Picts for long with nine hundred infantry and two thousand cavalry.'

'I don't plan to hold them,' Marcus said. 'I plan to destroy them, but first we must place our faith in the judgement of Julius Postumus Dulcitius.'

'Then may God truly help us.'

SWEAT

XXXVIII

Eboracum (York)

'If your brother wanted to regain my trust he should have sent you with his head in a basket.'

Valeria winced at the withering contempt in Dulcitius's tone, evidence, if any more was needed, that her mission might already be in vain. The words echoed through the great high-ceilinged chamber of the palace receiving room, accompanied by a snigger from the clerk at Dulcitius's side. A fire glowed pink in a metal brazier in the centre of the room and smoke gathered at the cornices to filter out through narrow windows set far up in the walls, but the shimmering coals made little impression on the chill air. Despite its grandeur the room smelled of rot, mildew and blocked latrines. Two officers of the Sixth legion sat wrapped in thick cloaks near the doorway, at an ornate table the size of a small boat. She recognized one as Terentius Cantaber, legate of the Sixth, a man whom Marcus derided as Dulcitius's bag-carrier. Evidently, they didn't share the clerk's amusement and their grave faces hinted that Valeria's arrival might have interrupted a serious discussion.

'With respect, lord,' she replied, 'I doubt that would further either of your causes.'

'And just what is Marcus Flavius Victor's cause?' Dulcitius demanded. 'Report after report confirms he has stripped the Wall defences bare. The Wall! The only thing that stands between Britannia and the vile corruption of the barbarian Picts—'

'The Wall and the spears of your soldiers, lord,' Valeria reminded him, to a grunt of approval from Cantaber's companion.

But Dulcitius chose not to be impressed.

'Do not lecture me, woman,' he hissed. The scorn in his voice made the hairs on the back of Valeria's neck rise like an enraged cat's. 'Even now you tell me your brother is riding south with his forces. Why south, and not east to where he could do what the Emperor pays him to do and keep the Picts north of the Wall? Because he has ambitions to follow in his father's footsteps—'

'I told you—'

'I served with Flavius Magnus Maximus,' Dulcitius would not be interrupted, 'an arrogant, greedy man with an insatiable hunger for ever more power; duplicitous and untrustworthy. He almost stripped Britannia bare and left me with a few hundred soldiers to hold back the Picts. Now you wish me to put my faith and the future of this province in the hands of a man who has proved himself to be even more unscrupulous than his father?'

'With the Votadini and Selgovae as her allies,' Valeria persisted, 'Queen Briga's army could number close to twenty thousand warriors. If you do not march to join forces with the Lord of the Wall, he must be overwhelmed along with every man in his command.'

'A fate that will be entirely of his own making,' Dulcitius said dismissively.

'And what of the fate of Britannia?' In her fury Valeria forgot the danger of making an enemy of the very man she had come to persuade. 'If Marcus is defeated and his horse soldiers annihilated how will the Sixth legion ever be able to force Briga and her Picts from the province? Without cavalry you are as helpless as a blind man groping his way along a cliff edge. Once they are south of Eboracum the tribes will swarm across the province with fire and sword. Briga won't face you in battle because she doesn't need to. Heavy infantry are too slow and unmanoeuvrable to hunt her down and pin her in place.' Terentius Cantaber rose from the table with a growl at this slight on his unit, but Valeria ignored him. 'She will split her army and force you to split your legion. Without my brother's cavalry you will clutch at her skirts, but they will always be out of reach. And all the time she will be wreaking havoc on the people of Britannia. No single town save Londinium and Eboracum has the garrison or the height of walls to keep her warriors at bay. You will be forced to watch as all the riches of Lindum and Glevum, Corinium and Isurium, Noviomagus and Verulamium fall into her hands and she slakes her blood lust on their people. Our people. The only thing she need fear is hunger, but she will have everything she requires long before Britannia's storehouses are empty. And when she has returned beyond the Wall there will be a reckoning. Rome will ask: how could this happen? Where was our brave *dux Britanniarum* while Britannia was being bled dry? How will you answer your Emperor, lord Dulcitius?'

The blood drained from Dulcitius's face and his right cheek twitched. 'I should have you whipped for your insolence,' he choked. He took a deep breath and made a visible effort to regain his self-control. 'None of this changes the fact that your brother is a traitor who has stripped the frontier bare of its defences and allowed, nay, encouraged, the Picts to invade us. Yet you expect me to go to his aid when I could be marching Britannia's most powerful military force into a trap.'

'Yes,' Cantaber intervened. 'Why should we trust your brother? Had we known of his plan the Sixth could have marched north days ago and been waiting for her at the Wall.'

'But that is the point.' Valeria didn't hide her exasperation. 'Marcus has placed the Picts at your mercy. He lured Briga south because he wanted her army to penetrate so deeply into the province it could never get out again. He doesn't want them stopped, he intends to destroy them. Utterly.'

'Yet he did not trust us enough to take us into his confidence,' the legate pointed out. 'You say he plans to bring them to battle at Longovicium, but even you admit that you do not know what awaits us there, or what his strategy will be. We only have your estimate that the Picts have twenty thousand warriors in the field, and that at second hand. We've always believed they could have at least twice that number. Lucti crossed the Wall with sixty thousand—'

'They included Scotti, Hibernians and Saxons,' Valeria pointed out, but she knew she was losing the argument.

'I do not dispute that,' Cantaber said. 'But my point remains. A moment ago you likened us to blind men groping in the darkness. That is precisely how we will be if we march north without properly scouting the route.'

'Your route is the north road.' Her head seemed filled with a fiery cloud. 'A road which you have travelled a hundred times, and of which your legion knows every cobble. If we leave in the morning you can be at Longovicium in six days and with your legionaries as fresh and ready for the fight as the moment they started.'

'It is as you say my legion,' Cantaber pointed out. 'I would not be doing my duty if I were to lead them into danger without taking the proper precautions. You will not deny that the Picts are capable of lying in ambush? There is also the question of your brother's loyalties.'

'If Marcus Flavius Victor is a traitor why would he have sent me here?' Valeria demanded.

'Why indeed?' Dulcitius said. 'Perhaps to lure us into that trap. Could it be that he has formed some kind of pact with this Queen Briga to share the island between them? Of course, that would mean he had sent his own sister to her death, because if it is true, I would have no choice but to order your immediate execution.' He shook his head. 'No, even I cannot believe that of our Lord of the Wall. Duplicitous as he is, he would never sacrifice you.'

'Then you will march?'

Dulcitius made a pyramid with his fingers and exchanged a glance with the legionary officers. 'I will think on it.'

'Then think quickly, lord.' Urgency filled Valeria's voice. 'Because if you do not arrive at Longovicium on time, everything I have predicted will come to pass in any case.'

'Oh, I think you underestimate your brother, my lady,' Dulcitius said with a thin smile. 'I believe we can depend on the Lord of the Wall to hold the attention of a few thousand savages for a day or two without losing his entire command. Senaculus here will direct you to your quarters. I will send for you when I have made my decision. Of course, I will expect you to remain as my guest whatever the outcome.'

'You're holding me hostage?' Valeria didn't hide her incredulity.

Dulcitius looked at her with genuine puzzlement. 'Do you really think Marcus wouldn't have taken that possibility into account when he sent you to me?'

Valeria stared at him.

How could she have been so blind?

'You should have trusted us.'

The voice came from behind as she walked down a long corridor to the quarters she'd been allocated in the east wing of the palace. Dulcitius's clerk had abandoned her with a hissed list of directions and now her spine tingled in anticipation of the knife point that could follow the words. She turned, still wary. Terentius Cantaber stood in the shadows of a doorway, well placed to simply disappear if they were interrupted. What was happening here? Conspiracy, or a shrewd instinct for survival in a city that reeked of it?

'It is not in my brother's nature.'

'Still . . . ?'

Valeria hesitated. Her inclination was to walk on, but she knew she would need this man's cooperation if she were to persuade Dulcitius to march to Marcus's aid. 'We are talking of trust?'

'You may not trust Dulcitius, but you can trust me. On my honour as a Roman soldier.' Cantaber paused, but if he expected an acknowledgement, none was forthcoming. 'I give you my word that the Sixth legion will march against the Picts. Dulcitius believes he commands, but the Sixth is my legion. Terentius Cantaber will not stand by behind these walls and leave Britannia to be ravaged by barbarians. It may take a little time, Dulcitius must believe it is his decision, but we will march.'

'Time is something we do not have.'

'Nevertheless, it has to be this way. Dulcitius is minded to sit behind these walls and allow your brother to reap the rewards of what he calls his "vainglory and perfidy". He has to be persuaded that revenge over your brother is less important than his duty to Britannia, or more accurately, as you sought so eloquently to convince him, his own self-interest. I must counsel patience.'

She drew in a long breath. 'Then I will accept your counsel, legate. But do not believe, like Dulcitius, that I am some pretty songbird to be caged at his will. If Dulcitius does not set off within two days I will find a way to join my brother.'

She turned and walked away.

Cantaber watched as the slim figure marched purposefully down the long corridor and an almost wistful smile flitted across his rugged features. 'A pretty songbird? I do not believe that for an instant.'

When Valeria reached her chamber, Leof was already there, unpacking her civilian clothing in readiness for the inevitable formal dinner that must accompany a visit to the *dux Britanniarum*.

'Leave that,' she ordered. 'I doubt Dulcitius will be in any mood for entertaining after what he's just heard.' She walked to the window. The houses between the palace and the river were ramshackle affairs, many of them already abandoned by townsfolk who preferred to live within the security of the fort's walls. Beyond the river those walls remained sturdy and all but impenetrable to anything but treachery or an army equipped with siege engines. It was a familiar enough sight, but it never failed to impress. Thirty feet high and encompassing an area of six hundred paces by four hundred, they were studded by no fewer than thirty enormous round towers. Inside, if Cantaber was true to his promise, the Sixth legion would be readying itself for the coming campaign. The long lines of supply carts outside the main gates seemed to confirm it, but they could just as easily be the sign of a city preparing for a siege. 'Come here, Leof,' she said. When the young Saxon joined her at the window she pointed to the east gate of the city, which was just visible from their viewpoint. 'There's a stand of trees just beyond the gateway. For the next two days and nights I want you to wait there with fresh horses. Tell Marius that he's to camp with the squadron on the north side of the river opposite and be ready to ride at a moment's notice.'

'And you, lady?' Leof studied her with concern.

'If it comes to it, I will find a way to reach you and we will swim our horses to join the others.'

'Are we to be fugitives then, in your own lands?'

'That depends on the lord Dulcitius.'

XXXIX

The Wall

Queen Briga breasted the final ridge and drew her pony to a halt. As she surveyed what lay at the foot of the gentle descent ahead a great cry burst from her throat. The unnerving howl was swiftly taken up by the three lithe grey wolves that never left her side and the entourage of misfits who surrounded her. Only Calista remained unmoved as she studied the Pictish queen.

The Wall had been part of Calista's life since her mother had first held her in its cool shade as an infant. She had been raised amid the raucous clamour and bitter-sweet scents of her father's brewhouse in the civilian settlement at Cilurnum, and exchanged her first kiss among the ruins of the lookout tower across the river. She'd long forgotten the impact it could have on someone who had never seen it before.

Briga had *heard* of the Wall. She had been *told* of its terrible majesty. It had been *described* to her in every detail. She *knew* the location of every fort and the number of auxiliaries who garrisoned each. Yet nothing had prepared her for the first sight of the astonishing stone barrier that separated her from her enemies. What manner of men had created this obscenity against the natural order? The height of three tall men, it stretched from horizon to horizon, the individual stones so closely engaged it might have been a single entity. Off to her left lay the fort at Hunnum, the lair of the feared Lord of the Wall, towers empty and battlements bare of soldiers as Calista had predicted. Ahead, on the line of the road where the queen sat her mount, stood twin towers guarding a double-arched gateway that carried the road north and south. As Briga watched, four Pictish scouts raced through the eastern arch and cantered towards her, their cloaks flying behind them.

The leader, a veteran warrior named Rhuin, leapt from his pony and knelt before her. 'It is as you said, Brenine, the fort is empty, the settlement deserted and the Wall unmanned. Alpin here has ridden as far as Vindobala and it is the same there. The way is open. There is water aplenty in the valley below and good camping ground on either side of the river.'

A savage joy raced through Briga's veins like an elixir, but before she could reply she was interrupted by another voice accompanied by the rattle of approaching hooves.

'What of Corstopitum?'

Briga suppressed a surge of irritation. The scout looked up at the queen and she nodded. 'Tell my lord Coel and his fellow kings what you found, Rhuin.'

Rhuin rose to his feet and addressed the three rulers who'd ridden up with their escorts. 'The gates are closed and the walls of town and fort bristle with soldiers. Their bolt throwers and boulder hurlers sit shoulder to shoulder and packed so tight a field vole could not wriggle between them.'

'Then we must invest the place with all the strength we have if we are to take their supplies,' King Luddoc of the northern Votadini urged. 'You have driven our warriors hard, Brenine. Five days of constant marching. They need rest and a sniff of the plunder you promised.'

Briga turned in the saddle to glare at him, and her wolves bared their teeth. 'There will be no rest and no plunder. Not yet. It was never my intention to invest Corstopitum. If we throw our entire army at the walls we may succeed, but at what cost and to what end? Scores of dead or injured warriors. And all for a few bags of grain. We will camp on the slope overlooking the town so they know the strength we can bring against them, but we will be on the move again before first light. A small force will remain, lighting many fires at night and showing themselves only occasionally during the day to confuse the enemy as to their numbers. Two hundred men will do. Your men, King Luddoc, since Corstopitum interests you so greatly.'

'Not mine.' Luddoc's suspicion of his companions was so great he risked outright defiance.

'Nor mine,' said Coel, with a grim smile at his fellow tribesman.

'I will supply the men.' Corvus made the offer to keep the peace, but he didn't hide his irritation. 'They will keep the defenders of Corstopitum occupied while we ravage the province. But King Luddoc is right, you have been setting too great a pace. Some of my older warriors will never last another day.'

'Then leave the old and the lame behind to fend for themselves or catch up as they can.' Briga had no sympathy for the weak. 'Because I will not be delayed seeking out a few hens and pigs in lands near as barren as our own. That is what the Romans will expect and have planned for. The greatest riches lie in the south of the province. Only the single legion at Eboracum stands between us and those treasures and already I can feel its commander's fear and confusion.' She waved a slim hand towards the empty fort at Hunnum. 'All this has been foretold. The Romans of Britannia are divided as never before, just as Rome itself is divided between east and west. What does Rome care about this island when the Empire is attacked from all sides like a deer beset by a pack of hunting dogs? Before the wall was built the peoples of this land were as one, and it is my pledge that they will be one again.'

Consternation showed on the faces of the three tribal leaders and Briga smiled at their timidity. How did men with so little ambition become kings?

'Yes. This will be one land. Pictland. You talk of plunder? Once we pass through that gate plunder is no longer our main objective, though there will be plunder enough for all. That is why we will stop only to fill our bellies, slake our thirst and rest our heads. If we meet the Sixth legion, we will trample its soldiers into the dust and leave their broken bones in our wake. Anyone who stands in our way will have a simple choice. Join us or be destroyed. We will take everything they have, including their lives. Londinium, not Eboracum, is the heart of Britannia. By the time we reach the city our numbers and reputation will be such that they will throw open the gates and beg for my mercy. And once we have Londinium we will keep it. Every town and settlement will have a Pictish overlord. Men in this army who think themselves rich thanks to two acres and a single cow will hold sway over a hundred British households.'

Coel and Corvus exchanged a glance of incredulity at this patent fantasy. 'But what of our own lands?' King Luddoc demanded. 'Do you expect us just to abandon them?'

'You have sons, lord king?' Corvus stifled a smile at Briga's question. Luddoc's reputation in the bedchamber was legendary and he was known to have twenty children by a dozen mothers.

'I have sons.'

'Then your eldest will hold your kingdom in your name. And the others can carve out kingdoms of their own from the lands we take in Britannia.'

'This is not what we agreed,' Coel pointed out.

'Circumstances change,' Briga replied, the glittering eyes narrowing. 'If you do not wish to lead your Votadini south to glory and riches, perhaps there is one among your tribe with more . . . appetite.'

'I have appetite enough and more,' Coel said. 'As you will discover when we meet the enemy.'

'Enough.' Corvus pushed his pony between them. 'We can only succeed in this endeavour if we are united. As the Brenine says, circumstances change and new opportunities arise. We would not be kings if we did not have the courage to reach out and take them. But what of Marcus Flavius Victor? What of the Lord of the Wall? He is not a man to be discounted lightly. Yet you have made no mention of him.'

'The Lord of the Wall has abandoned his garrisons,' Calista answered the question. 'Let that be sufficient.'

'Enough of this talk. The army will advance,' Briga ordered. The signaller at the queen's side blew a great blast on his *carnyx*, the long, curved bronze animal-headed horn used to pass orders to Briga's Pictish kings and clan chiefs. Moments later the vast horde that had waited beyond the crest of the hill moved forward in a rush, eager to secure the best camping grounds and watering places. The double gates were only wide enough to allow a dozen warriors or a pair of carts to pass through at a time, but Nechtan, Briga's senior commander, had foreseen the difficulty.

Groups of warriors trotted to right and left carrying ramps that had been prepared from foraged timber along the march. As the four rulers watched, the Pictish warriors swarmed up the ramps and across the Wall at countless points, leaving the gate free for cavalry and the supply wagons and cattle herds that followed in the army's wake.

'Nechtan knows his business,' Corvus growled softly.

'It's as well someone does,' Luddoc snapped. He pulled his horse round and led his escort west to where his tribe had been assigned a crossing point and to guard the right flank from a possible sally from Cilurnum.

'Our friend seems nervous,' Corvus laughed.

'Perhaps he's not so confident of our leader's strategy as you are,' Coel smiled.

'Our good fortune that the Romans left the door open for us.' Corvus looked towards the endless line of carts forming up in front of the gateway. 'Or we'd still be waiting here in the spring. Most obliging of the Lord of the Wall, don't you think?'

'I have scouts covering the western flank,' was Coel's response.

'And I the east.' Corvus swung in the saddle to survey the rising ground beyond Hunnum. 'If Marcus came charging over that hill with his cavalry, they'd be ankle deep in Pictish blood in the time it took to swing a sword.'

'But Victor isn't here. You heard the Keeper of the Shrine.'

Corvus produced a noncommittal grunt. 'Be careful what you say around the mighty Briga,' he warned. 'She doesn't appreciate being told she's wrong.'

'Would you have agreed to come if you'd known she was planning to put down roots in the south?' Coel demanded.

'What choice did we have?' Corvus shrugged. 'In any case my counsel still stands.'

Corvus called Awran from his place among the bodyguard. 'Round up two hundred of our old, lame and sick and find somewhere for them to camp among the Picts on the slope overlooking Corstopitum. When the rest of us move out they are to stay out of sight by day and set enough fires to imitate a whole army at night.'

'How long should I provision them for, lord king?'

'Briga wants them to stay here indefinitely, but we haven't the rations to spare. The Romans aren't fools. They'll work out what's happening within a few days. Tell them to stay for three nights, and when they've lit the fires on the third night they're to go home. And you're to go with them.'

'Home, lord?'

'Home, Awran. Queen Briga reminded me that I've left my sons to rule in my stead and I'd much rather it was someone I trust.'

Ahead, Briga urged her pony through the gateway by a passage kept clear by her bodyguards. Inside her a cold rage had replaced the earlier elation. Her enmity towards Coel had increased with each passing mile of the advance. Every time she gave an order he either made a scornful remark or suggested a different option. Briga's approach to war was simple. You ordered men to assemble, promised them plunder, kept them fed and then Nechtan did the rest. Coel, chieftain of the southern Votadini, had more acquaintance of war than most, apart, perhaps, from Corvus, whom she regarded as a mere brute. He had exposed her to ridicule and undermined her authority with his fellow kings, which was bad enough, but was that his only motive? Whatever the answer, it was enough. She called Calista to her side.

'You will find a way to get close to the king of the southern Votadini,' she said in a voice that invited no argument. 'Find out what goes on in his mind and what he says in his sleep. There is something in his eyes and in his voice I do not like.' She stared at Calista and her eyes seemed to glow with menace. 'It may be that he will require more than watching. Sickness and misfortune can sometimes be as dangerous on campaign as the enemy. Do you understand me, Calista?'

Calista lowered her eyes. 'I understand you, Brenine.'

'Then be ready for my signal.'

Drosten and Melcho had watched the discussions from a short distance away. 'It seems there is discord at the heart of our leadership,' Melcho frowned.

Drosten knew he would never have reached this far without his friend's help. Briga's 'gifts from the gods' had suffered terribly on the hectic march south, struggling to climb the steep scarps and boulder-strewn slopes north of the Wall without the benefit of hands, their stumps bleeding and strength fading. When Melcho had noticed Drosten dropping back, he allowed his pony to slow until he was level with the exhausted Pict. Without a word he'd dismounted and cupped his hands to help Drosten into the saddle. They'd taken turns on the pony for the last three days.

'You should not be here, Melcho,' Drosten said quietly. 'There is still time to turn back.'

'You wouldn't last a day without me.' Melcho kept his tone light and hoped Drosten didn't sense the brittle edge of fear the words contained. Marcus Flavius Victor's warning had echoed in his head from the moment Briga ordered her warriors into the saddle.

'*Never venture south of the Wall again.*'

In his dreams, sleeping and waking, the merciless hawk's eyes bored into his.

'*If there is a next time his warriors will return without their eyes and tongues.*'

Dread filled his mouth with sand and turned his bowels to ice. He stared at the gate. In his mind it became the gate to the Otherworld.

The last thing he wanted was to pass through. After he'd led the shambling column of mutilated warriors back across the Wall, the very heart
of him seemed to be filled with darkness. He dreaded the moment
sleep would force him to relive the chill morning at Alona. The
screams and the horror and the scent of blood and voided bowels. Yet
the instant he woke, he was seized by a paralysis at the thought of
meeting the eyes of the men who had returned without hands. *Why us
and not you?* They never spoke the words, but the sentiment was always
there. As was the guilt that weighed across his shoulders like one of the
great gathering stones the ancients placed upon the hilltops. *Why me?
Why of all those men did he choose me to remain whole?* Briga had
asked him that, on the day of Keother's terrible end. He'd been unable
to answer, other than to stammer about his good fortune. She had told
him he was chosen, not by Marcus Flavius Victor, but by the gods.
'Those favoured by the gods are useful to me,' she'd said. Since that
day he'd become, like Calista, a talisman of sorts, never allowed to
stray too far. Melcho, the Chosen.

'I said, leave me your pony.' The words came from far away and
when he blinked Drosten was studying him with a wary look.

'No,' he said. 'We will stay together and look after each other.'

'You are a good friend, Melcho.' Drosten managed a wintry smile.
'And a brave man.'

But Melcho knew it was not courage that drove him towards the
shadowy gate into the Otherworld, but the guilt at surviving whole that
would never leave him.

XL

Longovicium (Lanchester)

Marcus had gone over this ground in his mind so often he sometimes wondered if it was a product of his own imagination. But there it was laid out before him. He had visited Longovicium only briefly, and that many years earlier, and he was glad the landscape was largely true to his memory. He rested Storm at the top of the hill overlooking the fort from the west. For the last mile or so they'd followed the line of the underground aqueduct that served Longovicium, visible from the occasional flagstone protruding from the earth. But he'd forgotten the large holding dam it fed to the south of the walls, and the suspiciously well maintained pagan cemetery a little further off. The fort lay on a sloping platform overlooking the valley, with the Great North Road running through the settlement that stood beneath its eastern wall. Of similar dimensions to Vindobala, at one time it would have held a garrison of close to a thousand men, including a cavalry contingent. Now he guessed a maximum of three hundred, with the reluctant assistance of local militia who most likely spent the nights with their wives in the settlement that had grown up on either side of the road. The valley itself was perhaps five hundred paces across, with deceptively steep lower slopes. A narrow tree-lined river cut directly through it perhaps a quarter of a mile to the south of the cemetery, where a bridge carried the road over the stream. It was perfect.

A trumpet blared in the distance and he saw men scurrying to the walls of the fort in response to the long line of riders on the hill. 'I think it's time I introduced myself to the commander,' Marcus grinned at Caradoc. 'Have the quartermaster break out the best fare we have left and some decent wine. We'll entertain the officers tonight and I'll reveal my plans.'

'And not before time.'

Marcus ignored the muttered complaint and spurred Storm into movement. 'The regiments will make camp on the flat ground on this side of the river,' he called over his shoulder. 'But tell Sempronius and the others not to make themselves too comfortable. They won't be there for long.'

Two hours later Marcus sat at the head of a long table in the empty barrack block used as Longovicium's feasting hall. His long sword sat crosswise on the scarred planking to signify his dominion over those gathered. The fort's commander Aurelius Quirinus sat to his right and the others lined each side of the table. Sempronius, Rufius Clemens, Julius Pastor, Burrius of the Numerus Defensorum, by reason of his seniority, and Senilis, Rufius's cavalry commander, who Marcus had decided would control the lesser units. Hostilius Geta was a sullen presence at the far end, flanked by Caradoc and the young Picts Janus and Julius, and the legionary centurion from his cohort.

Marcus had ordered the creation of a crude sand pit on the table top, and when you looked closely it was possible to see individual elements of the landscape surrounding the fort. The assembled officers studied it with undisguised curiosity. Even Geta couldn't hide his interest.

'Firstly, Quirinus, I must thank you for the use of your hall and apologize for the unheralded nature of our arrival, but you will understand now, I'm sure, that I had reason for haste.'

'If you say the Picts are coming, I have no reason to disbelieve you, prefect.' Quirinus was still somewhat discomfited by the sudden influx of strangers, but he was soldier enough to accept it with decent grace. 'But surely we would have had word from the forts further north that they were on their way?'

'Briga is still far beyond the Wall,' Marcus assured him. 'We'll have ample warning when she crosses. The timing of our arrival is not a matter of luck, Quirinus, and together we're in a position to do Rome and this province a great service.' He looked round the table at the eager faces, mostly young. 'We will set a trap from which the Picts will have no escape. Your fort, with its stout walls, is here,' he jabbed with his knife at the mound of sand on the right side of the map. 'And here is the river,' he indicated a line that snaked from one side of the pit to the other. 'The north road, down which the Pictish invaders must come, runs past your walls to cross the river by the bridge at this point. How many *scorpiones* and *onagri* do you have available?'

Quirinus frowned. 'Christus save us, prefect, now there's a question. It grieves me to say we haven't broken out the artillery in years. Never had the need to. It's stored in one of the disused barrack blocks by the north wall. Maybe twenty engines, but we'll have to replace most of the ropes, check the springs and test the arms for strength before we even think about using them.'

'Then get your men working on them right away. Your head may depend on it.' The fort commander's mouth dropped open. 'That's not a threat, Quirinus. But if Briga breaches your walls it will be the best you can hope for. Rufius . . .' he addressed the commander of Verteris. 'How many machines did your men bring?'

'Six shield-splitters and the same number of *onagri*, all in good order,' Rufius said without hesitation and with an emphasis on the last four words that Quirinus didn't much like. 'They're packed on mules so they should be arriving within the hour.'

'Good.' Marcus nodded to Quirinus. 'Have them set up on the fort wall overlooking the valley. You have enough men to operate them all?'

'Of course,' Quirinus said. 'But I can't say how well they'll be aimed—'

A grunt escaped Caradoc and Marcus laughed. 'I doubt you'll have to worry about hitting your target. When it comes to it the Picts will be packed into that valley out there tighter than herrings in a pickle tub.'

'And then there's the question of manning the walls. Even if I rouse out the cooks, the clerks, the brewer and the armourer's mates, I doubt we'll be able to manage eighty men to each quadrant, and that's without any kind of reserve or a decent guard on the doors.'

'I can't spare you any of my infantry.' Quirinus pursed his lips in disappointment, but Marcus continued undeterred. 'The reason will become apparent later. What are your plans for the townsfolk?'

'There are places in the hills where they will be safe. I don't want them cluttering up the fort. I've sent word to the *curator* to be ready to move by morning.'

'Very well, but every able-bodied man between fifteen and fifty will help you defend the walls of Longovicium. The youngsters and the older men can look after the women and children well enough for a few days,' he stifled the other man's protest. 'Anyone with a hunting bow should bring it, with all the arrows he has, and any other weapons he can find. And boulders from the river. They may not have any military experience, but a fifteen-year-old boy or a tanner's labourer can drop a rock on a man's head as effectively as any trained soldier.'

Quirinus signified his agreement with a curt nod.

'So the fort will hold,' Marcus continued. 'And the Picts will march swiftly by beneath its walls, eager to cross the river and move beyond the range of your missiles. And that is where we will stop them.' He stabbed his dagger into the area north of the snaking line.

'How?' Geta demanded. 'How can a few hundred light infantry and a couple of thousand dismounted cavalry stop an army? Will Marcus Flavius Victor transform himself into Cacus the giant and fill the valley with his fiery breath?'

'You jest, tribune,' Quirinus scowled, 'but I am surprised a man who wears a cross at his throat would invoke the name of an imaginary monster when clearly it is God who will aid us against the pagans.'

'God,' with his right hand Marcus reached out and pulled his sword from its scabbard, 'a well-honed blade wielded by a strong arm, backed by a steadfast heart, and these . . .' From his left hand three objects clattered onto the table top and rolled to a halt just short of the sand pit. 'Every man in every regiment carries ten of them.'

'*Triboli*.' Rufius Clemens reached out and warily picked up one of the spiked pyramids. 'I haven't seen one of these for years.' He tossed the *tribolus* back onto the table, where it tumbled to a halt with one prong pointing to the ceiling. It was formed from four iron spikes joined together in such a way that one spike always ended upwards. 'You're a very devious man, prefect,' he grinned. 'Remind me never to cross you.'

'We'll scatter them in their thousands among the grass across an area a hundred paces deep on this side of the river. Among the *triboli* we'll dig hidden pits and fill them with sharpened wooden stakes – yes, even your warriors will dig, Ramios, sweat saves lives. If a charging man or a horse doesn't get a spike through a foot or hoof, they'll like as not step in a pit and break their leg.' The men around the table murmured their approval, imagining the attack breaking down in chaos and confusion and the Picts helpless against their swords.

'So we are to hold the far bank of the river?' Geta persisted. 'With fewer than three thousand men. That will only provide you with a single defensive line and a small reserve. All it would take is a few Picts to break through and your whole plan falls apart.'

'Not three thousand, Hostilius, one thousand. The cavalry will remain in the saddle where they belong.'

Geta puffed out his cheeks. 'So, our infantry are slaughtered where they stand, or worse, left to the tender mercies of the Picts, while your cavalry watch from a safe distance?'

Marcus ignored the intended insult and looked at the officers around the table. 'By the time the Picts reach here we will have been reinforced by the *dux Britanniarum* and the tribune's own Sixth legion, does that satisfy you?'

Geta snorted. 'Do these men know that Dulcitius hates you and believes you guilty of sedition and treason?' Marcus's grip tightened on the sword. He was beginning to wish he'd disposed of the young man on the march. 'What guarantees do we have that he will come to our aid?'

'Nothing is guaranteed in this life.' Marcus's hard smile sent Geta a message even a man as obtuse as he could not miss. 'My differences with the *dux Britanniarum* are a matter of record, and this latest misunderstanding will be resolved as those of the past have been. But no man can say our quarrels have had a detrimental impact on our joint military goal of containing the Picts. For all his dislike of me personally, Dulcitius has never failed to give me the support I required, nor I him. The Sixth will be here.'

Geta took heed of the message and bit his tongue. The others appeared satisfied, but Caradoc, for one, knew that Marcus's confidence wasn't entirely justified. Even if Dulcitius responded to Valeria's plea, timing was everything, and time was slipping away. Marcus had been certain he'd left himself ample leeway to create the defences that would stop Briga in her tracks, but now he was here the little rats of doubt gnawed at his self-assurance. There was so much to do.

'What of the cavalry, lord?' Sempronius asked quietly. 'You haven't mentioned our dispositions?'

'Our dispositions depend on information I do not yet have, Sempronius' – the words emerged more abruptly than Marcus intended – 'but you will know as soon as I acquire it. For the moment you and your men will help Rufius and his infantry dig their pits and scatter the *triboli*. Do not be economical with the spikes, every one might save a life.'

'Of course, lord,' Sempronius acknowledged. The others nodded their agreement.

'And Rufius, we need two diagonal passages through the pits and spikes that we can use in the event of an opportunity to counter-attack: place them here and here. Five paces wide, subtly marked. Make sure every man is aware of their position, but leave no clue for the enemy. Quirinus? I would like to take a look at your dam.'

The officers filed out to issue their orders and begin work on the defences in the valley. Marcus accompanied Quirinus from the fort's south gate and paused to study the scene below. Longovicium's civilian settlement flanked each side of the main road beneath the fort walls. At the moment it was a hive of activity as the inhabitants hurried to and fro among their substantial stone houses, filling carts and loading mules with their most treasured possessions. This was a prosperous place, its wealth built on generations of trade with the soldiers in the fort and serving the ceaseless civilian and military traffic that used the road. It was a sight that couldn't fail to inspire compassion, even in the man who had brought the villagers to this sorry state, but Marcus dashed any pity from his mind. His regiments and squadrons were camped in the open fields beyond the houses in the valley bottom. The infantry cohorts had set up their tents out of sight away to the right, beyond the winding course of the river which it would be their duty to defend to the last man. Already surveyors were marking out the area to be seeded with the *triboli* and studded with ankle-breaker pits.

'This way, prefect.' Quirinus's voice interrupted Marcus's internal debate. They followed the line of the underground aqueduct to the dam. The earthen wall rose above the rest of the landscape two or three times the height of a man, and when he climbed the turf bank Marcus remarked on the enormous volume of water contained within an area the size of an infantry parade ground.

'The one thing Longovicium won't run out of is water,' Quirinus chuckled. 'At least we don't have to worry about that. When the baths were working, we could freshen them up every couple of days and the latrines are as sweet-scented as honeysuckle. I had a survey done after Dulcitius gave me command of the fort. This is fed by the water of twenty springs that gather in a second dam, about twice as large, in the hills about five miles away. It can be a nuisance maintaining such a long pipeline, but I have a squad of men who work their way from one end to the other and then back again. They keep the channel clear and replace the flagstones the badgers pull out of place, the buggers. We have a constant flow for drinking and washing, and when we need more we just open the sluice a bit wider.'

'It seems a lot of engineering to supply one relatively modest fort.'

Quirinus didn't take offence at the reference to the scale of his command. 'Longovicium was once the *armamentarium* for every fort on the north road from Eboracum to Corstopitum. The factories here must have supplied about five thousand men with everything from pots and pans to blades, spearheads, maybe even helmets too.'

Marcus continued to stare out from the dam wall across the valley.

'I know what you're thinking, lord,' Quirinus said quietly. 'But it won't do. If you break the dam half the water will hit the houses in the town and the other half will just create a few puddles and the odd mud patch. You can't stop an army with this. And what are we to do for water at the fort if you try?'

'You'd have time to fill the fort's cisterns and you could use the bath pools as a reserve,' Marcus answered his question, but his thoughts were clearly elsewhere. 'No,' he agreed. 'It was worth considering, but you're right. We might knock down a few men and horses in the initial surge, but it wouldn't make Briga pause for a moment. Still, maybe there's another way. What if we could channel the water in the dam to the river? It would have to be at just the right moment, but if our defence was hard pressed it might make a difference.'

'Impossible.' Quirinus blew out his cheeks. 'It must be close on a third of a mile to the nearest point. Even with every man we have it would take weeks to dig a big enough channel. Not that we have enough spades and mattocks, or even carts to remove the spoil.'

Marcus nodded his understanding and let his eyes run from the fort south to where the road bridged the river. 'What if I could show you a way to do it using only a fraction of that effort?'

A bitter laugh escaped the lips of Longovicium's commander. 'You never give up, do you, prefect?'

'No.' Marcus led him from the dam wall and paced out the distance down the slope to just short of the north road. 'A hundred paces, more or less, wouldn't you say?'

Quirinus frowned. 'More or less, but we are still more than four hundred from the river,' he pointed out.

'That's true,' Marcus grinned, 'but this is as far as your men need to dig.' He took three steps forward and dropped into the drainage ditch that flanked the road's western edge. It was a good four feet deep and almost as wide. Like all roadside ditches within an hour's march it was maintained by the men of the fort's garrison. 'Your reluctant recruits from the village will have precious little to do before any battle. Have them dig a channel of similar width from the dam to this point and use the spoil to make a mound on top of the bank to divert the water into the ditch. The slope will do the rest. The flood will carry as far as the bridge. You may have to deepen the cut that carries the road drainage into the river, but that won't be too difficult.' He looked to the bridge where Quirinus had already set up a road block to stop civilians travelling north into the path of the Picts. 'And while they're at it they should tear down the bridge. No point in giving Briga an incentive to stay on the road.'

A trumpet blared from the fort, the harsh sound raising the delicate hairs on the back of Marcus's neck. When he turned he could see a man waving from Longovicium's walls. Quirinus frowned. 'I'm needed back at the fort.'

But Marcus was already on his way.

As he entered the gates he saw a Roman cavalry mount standing on shaking legs in a cloud of its own steam. The animal's nostrils flared as it snorted in each rasping breath, its flanks slick with white foam. The rider sat on the steps of the *praetorium* with his face in his hands. Marcus's heart stopped when he recognized the man, one of six scouts he'd ordered to watch sections of the Wall to warn of Briga's approach. 'Lucius?'

The soldier lifted his head at the sound of Marcus's arrival, but his eyes were so caked with sweat he might as well have been blind. 'Beg to ... Beg to rep—' Lucius's swollen tongue struggled to form the words.

'Get him some water.'

Quirinus dashed to a nearby cistern and returned with a brimming metal cup. Lucius drank deeply, then used some of the water to rub his eyes. He blinked into the winter sunlight. 'The Picts crossed the Wall at dusk yesterday, lord. I thought you would want to know. I rode through the night. This is my second mount.' He waved a limp hand towards the shuddering horse. 'I drove the first into the ground.'

But Marcus had stopped listening. Two days. She had stolen two days from him.

XLI

'You should let me go, lord. You are needed here.'

'No, Sempronius.' Marcus strapped on his sword belt and linked the scabbard to the metal hooks. He shrugged at his mail to test it for comfort around the shoulders. It seemed to become heavier with every passing year, but there was no helping that. 'There are things I must know that Lucius could not tell me. My guess is that the Picts will halt for a while to give Corstopitum a look over. It is a tempting plum filled with supplies and arms, but I've provided it with a formidable garrison and enough artillery to make it stick in Briga's craw. When she is thwarted by the fort's walls her warriors will want to plunder the surrounding countryside before they start south. By the time I reach them it will be just a matter of studying their line of march and their dispositions.'

'And if you're wrong?'

'If I'm wrong, I need to buy you time to finish the defences here and allow Dulcitius to bring the Sixth up from Eboracum.'

'We won't let you down, lord.'

'I know that.' Marcus clapped the younger man on the shoulder. 'If you're concerned about anything, look to Rufius. He's a miserable old bastard, but as good as any soldier I know.' A thought occurred to him.

'And have our cavalry move camp up into the woods beyond the crest of the ridge line.'

'You want us out of sight?' Sempronius looked puzzled, but Marcus saw no point in enlightening him further, even if he'd known what to say. He couldn't predict the future. He knew he should go down to the infantry line and talk to Rufius Clemens about his dispositions and his own doubts about Hostilius Geta, but he had no time. He had to find out how far Briga's army had advanced and what route she was taking. None of the other scouts had returned, which he guessed meant that the Picts had crossed as a single element around Corstopitum, but he couldn't be certain. By now they should be shadowing the enemy force, but they had no idea how vital time was. He needed information *now*.

He ducked out of the tent to where Luko sat his mount holding Storm's reins. The rest of the Ala Sabiniana were already in the saddle in two ranks facing the north road, their eagle shields strapped to their left arms – leaving hands free for the reins – and their dull green cloaks strapped behind the saddle. Marcus rode with Luko to where Caradoc waited in front of the long lines of horsemen. A few men watched from the walls of the fort overlooking the valley, but most were already hard at work either breaking camp for the move to their new positions or digging pits in the marshy ground in front of the river. Was there anything else he should have thought of? If there was, it would have to wait.

'Regiment will advance in line to the road and turn right into column of twos.' He nudged Storm into motion as Caradoc roared out the command.

Briga's entire being seethed with fury. It had taken hours to stir the army, gather the various elements together and cross the river to unite on the flat ground beside the Roman road south of Corstopitum. When they finally managed to combine, the fool Corvus announced that several score of his warriors had straggled off to hunt for loot in the town. Her first inclination was to leave them behind, but the king of the Selgovae announced airily that his warriors would never desert their tribesfolk and she was forced to wait while they were rounded up. Worse, when they eventually arrived at the rallying point she discovered two hundred of her northern Picts had been enticed to join them.

While they waited, a fight broke out between two of the rival clans of Votadini. Luddoc and Coel had watched with seeming unconcern as one of Coel's warriors ended up with his brain bashed in with a rock while a second man died in seconds from a spear wound in the groin. When she'd icily recommended that the two kings control their men, Coel had dismissed the skirmish as an insignificant episode in a decades long feud.

Now they were on the march, with Corstopitum an hour and more behind them, but she doubted they would cover more than five or six miles before making camp. Maintaining control of such a large force had proved much more difficult than she'd foreseen. In the hills north of the Wall it had seemed straightforward enough. Briga had simply led her straggling column of warriors through the narrow valleys and the others followed. She'd been content to allow the Selgovae and the Votadini to advance at their own pace.

It had worked until they'd reached the Wall, but there'd been growing friction between the tribes. In one incident the Votadini, who'd occupied the westernmost campsite furthest upstream of Corstopitum, had used the river as a latrine and mocked those below as they'd been forced to weave among bobbing turds to collect fresh drinking water. A small thing. A mere scratch on the body of the great alliance she had contrived to bring about. But scratches left unattended had a way of becoming festering sores. They had been Coel's men and she did not like the mocking look in his eyes when they met, as if everything she did was somehow humorous to him.

'I sometimes wonder if the Votadini are not deliberately slowing us down,' Nechtan stared venomously towards King Coel at the next break in the march.

'I can discipline our own people,' Briga said. 'The sight of a few heads on poles will soon ensure their obedience. But I can't execute

Coel's men without threatening the alliance. Even his enemies the northern Votadini wouldn't be happy to see their cousins die. He'd only take his tribe back north and like as not Luddoc would follow him.'

'That is true, Brenine, but we can alter the order of march so Coel and his warriors make up the rear of the column. That way if they are tardy they won't delay us, and if they are detached by a few miles it makes little difference. Let them eat the army's dust and see how they like it.'

To Briga's surprise Coel didn't take offence at her insistence his tribe make up the rear of the army.

'I'll be happier with Luddoc's spears in front of me where I can see them,' he laughed. 'Let Corvus worry about the backstabber.'

'My presence amuses you, lord?' Calista asked.

King Coel's smile widened. 'Your story amuses me, lady. The religious rites of the Votadini are hardly of sufficient appeal to attract so much interest, even in a priestess such as yourself. No, she has sent you to spy on me. Did she ask you to share my bed?' He laughed. 'You would be very welcome. The nights are cold and even a king's blankets let in the draught.'

'I serve the goddess, not kings or queens,' Calista snapped. 'I make my own decisions.'

'I believe you delude yourself, but that would not make you so different from so many others in this *army* of ours,' Coel nodded ahead to where Luddoc rode at the centre of his mass of warriors. 'What did she tell you to find out?'

Calista hesitated for a moment and then shrugged. What harm could it do? 'She wished to know your mind.'

'Then you may tell Queen Briga that I have nothing to hide from her. She knows I have brought my warriors here, not from any false loyalty, but because if I had not, she would have united with Luddoc to overthrow me and enslave my people. I have no love for her, just as she has no love for me. Where she leads, I will follow, but I have little faith in her ability as a commander. Those hills to our left.' Calista followed his eyes to the escarpment. 'Any prudent commander would have sent a patrol up there to check for enemy scouts. I am surprised Nechtan hasn't insisted upon it. If I was the Lord of the Wall, I would have men up there reporting on our every move.'

'The Lord of the Wall has followed his ambitions south,' Calista said. 'You have nothing to fear from him, lord king. The goddess has revealed this to me.'

'Truly? Then perhaps I am wrong to concern myself. But do not misunderstand me. Coel of the Votadini fears no man, nor woman. You may tell Briga I have made my bargain and I will honour it, but she would do well not to prolong her presence south of the Wall.'

'She means to make this land hers,' Calista pointed out. 'She has said as much.'

A bitter laugh escaped Coel's thin lips. 'She believes she is invincible, but the truth is she doesn't understand what she faces. Though the Romans are not the force they once were, long experience has taught the Votadini to respect them. If she puts down roots, this land of theirs will swallow her up. So you may also tell her that, come what may, King Coel has crops to plant in the spring and he means to be in his own fields with his own people when the sun warms the earth and brings the first touch of emerald to the forests.'

'You must—'

But the faint bray of a *carnyx* from the front of the column ensured Coel would never discover what he must or must not do. 'I think we must join our commander.' He nudged his mount forward, followed by Calista and his bodyguard.

By the time they reached Briga, Luddoc and Corvus were already crowded round the Pictish queen with their retinues. Coel nudged his mount through the crowd of bodyguards and Briga's squealing oddities. Briga was staring south to where the road disappeared into a wood and Alpin, one of her most trusted scouts, gesticulated towards the trees as he whispered excitedly into her ear.

'What's happening?' Coel asked Corvus.

'Our outriders report movement among the trees.'

'A trap?'

Corvus frowned as he considered the possibility, his single eye focused on the bare hillside above the trees. 'A strange place for one if it is,' he said eventually. He turned in the saddle to study the terrain around them. 'Only space for a few hundred men in that wood. Open hill to the east and little cover to the west. Unless they have a few thousand invisible friends they'd be fools to attack a force this size, even from ambush.'

Coel nodded his agreement.

'An army of this scale should just march over the top of them,' Luddoc gave his opinion, though no one had requested it. 'What is the woman waiting for?'

'She doesn't want to make a mistake,' Coel said. 'And she's right. Who knows what lies in those woods?' He turned to Calista. 'It may only be a detachment from the garrison at Vindomora, which lies not too far ahead, but better to be cautious when dealing with the Romans than risk any rash charge.'

As the three kings debated, Calista pushed forward towards Briga. The commander of the queen's bodyguard hesitated, uncertain whether to allow her past, but after a moment he nodded to the men barring her way and she advanced through the spearmen.

'These fools offer me nothing but riddles and wraiths.' Briga's voice had the jagged edge of forked lightning, but, though she hadn't turned her head, she spoke as if she'd summoned Calista's presence. 'There might be a hundred men in those trees or a thousand. What does the Goddess tell you?'

Calista's mind went blank and she fought to keep her hands from shaking on the pony's reins. She willed Coventina's words to emerge from her mouth as they'd done so often before, but the only result was a silence that lengthened as her panic grew. No experience had prepared her for this. What could she say? Suddenly she remembered Coel's dark eyes boring into her and it was his words that came to her. 'The goddess is not a military strategist,' she said, 'but I believe she would advise caution. The Romans have had a score of lifetimes to perfect the art of war. Perhaps it is only the garrison of the fort that lies ahead, but better to be certain than take a risk.'

'The gods send us a test.' Briga nodded thoughtfully. 'Nechtan?' The Pictish chieftain straightened. 'You will seek out the Mithiai warrior band and lead them in the advance upon the wood.' The Mithiai came from the thickly forested valleys of southern Caledon, every man a woodsman and a seasoned fighter. 'And send the men who rode with Keother to join the advance,' she said as an afterthought. Five hundred spearmen all told. It should be more than enough. 'You will advance cautiously. There should only be a few Romans, a scouting party, no more. If they dare to make a stand you may take their heads, but I want prisoners for the question.'

Marcus watched with Caradoc from the shelter of a clump of gorse on the crest of the hills to Briga's east, as the Picts sluggishly gathered a small force to advance against the woods where Janus and three squadrons of dismounted cavalry waited.

'Christus, they're slow,' Caradoc grumbled. 'We'll be here all day.'

'Janus knows what to do?'

'Of course he knows what to do, he's to do nothing. Hold them in place unless you tell him otherwise.' The old soldier looked longingly at the mass of warriors sprawled across the undulating plain below. 'No patrols. No flank guards. With another couple of regiments we could have really given Briga something to think about. Mind you, I'd have expected better from Coel or Corvus.'

'I don't want them worrying about their flanks just yet.' Marcus allowed his eyes to drift along the length of the column. 'What do you make of their dispositions?'

Caradoc peered down at the throng of warriors and their followers. A lifetime fighting the Picts had given him an unrivalled knowledge of their banners and war gear. 'Difficult to tell when they're all mingled together like that. Briga's wolf is up front where you'd expect it to be and I think I see Corvus's crow, Coel's bear and Luddoc's horse not far away.' Unwelcome news and Marcus felt a distinct twinge of the knife point near his heart. 'I don't know enough about Briga's clans to be certain, but there are bulls, boars, foxes, a leaping salmon that I take to be the Mithiai from beyond the Bodotria, and a serpent that used to be carried by Talorc's folk, but Christus only knows who carries it now. Thanks to Corvus's man Awran, I'm well enough acquainted with the Selgovae to say with some certainty they're that second great formation – if you can call it that – taking their leisure a little way up the road towards Corstopitum.' He shrugged. 'The Votadini must be bringing up the rear, though which of the cut-throats is the nose and which the arse-end is beyond the vision of these old eyes.'

'Good.' Marcus clapped the older man on the shoulder. From what he'd heard of Luddoc, he was almost certainly too proud to bring up the rear, which left Coel in that position. 'Then I've seen enough. Julius was not far wrong in his estimate, though more of them are farmers and the families of warriors than he reckoned . . .'

'The lord be praised. Easier to frighten and easier to kill.'

Marcus squirmed back through the gorse before he stood up, making sure his silhouette couldn't be seen against the skyline. He stopped abruptly when he reached the horses. 'Fool that I am.'

'What is it?'

'Supply wagons.'

'I saw no supply wagons.'

'Exactly. You can't feed an army of this size, however rapacious the Picts are, by living off the land. Cavalry can carry a week's rations and fodder at a push, but not infantry. These people are eating what they carry through the day and being resupplied when the wagons bringing food and ale reach them at night. That means the wagons are probably still passing through the Wall, or may not even have reached it.'

'So if we cut them off from their supplies, they go back home again,' Caradoc suggested.

'Perhaps, but if we let them return home they'll just be back in the spring or summer. I mean to encourage them to stay away on a more permanent basis. No, what I meant was that I've wasted a day and placed Janus and his squadrons' lives in danger for nothing. No matter how quickly Briga wants to advance she can only move at the speed of her slowest wagon or she will outrun her supplies.'

'If she set off two days and more before Julius expected her to, doesn't that mean she suspects something is wrong?'

'Of course she suspects.' Marcus pulled himself into the saddle. 'How could Briga, who has done what no other woman has ever done and not just united the Pictish tribes, but bent their rulers to her will, not be suspicious? But ninety-nine *pedes quadrati* do not make a *scrupulum*, no, nor a hundred and one. There is only one answer. It's possible she may defeat me, but she cannot defeat the arithmetic.' He saw Caradoc make the pagan sign against evil at his admission that victory was not certain. 'Briga's army can cover no more than six or seven miles a day. Her inexperience has bought me time, old man, and we have to use that time well.'

'What about the commander at Vindomora?'

Marcus took a drink from his copper water flask to rinse out his mouth and spat into the grass. 'He reports directly to the *dux Britanniarum*. I can't order him to abandon the fort, all I can do is suggest it. He may be right and Briga will bypass Vindomora as she did Corstopitum, but his men would add ballast to our defences at Longovicium. Come, if we don't go now Briga will reach the bridge before us.'

At last Briga's attacking force had formed some kind of line and a bray from a *carnyx* announced their advance. Marcus stared at the wood where Janus and fewer than a hundred men waited. He closed his eyes and said a silent prayer, though to what god it was directed he would never recall. If Janus returned without losing a man he would win. If not . . .

XLII

Melcho clutched his sword nervously as he advanced in the centre of the Pictish ranks towards the dark line of the forest. Nechtan had attached Keother's warriors to his own bodyguard because, in his own words, 'if we get into a fight, I don't want you getting in the way'. He was a tall, thin man with weatherworn features, a long nose and a pointed dirty-grey beard, and down-turned lips that gave him a permanently sullen expression. The top of his head was bald and brown as a hen's egg, but he wore what remained of his hair in a long ponytail. For all his grim demeanour, Melcho knew Briga valued him as a warrior and leader. In his right hand he carried a double-headed axe with all the ease of long use, while his left held an oval shield painted in an intricate spiral pattern. A pair of curved fighting knives were tucked into his belt, and another in his boot completed his armoury.

'Stay in line with me and keep your eyes open.' Nechtan's call to the men around him was echoed along the line to the outer flanks. He walked slowly, placing his feet with care, eyes roving between the ground just ahead and the first trees two hundred paces away. For all his entreaties the line of warriors snaked and undulated as the men tried to stay in formation with each other. They were five hundred strong, a great war band by any measure, that formed a single rank covering six hundred paces and more. Yet Melcho sensed this type of manoeuvre was alien to them. The Mithiai were great raiders, using stealth to snatch cattle, sheep and women from their neighbours. If a quarrel between two clan chiefs needed to be resolved it would be done in the traditional fashion, with agreed numbers of warriors meeting on open ground and showing their martial prowess against each other. Marching in the open to confront an unseen enemy was enough to make even the most seasoned warrior nervous. Melcho could feel the tension straining like a twisted rope and the urge to simply charge screaming towards the trees was as strong in him as in any other.

The sound of running feet on the turf made him look over his shoulder and he felt a surge of fellowship as Drosten ran up from the main force. 'The Brenine sent me to carry any messages you may wish to send, lord,' the mutilated Pict announced to Nechtan.

'The only message you will carry from me to the Brenine is the heads of my enemies,' the war chief rasped. 'Though I see you would find that difficult. But stay close in case I need you.'

Drosten and Melcho exchanged a nod and the younger man felt the tension drain from him at the sight of his friend. Melcho might be a member of what had once been Keother's bodyguard, but he had never made the mistake of believing he belonged. The others were mostly much older and years of imposing Keother's dictatorial rule and sharing his disorderly living had left them rough-edged and mistrustful of outsiders. Only the fact that they knew he enjoyed Briga's favour made him welcome among them. Before his misfortune, Drosten had been a true friend. They'd hunted and fished together, wrestled, fought, practised swordplay and never quarrelled. When he'd watched Drosten led to the stump he had wanted to cry out 'Take me instead', but terror – or perhaps it should be called self-preservation – had robbed him of speech.

He knew it would have made no difference. But every day since, Melcho had wished he'd had the courage or fortitude to offer that sacrifice. Was he a coward? The question continued to plague him and he feared the answer. Certainly, since they'd crossed the Wall he'd felt

312

a sense of oppression that was like living in constant shadow. Even Drosten's presence couldn't drive it away entirely, but it lightened his heart a little.

By now they were fifty paces closer to the woods and the warriors in the long line clutched at their weapons in anticipation of the final rush that could only be mere moments away. Nechtan had ordered complete silence until the enemy was in sight, but it went against all their warrior instincts. Even the most courageous warrior was the braver with a defiant roar in his throat and the pounding of it in his chest.

'Look!' The shout came from the left of the line where a man pointed his spear to the trees. A score of Roman auxiliaries broke clear of the trees waving spears and swords at the advancing Picts and roaring insults and challenges in their own tongue. Even as Nechtan turned to evaluate the threat a similar cacophony broke out to his right where more soldiers appeared to threaten that flank. The younger Pictish warriors replied with a howl of suppressed rage, but Nechtan's veterans kept them from making any foolhardy rush. The sight of the enemy had stirred Nechtan's blood as much as any man's, but he continued to study the wood through narrowed eyes. He'd expected the Romans to disperse like smoke when they recognized the size of his force, perhaps leaving a few men concealed among the trees to sacrifice themselves in an attempt to delay him. Instead, he faced a defensive line as long as his own, and a well-manned one at that. As well as the soldiers on the flanks he could see shadowy silhouettes standing resolutely among the trees, with others moving among them, their officers perhaps, providing encouragement before battle. Should he call for reinforcements? He had no doubt it would anger Briga, but it might be the prudent thing to do.

Yet something wasn't right.

'Quiet!' His command was taken up all along the line and gradually the cacophony subsided.

'What is it?' Drosten decided his status as Briga's messenger allowed him leeway to ask the question.

'You tell me,' Nechtan spat. 'How many men would you say we're facing?'

Drosten studied the wood. A score of soldiers were visible on each flank still throwing out their insults and challenges, but the bulk remained barely visible in the centre. Visible and oddly silent. 'Hundreds,' he frowned. 'But it's odd that most of them are so quiet.'

'Odd, because the bastards don't have a tongue,' Nechtan said through gritted teeth. 'Advance.' He raised his axe and set off for the trees at the trot with his personal guard in his wake. Behind him, the long undulating line of warriors dashed to take station on their leaders.

'They're running.' Melcho nodded to the flank where the soldiers had disappeared into the trees.

'They never intended to fight,' Drosten grunted between breaths. 'Only to delay us. But they've made a mistake. We'll hunt them down before they've gone another half mile, because they're in armour and that will slow them down. Nechtan can still slaughter the bastards.'

'Some of them want to fight.' Drosten followed Melcho's pointing sword to the centre of the wood ahead, where a line of shadowy figures stood, unmoved by the Pictish charge.

'Kill them,' roared Nechtan. 'Kill them all.'

With a roar the Picts charged through the stand of bushes that fronted the trees and into the wood. 'Bastards.' Nechtan slowed to an infuriated halt. He swung his axe and lopped the head from the nearest 'Roman'. 'Cunning bastards.' He picked the head up. A worn cloth sack filled with leaves and moss. It had been set up on a rough wooden frame, one of fifteen or twenty that held a dozen heads each. Some of them were topped with battered, rusting helmets from a previous age. He threw the cloth bag away and advanced deeper into the forest. The road was a little way to the left and he began to move diagonally towards it. Melcho, Drosten and the rest of his bodyguard followed.

'What's this?' Drosten dropped to one knee beside a small green heap among the leaves. Horse manure.

'Cavalry?' Nechtan couldn't hide his puzzlement. 'We were told the fort was garrisoned with militia infantry. Signal the—'

Drosten looked up to see a feathered arrow sprouting from the notch above his commander's breastbone. Nechtan pitched forward onto his face with a gurgling cry and a soft whirring sound filled the air.

'Down.' Drosten launched himself at the back of Melcho's knees, bringing him to the ground just as a shower of spears landed among the men around Nechtan, spitting one through the thigh and leaving another screaming as he clutched frantically at the long shaft pinning his lower belly. Within moments the clatter of hooves on the hard-packed earth of the roadway announced the withdrawal of whoever had thrown the spears.

Marcus counted the cavalrymen as they crossed the bridge, greeting the men by name and asking them how they fared. By the width of their grins it was clear they felt they'd done well, and a flicker of hope flared in his breast. The walls of Vindomora lay a hundred and fifty paces to the rear, but most of the garrison lined the south bank of the river to watch the return of the Ala Sabiniana's blocking force. The fort's commander, Antonius Vitalis, stood beside Marcus's horse with one hand proprietorially on the bridge's wooden parapet, a large silver ring set with what looked like a ruby glinting on his middle finger.

'You're sure I can't persuade you to come with us?' Marcus broached the subject one last time. 'I could certainly make use of these stout men of yours.'

Vitalis smiled his appreciation, but he shook his head.

'I have my orders, prefect,' he said, confirming Marcus's suspicion that some news of his alleged disgrace had seeped through from Eboracum. 'In any case' – a hint of regret there? – 'it's too late now.' It was true enough: if the garrison abandoned the fort, Marcus would have had to keep his horses' pace to that of the infantry, which would cause further unnecessary complication. 'But I promise we will buy you time,' the other man continued earnestly. 'Two hours at the very least.'

'You'll not take any unnecessary chances?'

Vitalis shook his head. 'We'll block the bridge and hold this bank, make a demonstration or two to keep them on their toes, then retire to the fort. The men are stout, but I can assure you Vindomora's walls are stouter still. If the Picts bypassed Corstopitum without a fight I doubt very much they'll try their hand against us.' He grinned. 'Though I wish they would for we'd make them pay dearly for their impudence.'

'Very well.' Marcus managed a smile despite his growing sense of foreboding. 'I'll leave you to it.' He stayed in position until he saw Janus's face, the last man of the last troop. 'If I count right you survived without losses?'

'Not a man and not a scratch, though we left them plenty to remember us by.' Janus was still glowing with the joy of his small triumph. 'I would have liked to delay them a little longer, but they smoked out our ruse more quickly than I'd expected.'

When Janus had crossed to the near bank the Vindomora militia began barricading the bridge with timber and sacks of earth.

'What's this?' The young Pict frowned.

'Our rearguard.'

'Then good luck to them.'

'I wish you God's favour, tribune.' Marcus turned to Vitalis and gave him a formal salute. He resisted the temptation to suggest leaving the bridge open to make it more of a lure for Briga's warriors and draw them on to its narrow confines: a commander did not give another advice unless that other was his subordinate.

Briga had planned to camp on the north side of the river, but the loss of Nechtan had shaken her more than she cared to show. As far as most of her host was concerned, he was just another veteran warrior who had followed her orders, but Briga, for all her personal vanity, knew better. Nechtan had been her guide in military matters and her general in battle. His death was like losing an eye or an arm. She was diminished, in her own eyes, if not her followers'. Her gaze drifted towards where her three allies sat their horses waiting for the order to make camp. All were experienced in battle, but could she trust any of them to take Nechtan's place? Not Coel, whom Nechtan himself had never trusted. Luddoc was so self-absorbed he was probably unaware of Nechtan's existence and would seek to supplant her the moment she gave him an opening. Corvus? A brute when she needed a brain. No, there was only one answer. For her own sake she needed to reassert her authority and prove to herself she'd absorbed what he had to teach her. She called the allied commanders to join her. The van of her army had halted among trees three hundred paces short of the bridge at Vindomora and she rode forward with Coel, Corvus and Luddoc until they had a view of the crossing and the fort beyond.

'We will make them pay for the loss of Nechtan.' She surveyed the barrier across the roadway and the small Roman force tasked with defending it. More soldiers lined the river bank to east and west of the timber crossing and she could clearly see the walls of the fort beyond it. 'Men will speak of their death agonies and shudder.'

'The river's not deep and the banks are scalable,' Luddoc pointed out. 'I say we can't let a paltry few hundred militiamen delay us again. We should ignore the bridge and throw the whole army across the river against them.'

'If we do that,' Briga countered, 'all it will achieve is to drive them into the sanctuary of the fortress walls. We will have a choice between either wasting time and men trying to winkle them out or leaving another garrison which will be a potential threat to our supply lines. No, I believe I have a more suitable strategy. Where is Rhuin?' She called for her chief scout.

An hour later Vitalis watched a mob of Pictish infantry warily approach the bridge as if their earlier encounter had left them confused about what tactics to use against the defenders. Eventually, their leaders formed them into a line, more solid in the centre than on the flanks. Vitalis guessed the bulk of the warriors would attack directly, while the others claimed the attention of his soldiers to east and west. He smiled, because it was exactly what he'd hoped for. An opportunity to bloody the Picts and give encouragement to his men before withdrawing into the confines of the fort. He had little doubt the barrier would stop the first enemy rush. If he could hold them in place long enough to do them some real damage, he'd be happier still. If they persisted, they would lose men. If they retired, he would stay in position until they attacked again and continue to do so until he judged the threat great enough to force him back to the fort. He'd promised Marcus Flavius Victor time and he would win the Lord of the Wall every last minute he could without risking his command.

'Looks as if they're frightened of us,' his senior centurion said as they watched the line edge forward.

'If they're not now, they will be once our shield-splitters start ripping into them.' He'd set up two of the bolt-throwing catapults on each flank of the bridge to provide a converging fire when the Picts bunched, as they inevitably must at the far end of the bridge. Two or three volleys would give them something to think about.

'Not that many of them, though. The way those horse soldiers were talking we were about to face a whole army.'

'This will just be the vanguard,' Vitalis said brusquely. 'The others will be along soon enough.'

By now the Pictish line was fifty paces from the bridge and he could make out the individual bearded faces roaring their incomprehensible insults and challenges. He tested the draw on his sword. Not long.

'Why don't the bastards charge?' Vitalis looked from his centurion to the enemy, who had inexplicably halted their advance and taken to hammering the shafts of their spears against their shields to make a sound not unlike distant thunder.

He felt the first stirrings of unease and he glanced to east and west, checking his flanks. 'Watch them for any tricks.'

A soldier's instinct told him he should retreat to the fort immediately, but he was a young man and duty held him in place.

The first frantic shouts from the fort confirmed he'd been correct. Desperately, he looked to his flanks. They remained clear and his mind reeled in confusion because he couldn't judge the nature of the threat or gauge how serious it was. It was only when the clamour from the fort increased that he realized his mistake. He looked back to see a rush of Pictish warriors surge round each side of the walls.

Rhuin had led Luddoc and his warriors in a wide arc that took them beyond the western Roman flanking guards. When they'd crossed the river they moved south for a mile before following the road back towards the fort. The only real uncertainty in Briga's plan was whether the Votadini could make their final approach with sufficient stealth to go unnoticed by the sentries. As it turned out only the last few hundred paces posed a problem and by then it was clear the ramparts were empty. The sentries, as Briga's witch had predicted, were drawn to the sight of the impending battle to the north. Luddoc laughed. Now the fort's garrison were laid out before them like hogs tied for a feast.

'Back to the fort,' Vitalis screamed, but he knew he'd left it too late. What remained of the garrison were reluctant to abandon their comrades. Already the Picts were forcing their way through the great double gate undeterred by the pitiful shower of spears that rained down on them from above. Once inside there would be no saving Vindomora.

The soldiers covering the flanks tried to outrun the warriors who closed in on the bridge like an enormous claw, but they were quickly cut down and hacked to pieces by the Pictish war axes. Blocked from any escape, something like a hundred of his original force formed a defensive wall around Vitalis. He knew they were waiting for orders, but terror rose in him like a rising tide and he feared he might soil himself. Beside him the centurion babbled a prayer. The thunder of feet on wooden boards announced the arrival of the original attackers. They were laughing now, crowing at their trapped enemy. On the outer edges of the Roman formation the Picts killed when the opportunity arose, but oddly there was no general slaughter. Gradually it dawned on him that they wanted prisoners and the awful reality of that fact made his earlier terror seem almost benign.

XLIII

They'd wasted a long, frustrating day while Terentius Cantaber worked patiently to convince Dulcitius that his career would be for ever tainted if he stayed behind Eboracum's walls. Still, it could have been worse. Cantaber had used the intervening hours to prepare his legion for the march, so they were ready to set out at dawn. Or, as it turned out, as soon after dawn as Dulcitius could be chivvied from his warm bed and sulky mistress. Yet Valeria, bred to the saddle, had to fight her frustration at being constantly confined to the leisurely marching pace and daily routine of the legion. The legionaries were all veterans, but as Cantaber explained, that did not mean they were conditioned for a campaign like this.

'We have been in garrison too long,' he admitted. 'It is not that the men are soft, but they do not have the miles in their legs at the pace you would wish them to travel. If I push them too hard we will lose one man in every four before we ever reach Longovicium.' Valeria felt like screaming that unless they reached Longovicium on time Marcus and his men would be slaughtered and the Sixth at the mercy of the Picts, but she bit her tongue. 'But rest assured I will do what I can.'

One thing she grudgingly admitted was that a legion on the march was an impressive sight. The soldiers kept formation in their centuries in a way an auxiliary unit never would, the long lines maintaining intervals and rank with remarkable precision. They carried their big oval shields slung on their backs, spears at rest on one shoulder and leather satchels containing their immediate needs hanging from a strap across the other. Their chain armour shone with the brilliance of constant attention and their helmets were uniform in pattern. A sword hung from every left hip on a belt that also carried a sheathed dagger and a pair of lethal *plumbatae,* throwing darts. They would provide Marcus with infinitely more likelihood of success against Briga . . . if she could get them to him on time.

The marchers rested for a few minutes every hour, leaning on their spear shafts because they were required to stay on their feet. Before the sun reached its height they broke their fast by a river or a stream where the horses could be watered. Eventually, they made camp five miles short of Isurium Brigantum, the town which in Valeria's mind had become the target for the first day.

Dulcitius had relented enough to allow her to ride with her own men and to pitch her tent among them. He even invited her to dine with him in the large tented pavilion that doubled as his living accommodation and headquarters, and with reluctance she joined him that evening. 'So you have what you wanted, my dear' – the wrinkled head swivelled towards her as they ate – 'but I sense you are still not quite pleased.'

'It would please me better if we moved with more urgency, lord,' she admitted. 'If Marcus is correct, the Picts will reach Longovicium in four days, perhaps less. We have already lost many hours.'

'Better to arrive late than not at all.' Dulcitius seemed pleased with himself and to her surprise Valeria realized he actually enjoyed being on campaign. 'No doubt the legate will have explained to you the logistical problems of moving large bodies of men across the country at speed. Yes, we have roads, but for infantry a road is just one long neck of a wineskin. Only a certain number of soldiers can move along it at any one time. Your legionary is not some over-excitable cavalry-man able to dash off across country to cause mayhem and then run

321

away again.' He affected not to notice the tightening of Valeria's smile. 'He can move at a specific pace and by and large that pace is dictated by the slowest of his accompanying supply wagons. He must be nurtured and maintained, so that when he reaches the field of battle he is neither exhausted, hungry, nor thirsty, but ready to fight with a sword in his hand and a meal in his belly. But, be reassured,' he wrested a shred of meat from a gap between two of his remaining teeth, 'General Cantaber is determined to camp at Albamus tomorrow and at Cataractonium the following night. We are well aware of the scale of this emergency.'

'I can ask no more.' Valeria lowered her eyes so he wouldn't see the anger in them. It had taken too long to persuade Dulcitius to move. No amount of reassuring words could change that. Yet she couldn't allow her frustration to lessen his enthusiasm. 'And I thank you for it, lord Dulcitius. You have been most patient with me.'

'What I cannot understand,' Dulcitius continued, 'is how a woman of your intelligence and strength of character could allow herself to become embroiled with your brother's intrigues without attempting to guide him back onto the path of common sense. If he had approached me with his true purpose at the start, we would have found some way of achieving the same outcome without putting Britannia at risk.'

Did Dulcitius actually believe this nonsense? Perhaps he did. She had known men so arrogant and bereft of self-awareness that, for them, the truth was whatever emerged from their mouths. If their next words contradicted it, those became the truth in their turn. Still, on balance it would do no harm to answer his question and give the impression she was prepared to confide in him.

'I did not guide Marcus, as you put it,' she accompanied the words with a sad smile, 'because he did not reveal his intentions until a few days ago. By then it was too late to do anything but follow his orders and try to persuade you to aid him.'

'For four whole weeks your own brother kept you oblivious of his intentions, and all the while he was building an army in front of your own eyes?' Dulcitius sounded genuinely astonished and Valeria winced inwardly at what was only the painful truth. Perhaps the *dux Britanniarum* wasn't the only person in this tent capable of self-deception.

'I'm sorry to say it is true.' The words almost choked her. 'He used everyone.' Only now did the scale of Marcus's deceit become clear to her. How else would he have persuaded Canalius to part with Sempronius and an entire cavalry wing from Cilurnum? *'Remind him that we're all following Dulcitius's orders.'* The words rang in her ears. 'Even me.'

Just where did the truth end and the lies begin? Suddenly everything that had happened over the last month moved into sharper focus. Was his determination that she shouldn't accompany him to meet Corvus designed to keep her safe, or was there another reason for her exclusion? She remembered the supplies that had appeared so fortuitously, like the Lord's miracle of the loaves and fishes. The way Marcus had used the priest, Ninian, to stir up the Christians at Brocolitia. Did his manipulation end there, or had the fire which ultimately drove the keeper of Coventina's shrine into Briga's arms been part of the plan all along? And to what purpose? What else was she missing? Of course, the raid on Aesica's miners' settlement. There was something about it that stank like last week's fish. The odd behaviour of the Picts and the even odder return of Janus and his squadron from their successful mission to recover the missing silver. Yes, their demeanour could be attributed to the apparently missing Julius and the two casualties, but there was something else that had affected every man in the patrol.

'Of course,' Dulcitius interrupted her thoughts with a sympathetic murmur, 'we must take into account the severity of your brother's wound. A man who believes he is dying cannot be altogether of his own mind.'

And how would you have known that? Valeria wondered. Caradoc had admitted channelling information of Marcus's movements to Dulcitius, but would he have mentioned his old friend's injury? Or was there more than one spy as Marcus had feared? A name appeared like a whisper in her head, accompanied by a face. Zeno? No, Zeno was no spy, but he had been in constant attendance upon Marcus. That was natural given the nature of Marcus's wound, but . . . Yes, that was what had blinded her to everything else. The wound. Twice she'd feared he would never take another breath, but each time he'd made what now appeared to be a remarkable recovery. On the day he'd seen her off on the ride to Eboracum the wound might never have existed. Zeno with his handsome, honest face and golden body certainly had questions to answer.

If he survived.

And that depended on the man opposite her.

'Two days to Cataractonium, then another three to Longovicium. That means we will be a day later than Marcus expects us,' she reminded Dulcitius.

'At the risk of repeating myself, the men must eat and sleep as well as march. I cannot provide them with wings.'

Valeria rose from her seat and bowed. There was no more to say. When she returned to her tent Leof was waiting. 'Are the horses ready?'

'As you ordered, lady,' the young Saxon said.

'Good. We probably won't need them for another few days, but best to be prepared.'

'I also have news.'

'What kind of news?'

'While you were with my lord Dulcitius, the legate paid us a visit. To inspect our camp, he said, but there was more. He took me aside and bade me memorize a message for you. Lord Dulcitius has scouts in the north. A constant stream of messengers bring him news of events there. He knows precisely where the Picts are and their rate of march. That means—'

'It means he can time his arrival just in time to claim victory.' Valeria frowned.

But how much sweeter would that victory be if it also encompassed the tragic death of Marcus Flavius Victor?

BLOOD

XLIV

Longovicium (Lanchester)

A shiver ran down Marcus's spine at the eerie *whippourwill* cry of a lone curlew in the gathering dusk. Curlews on the northern moors with the ice still forming on the ponds at dawn? A strange winter if they were, but these were strange times. More likely a scout who'd perfected the call and was using it to communicate with one of his comrades somewhere on the hill. But whose scout? If Briga's outriders were already in the forests up there watching his preparations, like as not they were all dead.

Darkness would come quickly, but there was still much to do. He was exhausted, slumped in the saddle and barely able to keep his eyes open as he followed the road into Longovicium with the fortress walls to his right. The houses on either side of the highway were old, but well built in stone with mostly tiled roofs, which would make them difficult to burn. Soon Pictish warriors would be swarming through these buildings bent on destruction and seeking plunder. Yet the walls and gardens, with their fruit bushes and apple trees, would provide a barrier against any frontal attack on the fort from this side. He'd considered fortifying one or two of the houses, but he knew he'd have been condemning the defenders to death. In any case, he needed the men elsewhere. The motley garrison of militia and householders would deal with any Picts who filtered through the buildings and tried to claw their way up the hillside.

'You know what to do?' he said to Caradoc.

The veteran cavalryman nodded and without a word turned off at the head of the leading squadron and urged his horse up the steep track past the north gate of the fort. The Ala Sabiniana would bed down on the high ground beside the dam, shielded from sight from the valley below by the fortress itself.

Marcus continued along the road to where Janus had ridden ahead to call together the Roman commanders. They gathered in a grain store on the southern edge of the settlement: Rufius, who would command the infantry; Sempronius, of the Second Asturians, three hundred strong; Julius Pastor, commander of the Ala Herculaea, two hundred strong; Burrius of the Numerus Defensorum, and Senilis who would command the combined smaller units who would fight independent of Marcus's direction. The glowering figure of Ramios, the German war chief, stood in the doorway. Their faces were dirty and etched with the same deep lines of exhaustion as his own and he guessed they'd worked through the previous night preparing the defences he'd ordered. Someone had thought to bring bread and wine and Marcus drank gratefully from a clay jar and swallowed a few bites of crusty loaf before he began.

'You can show me the river defences later, Rufius,' he told Verteris's commander. 'First we'll deal with the dispositions of the cavalry.'

He closed his eyes and tried to remember the positioning of the tribes that formed Briga's army on the march. When he'd been young, Brenus had spent many hours forcing him to memorize the pieces on a gaming board as he moved them around time and again, for just this type of occasion. It should have come as second nature, but he found that this time it didn't. That great scattered mass of warriors and camp followers on the plain would be funnelled by the terrain into the relatively narrow valley below the fort. Christus, the Picts were so many and the defenders so few. What had he done? Yet even as doubt welled up inside him, Janus, directly across the circle of puzzled commanders, winked at him and like a flickering candle the panic was extinguished. Marcus drew in a deep breath.

'Sempronius, you will position your men for the night on the high ground on the far side of the valley. Half a mile to the north should do it. We returned that way and there's a small dip behind the ridge line that will provide you with sufficient cover at dawn. I want patrols watching the Vindomora road through the night. Briga's scouts will be on the prowl. Make sure your commanders know to keep them from the hills, but they must not provoke or engage them. Use every ruse you can to make them think you're nothing but a few militia. That goes for all of you. Do you understand?' The cavalry commanders answered with a murmur of agreement. 'Julius,' he turned to Ala Herculaea's tribune. 'You will find somewhere similar on this side of the valley opposite Sempronius and the Second Asturians. You will launch the first attack on my signal. Look for a red flag waved from the tower above the east gate.'

'Attack on what?' Julius demanded. 'If you are correct there will be almost twenty thousand Picts filling the valley. Am I just to charge into their midst?'

'They will be in their tribal elements,' Marcus assured him. 'We watched them yesterday.' He crouched over a patch of thick flour dust and drew his dagger. 'Briga's Picts and their allies from beyond the Bodotria will be in the van, here.' He scratched a rough circle. 'Corvus follows. Then Luddoc and his northern Votadini and finally Coel bringing up the rear with their southern cousins. Your task will be to hit Luddoc as hard as you can.'

'And I?' Sempronius asked.

'You will begin your charge when Julius is part way down the slope and catch Luddoc on his left flank. He will be between a hammer and an anvil. Seek out the sign of the rearing horse that identifies Luddoc and his senior advisers. Do not allow yourself to be distracted by any other.'

'If there's nothing else I will see to my men,' Sempronius bowed. Julius Pastor walked out at his heels, clearly keen to discuss what they'd just heard.

'Burrius,' Marcus continued, 'your *defensores* will take station in the trees four hundred paces south of Sempronius and his Asturians, with Senilis's units opposite on the high ground left of the fort. You will attack the rear of Queen Briga's element simultaneously at my signal. Any questions?'

'Surely there's a simpler way of committing suicide?' said Burrius. 'My two hundred and,' he gestured to Senilis, 'two hundred more will be hanging on to the tail of a wolf twenty times our size. And if you're right,' he rubbed the toe of his boot across the crude flour map, 'Corvus and his Selgovae will be waiting to gobble us up like a fox in a hen coop.'

'Let me worry about Corvus,' Marcus said in a voice that allowed no argument.

'What about us?' Ramios the German demanded. 'My men have had enough digging. They want to fight Picts.'

Marcus realized he'd entirely forgotten his foreign allies. For a moment he considered placing Ramios under his own command, as he'd intended to do with the remaining cavalry detachments.

Rufius Clemens cleared his throat. 'We could do with all the help we can get, Marcus. I have nine hundred men all told, to defend a line close on a thousand paces in length. That's without a single spear in reserve. If Dulcitius comes up with the Sixth I'll guarantee to hold that line till Hades freezes over, but if he doesn't . . .' He shrugged. 'All it would take is a score of Picts to break the line and we're done.'

'All right.' Marcus studied the dusty map. 'Ramios, you and your men will take up a position here, on the rising ground to the right of the line. Publius and the Fourth Gauls on the left. That should give Briga pause if she considers flanking your line, Rufius. I should have thought of it earlier. You will be like the pillars that strengthen a gateway,' he explained for the benefit of Ramios.

'Pillars?' the German spat. 'I know nothing of pillars, but we will fight, yes?'

'Yes,' Marcus assured him. 'You will fight.'

Marcus and Rufius Clemens followed the other officers out into the gathering gloom. The stars were already showing as dull points in a sky the colour of pewter.

'Just enough time for you to show me your defences,' Marcus said as Rufius led the way down the slope from the settlement and across the marshy ground towards the river.

'You're a hard man to please, Marcus.' Rufius halted a hundred paces from the line of the river, marked by a band of trees on either bank. 'But I think you'll be satisfied.' Between the two men and the stream the ground was covered with tussock grass and a mass of low scrub that was thinner than Marcus remembered. 'What do you see?'

Marcus studied the ground in front of him, looking for the telltale signs of disturbance and carelessly discarded earth that would mark the pits. He shook his head. 'I see nothing.'

'Between here and the trees there are something like two thousand pits each just deep enough to snap a man's leg at the calf if he's lucky enough not to tread on one of the pointed stakes concealed inside it.' Marcus looked again at the ground, but he could still see nothing. Rufius and his men had achieved a remarkable feat of disguise in such a short time. 'Best for us if they come quickly tomorrow, because the grass and twigs we've used for camouflage will soon discolour and the pits will stick out like the pimples on a whore's arse. Between them we've scattered twelve thousand *triboli* . . .'

'Only twelve? I thought we'd carried fifteen thousand?'

Rufius gave him a wry look. 'I decided it might be sensible to save a couple of thousand to cover the flanks you'd left hanging in the air, but now we have the cavalry . . .'

'Is there anything else you think I've missed?'

'Well, to be honest, Marcus, apart from the fact that we're going to be outnumbered ten to one until that old slow-body Dulcitius arrives, your great plan appears to have more holes in it than a wine strainer. But let's not be too pessimistic. Come this way, and tread carefully, there might be one or two *triboli* that have strayed onto the lanes we've left in case we get the chance to counter-attack.' He led the way on a diagonal course towards the line of trees. 'There are four of them, each five paces wide, which might seem a lot, but Hostilius, who turns out to know something about these things, says they're in the right place. Any Pict charging directly at our defences won't even be aware when he's in the clear and the chances are he'll still have to negotiate ten or twenty pits and two hundred *triboli* on the way to the river . . .'

'Where you'll stop them.'

'Where we'll stop them.' By now they were making their way through the thicker brush close to the bank. 'A steep drop in most places,' he gestured down to the river bed five or six feet below, where the dark, foam-flecked waters flowed placidly among weed-covered rocks, 'and the same on the far bank, where they're in for a surprise.'

The surprise turned out to be a three-foot-thick wall of thorn bushes that created a solid barrier between the trees.

'That will hold them for a while.' Marcus didn't hide his admiration.

'Another of Hostilius's ideas,' Rufius told him. 'They're staked in so they can't be shifted without a lot of effort, and while they're trying to shift them we'll be killing them. Quirinus up at the fort has done us proud in the matter of throwing spears. He had about five thousand of the old-fashioned, weighted *pila* rusting away in an empty barrack block from the fort's time as an *armamentarium* – you know how it is, you have no use for the buggers, but you're worried somebody will turn up some day with a requisition form – and he very kindly provided us with four to every man. We also had a chat about artillery. He reckons some of his bolt-throwing catapults will be operating at the edge of their range and they'd be of more use down here.'

Marcus nodded. 'I agree.'

'So we have eight shield-splitters set up on earth platforms behind our line.' Rufius accompanied the words with a wicked grin. 'They have a clear field of fire that will converge three hundred paces out and just where you'd expect whoever was directing their attack to be.'

A young man in an officer's uniform appeared from the flank. Earth caked the skirt of his tunic and smudged his handsome features.

'You've been busy I see, Hostilius,' Marcus greeted him. 'And Rufius here tells me you've added some fine innovations to our defence, for which I thank you.'

Geta smiled modestly at the praise. 'The legate of the Sixth is a keen student of the military art,' he said. 'It's good that the dry old scrolls he made us read have had their uses.'

'I know you're keen to get back to your legion,' Marcus said. 'I had thought to send you south to inform the legate of our dispositions.'

Geta shook his head. 'I would not disobey an order, prefect.' He straightened. 'But I would rather be here with my men. They're up for this battle. They've seen me dig; now perhaps I can show them that I can fight.'

'Very well.' Something seemed to be wrong with Marcus's throat and the words came out as a sort of choked snarl.

'I just came to report that all preparations have been completed and are as you ordered.' Geta turned to Rufius. 'I still have some concerns about the enemy turning our flanks, but I would stake my life on the centre holding.'

'Then get the men fed and bedded down.' Rufius explained about the cavalry support and the young officer went away satisfied. They watched him go. 'A fine young man as it turns out,' Rufius said. 'It just shows you can be wrong about people.' Marcus chose not to supply the expected answer, and Verteris's commander continued, 'When do we expect the Sixth to arrive? I'd have thought we'd have had a message from Dulcitius by now.'

'No point in speculating,' Marcus said. He looked up the empty valley in the fading light. In a few moments the colour of the sky changed from an ethereal silver to the dull blue of a sword blade, and finally to black. Tomorrow that valley would be thronged with thousands of howling Pictish warriors eager to shed Roman blood. 'All we can do is wait.'

'Christus.' The word emerged from Rufius as a short gasp.

Marcus followed his gaze to where what started as a dull orange glow expanded to fill the northern sky.

'I thought Vindomora would hold her attention a little longer,' Marcus said almost to himself.

'They can't be much more than an hour away.'

'No, closer perhaps. But Briga has made her first mistake.'

· 'Mistake?'

'They could have been here an hour ago while the cavalry were still dispersing and all my clever plans would have come to nothing.' He gave the burning sky a last glance. 'Get some sleep, Rufius. You'll need it.'

XLV

A beautiful winter's morning, with the sun just peeping over the eastern skyline to dust the frost-tinted land with an ethereal blush of silver and gold. They'd saved one of the prisoners for just this moment. His name was Claudius, and he had no knowledge of his fate.

After Vindomora, Briga had decided to honour Coventina and thank her for the victory in a ceremony that would seal her pact with the goddess. She chose a river crossing on the line of march, overlooked on one side by a hillside where the great champions of her army gathered to observe the proceedings. King Luddoc complained that they would lose two hours of the day's march, but Coel supported Briga and said it would give encouragement to his men, who had taken no part in the battle at the fort.

Calista's role in the ceremony filled her with dread. She'd witnessed the cruelties Briga had inflicted on the survivors at Vindomora: the flaying and evisceration, men forced to watch their wives and families burn, then being hurled into the flames beside them, the long, slow agony of Antonius Vitalis. For all her hatred of the Christians was this what she wanted for Britannia? In truth Briga's appropriation of Coventina's divine qualities to suit her own will disgusted her. Whatever the Christians of Brocolitia might believe, no human had ever been sacrificed in Coventina's Well. Yet she knew that to flinch from what Briga regarded as her duty would at best damage her status with the queen and might lead to her own death.

They brought the prisoner forward through an avenue formed by Briga's misfits, who gibbered and mocked the naked Roman as he passed between their ranks. Claudius was a young man, lean and tall with arms tanned to the biceps and a snowy white torso and legs. He held himself erect as he was led to the river by a noose around his neck and with his hands bound behind his back, but his whole body shook and his terror was obvious.

Calista chanted the familiar lines of a song that hailed Coventina's deeds over the millennia, but her voice wavered and her fiercely clenched fists forced the nails of her fingers into her palms. Did she have the strength to do her part? She consoled herself that the prisoner's passing would be a hundred-fold easier than that of his comrades who had been tortured to death for Briga's pleasure. The queen sat on a chair upon a raised mound with a view of the river, with Fenrir, Geri and Freki at her feet, the three wolves hungrily eyeing the bound captive. Luddoc, Coel and Corvus sat their ponies impassively behind the hillock, surrounded, as ever, by their retinues.

As he approached the river, two of Briga's guards took the prisoner by the shoulders and hustled him down the bank into the knee-deep shallows. Calista followed, her heart thundering, and gasped as the freezing waters touched her exposed flesh. Claudius stared at her in bewilderment, his terror overcome for the moment by the sudden appearance of a young woman. Calista looked to Briga. The queen nodded.

'Do not struggle,' Calista said quietly. 'It will go all the easier for you.' The captive's eyes widened at words in a familiar language, but he frowned at the message they conveyed. She exchanged a glance with one of the guards and the man rasped a command. The second guard kicked the captive's feet from under him and with practised ease the two Picts pushed their prisoner back into the water until he was horizontal. In the same instant Calista bent to place her hands on Claudius's chest and forced his body beneath the surface. At first, he went rigid and she could see his blue eyes staring at her from the clear water, his mouth working in what might have been a plea for mercy or a prayer to his god. As he began to drown his body writhed and contorted, the thrashing legs churning the surface of the river to a froth. Calista struggled to keep her hands on his heaving chest and the guards, who had been instructed to release the captive and allow Calista to complete the sacrifice on behalf of Coventina, had to maintain their grip on the struggling Roman. Calista used all her weight to keep Claudius's upper torso beneath the surface. As the seconds passed she felt the strength drain from the young man. She saw the moment Claudius's blue eyes lost focus and his mouth stopped working and went slack. Three small silver bubbles escaped the young soldier's lips. A final convulsive twitch sent a pulse of energy through Calista that made her blink, and the body went still. Chest heaving as if it was she who had come close to drowning, Calista eased herself off the corpse and the guards allowed it to float away, bobbing gently over the rapids below, until the white blur disappeared around a bend in the river.

Calista raised her arms, the droplets that fell from her soaked dress glittering in the sunlight to create a halo of gemstones around her body. 'Coventina accepts Queen Briga's gift,' she called in a voice as rough-edged as a raven's cry. 'Nothing but victory awaits us now.'

The roar of acclaim that greeted her words seemed to shake the entire hillside.

Horns blared out the signal for the host to continue the march as Calista dragged herself from the river, weighed down as much by a sudden feeling of emptiness and exhaustion as by her waterlogged dress. She looked to the mound where Briga was already mounting her pony. The queen nodded solemnly to acknowledge her thanks, but some deeper message in the icy blue eyes made Calista uneasy.

'She senses a rival.' King Coel's words gave her a start. 'Sometimes when one is dealing with rulers it is wiser not to allow your light to shine too brightly.'

'I have done nothing but what was asked,' Calista said.

'That may be true.' Coel's agreement was accompanied by a twitch of the lips that she struggled at first to read. Pity? No. It was amusement, as his next words confirmed. Amusement at her naivety. 'But you may be assured she regrets it now. You do not understand because you did not see it. You seemed to grow in stature as the young soldier's life faded. When you raised your arms with the sun at your back you might have been the goddess herself – or a queen. You showed her your power.'

'The only power I have is through the goddess,' Calista insisted, but her words lacked conviction.

'Still,' Coel said gravely. 'Perhaps it would be better if you continue to ride with me for a while, so Queen Briga is given the chance to forget about your performance. I would like to know more about your Coventina.'

Calista stared into the dark eyes. Yes, now was the time. She made her decision. 'You once suggested I might share your bed, lord king?'

Coel froze; this wasn't what he had expected. 'Of course,' he said warily. 'You would be very welcome.'

'We would be alone and able to talk freely,' Calista continued. 'It may be that I only wish to talk?'

'Still you would be welcome.'

'Then I will share your bed, King Coel, and we shall talk of Marcus Flavius Victor.'

Briga led the advance on the gravelled Roman road with her wolves loping at her side. Her great host of Pictish tribesmen moved in a slow, aimlessly drifting mass across the gently rolling terrain to either side. Sometimes a tribe or clan would break ahead of the others, drawn by the sight of a farmstead or small settlement that held the promise of plunder, and she was forced to send messengers to discipline them. It irked her that, to her rear, the warriors of Corvus showed greater discipline now, clinging more tightly to his banner and keeping well away from their fractious traditional enemies.

Coel and Luddoc were further behind, out of sight, but not mind. She'd watched Calista ride off with the king of the southern Votadini and it only deepened the unease she'd felt following the ceremony. When Calista had arrived at her camp she'd regarded her as a pretty trinket to add to her collection of misfits, with the added attraction that she carried with her the prestige of Coventina's name. Briga had sought to capitalize on that name by ordering the sacrifice of the Roman militiaman, but when Calista had emerged from the river looking like the goddess herself, to the acclaim of the entire army, she realized she'd made a mistake. Now, she wondered if she'd compounded it by bringing Coel and Calista together. Coel was by far the most intelligent of her allies. Sending Calista to spy on him had seemed clever, but now that she had seen the keeper of the shrine's true power, she understood that she might have unwittingly created an alchemy with the potential to damage her own prestige.

Reluctantly, she thrust such thoughts aside. She could not be diverted by the mere possibility of intrigue. By now the Romans would have been alerted to her coming, the blazing pyres of the farms and settlements along the route incontrovertible evidence of her army's advance. She knew her enemy had an efficient signalling system which would carry the news within hours to Eboracum and Londinium. It gave her no immediate concerns. The Sixth legion, scattered in small garrisons across the land, like that of Corstopitum, would take many days to gather enough strength to face her. In any case, with such a host what did she have to fear? On the contrary she hoped for a confrontation, and the sooner the better. Her spies had sworn on their lives that no military formation of any note existed in the south of the province. The Romans depended on the Sixth for their security and once she had destroyed the Sixth the island was hers.

Of more immediate note was that forts like that at Vindomora flanked the Roman road every day's march or so, guarding the more important river crossings. That meant another awaited her an hour or two ahead. Rhuin had pointed to one of the marker stones that lined the road at intervals and interpreted the name as Longovicium. She hadn't yet decided what Longovicium's fate would be, though whatever happened she was minded to leave its commander a gift he would appreciate. Her decision would depend on his actions. If he was foolish enough to leave his walls and try to stop her, she would destroy him and kill every man. If he cowered behind them it was possible she would leave the garrison to wither, like a branch cut from a tree. Like Corstopitum, they could be dealt with later.

As they rode south the country became hillier and the Pictish host around and behind Briga seemed to be absorbed into the landscape so she only had contact with those closest to her. She felt another twinge of apprehension. If the Romans attacked now how would she control the response? She sent word to find Rhuin and when he rode up a few minutes later she demanded to know what his scouts were reporting.

'There is more open ground ahead for two or three miles,' he pointed south, 'and from the top of that hill a man can see smoke from what I take to be Longovicium. The road is overlooked to the east and the country is heavily wooded. We've seen signs of Roman scouts among the trees.'

'Only scouts?'

'They appear in small groups.' Rhuin shrugged. 'Ones and twos, never more than five. And my men know the difference between militia and auxiliaries. These are militia. When they're challenged they keep their distance. But they know we are here, Brenine.'

'And the fort?'

'We haven't been able to get close, but there is no sign of activity in the valley ahead.'

Briga considered for a moment. 'Position your scouts as a screen between the Roman militia and the fort.' Her look stifled any protest Rhuin might have. 'Keep them from reporting our numbers. If possible I want to draw the Roman commander and his garrison out to meet us.'

'As you wish, Brenine,' Rhuin bowed, but Briga knew he would have preferred her to allow the scouts to rove far ahead. Yet victory at Vindomora had proved the impotence of the small fortress garrisons to impede the great force she had gathered. If Longovicium's commander tried to stop her she would squash him like a beetle beneath a wagon wheel.

The *carnyx* blared to call a halt as Longovicium finally came into view. At first glance, there was no sign that the fort's commander had any intention of venturing out from behind his stone walls and Briga stifled her disappointment to study the way ahead. The road hugged the edge of a gentle slope and passed through a settlement of stone and wooden buildings directly below Longovicium's ramparts. Unless she wanted to come within range of the garrison's spears and arrows, she must necessarily vacate the gravelled highway and join her main force in the valley. Below her, the vale spanned a thousand paces and more in width, but the hills to east and west created a funnel that reached its narrowest point directly below the fort.

Corvus arrived first with his retinue to find out why they'd halted, followed minutes later by Luddoc, and finally Coel. Briga suppressed a surge of irritation as she saw that the king of the southern Votadini had left Calista with his tribesmen.

'Bigger than Vindomora and a more formidable position,' Corvus growled. 'We should leave it alone.'

'I agree,' said Luddoc.

'We should stay close to the east flank of the valley,' Coel said. 'They will have – what did the prisoners call them? – shield-splitters and *onagri* that could cause us many casualties if we stray too close. Are those houses occupied?'

'If they are, we will clear them, lord king,' Briga said tightly. 'But you will note that they protect our flank from any direct sortie from the fort.'

'A shrewd tactical observation, Brenine,' Coel agreed, but the mocking smile that accompanied the words irritated her even more.

'What about the hills?' Luddoc stared at the slopes to the east, topped by forest and scrub. 'And I don't like the look of those trees up ahead.'

'There are scouts in the hills, nothing more.' Briga didn't hide her impatience. 'Where there are trees there is usually a river, but this looks more like a stream. Hardly a formidable barrier, lord king, and by the time your Votadini reach it, it will be no barrier at all. Because

King Corvus and his men will bridge it for you, is that not so, King Corvus?'

'It will be my pleasure,' Corvus grinned, enjoying Luddoc's glare. 'We wouldn't want your precious warriors getting their feet wet, would we?'

'But first we will send Longovicium's commander my gifts.' Briga's mood lightened. 'Let Melcho the Chosen see to it.'

XLVI

Longovicium (Lanchester)

Marcus held his breath as the small contingent of Picts advanced hesitantly along the road towards the north wall of the fortress. From the tower above the north gate he had a view up the valley to where Briga would come. But he hadn't expected this.

'What in the holy name of Christ are they doing?' Quirinus muttered through clenched teeth. 'Is it some kind of probe? We've had no word from the scouts since dawn.'

'I don't know,' Marcus admitted. 'But I hope the bastards stay on the road. They must be a rare temptation for Julius, sitting out in the open like a doe basking in the sun. Christ only knows what he'll do if they decide to turn into the trees.' He watched as they approached ever closer, passing in front of the woods that hid the Ala Herculaea, and the little rise behind which the Numeri Exploratorum and Directorum waited. By now he could see that three carts accompanied the wary Pictish warriors. Finally they halted in an untidy huddle a shield-splitter's flight from the fort. Marcus sensed confusion among their leaders.

'I don't think they have much idea either,' Quirinus said. 'Mary, mother of God, is that one of ours?'

Four or five men began unloading an instantly recognizable object from the back of one of the carts, hurried on by the kicks and punches of their companions. At least one of the sufferers wore a military tunic, but Marcus wasn't certain whether Quirinus was referring to the men or the *onager* – the first of two as it turned out – they were setting up on the road facing the fort.

'How much damage do they think they can do with a pair of *onagri*?' Quirinus sounded almost insulted at the slight to his command.

'I don't know,' Marcus repeated, 'but I think we're about to find out.'

'Will this do?' Melcho demanded.

'I – I – I think so, lord.' One of the prisoners Briga had spared to deliver her 'gifts' had been chosen for his knowledge of the Pictish tongue.

'I'm not your lord, and you'd better not miss,' the young Pict said in a voice made harsh by unease at being placed in this exposed position.

They manhandled the two weapons from the carts and set them up on the road. A bare three hundred paces to the south Melcho could see men watching impassively from the walls of the fort. All it would take was a swift sortie by a score of the defenders and they'd be fleeing for their lives. It seemed to take an age to position the two catapults, as the Romans called them. They had to be secured by metal pegs hammered into the surface of the roadway and then the terrified prisoners conducted a nervous debate over whether a wheel had to be turned four times or five.

'Get a move on.' One of Melcho's companions lost his patience and began hammering the Pictish speaker with his spear butt.

'Leave the poor bastard alone,' Melcho snapped. 'It won't get this done any quicker.'

Eventually the men seemed satisfied, but their leader approached Melcho nervously. 'We would like to attempt a ranging shot, lo— sir.'

'A what?'

'We would like to make a first attempt. It may fall short – or long – it depends on the torsion of the rope and the force of the wind, which is against us. You have to understand,' the man was almost weeping, 'we are not accustomed to this type of ammunition.'

'Very well.' Melcho drove the pity from his heart. 'Continue.'

Melcho blinked at the loud *whump* as the released throwing arm struck the leather cushion on the crosspiece and the catapult bucked like a fractious pony. Men ran forward to refix the restraining pegs. By some freak of good fortune, or the professionalism of the operators, the first missile soared over the walls into the centre of the fort. This time they loaded both *onagri*.

By the time the missile was recovered and placed before Marcus in the tower, the fort was under an intermittent, erratic bombardment. He grimaced as he recognized the agonized features on the decapitated head.

'Poor . . . ?' He shook his head; the name escaped him.

'His name was Antonius,' Quirinus offered quietly. 'My counterpart at Vindomora. That means they must have taken the fort.'

'More likely he never made it back from the bridge. Briga is no fool and the position was ripe for flanking. I tried—' He shrugged. 'We can expect the rest of the garrison to follow him.'

'Should I . . . return fire?'

'There's no point and you'll likely be glad of the ammunition later.'

Quirinus nodded. 'I'll have them gathered up for a proper burial. Best if we let these barbarians do what they've come to do and return to their bloodthirsty queen.'

He turned away and Marcus mused that if Quirinus thought lopping off a few heads made Briga bloodthirsty he had a lot to learn. She was simply sending them a message. A message Marcus was not displeased that the garrison of Longovicium would receive. No matter how bad things got later, there would be no talk of surrender now.

'That's enough.' Melcho was surprised at the authority that came so naturally to him. The warriors Rhuin had chosen to escort the catapults had no interest in leadership, they were happy to be led.

345

'We've only used fifty heads,' one of the men pointed out.

'Do you want to be here all day?' A muttered chorus of 'No.' The men had become more restive with every passing moment, looking to the tree-covered hillsides around them. Melcho experienced the same feeling that they were being watched, and not just from the fort. 'Then do what needs to be done and let's get back.'

From the tower Marcus winced as he saw the prisoners being forced to their knees and the swords flashing in the damp sunlight. He was about to turn away when a distant thunder alerted him. Not thunder, but the sound of thousands of spear butts and sword pommels being hammered against wooden shields, accompanied by a cacophony of blaring horns. The sounds of the Pictish army announcing its presence.

A murmur of unease ran through the men on the walls. 'Quiet,' Marcus rapped. 'Get Quirinus back up here.' He spared time for a glance to the south, beyond the river, but the road was empty. Where in Christ's name was Dulcitius? 'Signaller. I want green flags waved from the east towers and the south wall. And keep waving them until I tell you to stop.' The green flag was the signal to Rufius at the river and the cavalry regiments on the hill to prepare for battle. It was all a matter of timing.

They came like a dark shadow spilling down the valley and over the lower slopes of the surrounding hills. At this distance their approach appeared painfully slow, but nevertheless the relentless advance sent an icy knife point running up Marcus's spine. So many of them. And this was just the vanguard of Briga's Picts. Yet experience told him his eyes were deceiving him. They looked as if they covered every blade of grass, but barbarians didn't march in compact units. They didn't march at all. They walked or shambled or trotted as the mood took them and they would be in loose formation in their clans and family groups, each under some sort of banner, however ludicrous. A fox's skull. A deer's antlers. Scraps of cloth in any colour that took their chieftain's fancy, some with painted symbols, but most without. Some, like Briga's wolf banner and Luddoc's prancing horse, were elaborate affairs. For a few years Lucti, Briga's unfortunate predecessor, had marched beneath the entire skeleton of one of his uncles, a hereditary enemy who'd met the sorry end that awaited so many Pictish kings.

He looked to the hills and the river for any sign of activity or hint of threat, but his officers had done their work well and all that awaited the advancing Picts was a pastoral swathe of stubble field, rough grazing and bogland. Everything was falling into place. The only question was whether the plan that had seemed so perfect in his head would stand the test of contact with Briga or be exposed as a bloody fantasy. That depended on what happened next.

He stared at the rolling tide of warriors and tried to identify Briga and her entourage in their midst, but for the moment they were too far away.

Briga rode at the centre of her host flanked by her personal guard of mounted spearmen and followed by a cloud of her misfits. Rhuin, his scouts now returned from their mission on the flanks, assured her that the buildings of the settlement were empty. She'd ordered them burned, but the scouts discovered that anything flammable inside the shops and houses had been soaked in water so nothing would catch light. It was a concerning sign of the fort commander's efficiency and an indication that he wanted a clear line of flight for his catapults. To combat this she'd contrived to have the van of her force veer left away from the fort, but because of their sheer numbers many would still be in range of the missiles. The captain of her guard tried to steer her towards the far slope, but Briga maintained her course unerringly down the centre of the valley. The goddess would protect her. The thought brought an image of Calista's face. Should she call the keeper of Coventina's shrine forward to bask in the light of her forgiveness? On balance, no, better for her to stay in the shadows a while longer. Calista might believe Coel could be her protector, but a loaf baked with a hint of red cap mushroom or Edin's bane would change that. She had watched the results with interest when one of her rivals had become careless. Visions and delusions of might, followed by agonizing cramps and the bloody flux. Within days the consumer became a walking corpse, then a state like death itself, before the last breath. She had buried him alive.

She glanced to the fort on the hillside. Those formidable walls studded with their many towers. Another three hundred paces and she would be directly below them. Was the commander quivering in fear at this evidence of her might, as the fool at Vindomora had trembled at the sight of the knife? On balance she thought not. Some sense told her that this man would be seeking any opportunity to damage, hurt or delay her. Perhaps she *should* invest the fort. She had an urge to face the Roman whose defiance she felt even here, meet his eyes and drag him from behind his great grey walls. It would be a matter of a moment to issue the order.

But she wanted to be as far south as possible before she met and destroyed the Sixth legion, Longovicium was a formidable stronghold and a siege would delay her for days at best. And for what? A fleeting moment of satisfaction as his blood sprayed scarlet in the cold air? No, Nechtan would advise against it. It was enough that he should stay behind his walls and look on as Briga's invincible wolves marched past his gate while he watched, helpless. He would see them now, from that fine vantage point: the great flowing mass of Pictish warriors, their spear points gleaming, bodies painted with the records of their deeds and lineage, the finest their people could provide. Corvus and his Selgovae: for all his sullen impenetrability, a great king and a great warrior whose crow banner would fly over the corpses of the Sixth legion even as the crows themselves feasted on their eyes; and the feared Votadini, divided now, but not for long.

'Brenine!' Rhuin forced his way through the Pictish warriors on his pony. He had an odd light in his eyes. 'Romans in the trees ahead.'

Briga felt a surge of elation. The Roman commander had decided to challenge her. He wasn't in the fort at all. How many? It didn't matter. The garrison could only number a few hundred at most and he must have stripped it to defend this pathetic little barrier to her ambitions. A delaying tactic, nothing more, but this impudence would be punished. None of them would escape this time.

'Attack with half of our warriors. We will crush them like a nut beneath a quern stone. Let Nechtan lead the charge.'

Rhuin gave her curious look. 'Nechtan is dead, Brenine.'

She blinked. How could she have forgotten? 'Then you must lead them yourself, noble Rhuin. Remember, I want the Roman commander taken alive and brought to me.'

XLVII

It took longer than Briga would have preferred for Rhuin and the warrior princes of the Picts to chivvy their spearmen into three rough lines across the pasture, fields and marsh of the valley bottom. By now the sun was directly to the south and so low in the sky she had to use her hand to shade her eyes. The scouts had been stopped short of the tree line by a shower of slingshots, arrows and throwing darts and when they returned they spoke of Romans in their hundreds beyond the stream. She had pondered a flanking movement of the kind that had proved so successful at Vindomora, but that would take even more time to organize. An attack on the right would be exposed to the catapults on the fort walls, while on the left the terrain was much steeper.

At last they were ready, her great lords, at the head of their tribes and clans, each with his own banner and a mounted retinue perhaps twenty strong. A *camyx* blared out the signal for the advance and Briga nudged her pony forward in the wake of the advancing warriors, calling for her throne to be brought forward to where she could view the coming victory.

Rhuin rode at the centre of the Pictish line, squinting against the glare of the sun. Though his sight was impaired he savoured the warmth on his face that spoke of the eventual return of spring and the planting of the fields. That same warmth was replicated in his heart, for Rhuin's standing among his people had never been greater. It was he who had guided King Luddoc and his warriors on their long march around the flank at Vindomora and led a contingent to take the fort gates while Luddoc attacked the enemy holding the bridge. Briga had rewarded him, a simple hill farmer, with a chain of silver links and the promise of a lordship of his own. He wore a mail vest that had belonged to a Roman officer and carried the man's sword at his waist. To his right and left, the fluttering banners of the Fortriu, the Mithiai, the Sil Conairi and the Fib, while at his back marched the men of Caledon. Rhuin lacked the patience or skill to design a banner of his own, but he had solved the quandary by appropriating the severed hand of Vindomora's commander, still with its jewelled ring, and mounting it on a pole.

A mixture of apprehension and exhilaration surged inside him as the pony moved easily to his nudged commands and he led his men towards the stream perhaps five or six hundred paces ahead. The sunbeams slanted through the trees like a thousand polished sword blades and created pools of light and shade on the pattern of fields and grassy sward in front of the river. A glint among the foliage caught his eyes, but he dismissed it as a patch of melting frost or water pooled in a hoofmark in the mud.

The number of defenders his men had reported on the far side of the stream had troubled him at first, because, from what he knew of Roman garrisons, they seemed too numerous for a fort even on the scale of Longovicium. If the commander had recruited every able-bodied man from the settlement he'd still have had to strip the fort bare to properly defend this line. However, he remembered the subter-fuge the Romans had used in the wood before Vindomora and consoled himself this must be something similar. In any case it didn't matter. He almost laughed at the thought. Briga had given him command of almost five thousand warriors. Great kings had led entire armies containing fewer men. They would sweep across the stream, tear the defences aside, slaughter the defenders and he would present their commander to Briga, naked and bound, for her pleasure.

By now the leading rank was directly opposite the fort and Rhuin spared the towering grey walls an apprehensive glance. He did not fear a counter-attack against his right flank because he'd left scouts among the houses of the settlement and they would provide ample warning of any movement. What did concern him was the power of the catapults he knew lined those walls. Melcho had told him how the machines, manned by men who knew them, had effortlessly thrown the heads from Vindomora over the fort walls four hundred paces distant. The flank of his attack was much closer than that to Longovicium and he wondered why they weren't already the target of the fort's missiles.

The long line of warriors rippled and snaked as they advanced, men's feet slowed by fear or apprehension, or quickened by the spear butts of the second line urging them forward. Rhuin's horse lords, in contrast, hauled at the bridles of their mounts to keep them in check as the ponies, sensing the excitement of the men in their saddles, strained towards the inviting broad swathe of fields and grassland ahead.

Less than four hundred paces now and the dark line of trees seemed much closer and more forbidding. Not all warriors are heroes and Rhuin knew the timid among them would be feeling the increasing tension of approaching battle. That tension would quickly spread to the others if he didn't do something about it.

'Let's hear some noise,' he called over his shoulder. Slowly at first, but building in tempo and volume, the men behind him began a rhythmic chant and clashed their spear shafts against the wooden boards of their painted shields in a thunderous rattle that spread quickly through the ranks to right and left. The *carnyx*-bearers of the individual tribes added to the clamour with a braying cacophony that echoed across the valley and made the heart soar.

Now the pace quickened of its own volition as the warriors matched their step to the beat of the shield panels. Still a walk, but a walk that now seemed to eat up the ground as the frustrated ponies, excited by the noise, danced and skipped in front of them. Even Rhuin's mount, honed to the obedience required of a scouting pony, bucked beneath him and fought the bit.

'Behave, you bastard,' the Pict muttered. 'Soon, boy. Soon.'

As if their own commander had vainly echoed the words he caught his first sight of the defenders. A dozen men broke cover to appear in front of the stream shaking their spears and howling what must be insults. Other groups appeared along the line, mimicking the first, and a growl went up from the warriors around Rhuin at the sight of their enemy, the sound of a hunting dog with the scent of blood in his nostrils. The growl grew into a roar of hatred and menace.

At two hundred paces the roar was echoed by a great shout from the trees that sent a shiver through Rhuin. That volume of noise didn't come from a few hundred men. 'Stop,' he cried, but his voice was lost in the tumult and the warriors around him were already surging forward in response. What choice did he have? He urged his mount forward so he was leading the charge.

'Idiots.' Marcus shook his head. 'I told Rufius to keep them quiet until the Picts were on the point of their swords.'

'Christ our lord save us.' The whisper came from the top of the tower steps at Marcus's back. He felt a surge of pleasure at the sound of a familiar voice, but the welcome must wait.

'What news of Dulcitius?' he demanded.

But Valeria only had eyes for the great host that filled the valley below the fort walls and as far north as the eye could see. 'The Picts alone would have been enough, but Corvus, Luddoc and Coel? You have destroyed us, brother.'

'No,' Marcus shook his head. He waved a hand towards the Picts advancing down the valley. 'All you see is numbers. What I see is Briga exactly where I want her. If you are truly a herald for Dulcitius we will destroy her.'

'Dulcitius has his own plans.' He saw how tired she was now, the russet hair plastered against her brow with sweat, helmet hanging from the limp fingers of her right hand. 'And they do not include making a hero of Marcus Flavius Victor.'

'But he is coming?'

'He is coming,' she admitted. 'But he is coming at his own pace. He has had men watching you for days, Marcus. He has studied your every movement, and the Picts', too. Dulcitius will come at a time of his choosing. A time when you have been bled dry and are crying out for either Briga's mercy or Dulcitius's aid. I have brought another hundred and fifty spears to share your sacrifice.'

But Marcus wasn't listening. 'How far away is he?'

'Last night he camped south of Vinovium.' Something between a sigh and a sob escaped her salt-caked lips. 'If he hurried, he could be here by dusk. But he will not hurry.'

'Then why are you here,' he demanded, 'when you could have been urging him to move faster?'

'You seem to have the impression he looked upon me as his adviser.' Fury coated Valeria's words with venom. 'When the reality is that when you sent me to him you handed him a hostage. I only escaped last night with the help of Terentius Cantaber. It was he who gave me the Sixth's cavalry contingent. A hundred and fifty spears, Marcus. At least try to appear grateful.'

'I am grateful,' Marcus protested. 'But Dulcitius . . .'

She stared at him. 'Tell me we can still win.'

'You will see.' He met her gaze. 'We can win.'

Despite the evidence of her own eyes, Valeria chose to believe him. 'Where can we be of most use?'

'Where else but by my side?' Marcus managed a smile. 'The regiment is already in the saddle at the head of the little wooded vale to the north-west. Join them there and get something to eat and drink. But be quick. It will be a matter of minutes.'

He watched her hurry off and turned back to the valley where the Picts were approaching the marshy ground in front of the river in a concerted rush led by their horse-borne chiefs.

They would win. Somehow, they would win.

'Why have we stopped?' Calista asked Coel.

The king raised himself in the saddle and peered south. 'Either the

Brenine has changed her mind about attacking the fort' – he waved a hand in the direction of Longovicium, though neither fort nor settlement was visible because of the valley's twists and turns – 'or the Romans are up to their delaying tactics again.' He fixed her with his shrewd eyes. 'The latter is more likely.'

She had spent the night beneath his blanket, but not for the purpose his followers believed. Huddled close against the cold, Calista had passed on the information she'd been given by Marcus Flavius Victor, aware that if she had mistaken her man, she was unlikely to live to see the dawn. At first Coel was suspicious, but his surprise at the identity of the messenger was offset by the fact that he was hearing what he'd hoped to hear. They'd talked in whispers long into the night, before Coel said: 'We are agreed?' She'd sensed his growing desire as the heat from their bodies mingled, but somehow they both decided this wasn't the time. When she woke he'd been gone.

'Then it is time,' she said.

Coel nodded and called up his senior commander. 'Alert the men to be ready for battle. We will leave them in their present positions, but our horse will assemble on either flank. And have the men wear the token I provided in honour of the Lady Calista. Pass the order by word of mouth. No trumpets.' He pulled a white cloth from a bag tied to his saddle and offered his right arm. 'Perhaps you will do me the honour?' She tied the cloth round the leather tunic he wore over his chain armour. He smiled. 'Now no one will mistake us for anything but what we are. The southern Votadini.'

He stared ahead to where Luddoc's men were taking advantage of the halt to rest their legs, either sitting or crouching in the damp tussock grass of the valley bottom. 'Luddoc killed his own brother to take the crown he wears and his treachery is the stuff of legend, but here I can trust him, because I can watch his every move.'

'I should go,' she said.

He reached across to gently touch her cheek. 'Fare well.'

'And you, lord king.' She set her pony towards the western slope.

XLVIII

Rhuin hefted his spear in his right fist and brought up his circular shield to protect his chest. They were a hundred and fifty paces from the line of trees now and he reined his pony back slightly to allow the warriors jogging at his rear to keep pace. The initial rush had quickly faded to a trot as the attackers encountered the marshy ground closer to the river and realized how much further they had to go. Even so, he knew many of the older warriors would be blown by the time they reached the enemy. The line of the river slanted across the valley bottom from the west, where it was closest to the fort, to the east, where it was more distant, before following the terrain south. Four good bowshots would cover the length and he consoled himself that, despite his earlier concerns, it could only be lightly held. The defiant roars and mortal insults of earlier had long since been replaced by rasping breaths and his ears filled with the bellow of the *carnyx*, the thunder of stamping hooves, jingling horse brass and the pounding feet of the men closest to him. His heart hammered in his chest with the exhilaration of the charge. All he wanted was to bathe his spear in Roman blood.

Rhuin had trained in war since he'd been strong enough to hold a wooden stave, battered black and blue by older warriors until every movement became second nature. As he approached the scrub bordering the river he held the nine-foot ash shaft loosely in his right hand and his mind automatically went through the sequence of thrust and counter-thrust, parry and the roundhouse swing that could leave even a man in an iron helmet senseless and vulnerable. The river bed, though likely rocky, would barely check the pony's progress after so many days without rain. His enemy would be waiting on the far bank, of course, but by the time he'd plunged the spear point into the first quivering body, his warriors would be with him, eager for the slaughter. The work of a moment to drop the spear, draw his iron sword and turn to attack the flank of the Roman line. But where was the whistle of passing slingshots and the soft, spine-tingling *zzzip* of their arrows? The Romans had few bowmen, but surely the defenders would contain a decent number of slingers? Closer, and ever closer. It was still difficult to see properly because of the low sun slanting through the trees, but he chose a wide gap between two stout oaks. He could almost hear the screaming already.

But the screams, when they came, were from behind him.

He risked a glance over his shoulder to see men tumbling into the grass, clawing at their feet – a cry and a sharp snap and someone nearby fell shrieking and flopped forward, his leg twisted horribly – most of the first line were mowed down as if a scythe had swept across them. What sorcery was this? But they must go on, there was no turning back now.

'Forward,' he roared, directing his words to the horsemen on either side who appeared so far untouched. 'To the river. Kill the bastards!'

But even as he called out the words the horse to his left dropped a shoulder and went tumbling, legs flailing, crushing its rider beneath its body. Rhuin swallowed. 'Epona save us.'

But Epona wasn't listening.

He was a dozen paces from the trees and could actually see into the stream bed when he heard a shocking crack as his mount snapped its foreleg in a pit and he was flying through the air. The spear point bit into the earth and half-spun him so that his skull, which would have been crushed by a boulder, only suffered a graze that tore his scalp, but a bolt of fire shot through his side and he knew his left shoulder was broken. With a stomach-churning somersault he found himself lying on his back in the stream bed with the breath knocked out of him. As if in a dream he watched warriors who had survived the pits and the *triboli* splash through the shallow water and climb the south bank.

But something was wrong.

Instead of clawing their way up the three or four feet of earth to attack the defenders, the Picts were left tearing impotently at an immovable barrier blocking the top of the bank. Now the air was filled with the rhythmic grunt of the Romans driving their spear points home through the bushes into flesh, sinew and viscera, the cries of terribly injured men, roars of triumph and the pathetic moans of the dying.

Rhuin's head still spun from the fall, but he knew he must do something or the attack was lost. He levered himself up and dashed blood from his eyes, awkwardly drawing his sword from its leather scabbard. More men poured into the stream bed, but others reached the north bank only to fall senseless or dead into waters that were already running pink. No shortage of slingers or bowmen now, his numbed mind told him. Someone took him by the right arm, but he shrugged him off. His left hung helpless and felt like a bar of glowing iron.

'To me,' he called. Eight or ten men within hearing distance answered his rallying cry and crouched in the stream bed beside him as lead slingshots and arrows and spears whispered past inches above them. Two or three he recognized as men from his own tribe, four were certainly Mithiai, the others might have been of any Pictish clan. Most had the quivering, tightly wound look of hunting dogs ready to be loosed, one or two were wide-eyed with terror. They would have to do.

'You and you,' he nodded to two of the Mithiai. 'We will keep the defenders busy while the others tear the barrier down. Now!'

As one they rushed up the bank. The warrior to Rhuin's right fell instantly, one eye turned to pulp by a lead shot. Another of his comrades ran to take his place. Sweat pouring from his forehead to mingle with the blood streaking his face, Rhuin hunched his shoulders and dug his feet into the muddy soil of the bank, scrabbling upwards until he found an unstable perch from which he could use his sword. The two spearmen ignored what was going on around them and concentrated on the shadows behind the prickly wall, stabbing their spears at any target that came close as the others tore at the thorny barrier until their hands bled.

A despairing cry. 'It's staked in place.'

'Keep trying,' Rhuin snarled. He was at the lowest level of the barrier and he noticed a slight gap beneath it. One of the wooden stakes was visible just a few feet away. He worked his way up and wriggled beneath the piled bushes, ignoring the agony of his shoulder, thorns tearing at his injured head and the exposed flesh of his neck. Too far away to reach with his good hand, but he hacked desperately at the rough-hewn peg with the edge of the sword, knocking away splinters of bark. A shout of warning and a pair of feet appeared beside the peg. Rhuin twisted and stabbed with the point, rewarded by a howl of pain and the feel of the metal sinking into the hard muscle of the man's calf. He hauled the sword clear with a flicker of scarlet and returned to slashing at the stake.

'Watch out!'

He looked up at the warning cry from the neighbouring spearman. The last thing he saw was a pair of demented, red-rimmed eyes above a snarling mouth, and a flash of metal. Darkness. The deepest darkness of the soul. In that instant he knew one eye was gone, probably both. Before he could register the horror of his wound, a spear plunged into his back just below the neck with the force of a hammer blow. The Roman chain armour he wore would turn a sword edge, but even the close iron links couldn't stop a direct thrust from a spear, and the needle point penetrated deep enough to sever his spine. Curiously, after the initial punch of the weapon he felt no pain. Hands grabbed his legs and hauled him out of the thorns. Someone laid him gently against the earthen bank of the stream. Left unaided, he slumped sideways onto the stream bed. He could feel a moss-covered stone against his cheek and smell the water flowing inches away. A curtain of fire seemed to have fallen across his eyes and a hundred red-hot needles brought a hundred different levels of pain. He drifted in and out of consciousness and woke – did a blind man wake? – at one point with a terrible thirst. He would dearly have loved to reach out and scoop up a handful of that wonderful liquid he could hear burbling over the stones, but for some reason he couldn't get his hands to work.

The sound of fighting faded and his delirious mind searched for a familiar memory to cling to, like a drowning man reaching out for a piece of driftwood. In the darkness of his subconscious he struggled to picture the wife and children he would never see again, but they flittered across his mind like the ghost of a deer half-seen through the undergrowth of a gloomy forest run. He would have wept, but he didn't know how.

XLIX

Drosten and Melcho sat their ponies uneasily among the retinue of misfits and bodyguards surrounding Briga. The queen occupied her throne in a cart that had been placed on an elevated mound. Melcho had used his new-found influence to persuade Briga that Drosten would be more useful to her on horseback. The wolves Fenrir, Geri and Freki circled Briga's cart restlessly as if they could already scent the blood about to be spilled a few hundred paces ahead.

Briga's heart raced as she watched the ragged lines of warriors set off to attack the Romans defending the river. Slowly at first, but then more quickly like an unstoppable wave approaching a beach, their advance accompanied by a curiously mistimed dull roar.

'Let us move forward to be in position to take advantage of Rhuin's victory,' she ordered.

But before she had time to prepare a voice called out, 'What's happening there?'

When she looked again, the first line of distant attackers had disintegrated, reduced to a scattered collection of individual warriors who trotted on towards the trees, led by a few horsemen who disappeared one by one in their turn. 'No,' she whispered. But the second line of warriors followed the first with the same result. The intact third line staggered to a halt and she could see them milling in confusion.

'You,' she pointed to Melcho. 'Go forward and find out what has stopped them. I need information and I need it quickly.' She watched Melcho ride off, his mount's hooves kicking up sods of muddy turf in its wake. A surge of panic swept through her. What should she do? For a moment she wished Nechtan were here to advise her, but instantly thrust the thought aside. The attack had been halted, but for what reason? Superior numbers? She looked at the fort on the hill. Substantial enough, but it could hold no more than a few hundred men, and judging by the movement among the catapults on the walls it did not lack defenders. Not numbers then. Whatever the reason, she understood that doing nothing was out of the question. She must act. She had overwhelming strength. She would use it. She slipped from the throne into the saddle of her waiting mount.

'Sound the advance,' she cried, and within moments the valley echoed again to the blare of the *carnyx*.

It took time to coax the great host into motion once more, but eventually they moved forward in the wake of the attackers. By now the third line had resumed the attack, but their progress was hesitant and wary. Thousands of seasoned warriors halted by a few hundred cowards hiding behind a shallow stream. The fury grew inside her like white heat as she reined to a halt in the centre of the valley perhaps four hundred paces from the river.

Melcho rode up and forced his pony through her bodyguard. He had something in his hand and leaned across to hand it to her. Briga took the object, wincing as she pricked the ball of her thumb on one of the four needle tips of the iron pyramid. 'The ground before the river is sown with thousands of these,' he said. 'There are cunningly placed pits too. Hundreds of our people are crippled or maimed. The others are confused and they have few leaders left. Rhuin is dead. The bravest of his men are still attacking, but there is some sort of barrier in the wood and they can't reach the enemy.'

'Then take—'

Her horse reared as something hissed across its front. In the same instant a wet thud was followed by the dual screams of a man and his mount. When Briga recovered her senses one of her bodyguard was down, pinned by his own horse as it kicked and flailed in the grass with a four-foot arrow through its middle and its entrails bulging from the gaping wound the missile had caused. Its rider had lost his leg at the knee, severed by the same arrow that impaled the horse. Melcho dismounted and took a war axe from another of the stunned bodyguard and chopped through the animal's spine with a single blow. A second giant arrow hissed by a few feet away, but the trajectory was too high. A third, from the opposite flank, ripped an arm from one man twenty paces away from where they stood and tore a gaping hole in the chest of another fifty paces on.

'Brenine, you must go back,' Melcho shouted. 'You are too vulnerable here.'

Briga bridled at the order, but she knew there was sense in it. Reluctantly she returned to the mound and resumed her place on her throne.

Despite his generous gift of shield-splitters to Rufius Clemens, Quirinus still counted twenty-four catapults on his rampart, and he congratulated himself that he'd deployed them well. Twelve *onagri* and four shield-splitters, more properly known as *scorpiones*, stood on the eastern wall, directly facing the enemy. The Pictish commander had arranged her line in an arc that avoided the area in front of the fort, yet to Quirinus's mind that counted for little. Much of that quarter of the field would be shielded by the houses from his missiles in any case, and from the elevation of the fort walls an *onager* could send its bucket-sized boulder almost the entire breadth of the valley. The *scorpiones* had less range, but they still generated enough power to send their big arrows into the outer reaches of the massed ranks to their front. When accuracy was required the *onager* and the *scorpio* had a similar rate of fire, but blessed with a huge target like this, a *scorpio* could launch its missiles at twice the rate of an *onager*. The other catapults he'd divided equally between the north and south walls where they could flay the Picts in the van and rear of Briga's force.

Marcus had taken up a position in Longovicium's eastern gate tower, though his feet were itching to take him back to his command. He'd watched the Pictish attack crumble as it struck the line of *triboli* and pits and was satisfied Rufius and Hostilius could hold . . . for the moment. That was the key; he must not be blinded by Briga's early failure. She had warriors and to spare. She would come at the line again, and again. That was why he delayed. He wanted – no, needed – to know how she would react to what happened next. There were still so many things that could go wrong.

The wounds caused by the *scorpiones* were spectacular, but it was the great boulders launched by the *onagri* that the warriors of Briga's army came to dread. How much damage they caused depended on the trajectory of the missile. If the captain in charge set his machine to throw in a high arc the boulder would crush a single man, perhaps two, and wound a few of those around them with splinters of bone. But it was a low trajectory that caused most casualties. On the first bounce the missile might kill a single man or destroy a file of warriors as it skipped, but its momentum would carry it on to smash four or five more before its energy was spent. Not even the most hardened fighter who had looked upon the victim of a direct strike from an *onager* would ever forget the sight. A torso with no head was one thing, but a human being torn asunder with heart, lungs and vitals exposed among splinters of broken ribs and backbone was quite another. Half men, their legs removed at the hip. Even a glancing blow would remove an arm, leaving a man alive with his beating heart exposed and condemned to a long, excruciating death.

These terrifying man-killers targeted the massed ranks of Briga's army with specially selected river boulders the size of a water bucket and larger. Their targets learned to watch for the flight. At first a dark streak above the fort's parapet, then an apparently long, slow climb before the stone plummeted earthwards at incredible speed. It seemed simple enough to judge where the missiles would fall, but the reality was different. A man would dance to right, or left, and have time for a last curse as he found himself directly in the boulder's path, or he'd be transfixed by sheer terror and it would save his life.

Briga watched the dark specks arcing across a winter sky of perfect blue, apparently harmless until you saw the way the crowd of warriors seemed to pulse where they fell, panic spreading like the rings from a stone dropped into a pool. Every impact felt like a dagger in her heart and for a moment her mind froze.

'Brenine,' Melcho urged. 'We must do something.'

Yes. Something. She took a deep breath. What had she been about to order?

'Take another thousand men and reinforce the attack on the Romans at the river.' A shudder ran through her, but it was her body regaining control of itself. 'Their toys have no fears for us now.'

Melcho blinked at this sudden new elevation in his status, but he didn't hesitate. 'We'll need every axe we can get,' he told her, remembering the reports of an immovable barrier of thorns.

'Very well. Blaid?' she called to the keeper of her wolves. 'You will go with Melcho and let my lords know he carries my authority. Every man from this point forward who carries a war axe will accompany him and destroy the Romans for me. The first ten men to break through will have rewards beyond their imagination.'

'But Brenine,' Blaid pleaded. 'My children.'

'They will be safe with me,' she reassured him almost gently. 'Now go.'

As Melcho rode off with the wolfmaster at his heels Briga tried to ignore the screams from behind her and concentrate on what was happening at the river. Should she order Corvus and his Selgovae forward? No. All it would do was bring his two thousand within reach of those terrible machines. Better for now that he stay where he was. She had men enough for the task. But there *was* something she could do.

She looked for someone to carry the message, but the only person left apart from her misfits was the cripple on his pony. 'Can you ride without hands?' she demanded.

'Would I be sitting a horse if I couldn't?' Drosten snapped. There was no disguising the insolence in his tone, but that reckoning could be considered later.

'Then ride to Beli and the Sons of Feradach. They will climb the hill and outflank the defences on the left. When they are past the Romans they are to turn and attack them from the rear.' The Sons of Feradach were five hundred strong and farmed the lands of Mounth. They were positioned on the left of the army and well placed for the manoeuvre. 'But do not tarry. I will have further work for you.'

From his vantage point in the tower, Marcus wondered at the steadiness with which the Picts endured their flaying at the hands of Quirinus's artillery. Brave men, but enemies, so they had to die. He looked to the north for some sign that Corvus and the others were advancing to join the attack, or launch a new one against the fort. He could see the crow banner at the centre of his host, and that must be Luddoc to his rear. He felt a momentary panic. Christ forbid that Briga had moved Coel forward. No, it must be Luddoc. The Selgovae and Votadini looked almost detached from the blood-letting not so far ahead, almost as if they were bored.

Patience. You must not act too soon.

'They're bringing up more men.' Marcus turned to where Quirinus was pointing. 'A lot more men. Can Rufius hold, do you think?'

'If he doesn't, he's dead,' Marcus snapped. Quirinus turned away to hide a smile at this sign of nerves. All right for you, Marcus thought, safe here behind your walls. His eyes caught a flicker of movement on the steep slope to the east. Hundreds of Picts creeping through the gorse and dead ferns towards Rufius's right flank. There was no time to send a messenger to warn him. It wasn't unexpected. With luck, Ramios's dismounted Germans would hold them in place until Rufius could send a century to support him.

He looked to his right where two nervous-looking civilians crouched behind the parapet holding red flags.

'In Christ's name what are they doing?'

Marcus spun round at Quirinus's shout.

'Where?'

'The top of the slope. Look.'

At first Marcus could only see the Picts struggling to reach the crest of the hillside in a long, apparently breathless straggle. Then Ramios and his hundred German riders swooped from the treeline like a hawk stooping on a mouse.

'Idiots,' Marcus groaned. 'I'm surrounded by idiots.' But the words were tinged with pride. Because Ramios had chosen his moment to perfection. One hundred riders against five hundred Pictish warriors. A prudent man would have charged in column – a rapier thrust that would have cut the Picts to the heart and allowed him to withdraw. Ramios had no time for rapiers, he preferred the scythe. He attacked in extended line, so every man had an opportunity to pick a target among the exhausted and bewildered enemy. The Germans had the slope in their favour, the Picts had no time to form a defensive line. They barely had the opportunity to bring their spears up before Ramios was on them. Fifty men must have fallen as the Germans broke through the warriors at the top of the slope, and fifty more when they hit the Picts still making the climb. They reached the valley floor with every man still in the saddle. 'The silly bastard will have a lot more trouble getting up that hill than he did coming down,' Marcus predicted.

But Ramios had no intention of turning back. With a precision that would have delighted the Ala Sabiniana's horse-master, the German warriors moved from line to column of fours and continued their charge just beyond the belt of pits and *triboli*, through the Picts attacking Rufius's defences. Their arrival was so sudden that barely a man tried to stop them. Those who noticed, saw mounted warriors in furs and leather tunics who bore much more resemblance to their own cavalry than they did to any Roman.

An odd sound reached the men in the tower. Quirinus shook his head in disbelief. 'They're cheering them. Saluting their courage.'

A harsh bray escaped Marcus. 'Courage my arse,' he laughed. 'They think they're Picts riding to attack Rufius's other flank.'

Ramios must have reached the same conclusion, because they saw he'd sheathed his sword and was waving to the enemy as he rode past. Marcus watched the little column of riders until they reached the safety of the rising ground to the north. On the opposite side of the valley either Rufius or young Geta had finally sent out a force of infantry to hasten the Picts' retreat down the slope.

He turned his attention to the great mass of warriors still waiting in the north, but there was still no sign of movement. Should he . . . ?

Quirinus cleared his throat and Marcus turned to find a slight figure standing in the shadow of the stairway. A shiver ran through him.

'It is as you intended,' Calista said.

'I thought—'

'Briga's way is not my way.'

It was time.

'Make the signal,' he ordered the two bannermen. He turned to her. 'Will you come with me?'

She shook her head. 'My future lies in the north. The goddess has foretold it. If you ever have need, look for me there.'

L

Hidden amid the trees on the hillside north-east of Longovicium, Sempronius tightened the strap on his helmet for the fifth time and tested the draw of his sword. The distinct formations below him in the valley bottom stood out clearly in the midday sunlight like pieces on a gaming board and frankly they terrified him. He had marked his target, Luddoc's flying horse banner, as Marcus had ordered, but Luddoc's force alone must number upwards of two thousand, while the massed tribes of Corvus and his Selgovae and Coel and his southern Votadini waited less than a bowshot away. He knew he should rejoice at this opportunity to at last show the prowess of the Second Asturians, but all he felt was resignation. The mere sight of Briga's army convinced him he would not survive today.

From his vantage point he could just see Longovicium's gate towers. A dozen times in the last ten minutes he'd been convinced he'd spotted a flash of red, but it had proved to be only the sun glinting on armour or some other distraction. A distant hum told him of activity elsewhere, but the contours of the hill shielded most of the valley from him so he didn't know if it was the battle Marcus had sought or the sound of Briga's Picts slaughtering poor old Rufius and his lads at the river. He let out a deep breath. He had spent the morning inspecting his men and passing on Marcus's curiously cryptic instructions. What did it mean? None of them would find out until they came within sight of their enemy, and what good would it do them then? All they could do was wait.

'There, lord. In the tower. The signal.'

Sempronius stared at the fort. At last. Two red flags. He discovered he was smiling. The kind of wolf's smile Marcus wore when he was planning something utterly devious. He turned to his officers. 'Regiment will advance at the walk. Remember. Not a sound until they're on the point of our spears.' One thing was certain, he was damned if he was going to wait until Julius Pastor and his Ala Herculaea were halfway to the enemy.

They set off down the slope at an angle. Ten close-ranked squares of thirty men, their mounts snorting with excitement and chewing at the bit, spears at the port on their right shoulders and big round shields protecting their left sides. They were approaching Luddoc and his warriors from the rear of his left flank, which was perfect. Or it would have been if they didn't have another four or five hundred paces to go, the last hundred of it across open stubble field and pasture. Christus save us there were a lot of them. He cast a wary glance at Coel's southern Votadini, directly below and clearly at battle readiness, spears and shields in hand. Some of them were staring directly at him, but not a man made a move or a sound.

The slope eased a little and he nudged his mount into a trot and twitched the reins to change the angle of approach so he could wheel the regiment to bring it against the head of Luddoc's force. Isolate him, Marcus had said. Cut down his bodyguard and any of his lords who stand with him. Be ready for any eventuality. What eventuality? Pastor and the Ala Herculaea should be close by now, but he could see nothing of them on the far slope. Ah well, three hundred, or five, what difference did it make?

Coel saw the disciplined squares of cavalry break from the cover of the trees and make their way steadily across the hillside. 'You know what to do?' he said to his commanders.

'Yes, lord . . .'

He knew they had questions, but he had no answers. Only one thing was certain. 'Kill only if you have to,' he said.

'Now?'

'We wait.'

Now there could be no doubt they'd been seen. Confused shouts erupted from the resting Votadini. If the warriors managed to form a defensive line Sempronius knew his men would all die for nothing. Individual warriors on the outer edge of the massed men reached for their spears and shields, but most still didn't perceive the scale of the threat.

'First two squadrons will remain in square,' Sempronius called over his shoulder. 'The remainder will form line.' The manoeuvre had been agreed before they set off and it took only a single trumpet call to see it carried out. He looked up at an echoing blast and saw with satisfaction that the Ala Herculaea were hurtling towards Luddoc's men from the opposite side of the valley, causing further confusion in the enemy ranks. They reached the flat ground of the valley bottom and he cursed as his horse almost stumbled. Cut the head off the snake. The order had been quite specific. What happened afterwards wasn't worth concerning himself about. The leading squadrons in column appeared on his right flank. Ahead, Luddoc's rearing horse banner fluttered above a milling group of riders perhaps forty strong and he twitched the reins so the nose of his mount was pointed directly towards them. He found that he was holding his breath and forced himself to suck in some air. Fifty paces, Christus save us. The warriors around the banner were armed with swords, not spears, and he could see the panic in their eyes. He roared his thanks to God like a battle cry. In a blink the Asturians were among them. Sempronius's spear took a bearded man in the chest and glanced from his mail upwards into his throat killing him stone dead. He hauled his long sword clear of its scabbard, swung it at a second man, missed completely and almost fell out of the saddle. Where was he?

'Remember, I want the king alive,' he roared to anyone within hearing. 'Kill the rest if you must, but I want him alive.'

Men were fighting and dying in a confused throng all around him. Someone cut at his arm as he circled his horse seeking the banner, but he barely noticed the blow and before he could react the warrior was gone. Screams of men and horses. Snarling Pictish faces. One of his own, unhorsed and with half his jaw missing, hacking at the legs of a Pictish nobleman's mount as the Pict split his skull with a war axe. Not so far away the Ala Herculaea, who had performed a mirror image of the Asturian manoeuvre, fought for their lives in a bloody melee. Sempronius risked a glance behind him to where the remainder of his command had formed a wall between the king and his warriors, and were dying to keep it intact. Nothing to be done about it, but for their sacrifice to be worthwhile he had to take Luddoc alive.

The standard-bearer must have been killed or knocked from the saddle in the first rush, because the banner suddenly reappeared above a group of warriors that pulsed and snarled around their dismounted king at the centre of a ring of Roman spears. Luddoc, as brave as any, fought to reach his tormentors, but his bodyguard of noblemen kept him from the spear points even at the cost of their own lives.

Julius Pastor appeared at Sempronius's shoulder, helmet gone and blood pulsing from a cut on his cheek to sheet his chain armour. 'We have him, what in the name of Christ do we do now?'

Sempronius shook his head, too weary to articulate his own despair. He looked up and saw his doom. Two hundred Pictish horsemen galloping to their king's aid. Then he saw the white cloth on the leader's arm. 'The white cloth,' he croaked. 'The Lord of the Wall said—'

'Look for the white cloth. Whoever wears it is a friend.'

Odd friends, smashing aside the wall of spears that had been keeping Luddoc's warriors at bay and exchanging blows with the men who wielded them. 'Hold,' Sempronius found his voice. 'The men of the white cloth are our allies.' Too late to save many, but the Roman wall was quickly replaced by a Pictish one, the riders snarling at their tribesfolk to stay back.

Sempronius slumped in the saddle. Almost absently he noticed blood leaking from beneath his mail and dripping from his left hand. When he looked up, he found himself the focus of a pair of merciless dark eyes. He had never met Coel, but he recognized a king when he saw one.

'Lord . . .'

'Go,' Coel hissed, and Sempronius saw he was wound tight as a bowstring. 'You have done what you came to do.'

'My men,' Sempronius persisted. 'The wounded?'

'They will be safe with me. But go now before I kill you myself.'

Something stirred inside Sempronius, something hot and bright that grew and multiplied until it filled him beyond bearing. He saw the faces of all the dead men who'd fallen to present Coel with Marcus Flavius Victor's gift. In that instant he knew he had to kill this—

'Come,' Julius Pastor took his arm. 'We are no good to Marcus dead.'

They gathered their bleeding and exhausted troopers together and rode off towards Longovicium past the flank of a curiously passive and immobile host of Selgovae, whose leader didn't even spare them a glance.

'A man would be unwise to depend on the gratitude of kings,' Pastor observed with a bitter laugh.

But Sempronius's mind was elsewhere.

They had another battle to fight. And this time it would be a battle for survival.

Coel gave orders for the Roman wounded to be cared for and the dead to be treated honourably. Every eye was on him as he slipped from the saddle and removed his iron helmet, but he barely registered the interest. His fingers touched the golden circlet that ringed his brow and he realized he'd been wearing it for so long it had almost become part of him. He eased it free and pushed his way through the mounted Votadini warriors who had replaced the Romans around Luddoc. The king's bodyguard eyed their fellow tribesmen warily, but Coel didn't break stride as he advanced until the sword points were almost touching his breast.

'We are all Votadini here,' Coel called to them. 'You have nothing to fear.'

'Don't listen to him.' Luddoc stepped clear of his guard, sword in hand. 'He has betrayed you to the Romans and murdered your kin.'

'You have been brought here by a fool, on a fool's quest.' Coel ignored the other man. 'We should go home. Now.'

'Coward,' Luddoc sneered.

Coel took a step back, but only to lay the golden circlet on the damp grass.

'You have always coveted my kingdom, fool. Well if you want it, you will have to fight for it. In the old way.'

LI

Briga watched in dismay as the pathetically few Roman cavalry destroyed Beli's flank attack, and in disbelief as they traversed the entire field filled with her warriors to escape. She pounded the side of the cart with her fist and screamed that she'd have Beli's head if he wasn't dead already. Drosten watched her tantrum with weary detachment. She'd had him ride back and forth to Melcho four times demanding to know when he'd break through, and his forearms were stripped raw by the constant action of the reins. All Drosten could tell her was that the axemen were doing their job, but it would take time to remove the thorn barrier entirely. Melcho had no doubt they would prevail, the spikes and pits held no fears for them now, but more and more of his men were dying on the points of Roman spears, and falling to Roman slings, arrows and deadly, weighted throwing darts.

'Go forward and tell him I demand he breaks through now.' The queen's voice was like the rasp of a saw. Drosten remembered the first time he'd seen her, on the day Keother died, a goddess who'd seemed to radiate power and with the gift of life and death at the tip of her long fingers. She looked much older now, the black band framing her eyes streaked with tears and the red paste of her lips smeared across her cheek. Diminished, was how he would describe it, not in stature, but in authority.

'He does not need your demands,' he replied. 'He needs more men.'

Briga flinched as if she'd been slapped. Drosten knew she would probably kill him when this was over, but he found he didn't particularly care. He watched the bright lips work and waited for the death sentence, but gradually she regained control.

'Enough of our people have died. Let the Selgovae bleed for a change. Tell Corvus that we have opened the way. He should bring every man he has forward to destroy the enemy.'

Reaching the Selgovae meant Drosten must ride beneath the walls of the fort. The Roman artillery continued to take a steady toll of the still waiting Picts, but the fall of the boulders and arrows was more intermittent and he suspected the operators must be tiring. He chose a line that took him up the centre of the valley away from the more crowded eastern slope. Here and there men tended warriors who'd been injured, or more often the shattered bodies of the dead. An occasional boulder still with pieces of flesh stuck to it, or a red smear in the grass, told its own story. He ignored the missiles that passed overhead and sought out the crow banner of Corvus.

The King of the Selgovae did not even deign to look at him when he delivered Briga's message.

'This is no business of mine.' Corvus studied a group of horse soldiers straggling up the slope towards the fort. 'The Selgovae will fight when we reach the south and there is silver and gold to be plundered as your queen promised. If there is a bump in the road, let the Picts flatten it. There is no glory in brushing aside a few auxiliaries,' he said with airy dismissal. 'You may tell the Brenine that I am saving my warriors for a proper battle when we meet the Sixth legion.'

Drosten stared at the bearlike chieftain in disbelief. Eventually the single eye dropped to acknowledge his presence. 'I would suggest that you carry your request to the Votadini, but it appears they are occupied for the moment. And,' he sniffed like a hunting dog testing the air, 'your queen may require your presence sooner than you think.'

Because the Romans weren't finished.

Burrius and the Numerus Defensorum attacked first, from the east, and their target was the left flank of Briga's rearmost troops, not so far from Drosten and the Selgovae. Drosten saw them break cover from the trees at the top of the hill. A few hundred horsemen attacking several thousand of Briga's as yet unblooded warriors. A mere pinprick, but still . . .

'Will you not move to support them now?' he demanded.

But Corvus remained unmoved. 'No business of mine,' he repeated, shaking his great head.

Drosten kicked his pony into motion to return to face the queen's unpredictable reaction. Once more he stayed to the west of the mass of warriors. They too had seen the Roman cavalry and whoever commanded this tribal group was quick enough to react, for spearmen were running to where the cavalry would strike and creating a wall of metal and shields. But a nagging doubt gnawed at his mind. Why should such a weak force, however brave, spend their lives so pointlessly?

He had his answer soon enough, because before the eastern attackers were two thirds of the way down the hillside he heard the thunder of hooves from his right. When he looked up, what appeared to be a whole army of cavalry was pouring down the *western* slope from a valley close to the fort. Drosten felt a stab of fear at the sight of the great wave of horsemen thundering towards him and he swerved his pony towards the sanctuary of the main body of Pictish warriors. In Taranis's name where did they get so many cavalry?

The attack against Luddoc by Sempronius's Asturians and Julius Pastor's veteran Ala Herculaea had been so central to Marcus's plan he'd given them no further task when they'd completed it. There was also the small detail, which Sempronius pondered as he rode up the slope towards the fort, that the Lord of the Wall couldn't be certain how many of his horse soldiers would remain alive after their charge.

It was only as he marvelled at his survival and that of another four hundred men of the Second Asturians and Ala Herculaea that the young commander decided they were well capable of doing more. The only question was what? What would the Lord of the Wall do under the circumstances? The answer came when he saw Senilis forming up the pathetically few troopers of the Numerus Directorum and Numerus Exploratorum for their attack on the Pictish rear. He looked towards Julius Pastor and the ironic shake of the head told him they were of the same mind. He gave the orders to join the units converging on the top of the slope.

Marcus's instructions to the cavalry attacking Briga's rear had been clear. Hit and run. Cause as much mayhem in as short a time as possible and get out to fight another day. But that had been with a mere two hundred horse soldiers on the west slope. Thanks to Sempronius's reinforcements Senilis now had six hundred cavalrymen under his command. Many were exhausted and battered, it was true, but still two full regiments, and he saw the opportunity to do the Picts some real damage. He formed them up in two lines behind the crest of the hill.

The Numerus Defensorum were five hundred paces from the Picts and closing fast. At the canter, a cavalry horse could cover three hundred paces in the time it took a man to count to fifty. Sempronius counted off the number in his head before the order came to advance. For the moment all the enemy's attention was on the east side of the valley. He could see hundreds of spearmen already forming a line that would force the *defensores'* commander to swerve away if he didn't want his men to be slaughtered. But by now Burrius would see the cavalry on the opposite side of the valley. He would know every second he bought them would count in lives saved. Sempronius heard the sound of a cavalry trumpet braying and his heart went out to the man, because that too would keep the Picts' attention on the smaller force.

They were three hundred paces short of the Pictish flank when the Picts finally realized they were being attacked on two sides, and that the greater danger came from the west. Spearmen began to form a ragged line, but Sempronius laughed because they were too late. A few dozen men would not stop six hundred charging horsemen. Beyond them the great majority milled like so many sheep, and all his experience and training had taught him that infantry caught in the open order were just targets. Hit and run. Yes, they would hit and run, but by the bones of Christ they would give this Briga something to remember.

Most of the troopers who'd made the first charge had lost their spears, but they had swords and a man on a charging horse who knew his business would be inside a spear point and gutting his opponent in the time it took to blink. They seemed to fly across the flat ground of the valley bottom and he was among the enemy almost before he realized it. A Pict with a spear darted the point towards his chest and he swept up his blade to knock the shaft aside so the bright iron flashed past his shoulder. No time to bring the sword round, but the horse hammered the man aside with its shoulder, snapping at his face with its teeth for good measure. Everything was instinct now.

Sempronius knew he should be aware of the heartbeat of battle around him, ready to give his signaller the order that would direct his troopers, but with so many Picts to kill there was no need. A man wielding a war axe appeared in front of him and he nudged his mount left to bring the Pict onto his sword. A more experienced warrior would have stood his ground and killed the horse, but this one allowed Sempronius to place him just where he wanted. He saw the conviction in the narrowed eyes turn to fear, the momentary hesitation as the young warrior realized his mistake, the shriek and spurt of bright blood as the sword chopped down and the hand holding the axe fell to the ground.

They were close to the centre of the Pictish force now. At last, the mass of Briga's warriors realized the eastern charge had been a feint and hundreds sprinted to engage the horse soldiers who had sliced into their ranks from the west. Sempronius turned his mount and risked a glance to his left where a score of small skirmishes were being played out. Yet more Picts were coming from the south to converge on the Roman cavalry and even as he watched two or three horses went down under the sheer weight of numbers. Time to go. He looked for his signaller and had a moment of panic until he realized the trooper had only strayed a few paces away.

'Claudius,' he shouted.

The signaller turned towards him and he saw the young man's eyes widen in alarm. Too late. He felt his horse lurch beneath him as a Pictish nobleman ran from his blind side to hamstring the beast. Sempronius fell with a force that knocked the breath from his body and momentarily deprived him of his senses. His hand scrabbled for his sword as some object blocked his view of the sky. The last thing his brain registered was the flicker of sunlight on the axe edge that carved his face in two.

Briga's rage when she heard of Corvus's refusal to advance made her almost incoherent.

'What . . . what did he say?'

'He said there is no glory in brushing aside a few auxiliaries,' Drosten repeated Corvus's words. 'If there is a bump in the road, let the Picts flatten it.'

'And he did not move even when the Romans attacked?'

'No.'

'When this is over, I will have the traitor fed to my wolves.' She looked to where Blaid stood calming Fenrir, Geri and Freki. 'These Roman cavalry, how strong was the force?'

Drosten shook his head. 'It was difficult to tell. Hundreds certainly, perhaps as many as a thousand. But the warriors you sent drove them back with great slaughter,' he assured her.

Briga drew a long breath and stared up towards the fort. 'We will soon be free of this place,' she said. 'Your friend Melcho the Chosen sent word that the barrier is almost gone and the defenders weakened by exhaustion.'

'The cavalry . . . ?'

Briga did not know where they came from, but she knew one thing for certain.

'The Roman power is spent.'

But she was wrong.

LII

Marcus ran from the tower and out of Longovicium's south gate to where Luko waited with Storm. Valeria's Saxon, Leof, placed his battle helmet over his head and helped him into the saddle. His sister rode from the rear of the fort to join him with the men of the Ala Sabiniana, Ramios's hundred Germans and the troopers she'd brought from the Sixth legion.

Marcus had accepted Dulcitius wasn't coming now. If he wanted to defeat Briga, he must do it with the men at his disposal. He'd watched Senilis's headlong charge into the rear of Briga's Picts and he could have wept at the sacrifice he witnessed. But that sacrifice had not been in vain. The attack had drawn thousands of Pictish warriors from where they had waited by the queen. Thousands more were entirely focused on a final devastating assault on Rufius's increasingly weakened line. He would ride with Valeria's squadron today, to glory or to death. He would never have a better chance.

'Kill the queen,' he called. 'And the Picts will melt away like snow in spring. Kill their queen and they will bow their necks for your swords.'

He had no idea whether either was true, but it was what warriors expected to hear on the day of battle and those closest to him shouted their approval. They moved slowly out into the open in their squadron squares, but Marcus quickly increased pace to the trot and led the regiment in a curve that would bring them south of the buildings of Longovicium's settlement. Ten squares in two lines abreast, with around two hundred and fifty men riding in a single unit as a reserve, though what Ramios would make of his orders only God knew. The houses would shield their initial advance, but equally Marcus would be blind to any changes in Briga's dispositions.

When he'd last seen them, the great majority of her warriors were either in the south attacking Rufius at the river or to the north celebrating the blood-letting that had driven off Senilis's horse. Marcus calculated that neither of these forces could react quickly enough to oppose his charge against Briga herself. That said, she still had something like two thousand men in close proximity and everything depended on how those men deployed at the first sight of Roman cavalry a bare three hundred paces away. He felt calmer now than he'd done at any time during the day. The rhythm of the horse beneath him and the muted rumble of thousands of hooves banished the nerves that plagued even the most experienced veteran on the verge of battle.

The harsh bray of a *carnyx* came from somewhere near the river on the right, from where the Picts *could* see them. A warning call or the signal for another Pictish attack? Only time would tell and that time would be soon. They emerged from behind the houses to see the entire field laid out before them. A shiver of dread ran through Marcus at the sight of warriors converging on Briga's wolf banner where some enterprising nobleman was already forming the wall of shields and spears that might spell their doom.

He reacted instantly to the threat with a change of formation. 'Sound Form Cuneus.' Valeria's signaller blew the familiar call and the smooth transition began that the squadrons had practised so often. Time, they needed time. It would be close, and if the alignment was only half-formed, likely they would all be dead, but Marcus knew he'd no other option. Valeria's riders were positioned at the centre of the front rank of five squadrons, with Caradoc on her right. While they maintained position the three outer squadrons dropped back to form up behind them, while the rear squadrons slowed to make room. The Boar's Head, a close-packed triangle of horsemen three hundred strong that rode like an arrow aimed at the very heart of Briga's army. A regiment charging line abreast would be hard pressed to break a wall of shields, but the Boar's Head, with steadfast warriors of valour and will at its point, at least had a chance.

A shallow drainage ditch appeared beneath Storm's hooves, but the stallion barely broke stride.

Marcus glanced at Valeria to his left, her face a mask of concentration, spear held easily in her right hand and the bright point glinting in the sun. A little behind her rode Zeno, who'd left his assistants to take care of the wounded from the battle at the river, with the assurance that anybody could fashion a tourniquet or lop off an arm. Leof rode behind them, his long golden hair streaming from beneath his helmet.

Valeria would follow him to the gates of Hades and beyond, and her squadron with her, and so, for different reasons, would Caradoc. The old man rode with his head low over his horse's ears and, as if he sensed Marcus's eyes on him, he looked to his left and grinned as their eyes met. When a man rode into battle beside another all the old enmities were forgotten. Caradoc had done what he'd done out of loyalty because he'd believed Marcus was bent on self-destruction, and perhaps he wasn't wrong, but that was in the past now. All that mattered was the wall of shields ahead and the men behind it who wanted so desperately to kill them all. Behind Caradoc rode Senecio, his bow more deadly than any spear and the arrows already arcing to plunge into the enemy ranks, and Ninian, whose muttered prayers were now of as much use as any further military wisdom Marcus could impart.

Janus and Julius led different squadrons in the second rank. A dozen years since he had found them standing back to back and ready to fight to the death amid the burning ruin of their settlement. He felt a welling inside, an upsurge of pride that he led such men. In a way, he thought of them as his sons, and an image of his true son appeared in his head, fair hair hanging across dark, bewildered eyes. With the vision came an urgent desire to survive. He'd wanted a son who was a warrior, but an eight-year-old boy was barely formed. He could see that now. Why hadn't he seen it then? What chance had he given young Bren? Why would any father turn his back on his own flesh and blood? He didn't know the answer, but, if he lived to see the sun set, he would do every-thing in his power to change it. All this in a few heartbeats, with the muddy earth blurring beneath Storm's pounding hooves and every snorted breath taking them ever closer to a defensive line that thick-ened and became stronger even as he searched for some weakness.

A hundred paces.

Valeria's signaller must be lost in the moment because he repeated the call to form *cuneus* over and over again in a constant braying clam-our that drove the horses to a new frenzy. It took courage to stand in a shield wall with three hundred charging horses thundering towards you like a living avalanche, looming larger and more deadly with each pounding heartbeat. Some warriors had that courage and some didn't. Men would be pissing and fouling their breeks behind those painted shields and that thought pleased Marcus. 'Kill them,' he roared, as much to ward off his own fears as to instill bravery in those around him. 'Kill every last one of the bastards.' The cry was taken up by hun-dreds of gaping mouths around him and three or four of Valeria's riders were so consumed by battle madness they forged past the *draco* banner to lead the squadron.

'Get back in line!' Valeria shouted the order, but her cry went unheard or unheeded.

Fifty paces.

In God's name make them break now. Marcus could see a few men running from the defensive line, but he was still faced by a solid wall of shields in the hands of resolute warriors, punctuated by those wicked spear points that were a few moments from snatching his life. He felt Storm's confusion and struggled to hold him steady. For all his train-ing, every deep-rooted instinct screamed at the horse not to charge home. Would he stay the course or would he twist clear? For a moment everything was in doubt. He could hear Valeria cursing her mount with words that he doubted many Christians would know.

Snarling, bearded faces recognizable as individuals behind the shields. Teeth bared in terror or defiance.

Twenty paces.

He nudged Storm a little to the left and levelled his spear through a gap in the riders half a length ahead, at a shield bearing Briga's symbol of a howling wolf and held by a grey-bearded veteran.

Ten.

'Mary mother of God save us.'

A war axe came spinning from behind the shield wall and by ill-fortune or design the heavy blade struck deep into the snout of the lead horse, making the beast swerve. Its new course took it directly into the path of the animal to its right and both of them went down, taking out the legs of a third. Three tumbling battering rams of uncontrolled meat, muscle, bone and sinew, each weighing as much as a fully loaded cart, smashed into the Pictish line and tore a gaping hole in the defenders. Marcus let out a great roar and the elixir of battle sent a surge of fire through his veins like one of Zeno's potions. He swerved for the centre of the gap with Luko and Valeria keeping pace at his side. Some brave soul stood up in the centre of the carnage of dying horses, broken men and shattered shields and Marcus's spear twitched instinctively to the left to take him directly in the midriff. He felt the moment the point entered flesh and split the bones of the man's spine. 'Too deep,' he muttered to himself as the spear shaft was wrenched from his grasp. He reached for his sword. Where was Briga?

His eyes searched for the wolf banner above the mass of milling men in a valley bottom trampled to a morass of clinging mud by thousands of marching feet. Little groups of warriors held their ground against the Roman cavalry, but for now there was little cohesion or order to the defence and most of the Picts were only interested in survival. Clearly that would change, because away to his left someone had put together an organized force of warriors from the earlier fighting and they were already racing to their queen's support. Then he saw it, a little to the south. He pointed with his sword and Valeria nodded that she'd also seen the banner. No sign of Caradoc, but Julius and Janus and their squadrons were still with him. Not enough, the thought cut through the exhilaration of battle, but he thrust it aside and drove Storm to where Briga waited.

'There,' Valeria called. He saw her now, seated on her ludicrous throne in the midst of a battle, but still imposing in her cloak of scarlet. Features undistinguishable yet, apart from the band of black that created a mask around her eyes, and made to seem taller by the starburst of lime-washed hair that surrounded her head. He had her now. With the squadrons of Janus and Julius keeping his flanks secure, he closed on the Pictish queen. Without warning a bizarre band of cripples and oddities appeared like a swarm of wasps to attack the leading riders. Marcus beat away a man – a dwarf, his disbelieving mind confirmed – who tried to grab his reins, while, with the snap of yellow teeth and a spray of red, Storm sent a muscle-bound giant reeling with half his face missing. Marcus had heard of Briga's misfits from Julius, but nothing had prepared him for this madhouse. To his left a beautiful naked girl disappeared shrieking beneath the hooves of Luko's mount.

While the misfits were dying, Briga's bodyguard took advantage of their sacrifice. Somehow the score of mounted spearmen eluded Janus on the left and struck Marcus's flank like a lightning bolt. Luko swung his dragon standard like a club and knocked one man from the saddle, but another rider rammed Storm in the side with such force that Marcus heard the snap of the horse's ribs. He just had time to swing his left leg clear of the collision before he was flung through the air with his sword in a death grip. The landing drove the breath from him and the impact broke the chin strap on his ornate helmet and knocked it from his head, but the soft ground saved him from any real damage. He struggled to his feet in time to parry an axe stroke from a roaring Pictish veteran that would have cleaved him in two at the shoulder. The problem with an axe was that your first blow had to be certain, because it was too unwieldy to get back in position and Marcus barely looked to see the effect of his sweeping cut that sliced across the top of the man's nose and turned both his eyes into bloody ruin.

Drosten had never felt so helpless. He watched the battle in mute horror as he stood by the throne awaiting the queen's next order. When he recognized the tall warrior struggling through the mud towards them hot bile rose in his throat. 'He is here.'

Briga followed his eyes to the man trudging implacably towards her. She shook her head in disbelief. 'The Lord of the Wall? How . . . ?'

But that didn't matter. Marcus Flavius Victor might be a man alone, but she had no doubt of her fate if the Roman reached her. She looked around for help, but every surviving spearman within call was engaged with the enemy. Even her misfits had sacrificed themselves for her. All that remained was Drosten, and she almost laughed. A helpless cripple? Yet hundreds more of her warriors were coming from the north to press what she now saw was a pathetically small band of Romans. All she needed was time. And she did have one more weapon.

'Fenrir, Geri, Freki.'

The wolves had been sitting at her feet and now they rose, lips drawn back from their teeth in a silent snarl, lean, long-limbed grey shapes, their winter fur mottled and thick. Briga pointed at Marcus.

'Kill,' she cried.

'No!' Blaid emerged from where he'd been resting beneath Briga's cart, exhausted by a day of constantly carrying messages.

Briga hissed at him to be still.

The battle seemed to fade as Marcus watched the wolves stalk silently over the muddy ground towards him, spread out in a half circle so he wouldn't know where the first would strike. The instinctive co-ordination and exact placing told him this was a trained manoeuvre and not the first time they'd performed it. Geri and Freki drifted to his left in a low crouch, their merciless grey-green eyes never leaving him, fangs bared and edging ever closer. Fenrir stayed well to the right, keeping his distance, but a menacing threat at the outer edge of Marcus's vision. Marcus's chain armour would protect his body, though his arms and legs would be vulnerable. A great clamour drew his attention and he risked a glance to where the bulk of his troopers were struggling to keep a mass of Picts at bay. That single lapse of concentration was all the encouragement the wolves needed. Geri and Freki darted in, lean bellies brushing the ground, snarling and snapping at his legs and forcing him to spin left. It was only when he swept his sword to drive them away that he realized his mistake. A grey blur launched itself silently from his blind side in a great leap that brought Fenrir's fangs to his exposed neck. So close he could actually smell the wolf's rancid pelt and drool from the open jaws struck his face before Leof's sword smashed down to chop the animal out of the air.

'Lord, we have to get out now.' The Saxon handed him his helmet with shaking hands. 'It may already be too late.'

Marcus looked up trying to disguise his relief. Valeria sat tall in the saddle holding the reins of two mounts, one with blood coating the saddle. 'Leof is right, Marcus.' He'd never heard her sound so grave. 'We're being slaughtered. Caradoc fell trying to break the line and only two of the rear squadrons managed to follow Janus and Julius through the gap. They're pressing us on all sides. If we don't get out now we never will.'

Marcus took the reins of the bloodstained horse. He looked to where Briga stood fewer than twenty paces away behind a rapidly forming wall of shields. He sheathed his sword. It was over. He'd failed. But when Leof moved to help him into the saddle, he noticed an abandoned spear half-hidden in the mud at his feet. With one movement Marcus scooped up the shaft and hurled it in an arc over the heads of Briga's spearmen.

Briga watched the flight of the spear, transfixed, as it soared through the still air towards her. She was almost disappointed when Drosten's face appeared in front of hers and he wrapped his truncated arms around her. Too late. She felt the shock of the spear's impact as it hammered Drosten against her. A dull pain in her chest. She saw his eyes bulge, heard the terrible groan and his last breath touched her cheek like a kiss. Briga moved her lips to his and sensed the final vestige of life leave him. She pushed Drosten's body away, noticing the point of the spear projecting a finger's breadth from the dead man's chest. Wonderingly, she touched the chain armour between her breasts, but all she felt was a dull ache. Drosten fell backwards, instantly forgotten, twisting to land face down in the mud, the spear quivering like a banner pole in the wind.

Briga turned her attention to her nemesis, mounting his horse to flee as her warriors closed in on all sides.

'You may run, Lord of the Wall, but there is nowhere to go,' she shrieked. 'Eventually you will be brought before me in defeat. Your agony will be long and painful. At the end you will pray for death, but Briga will refuse it.'

Below her Blaid knelt in the mud sobbing, while Geri and Freki struggled to drag Fenrir, his back broken, but still able to whimper his agony, towards the wolfmaster.

LIII

Calista arrived back among the Votadini to find Coel stripped to the waist ready to join Luddoc in a makeshift ring that had been formed from a string of knotted reins arranged on the grass. The circle measured twelve paces across, more or less, as Votadini convention required. Each king had armed himself with a sword and would fight barefoot on the trampled grass.

It was Coel's habit to carry a superbly decorated ceremonial sword, but Calista noticed he had switched the weapon for a more functional iron blade that shimmered with a dull blue-grey light. He'd told her of his intention the previous night when she'd passed on Marcus's instruction for the Votadini to wear white to identify them to the Roman cavalry. At that point she'd still not decided where her future lay, but Coel assumed she would remain with his people.

'Pray to your goddess that I prevail tomorrow. If I live, I pledge you will want for nothing.'

'Am I to have no say?' she demanded. 'Is Calista, the keeper of the shrine, to be nothing but a gaming piece exchanged for barter between two men?'

'Very well,' he'd conceded. 'If I live, you will do as you please.'

Now he stood in the ring opposite Luddoc surrounded by the elders and champions of their tribes, the breath of both men misting the cold air above them. Neither king carried a shield and she asked a warrior standing nearby why they rejected the protection.

'This is a fight to the death.' The man looked at her as if she was a fool. 'The only protection they need is their sword and the favour of the gods. Besides,' he grinned, 'Coel reckoned that if Luddoc had a shield he might still be hiding behind it when night fell.'

A priest entered the ring and stood between the combatants. He picked up the circlet of gold Luddoc had laid beside that of Coel, and raised it ceremonially above the king's head. 'This is the crown of the Votadini held by the line of King Luddoc for time immemorial.' He ignored the jeers of Coel's supporters. 'And this the crown of King Coel,' he picked up the second circlet, 'who claims both by virtue of *his* lineage.' This was the signal for the men of north and south to begin the chant of their king's ancestry and within three or four generations it was clear why they were fighting. The chanting synchronized and the warriors of both sides cheerfully took up the rhythm: '. . . son of Madog, son of Owain, son of Luddoc, son of Madog, son of Fergus . . .'

When the ritual ended the priest raised his arms. 'This is a fight to the death, in the old manner. The prize is the crown of the Votadini. Every warrior here will abide by the decision of the gods. Any man who is forced from the circle will be returned to the fight. Any man who steps out of the circle voluntarily through fear or because of injury will go to the fire. Anyone other than the challengers who enters the circle for any reason will go to the fire. Do you understand?'

Neither king deigned to answer. Luddoc hunched his broad shoulders and swung his sword in a series of measured practice cuts that hissed through the chill air. Coel watched his opponent with his blade hanging loosely at his right side. There was a stillness to him that sent a shiver through Calista. This was a new Coel. Cold as ice and as hard and unyielding as the blade he wielded.

'Begin,' the priest cried, and stepped out of the circle.

Both men moved swiftly to dominate the centre of the ring, but it was Coel who took advantage, forcing Luddoc to circle just out of reach seeking a weakness. Coel's sword followed his opponent, ready to react to the inevitable attack, but for the moment Luddoc only darted tentatively with the point.

'He's better than this,' Calista's companion muttered. 'It's a ruse.'

A few moves later her informant was proved correct. Luddoc's dart turned into a full-blown thrust intended to pierce Coel to the spine, but this too was a ruse. At the last moment he twisted the blade away from the expected parry and cut upwards so the point would have scythed through his enemy's viscera and breastbone. But Coel had already danced beyond the reach of the sword tip and when Luddoc darted back to await his counter-attack, he found his opponent staring at him without any discernible expression. Still Coel allowed his rival to take the initiative and it was Luddoc once more who probed and danced seeking a decisive opening.

'He plans to wear him down.' Calista's neighbour didn't hide his disappointment, but the northern Votadini roared their king's every step and twist.

Another thrust from Luddoc, and Coel parried before dancing clear with the clash of metal ringing in his ears, the first time the two blades had touched. This time Coel swept instantly into a counter and Luddoc had to use every ounce of his skill to avoid the blizzard of iron that assaulted his eyes and sought out his body. When he eventually danced clear, feet skirting the reins of the circle, the king of the northern Votadini's chest was heaving and Calista convinced herself she could see doubt in his eyes.

'Too slow. Too slow.'

It was obvious now, even to Calista. Luddoc had all the skills of a warrior and was as brave as any man could be brave, but Coel was just as efficient, and, more important, he was faster. As long as Luddoc could bring his edge up to parry he was able to keep Coel at bay, but he never came close to touching him. Gradually an uneasy murmur could be heard from the northern warriors.

Desperation made Luddoc reckless and he risked everything to get close enough to kill Coel. He feinted low and right, flicked his sword into his left hand and scythed at Coel's exposed stomach. It was a good trick that would have disembowelled most other men and left their guts lying on the trampled grass. Not Coel. He swayed back so the blade passed a hair's breadth over the taut muscle of his stomach and at the same time managed to flick his blade so the tip scored Luddoc's cheek, causing a ragged wound that dripped blood onto his chest.

Coel took a step back, as if to examine the results of his swordsmanship, and Calista saw a frown that made her suspect Coel had intended to take Luddoc's ear. The ear came later. First a lightning thrust impaled Luddoc's left arm and ensured there would be no more clever switches. More wounds followed until the king of the northern Votadini's torso shone with gore. Suddenly one eye was gone and the other masked with blood from a scalp wound. She willed Coel to finish it, but he told her later that his new northern subjects must learn the price of disloyalty. It was not cruel, he said. Just necessary.

By the time Coel tired of tormenting him, Luddoc was close to collapse, but still he swung his blade where he judged his enemy to be. At last the king of the southern Votadini slipped behind his rival and slashed his blade across the sinews of Luddoc's ankles to bring him to his knees with a cry of torment and frustration. For a fleeting moment Luddoc raised his blinded eyes as if seeking a last glimpse of the sky, before Coel put all his strength into one final blow that took his enemy's head from his shoulders. Ignoring the roars of acclaim from his supporters he knelt by Luddoc's side and arranged his body with hands on chest and his sword beneath the clutching fingers.

'Kneel,' he shouted, and every warrior dropped to his knees. 'And I will count you oathsworn to the king of all the Votadini. There will be no more bickering or raiding, we are one people now. I, your king, will be the arbiter of all disputes. If any man cares not to accept that reality or my rule he should leave now and find another king to serve.' Not a man moved. In the silence, the dull roar of the fighting less than a mile to the south was just discernible. 'Luddoc brought you here on a fool's errand. The Picts are no friends of the Votadini. He was a fool, but a brave fool, and he died well. We will carry his body with us and bury him with the honour he deserves. The keeper of Coventina's Well will ride with us, and we will build the goddess a new sanctuary at Caer Eidinn. Prepare to leave; the sooner we are quit of this place the better.'

He walked to where he had left his clothing and an awestruck servant came with a bucket of water to bathe the few minor wounds he'd suffered and wipe away the sweat of battle. Calista joined them and took the cloth from the servant's hand. Coel nodded and the boy left them alone.

'You will not go to Marcus's aid?' She dabbed at a cut on his left breast. 'He could be dying up there.'

'That was not in our agreement,' he said. 'Marcus would be the first to tell you that a commander or a king cannot allow himself to be swayed by friendship. He knew the odds the day he marched.'

'A new well and shrine for the goddess at Caer Eidinn?' Calista frowned. 'You said that if you lived I could do as I chose.'

'Choose then.' He softened the words with a smile. 'But you will like Caer Eidinn.'

LIV

Aurelius Quirinus had never felt more helpless as he stood on the parapet of Longovicium and watched Marcus's few hundred cavalry charge into the Picts and what appeared to be certain defeat. Even if the Ala Sabiniana managed to kill the Pictish queen very few of them were likely to come out of the valley alive. Of course, Marcus would have known that when he'd ordered Quirinus to stay behind his stout stone walls and hold Longovicium to the last. No sign of the Sixth legion and the unlikely miracle Marcus had so confidently predicted. Quirinus took a last look at the battle below. He liked to consider himself a veteran, though he knew the young men of his command only thought of him as old. But nobody lived for ever. Even an old man with a couple of hundred warriors could do something. The question was what?

He'd kept up his hail of *onager* and shield-splitter missiles until the attack had made it impossible to tell friend from enemy. The machines were idle now and so, more importantly, were the men who crewed them. It seemed to Quirinus that a hundred and fifty stout men could hold these walls about as effectively as two hundred and fifty. In addition to his regular garrison he had a hundred civilians, most of them former soldiers or members of the local militia. That made up his

395

mind. He'd take the majority of his regulars to join the battle and leave fifty to stiffen the civilians' resolve.

There was no question of following Marcus's cavalry down the slope and getting swallowed up in that gigantic Pictish maw, but Rufius Clemens would certainly appreciate his help. Before Marcus launched his charge the Picts in front of the river were as thick as fleas on a badger. Rufius's men had been fighting for almost an hour without respite, which was a lot to ask of any soldier, even behind that well-constructed barrier. Quirinus issued his orders.

The little column left the fort by the west gate, out of sight of the Picts, and made their way along the brow of the hill towards the river. It was only when they reached the ditch Marcus had ordered dug that Quirinus remembered the dam. He shook his head. Timing was everything, the Ala Sabiniana's commander had said, but he was no longer here to decide the timing and in any case time was running out. He ordered eight men to follow him up to the dam wall, where a section of the clay and stones in the centre, above the ditch, had been hacked out and the gap shored up with wooden boards and timber props.

'Get rid of the wood,' he ordered, 'and let's see what we've got.'

The section drove deep into the wall, but there was no sign that simply removing the props would be enough to breach it. He reckoned what remained was the length of a sword blade at most. Fortunately, the men who'd dug it out had been in so much of a hurry to get back to the fort they'd left some of their tools. He picked up a mattock and threw it to the burliest of his men. 'Here,' he said. 'Get digging.'

The remaining clay must have been thinner than he'd realized, because the soldier only made two solid stabs with the mattock before it began to ooze dirty brown water. Quirinus ordered the man to stand clear. Within seconds the clay around the break crumbled and the original trickle became a spurt that erupted while they watched to an enormous rush as the middle of the dam broke away entirely. It made a fine spate as it poured down the new ditch into the drainage ditches that flanked the north road, but he couldn't help feeling disappointed in Marcus. As a weapon of war it seemed rather pathetic.

'Right,' he said, 'enough of this, let's get where we're needed and do some real soldiering.'

Marcus looked around him and felt something like despair.

How many were left out of the six hundred or so cavalry who'd charged with him? Three hundred. No more. Among them were most of Ramios's barbarians, who'd survived remarkably intact, and the depleted squadrons of Janus and Julius. Caradoc and his men had suffered the worst of the casualties after coming up against part of the line that was three or four shields deep. Caradoc should have turned away and tried elsewhere, but he had been determined to support Marcus and Valeria or die in the attempt. No one had seen him fall. That was the way of war. Horse and man had simply charged into a wall of spears and never come out again. By some miracle Senecio and Ninian had fought their way through. The former priest had lost helmet and shield, but managed a shy grin that Marcus struggled to return. Surprisingly, Valeria's squadron, at the very heart of the attack, had fewer casualties than most, and Zeno was still tight to her flank like one of the guardian angels the priests made so much of. Marcus had brought them all here to their deaths, and for what?

Only their discipline and the ability to maintain a tight formation had saved them so far. When he'd been forced away from Briga they'd ridden almost aimlessly looking for a way out of the trap, still powerful enough for the moment not to make them a target for any but the strongest Pictish force. That would likely continue as long as they kept on the move, but the horses were tiring with every passing minute.

'What do we do?' Valeria's voice held no fear, only a hint of weary resignation, which probably hurt him more. She expected to die. The realization prompted a dull fury in Marcus that cleared his mind of the hopelessness that had dogged him since he'd seen Briga survive his spear. Somehow, he must get them out.

They'd been riding in a circle, avoiding the most aggressive-looking bands of Picts, and their turn had brought them to the centre of the valley just south of Longovicium. The steep slope where Ramios had ambushed the Pictish flanking attack was just to their right. It might be possible to force their horses far enough up to enable them to create some sort of redoubt. But first they'd have to fight their way through the Picts who'd congregated at the bottom of the slope seeking a weak spot where they might break through. For the moment, Rufius's defence seemed to be sound enough, but that couldn't last. By now his men would be exhausted, their strength depleted by casualties. Marcus made his decision.

He moved his mount close to Valeria's.

'Follow me to the east side of the valley.' He saw the doubt in her eyes. 'We won't be stopping,' he explained. 'Before we reach the slope we'll wheel right in a half circle and charge across the line of Briga's attack as Ramios did. That's the last thing they'll be expecting. At best, some of us will get through to the far slope and safety. At worst, we'll take some of the pressure off Rufius and Hostilius. A few of us might fight our way through to his lines.' He waited for her reaction. 'If you have a better plan, now's the time.'

She actually laughed, this wonderful sister of his, whose only blemishes after half an hour of battle were a smudge of earth on her cheek and a few splashes of blood on the mail of her sword arm. 'Death or glory. Is that all you ever have to offer, Marcus? It's a good plan, and you're a good man, whatever you'd like others to think, but God will guide us through this.' She drew out the little silver cross she wore at her neck and kissed it. 'Have faith in him, brother.'

Marcus set a course through an avenue of Picts who tightened their grip on their war axes and eyed the three hundred horsemen hungrily, for all the world like a great pack of Briga's wolves.

When the contents of the dam reached the river, they created a wall of muddy water a sword's length deep that swept between the banks with enough force to knock a man off his feet and to carry away many of the wounded and the countless dead. Rhuin, more dead than alive, wasn't even aware of the deluge that drowned him or the sudden cry that went up from the already demoralized warriors.

'Coventina has deserted us!'

From her heightened position on the cart, Briga saw that Marcus had made a fatal mistake.

'He is trapped,' she howled with the laughter of relief. 'The bards will sing of Briga's victory at Longovicium for a hundred generations of men.' She turned to where a great shout erupted from the north and snorted. 'And here is that thief Corvus coming like a carrion bird to make sure his Selgovae do not miss their share of the spoils. Go to Melcho and tell him I want the Lord of the Wall alive for my pleasure.'

The order was to Blaid, who had been sitting beneath the cart beside Drosten's still body, stroking dead Fenrir's fur and with the heads of Geri and Freki on his knees. He pushed them away and without invitation jumped into the cart beside the queen.

'You fool.' Blaid's voice was thick with contempt. 'There is no victory.' He pointed to the north. 'You are looking at your doom. Are you so blind you cannot see Corvus is not supporting us, but attacking like the backstabber he is? Do you not see that our warriors are running away from the river or the Roman column on the north road that must be the Sixth legion—'

Whatever else Blaid was going to say was stilled for ever by the dagger Briga plunged into his throat. She pushed the soon to be corpse over the wall of the cart to join dead Drosten and thought nothing more of him except to look where he'd been pointing. The glint of sunlight on spear points and armour. A streaming banner. 'It cannot be,' she whispered. 'The Sixth cannot come from the north.'

She heard a soft growl. Geri's leap took the wolf into the cart and her jaws clamped on Briga's wrist, breaking the delicate bones and making her shriek with the pain of it. Freki was a heartbeat behind and the weight of her impact knocked Briga flat. The grey eyes bored into hers and she choked at the stink of Freki's breath. She would have screamed again had it not been for the yellow fangs that clamped on her throat.

LV

'What are they shouting?' Marcus called to Janus, more to gain time to steady his reeling mind than to elicit information. One moment he'd been steeling himself to charge the horde of Picts attacking Rufius's over-stretched line, the next the attackers were running back in apparent panic, those closest to the river infecting the others as they fled.

'Some of them are saying that Coventina has deserted them,' Valeria said. Marcus's heart seemed to stop at the mention of the goddess, but Janus's dazed expression told of something of even greater import. 'But there are more and more calling out that the queen is dead and they've been betrayed.'

Briga dead? How could it be? Marcus looked north to where the cart with the throne stood out in solitary isolation on its mound like a grand funeral monument of old. Warriors still fought on the ground beyond, but for the most part the Picts were avoiding the area as though it were cursed. Those from north and south of the battlefield – they still counted in their many thousands – sought the illusory sanctuary of each other's company, gathering together in a great leaderless, dispirited mass at the bottom of the eastern slope, their southern flank bounded by the river. Beyond them, Rufius's incredulous defenders edged warily from the trees.

'Send a messenger to tell them to stay where they are,' Marcus growled. 'This is not over yet.'

'They're beaten,' Valeria said, with a nod towards the ever expanding host of Picts, 'but they'll still take a lot of killing.'

'I want to see her body.'

They walked their horses through the detritus of war towards the hummock. Gone was the ear-piercing clamour of battle and the stomach-clenching terror that accompanied it. Only the silent dead remained. The dead here were mostly victims of Quirinus's *onagri* and *scorpiones*, lying beneath blankets weighted with stones to conceal their shattered bodies. Small groups of Picts made their way furtively across the field looking neither right nor left, in the unlikely hope that ignoring the Romans would save them from attack. Yet they remained, for the moment, unmolested. Storm was there, a still dark mass with blood from his torn lungs staining mouth and nostrils, and Marcus had to choke back a sob at the sight of his companion of all these years. A wavering line of bodies halfway to the settlement had the look of the debris deposited on a beach by an incoming wave. It contained the corpses of many friends as well as enemies and he felt a melancholy pang at the thought of Caradoc lying unmourned among them. But the dead would have to wait.

'Who was it fighting the Picts in the north?' Valeria spoke in the past tense because the sound of battle had faded there as Briga's disheartened warriors retreated in droves to join their comrades.

'Corvus, I think.' Marcus frowned. 'But I have no idea why.'

'He saved us.'

'Perhaps . . .'

'Corvus was part of your plan all along, and you didn't tell me?'

'Would it have made a difference?' It didn't seem to matter now. 'I couldn't be certain what he'd do. It wouldn't be the first time he broke a pledge for his own profit.'

'And Coel and Luddoc?'

'Not Luddoc.' He was suddenly very weary. Probably best she didn't know the detail of his pact with Coel. They dismounted as they approached the mound. Briga's surviving wolves lay by the corpse of their sibling, the extent of their grief somehow self-evident. Marcus made a wide circle to avoid the animals, but they ignored him.

Closer to the cart, a man in a wolfskin cloak lay staring through dull eyes at the pale clouds passing overhead. Beside him, the warrior who'd sacrificed himself to save Briga had the spear still projecting from his back. Marcus pulled it free, turning the body so he could see the face. It wasn't the agonized features that shocked him to a degree that surprised him, but the stumps of the severed wrists. He studied the face with more intent: sallow and sunken in death, with the lines of his suffering written across it like the cuts of a knife, but finally at peace. Not a face he recognized from that blood-soaked glade at Alona, but this man had been there and the price he had paid for it pierced Marcus like a knife. Could a soldier's heart come close to breaking for his enemy? Did the Lord of the Wall have a conscience after all? He swallowed the lump in his throat and covered the dead face with the cloak.

'She almost killed us, but Mary, mother of God, she didn't deserve to die like this.'

Marcus went to where Valeria stood looking down into the cart. Briga lay on her back by her throne, startled eyes staring from the black mask and a mess of torn flesh where her throat should be.

'Yes, she did.' Marcus's sympathy had limits. 'All this is her doing.'

Valeria looked up sharply and words might have been said, but for the arrival of a grinning King Corvus, who slid from the saddle to join them. 'Marcus, my friend. Lady,' he bowed to Valeria. 'You are even lovelier than I remember.' He ignored the hiss the comment prompted. 'So the bitch really is dead; I wanted to see it for myself.'

'Why did you attack the Picts?' Marcus asked quietly.

'What, no thanks, no expressions of astonished joy?'

'It wasn't part of our agreement.'

'No.' Corvus's grin grew wider, like a man who knew a joke no one else could see. 'But a man does himself a service whenever he takes the opportunity to kill a Pict, eh?'

'Then why aren't you killing them now?' Valeria said. 'At least you must want them as slaves.'

Corvus turned his single eye to the great throng. 'When I look upon my fellow Celts, I do not see slaves, I see trouble. Having them in my household or in my fields would be like giving a home to one of those giant cats on your Roman statues. Interesting, but dangerous. No, I will take their supply wagons if that bastard Coel hasn't already stolen them . . .' he gave Marcus a sly look, 'and the other half of my silver.'

Marcus sighed. 'Leof,' he removed a gold ring from his finger, 'take King Corvus to the fort. There's an iron-bound chest in tribune Quirinus's strongroom. This ring will give you my authority.' He waited until Corvus was in the saddle. 'And don't forget to give him the key.'

Corvus laughed.

'My thanks. Lady,' he bowed his head. 'Should you ever have the urge to become a queen there will always be a welcome for you at Ail Dun. You still haven't seen them, Marcus?'

'Seen who?'

'The reason I became your comrade and saviour.' As he rode off he waved a hand towards the Great North Road and Marcus finally noticed the long column of marching soldiers. The unmistakable sound of an infantry trumpet filled the valley and the men deployed into line in a single smooth movement.

'Dulcitius?' Valeria didn't hide her disbelief.

'Dulcitius wouldn't come from the north.' Marcus suddenly felt an overwhelming sense of relief. 'Demetrius.'

'Demetrius from Hunnum?'

'Don't sound so surprised. I gave him the authority to gather infantry from every fort between Cilurnum and Banna and follow Briga south. Another six hundred men. That will give the Picts something to think about.'

As it turned out, the Picts had already been doing some thinking.

'I've talked to them, lord,' Janus announced. 'And I don't think we need to have any more people dying.'

'Isn't that for me to decide?'

'They say their gods have deserted them and their queen betrayed them, lord', Julius said. 'They don't want to fight. They're prepared to surrender in return for safe passage home with their new king. He'll give pledges and provide hostages, maybe even pay tribute, lord.'

'Corvus won't like it.' Marcus pursed his lips at the thought. 'He expects us to slaughter them.'

'Corvus isn't here, lord,' the brothers chorused.

'And who is this king?'

'They want to tell you that themselves, lord.'

Before they set off for the Picts, Valeria handed Marcus a scrap of parchment. He read it and nodded before walking with the twins to where a small group of warriors stood around a young man holding a green branch.

'Who is he?' Marcus demanded.

The harshness of his tone made Janus dart a worried glance at his commander. 'His name is Melcho. He led the attack on Rufius. A man of no lineage, but Briga's nobles praise his courage.'

Marcus nodded and strode to meet the young man. Melcho met his gaze without flinching. That face? Yes, he remembered now and he saw that Melcho knew it. His last words at Alona flashed through his head. *'Never venture south of the Wall again.'* Melcho would recall those words and the threat they carried. What kind of courage had it taken to march out and confront the man who pronounced them?

'You speak for your people?'

'I do.'

'Then speak.'

Melcho repeated what Julius had said.

'And you are their new king?'

'No, lord.'

'Then who is?'

To Marcus's surprise Melcho pointed behind him. He looked over his shoulder into the worried face of Janus.

'You?'

'They value a great warrior,' Janus said modestly. 'But they also hope for a more peaceful and profitable relationship with those south of the Wall. They followed Briga more out of fear than anything else, lord, I ask you to give them a chance.'

Marcus studied the young Pict. There was sense in what Janus said and he had a feeling Londinium and Rome would agree. Better a peace bought without further casualties and the promise of profitable trade, than the constant threat of war.

'And you'll give me hostages?'

'He was mostly thinking of one hostage, lord,' Julius said.

Marcus considered for a moment. Corvus certainly wouldn't be happy, and neither would Coel, but it was not his place to make them happy. He guessed that without Briga many of the Picts would drift north again and begin squabbling among themselves. Like as not, Janus would have grasped a wolf by the tail, but he'd learn quickly or the wolf would eat him. Whatever happened, the tribes beyond the Wall would keep each other occupied for years to come. In any case, he thought, as he looked out over the blood-soaked field where the buzzards and ravens were already circling, he'd had enough of killing for today.

'Very well,' he said, and the twins grinned. 'But you'd better be on your way soon. I've just had word that Dulcitius and the Sixth are less than three hours away and I doubt he'll be quite as obliging.'

He walked back towards Valeria. What was it about battle that made a victory feel like a defeat? So many brave men dead. Brave men on both sides. This was what he'd planned and worked and schemed and risked all for. Now that he had it, all he wanted was to be done with it. Yet Marcus Flavius Victor could not escape his destiny any more than his father Magnus Maximus had been able to escape his.

And now he understood where his true destiny lay.

In far-off Saxonia where he would find his son.

Historical Note

The Roman Empire in the year AD 400 is a very different animal from the Rome of the first century I'd become so familiar with during my journeys with Rufus and Valerius. For a start, there was not one empire, but two, the eastern, ruled from Constantinople, and the western, ruled at different times from Rome, Milan, and Ravenna. Ultimate power lay with two brothers, Arcadius, in the east, and Honorius, in the west, the sons of the Emperor Theodosius I, who maintained an uneasy, sometimes fractious alliance. Honorius, the younger, owed his grip on the purple to his military adviser, the famous general Stilicho, whose Germanic roots could be a benefit or a bane, depending on the current Imperial mood towards his tribesfolk, which swung erratically between the contemptuously cordial and the genocidal.

Organizationally, Britannia too had changed. Civil power remained largely in the hands of a bureaucratic elite in London (Londinium), but that of the military was focused on York (Eboracum), base of the Sixth legion, the sole remaining legionary formation in the province, and the headquarters of the *dux Britanniarum*, its military commander. More confusingly, for administrative purposes the province was split into four: Britannia Caesariensis. Britannia Prima, Britannia Secunda, and Maxima Caesariensis, whose precise locations and functions remain a subject for debate. For this reason and for the sake of continuity, I have chosen not to refer to the existence of the sub-provinces in *The Wall*.

Christianity finally became the official religion of the Roman Empire in AD 380, after decades of debate over its legal status and, indeed, form. One of the great challenges of researching and writing *The Wall* was to unravel to what extent the new religion had become institutionalized in the military and civilian lives of the people of Britannia after centuries of paganism. How quickly was Rome's pagan symbolism, all-pervasive since the conquest, replaced by that of Christianity?

Like his predecessors of three hundred years earlier, the Roman soldier at the cusp of the fourth and fifth centuries carried a sword or a spear, fought from behind a shield and either marched or rode into battle. Plate armour had largely been replaced by the more flexible chain or ring, but his helm was still made of iron or brass, even if the design was different. What had changed, radically, was the organization of the army in which he fought.

A legion – the major fighting unit of the Roman army – which had a nominal strength of five thousand men, and perhaps more, in AD 100, now contained, at most, three thousand, and where Britannia once had a garrison of three or four legions, she was now probably only defended by a single one. Auxiliary units that had between five hundred and eight hundred men in AD 100, the provincial, previously non-citizen soldiers who supplied Rome's light infantry and specialist troops, usually numbered fewer than three hundred in Marcus's time. Yet as suggested by the *Notitia Dignitatum* – a directory of Roman units at the beginning of the fifth century – it appears possible some auxiliary formations were part of the garrison of Hadrian's Wall almost from beginning to end, a few perhaps even inhabiting the same forts throughout.

So, who were they defending Britannia from, and why?

The first reference to the Picts appears in an anonymous panegyric of AD 297, and a few years later another refers to the 'forests and marshes of the Caledones and other Picts', indicating the Picts were a confederation of tribes rather than a single entity. We assume the word Picti means 'painted people', a suggestion apparently borne out by the poet Claudian's reference around AD 402 to soldiers who had 'watched the life leave the tattoos on a dying Pict'. Whatever their method of decoration, there is no evidence that the tribes of what is now Scotland considered forming great tribal alliances before the Romans took an interest in the area around AD 80. In essence, the Romans created their Pictish enemy.

It was always my intention that the Wall itself should be the heart and soul of this book: the places, the people (the book is populated by many of those recorded on the altars and gravestones discovered in its environs) and the vistas. By the time Marcus Flavius Victor leaves Hunnum for Segedunum this extraordinary structure had dominated the northern landscape and, to a great extent, dictated Rome's strategy for ruling and defending Britannia, for two hundred and eighty years. During that time, it had been abandoned, rebuilt, repaired, and, if you'll excuse the management speak, repurposed.

Why did Hadrian have the Wall built? It looks like a defensive barrier, and to a certain extent acts like a defensive barrier, if not a very efficient one. The number of gateways in the original design, and their positioning, suggests a considerable element of control over north–south passage and vice versa, indicating an amicable and profitable relationship with the locals, accompanied, presumably, by a substantial income from tax. Unlike his predecessors, Hadrian saw no reason to absorb the north of the island into the Empire. He had already created a wooden palisade in Germania to fill the gap between the Rhine and the Danube. At a time when his reign was unpopular it may have made sense to him to create something on a grander scale as a projection of Rome's and the Emperor's power.

What is more puzzling is that it went against every tenet of current Roman military strategy. Rome's was a mobile army. Its legions could cover the ground at a remarkable pace, accompanied by flexible, specialist units of auxiliaries on foot and horseback, and strike the enemy with devastating force. An army of manoeuvre that did not, unless in the utmost extremity, fight from behind walls. Now, and for the greater part of the Wall's active life, Hadrian ensured that the function of between five and ten thousand highly trained soldiers would be primarily defensive.

During the latter part of the fourth century the structure of the army changed, garrisons were reduced and forts abandoned. Identifying which ones is the great difficulty for the author recording the final years of Roman Britain. Undoubtedly, cavalry, with their greater mobility, will have become increasingly important.

Lord of the Wall is a fictional rank, but it made sense to me that the Wall garrison must have had a single guiding hand closer than Eboracum, where the *dux Britanniarum* would have had myriad responsibilities. Hopefully you think Marcus Flavius Victor is worthy of it.

Glossary

ala – auxiliary cavalry wing composed, in late Roman times, of three hundred horsemen in ten squadrons.

arcani – units of frontier scouts based in Roman Britain, they acquired a reputation for being too close to the tribes beyond the Wall.

auxiliaries – originally non-citizen soldiers serving as light infantry and cavalry in the Roman armies. Later auxiliary units would be composed of locally recruited warriors from nearby tribes.

buccellatum – Roman iron rations, very hard biscuits.

carnyx – curved horn used by the Celtic tribes.

centurio regionarius – legionary centurion tasked with military and administrative supervision of a particular geographical area, in this case the coastal forts of Cumbria.

comitatenses – the late Roman field army.

Constantinopolis (Nova Roma) – capital of the eastern Roman Empire, now Istanbul.

Coventina – Romano-British water goddess, celebrated at her shrine Coventina's Well at Carrawburgh (Brocolitia).

cuneus (also known as the Boar's Head) – a compact arrow-head formation used by Roman infantry and cavalry to break up enemy formations.

Damnonii – Celtic tribe who inhabited the area surrounding the Clyde valley in south-west Scotland.

decimation – a brutal and seldom used Roman military punishment where one man in every ten of a unit found guilty of cowardice or mutiny was chosen for execution by his comrades.

draco – the dragon standard carried by military units in the late Roman army.

Duoviri – joint magistrates who held administrative power in a Roman town or city.

dux Britanniarum – commander of the northern military units of late Roman Britain, one of three major commands listed in the *Notitia Dignitatum*, along with the *Comes Britanniarum* and the Count of the Saxon Shore.

fustuarium – brutal Roman military punishment where a soldier was ordered to be beaten to death by his comrades.

Goths – German-speaking tribes from east of the Danube who migrated across the river and demanded to be part of the Roman Empire (eastern and western tribes are known respectively as Ostrogoths and Visigoths).

hack silver – silver cut from large pieces of tableware and used by the Romans as currency to bribe or pay Celtic tribal chieftains during negotiations.

iugerum – Roman unit of land measurement of about one quarter hectare.

limitanei – auxiliary frontier troops of the late Roman Empire. All of the units manning the forts of Hadrian's Wall would have been *limitanei*.

lucana – dried sausages that formed part of a soldier's rations on campaign.

medicus – a Roman doctor.

Mithras – an eastern deity favoured by Roman soldiers until the advent of Christianity; his attendants were Cautes and Cautopates.

Novantae – Celtic tribe who inhabited what is now Dumfries and Galloway in south-west Scotland.

onager – Roman catapult for throwing heavy missiles like river boulders.

pes quadratus – Roman measurement of area, one square foot.

Picts – tribal federation which occupied much of what is now Scotland north of the Forth–Clyde isthmus; it probably incorporated what were the Caledonians, Maettae etc.

praetorium – the commandant's living quarters in a Roman camp or fortress.

prefect – Roman military title still in use in later times, cavalry commander (though the term may have had multiple uses).

principia – the headquarters building in a Roman camp or fortress.

scorpio – bolt-firing Roman light artillery piece.

Scotti – Celtic tribe from Ireland which joined with the Picts and Saxons to raid Britannia.

scrupulum – Roman measurement of area: one hundred *pedes quadrati*.

Selgovae – Celtic tribe which inhabited the lands of what are now the central and western Borders of Scotland.

stipendium – the pay of a late Roman soldier, often paid in kind rather than money.

tribune – Roman military title still in use in later times, commander of an infantry or cavalry unit.

valetudinarium – a Roman military hospital (could be temporary or permanent).

Vandals – a Germanic people who migrated westward into the Roman Empire under pressure from more powerful tribes in the east. In the late fourth century they supplied soldiers for the Empire, including the famous general Stilicho.

Votadini – Celtic tribe who inhabited eastern Scotland south of the Forth estuary, later immortalized in the epic poem *The Goddodin*.

Acknowledgements

Firstly, I have to thank my editor Simon Taylor for the opportunity to embark on a new journey with Marcus Flavius Victor, the production team at Transworld for helping me make it what it is, with a special word for Stephen Mulcahey for his superb cover image, and Stan, my agent at The North Literary Agency. Also my wife Alison for her unstinting support and my family for cheering on from the sidelines. Research is at the heart of all of my books and I couldn't have written this one without feeding off the knowledge and insight of many others. *Hadrian's Wall* by David J. Breeze and Brian Dobson was the book I turned to most, but Mike Bishop's *Per Lineam Valli* website (https://perlineamvalli.wordpress.com) is another fantastic resource, along with his peerless *Roman Military Equipment from the Punic Wars to the Fall of Rome* (written with J. C. N. Coulston). *The Late Roman Army* by Pat Southern and Karen R. Dixon helped me navigate through a whole new way of military life. I'd also commend Alistair Moffat's *The Wall*, and Philip Parker's *The Empire Stops Here*. Only fragmentary references to the Picts by Roman historians survive, and I'm grateful to *The Picts: A History* by Tim Clarkson for guiding me through them. For a more graphic insight into their symbolism see *The Pictish*

Symbol Stones of Scotland edited by Iain Fraser. Finally, for anyone looking to steep themselves in the history, archaeology and life as it was lived on Hadrian's Wall I'd highly recommend signing up to Newcastle University's Futurelearn course, *Hadrian's Wall: Life on the Roman Frontier*, if it's still available.

ABOUT THE AUTHOR

A journalist by profession, **Douglas Jackson** transformed a lifelong fascination for Rome and the Romans into writing fiction. His first two novels were the highly acclaimed and bestselling *Caligula* and *Claudius*, while his third novel, *Hero of Rome*, introduced readers to a new series hero, Gaius Valerius Verrens. Eight more novels recounting the adventures of this determined and dedicated servant of Rome followed, earning critical acclaim and confirming Douglas as one of the UK's foremost historical novelists. He has also written adventure thrillers under the name James Douglas. Douglas Jackson lives near Stirling in Scotland.